THE GOOD MOTHERS

CAITLIN WEAVER

Storm

PUBLISHING

Ebook ISBN: 978-1-83700-168-2
Paperback ISBN: 978-1-83700-170-5

Cover design: Eileen Carey
Cover images: Getty Images

Published by Storm Publishing.
For further information, visit:
www.stormpublishing.co

ALSO BY CAITLIN WEAVER

Such a Good Family
Things We Never Say
The Perfect Plan
Who We Used to Be

To my nieces, Eira Rose and Ovedia Arlys.
May you find your circle of women and always keep them close.

ONE

The car came out of nowhere—at least, that's what Lacey told herself after she hit it. She'd been squinting at her phone in her lap, trying to make out the next turn on her GPS app when the crunch of metal caused her to whip her head around. It was a residential street and she wasn't even going that fast, so at first the impact didn't register. She hit the brakes, trying to determine where the noise had come from.

"No, no, no," she breathed, as she saw, in her passenger side mirror, a cherry red Chevy pickup truck with a long scrape down the side of it, ending near the bumper where there was a yellow bumper sticker that read, "The more people I meet, the more I like my dog."

"Please, no," Lacey muttered, reversing for a better look at the damage. The scrape started as a faint line near the rear bumper and ran the length of the truck bed before spreading out and deepening into a gouge at the driver's door.

"Did you just hit that car?" came a voice from the backseat. Her eight-year-old, Elliott, sat up straight out of his usual slump and rolled down his window for a better look. His hair, dark blond like hers, begged for a haircut, shaggy around his ears and on the back of his neck.

"I didn't see it, OK?" she defended herself. In fairness, the truck *was* parked more than a foot away from the curb. Still. She clenched her jaw. The clock on the dashboard blinked forward. Eight thirty-seven a.m. They were late. Late to the one appointment where she absolutely had to make a good impression.

"How could you not see it, Mommy? It's the only car parked right here." Elliott widened his eyes, pale blue like his father's, and gestured to the empty street. Despite her growing panic, Lacey's heart momentarily snagged on the sweetness of the word "mommy." At eight, Elliott was still mostly a little boy; only rarely did she see flashes of the older boy he could become, the one who rolled his eyes and called her "Mom."

"I was looking at the map," Lacey cried, her voice pitching higher. "It's not like I meant to—" She stopped, squeezed the steering wheel with both hands and took a deep breath. *Stay calm,* she reminded herself. *If you stay calm, Elliott will stay calm.* Emotional co-regulation, the therapist had called it. The therapist she could no longer afford.

She took another breath and glanced around. No one was on the street. She should leave a note, or knock on the door of the house the truck was parked in front of. The truck was shiny and new looking, nothing like her rust-spotted 2005 Ford Fiesta. Her stomach lurched, thinking of the expense to repair it. Her car insurance would go up—wait, had she even paid her last insurance bill? She could picture it, sitting on top of a stack of papers on the counter at their old house, but that was months ago. Had she even packed those papers when she and Elliott moved to her sister's? Or had she just swept the whole stack into the recycling bin in her frenzy to get out? She'd always prided herself on being organized, but ever since she and Judd had separated, her life felt like a ball of yarn unraveling from both ends.

She pushed her long, sideswept bangs out of her eyes—Elliott wasn't the only one who needed a haircut—and pinched the bridge of her nose. Then she sat up and squared her shoulders. "Roll up your window, please," she said to Elliott as she put her car in drive and eased forward again.

"Whoa, Mommy, shouldn't we, like, call someone? Or try to find the owner of the truck? I mean, we can't just, like, leave, can we?" In the rearview mirror Elliott's forehead was scrunched as his anxiety rose.

"I'll call them," Lacey promised in a soothing voice, accelerating now, and taking the first right turn that would get her off that street and away from the red truck.

"But how?" Elliott demanded. "We don't even know who the truck belongs to."

"I'll find them," Lacey lied, looking in the rearview mirror and giving her son her best there's-nothing-to-worry-about smile, even as her stomach churned in response to her moral failing. "It's just that we're really late right now, buddy. But I'll come back later, I promise." There was a twinge deep in the middle of her chest. What kind of person had she become? The kind who lied to her child, that's who. And now, the perpetrator of a hit and run.

She gritted her teeth and swallowed down the guilt rising in her throat. She would do better, she would. She just needed to catch a break. Slipping her hand into her pocket, she fingered the scrap of paper she'd ripped from the flyer in the coffee shop, where'd she jotted down the address they were headed to.

This had to work out. She was out of options.

Five minutes and a short drive later, Lacey peered up at the house she'd parked in front of. It was larger than she'd expected, but not as new as many of the homes on the street. Unlike the houses on either side, it did not have a fresh coat of paint or a front yard with tidy landscaping that looked straight out of HGTV. Still, with its wraparound front porch and bright yellow door there was something warm and inviting about it. Out the front was a towering oak tree that shrouded the second-floor windows, and on the lawn a *Frozen*-themed bike with training wheels lay discarded.

Lacey looked down at the paper in her hand, then back up to

the wrought-iron numbers attached to the house. 811 Wildwood Lane. This was it.

"Can't I just wait here?" Elliott asked. After the excitement of the accident (*minor accident*, Lacey told herself) he had wilted back into his usual slouch, looking like he wanted nothing more than to melt into whatever piece of furniture was supporting him.

Lacey shook her head. "They want to meet you, too, buddy. And there'll be some other kids to play with." Her heart beat a drumroll in her chest.

"Why do we have to do this, anyway?" he mumbled, shoving his hands into the pockets of the hoodie he'd insisted on wearing despite the sticky late-August heat. "This place looks stupid. Why can't we just stay at Aunt Sarah's?"

The muscles in Lacey's neck tensed at the mention of her sister. She also wished they could continue living in Sarah's expansive Tudor Revival home with its rainfall shower heads and refrigerator that remained magically full of fresh produce, prime cuts of meat, and the expensive Greek yogurt Lacey loved but almost never splurged on.

Growing up, Lacey never would have guessed her younger sister would be the one living the picture-perfect life—happily married with two kids in a big house in an affluent New Jersey commuter town only a forty-minute train ride from New York City. Sarah's front yard even had a *literal* white picket fence. That life was supposed to be Lacey's. Sarah had always been the wild one, cutting class, sneaking out to parties, and washing out of college her first year before finally limping across the graduation stage five years later.

Lacey, on the other hand, had done everything right. She followed the rules, made responsible choices, checked all the boxes. And yet here she was, facing divorce and effectively homeless.

A flicker of envy rose in her chest as she pictured Sarah's life: shuttling kids to soccer practice, filling a Costco cart without once calculating how much was left on her credit card or worrying if the tank of her giant SUV was too expensive to top off.

"Does this place have a pool?" Elliott craned his neck toward 811 Wildwood. "Aunt Sarah's house has a pool."

"We can't stay at Aunt Sarah's anymore, OK?" Lacey's voice was sharper than she intended. *And that's your fault*, she wanted to add, a pang of guilt reverberating in her chest as soon as the words formed in her mind. Elliott couldn't help who he was.

"Your brain works differently than other kids," she'd told him when she and Judd had gotten his ADHD diagnosis a year ago. "And there's nothing wrong with that. You just need different strategies for managing your emotions and your impulses." Different strategies, along with occupational therapy and medication, both of which his father was firmly opposed to.

"Is it because of what happened with Cole?" Elliott asked in a small voice. "Is that why we have to leave?"

Lacey could taste the banana she'd had for breakfast in her throat as she flashed back to the horror on Sarah's face when, during one of his outbursts, Elliott had pushed seven-year-old Cole, toppling him over onto Sarah's stupid, expensive coffee table with its glass top and heavy metal edges. Who had furniture that unforgiving with small children around? People whose children didn't suffer from severe emotional dysregulation and lack of impulse control, that's who.

Cole had hit his head. There had been a lot of blood and a visit to the ER that resulted in stitches. The worst part was that Elliott hadn't even been mad at Cole; he'd been upset with Lacey for taking away his screen time. Cole had just been the closest target.

Lacey turned to face her son in the back seat of the car. "What happened with Cole was not great," she said.

"I said I was sorry." Elliott's small face rearranged itself into a look of such acute remorse it made Lacey's chest ache.

"I know, sweetie." She reached back and squeezed his hand. "I know. And that's not why we're moving." It was, though. Sarah had asked them to move out the next day.

"Brett doesn't think it's a good idea to have Elliott here anymore," Sarah had said, biting her artificially plumped lip in a way that suggested her husband—a finance guy who'd swooped in with his country club membership and family money and finally tamed Lacey's sister—wasn't the only one who thought it was time for them to go.

"Of course, I understand. We'll be out of your hair as soon as possible," Lacey had replied, unable to tell her sister the truth: that she had nowhere else to go. In that moment, instead of meeting Sarah's eyes she'd focused on a spot in the middle of her sister's forehead, which was smooth and wrinkle-free, just like everything in Sarah's life.

Shaking the memory from her head, Lacey released Elliott's hand and unbuckled her seatbelt. "Let's go," she said.

Up on the porch she rang the doorbell and surveyed her surroundings as she lifted her thick, shoulder-length hair away from her sweaty neck. Next to the front door was a long row of shoes in varying sizes. A pair of boys' Nike high tops sat next to a pair of women's Birkenstocks in an expensive-looking, buttery yellow color, followed by two tiny rainbow-colored Crocs. Lacey tried to remember when Elliott's feet had been that size. When he was two, maybe? Three? He'd been deliciously chunky back then, his chin disappearing into his neck when he smiled. Now he was bony and angular, a side effect of his medication, which suppressed his appetite. Medication Judd didn't want him to be on.

There was a sturdy-looking rocking chair and a patio couch further down the porch and around them stood tall, lush potted plants that looked well-cared for. The couch was piled with plump pillows and a quilt, and a book was splayed open on the coffee table. Lacey felt the pull of the comfortable setting. She could imagine sipping her morning coffee in the rocking chair, or stretching out on the couch under the pleasant breeze coming from the ceiling fan. She closed her eyes for a second as she pictured it. What she wouldn't give for a nap. She was so tired lately her bones felt heavy, like it was an effort just to carry them through the world.

There was a scraping sound as the front door unlocked and opened. A small girl stared up at Lacey, her brown eyes wide with excitement. She wore a flouncy teal-colored dress that Lacey recognized from a Disney movie over a yellow bathing suit, and her hair was pulled back tightly from her face and then exploded in a small black poof on the top of her head.

"Mommy, they're here!" she called in a trumpet-like voice. Then she slammed the door and Lacey heard the pounding of feet receding.

Lacey shifted on her feet, her heart rate accelerating. This house had to work out. Back at Sarah's their bags were packed. She'd promised they'd be gone by the weekend, but where? Once upon a time, Lacey had friends—a lot of them. She'd been Homecoming Queen in high school, for God's sake. But when Judd came along, she'd fallen so hard for him she'd let herself become consumed by the relationship, despite her mother's warning that he was "a wild card, best-case scenario."

The few friendships she'd managed to hold on to had quietly dissolved during the pandemic, lost in the chaos of Judd's transformation from the freewheeling, funny guy with a thousand interests —the man she'd fallen in love with—into an internet conspiracy theory-obsessed recluse and self-proclaimed Bitcoin expert.

Tears pricked her eyes as she leaned forward to press the doorbell again. Maybe they could sleep in her car. She could tell Elliott they were camping.

Before Lacey's finger reached the doorbell, the door swung open, revealing a woman with a petite, athletic frame, dressed in a shapeless beige shift. On Lacey, the dress would have looked like a potato sack, but on this woman, it draped perfectly, as if she'd just stepped off a runway. Her face was angular yet soft, with high cheekbones, full lips, and deep-set brown eyes that flickered with a hint of suspicion. Upon seeing Lacey, though, they crinkled as she gave a warm smile.

"You must be Lacey," the woman said. "Come in." Her voice was breathy and as Lacey stepped past her into the house she caught a whiff of her perfume, something with hints of cedar and citrus. "And sorry about Linden." She glanced at the little girl who'd answered the door, now peeking out at them from down the hall. "She gets excited about visitors."

Inside, Lacey found herself standing beside a built-in row of hooks, each holding a brightly colored kids' backpack. She gazed down a long hallway that opened into a sun-drenched living room. A colorful rug lay scattered with Hot Wheels cars and half-dressed dolls, while an inviting L-shaped couch sat nearby, a small stack of children's books resting on one corner. By the window, a table crowded with houseplants caught the light. The air smelled like lemon cleaner and freshly baked cookies. A thought rose to Lacey's mind unbidden.

This is what home is supposed to feel like.

Elliott stayed close to Lacey, and the woman turned her dazzling smile on him, revealing a small gap between her two straight, white front teeth. "And who is this handsome young man?" she asked.

Elliott stared mutely up at her as if mesmerized.

"This is Elliott," Lacey supplied.

The woman nodded and reached out to ruffle Elliott's hair. It was the kind of uninvited touch that, from anyone else, would have triggered a surge of mama-bear protectiveness in Lacey. But with this woman, it felt natural. Lacey found herself half wishing she'd reach out and smooth Lacey's hair, too.

"I'm Regina Cho," the woman said. "And it's wonderful to meet you." She turned to sweep a graceful arm out toward the interior of the house. "Welcome to the mommune."

TWO

Elliott's brow furrowed as he eyed Regina. "What's a mommune?"

Regina gave a breathy laugh. "Like a commune of moms. That's what we call ourselves," she said, grinning at Lacey like they were old friends.

Elliott still looked puzzled, but curiosity drew him a step closer to Regina. "What's a commune?"

Regina's face turned serious as she addressed Elliott. "I can already tell you're very smart because you ask good questions." Her tone was calm and direct, the way you'd speak to another adult, not the exaggerated singsong most people used with kids. Elliott's shoulders straightened with quiet pride.

"A commune," Regina continued, "is a group of people living together and sharing responsibilities. Everyone who lives here helps each other, whether it's cooking dinner, packing lunches, or watching each other's kids." She glanced at Lacey and added with a playful wink, "But don't worry, there's no hard labor—unless you count laundry—and we have wine."

Lacey smiled and exhaled, her shoulders finally easing. She and Elliott slipped off their shoes and followed Regina into the kitchen. For the past three days, she and Regina had been emailing back and forth after Lacey had spotted the flyer at the library, a bright burst of hot pink on the bulletin board that caught her eye when she'd left Elliott in the kids' section with a stack of *Dog Man* books and gone to the restroom for a quick, desperate cry.

SEEKING RESPONSIBLE SINGLE MOM TO JOIN OUR HOUSEHOLD.
MOTHERHOOD CAN BE LONELY AND WE SUPPORT EACH OTHER!
SEEKING SOMEONE WHO WANTS A COMMUNITY, NOT JUST
ROOMMATES.
GREAT NEIGHBORHOOD WITH GOOD SCHOOLS.

The rent was cheaper than any of the dismal apartments she'd seen. Right there in the library, Lacey had pulled out her phone and sent a message to the email listed, trying hard not to get her hopes up. But now, here was Regina in person, every bit as warm and friendly as she'd seemed in their flurry of emails.

In the kitchen, Linden sat ferociously chewing a bit of toast, peanut butter smeared across her small face. Across from her was a woman in a dark pink and orange silk robe, the bright colors striking against her deep brown skin. She gave off a regal air, her hair buzzed close to her scalp the perfect complement to her large brown eyes and sculpted cheekbones. Though she was basically still in her pajamas, somehow next to her Lacey felt like the under-dressed one.

"Nanette," Regina said, gesturing to the woman, "meet Lacey."

"Hi." Nanette raised her half-full coffee cup in salute, the stack of jade bangles on her wrist clinking together like wind chimes. "This is Linden," she added.

"They've met," Regina said, then turned to Linden. "Honey, what did we say about answering the door?"

Linden swung her feet under the chair, staring down at her plate. "That I should let a grown-up do it," she mumbled.

"That's right," Regina said with a firm nod. She tucked a lock of her wavy, dark hair behind her ear.

Linden's eyes turned to Elliott. "Do you know how to play hide and seek?" she asked him. "Because I do."

"Uh, yeah," Elliott scoffed. "I'm eight."

"Be nice," Lacey muttered through gritted teeth.

"Well, I'm five," Linden shot back, scrambling out of her chair and placing her hands on her hips. "Let's go."

Without another word, she spun on her heel and ran out into the hallway and up the stairs. Elliott hesitated, glancing at Lacey, then shrugged and followed.

"Is he OK...?" Lacey's voice trailed off as the kids disappeared up the stairs. Had she remembered to give Elliott his medication that morning? He was like a different kid when he didn't take it, his emotions on a hair trigger.

Nanette waved a dismissive hand. "Linden will show him the ropes."

Regina laughed. "She basically runs the house."

"True," Nanette said, rolling her eyes as she took another sip of coffee.

"Coffee?" Regina offered, already filling a mug for Lacey. Her movements were smooth and precise, like a ballet dancer.

"Thank you." Lacey accepted it gratefully. She hadn't dared step into the kitchen at her sister's house that morning—she'd been too afraid of running into her brother-in-law.

"I heard the word 'coffee.'" A petite woman with long dark hair breezed into the room. She wore pale pink pajama pants and a faded purple T-shirt that read *Bless Your Heart*. Her pale skin had an almost luminescent quality and her deep-set hazel eyes radiated warmth. "Any chance y'all could give me mine in IV form?" she asked, her honeyed drawl immediately putting Lacey at ease.

Regina laughed. "Lacey, meet Tavia."

"Nice to see you, honey." Tavia extended her hand, her grip surprisingly strong.

Regina picked up another mug and filled it for her. "Early morning?"

Tavia winced. "Is four-thirty even considered morning?"

"It's the two-year sleep regression," Regina said with a sympathetic shake of her head. "The twins went through it at her age. I thought it would never end, but one day—poof—it just did." She snapped her fingers and glanced at Lacey. "Maddie and Max, my kids, are eight now, like Elliott."

"Well, Grace just passed out in her crib two minutes ago, praise the Lord," Tavia said, taking a greedy sip of coffee.

Maddie, Max, Linden, Grace. Lacey tried to keep up with all the kids' names being thrown around. She wondered how many of them lived here with these three women.

Regina turned to Tavia. "Next time, hand her off to me and go back to bed. I'll take a shift."

"Don't think I won't," Tavia said with a tired shake of her head.

"I'm running errands with Linden later," Nanette said. "I can take Grace along and give you a break."

"Mom, have you seen my charger?" A boy with Regina's sharp features burst into the kitchen, holding a remote-control car.

"Where did you leave it?" Regina asked.

The boy pushed his black-framed glasses up his nose. "I don't know."

Linden came barreling back into the room, scrambling under the table. Elliott chased after her. "I see you!" he called.

Regina wrapped an arm around her son and pulled him toward Elliott. "Max, this is Elliott. He and his mom, Lacey, are thinking of moving in."

Max gave Elliott a half wave. "Wanna see the racetrack I built in the backyard?"

Elliott's eyes lit up. "Sure!"

"C'mon." Max was out the back door before Lacey could say a word.

"Hey, wait for me!" Linden called, pushing out from under the table and darting after them.

Lacey glanced at Regina. "Are you sure...? Elliott can be..." She trailed off, anxiety gnawing at her.

"They'll be fine," Regina said with a dismissive wave. "Let's sit and get to know each other." She pulled out a chair for Lacey and leaned forward. "Why don't you tell us about yourself and what you're looking for in a living situation?" There was a breezy confidence in the way she spoke, a kind of cool older sister vibe, that made Lacey want to impress her.

Lacey flushed as all three women's eyes turned to her. She was already taken by the easy, supportive vibe between them. It felt almost sisterly, or at least what she imagined sisters should be like. Not like her and Sarah. *This is what I want*, she thought. *Someone to hand me a cup of coffee in the morning. A minute to breathe while someone else watches my child. A safe place where I don't have to walk on eggshells. Somewhere I can get my life back on track.*

The weight of everything she'd endured in the past few weeks since leaving Judd crashed down on her, and tears welled in her eyes. She could still see the unhinged fury in his eyes when she told him she was leaving. The way he tore through the house, searching for Elliott's pills to flush down the toilet, ranting that she was a terrible mother for letting Big Pharma poison their son. And then his final blow—a threat to seek custody—that sent an icy chill through her.

"Well, I'm, um..." Lacey's voice broke. She buried her face in her hands, her shoulders shaking with sobs she'd been holding back for too long.

"It's OK." A hand squeezed her shoulder. She looked up to see Regina's concerned but understanding eyes. "Every one of us was in that exact state when we moved in," Regina said gently.

Lacey let out a watery laugh, wiping her eyes. "I don't know about that. Everything's so messed up right now."

One side of Regina's mouth curved upward. "Try us," she said. "You'll find we're a pretty understanding bunch."

Lacey bit the inside of her cheek. She had nothing to lose. "I'm getting a divorce," she said, the words spilling out in a rush. "At least, I'm trying to. Judd, my husband, has become someone I don't even recognize anymore. He thinks 5G causes cancer and that the government is poisoning us through flu shots. He emptied our joint account when I asked for a separation and because I'm the kind of disgustingly naïve woman who never kept money of her own, I'm totally screwed. And Elliott has ADHD. Like *bad* ADHD. He's a total handful. Acts out, struggles socially, the whole deal. But medication and therapy are helping—except Judd doesn't believe in those, either. Oh, and I hit a parked car on the way here and... well, I basically fled the scene." She exhaled sharply. "Whew."

The table fell silent. The women stared at her and a wave of nausea swept over Lacey. What was she doing? This was an interview, and she'd just aired all her dirtiest laundry.

"I'm sorry," she stammered, pushing back her chair. "Where's the bathroom?"

Regina pointed. "Down the hall on the left."

Inside the small bathroom, Lacey splashed cold water on her face. Her tired brown eyes stared back at her, bloodshot and puffy. She patted her face dry and squared her shoulders. There had to be a way to salvage this. She'd beg if she had to.

As she stepped into the hallway, she heard whispers from the kitchen.

"She seems unstable," Tavia murmured. "Desperate, even."

"A little like you when you showed up on my doorstep?" came Regina's voice. Her tone was pointed but not unkind. "We don't judge, remember? We've all been there. Besides, a little desperate isn't a bad thing, is it?"

The other two women laughed.

Lacey felt the flush on her face deepen. Not that she blamed them. She *was* desperate. She squared her shoulders, resolving to pull herself together and try to rescue her first impression. She needed this.

Clearing her throat, she stepped back into the kitchen. The women leaned away from each other, all smiling too brightly.

"Wow, I'm really sorry," Lacey said, gripping the back of a chair. "I've been under a lot of stress. But I'm a responsible person, I promise. I'm clean, conscientious, and—"

"Lacey." Regina held up a hand and offered a warm, disarming smile. "No apology necessary. We're here to help."

THREE

Lacey's body tensed at the sight of her sister's dark blue BMW SUV gleaming in the driveway as she and Elliott pulled through the wrought-iron gate. She'd been hoping Sarah wouldn't be home, that she and Elliott could slip downstairs to the in-law suite in the basement without crossing paths.

Elliott, however, lit up. "Does that mean Cole is home?" He scrambled to unbuckle his seatbelt before the car had even rolled to a stop. "Can I go play with him?"

Lacey's fingers tightened on the steering wheel. "Let's just head downstairs," she said.

"But downstairs is so boring," he groaned. "I haven't done anything fun today."

Lacey met his eyes in the rearview mirror. "Playing Hot Wheels in the backyard with Max wasn't fun?"

Elliott hesitated, then grinned, the gap from his missing front teeth widening his smile. "Yeah, Max and Maddie have cool toys. Can we do another playdate with them soon?"

Lacey inhaled, steadying herself before forcing a smile. "I really hope so, buddy."

At Regina's—Lacey still couldn't quite bring herself to call it *the mommune*—Elliott had disappeared into the backyard with the other kids while she sat at the kitchen table, trying to convince herself she hadn't completely blown the meeting with her emotional breakdown and subsequent oversharing. Regina, Nanette, and Tavia had been kind, but the moment the kids came charging inside, grass-stained and grinning, demanding popsicles, Regina had risen from the table, signaling an end to the conversation.

"Well," she'd said, offering Lacey her hand, her chiseled face unreadable. "We've enjoyed meeting you. We'll be in touch."

Lacey had spent the drive back to Sarah's biting the inside of her cheek, trying not to cry as she asked herself the same exhausting question: *Where will we go if this doesn't work out?*

Lately, she had spent a large part of her energy holding back tears as she reassured Elliott everything would be OK. Then, at night, when she finally heard his breathing slow beside her in the bed, she'd tell herself *now* was the time to break down, to let it out, to have a good cry. Except nothing ever came. Instead, her mind filled with numbers—the dwindling balance in her bank account, the number of pills left in Elliott's orange prescription bottle before she'd have to scrape together the copay for a refill, the count of days they'd been at Sarah's and how close they were to wearing out their welcome.

Her life felt like an impossible math problem, the kind where the numbers were always too much or too little. Never just right.

She and Elliott got out of the car and Lacey braced herself as they stepped through the side door of Sarah's house, but all was quiet.

Elliott veered toward the kitchen. "Can we make banana bread?" he asked eagerly. Baking had always been one of their favorite things to do together, one of the few activities where Elliott could truly focus. He'd measure each ingredient with careful precision, stir the batter exactly twenty times, then watch the oven clock tick down while sweet, familiar scents filled the air. Lacey loved it almost as much as he did. There was something deeply reassuring about combining a handful of messy ingredients and knowing exactly what you'd get in the end. But they hadn't baked in weeks, not since moving in with Sarah, whose immaculate kitchen felt too museum-like to risk sticky, flour-dusted counters.

Lacey caught his shoulder, steering him toward the basement stairs. "Not today, buddy, I'm sorry."

"But I'm hungry," he said, shaking off her hand. "I want a snack."

"I have snacks downstairs," she said, hoping her emergency stash of granola bars hadn't run out. "Come on, let's give Aunt Sarah some space."

He frowned. "Why does she need space?"

Lacey bit her lip. *Because maybe if we're so quiet she forgets we're here, we can stay. Because otherwise, I don't know where we're going next.*

"I think you've earned some screen time," she said lightly. "For being so well-behaved at the, um, playdate."

Elliott perked up, but not before casting a wistful glance toward the sun-drenched kitchen. "Do you have croissants downstairs?" he asked.

Sarah always kept fresh pastries from the local bakery in a special ceramic Le Creuset bread box on the counter.

"Let's see what I have," Lacey said, relieved when he followed her downstairs.

The spacious downstairs guest suite had been meant for their parents, who'd sold Lacey and Sarah's childhood home two towns over and retired to Virginia Beach a few years back, living modestly on their public school teacher pensions. But just a year after settling in, their mother had been diagnosed with aggressive ovarian cancer, and three months later, she was gone. Their father followed almost exactly a year later of a heart attack.

Lacey had just settled Elliott on the bed with his iPad, headphones, and a *Star Wars* movie when her phone rang.

At the sight of Judd's name on the screen, anxiety shot through her, followed by a wave of deep, aching sadness. There had been a time when seeing his name light up her phone sent a thrill through her body, when a call from him meant something good—plans for the weekend, an inside joke, a reason to smile. She remembered the first time she'd spotted him across the lecture hall at Rutgers. One look at his tousled dark hair and easy grin, and she'd felt something electric bolt through her. They were inseparable almost instantly.

He was two years older, and the next year when he graduated and got a job designing websites for a company in the city, she'd felt so grown up. She was dating an actual adult with his own apartment on the Upper East Side. It had all been so exciting, until she stared down at two pink lines on a pregnancy test at the start of her junior year.

The phone buzzed insistently in her hand, startling her out of her thoughts. Judd was the last person she wanted to talk to. But there were things they needed to discuss—namely, getting mediation started so they could finalize their separation and divorce.

Glancing at Elliott, who was fully engrossed in his movie, she slipped into the bathroom and closed the door.

"Hi," she said cautiously.

These days, she never knew which Judd she was going to get— a flash of the old one, lighthearted and quick to laugh, the one who made impulsive but reasonable decisions, or the new one, dark and angry, the one who ranted about fluoride in the water and called Elliott's doctor a quack for diagnosing him with ADHD.

"We need to talk," he said tersely.

"I agree," she said, forcing a friendly tone. She had learned that placating him, at least at first, was the only way to have a conversation that didn't end with him hanging up and flooding her phone with all-caps texts and links to obscure, unvetted scientific articles that *clearly*, INDISPUTABLY proved she was wrong about everything.

"I got a letter from the school saying Elliott isn't registered yet," Judd said. "School starts next week, Lacey."

She sank down onto the plush white rug next to the bathtub. "You're right, it does," she said, struggling to keep her voice even. "And Elliott *will* be registered, it will just... likely be at a different school."

A pause. Then, flat but sharp, "And why would that be?"

Lacey swallowed. "Well, as you know, we're staying with Sarah right now, so Elliott will—"

"Sarah's kids go to private school."

"Yes, absolutely, they do," she said, her words slipping into the same careful, singsong tone she had once used to coax a toddler Elliott into naps. "But she's zoned for a different district than we are, so theoretically, Elliott will be changing schools."

"Elliott will be going to *his* school," Judd snapped. "You're the one who's always going on about how he needs routine, familiarity. So get your ass in gear and get home."

Home.

Lacey closed her eyes and let her forehead rest against the cold marble edge of the tub. She pictured the modest Craftsman on a quiet, leafy street. It was nothing like Sarah's sprawling house, but it had been theirs. The backyard, cramped but cozy, had been the scene of many summer barbecues, Judd at the grill, a beer in his hand, holding court with the other dads. He had always had that way about him, magnetic, effortlessly charming, able to talk to anyone.

But during those long months of lockdown in 2020, something had shifted. The man who used to light up rooms slowly began to darken them. Instead of coming to bed with her to watch late-night comedy shows, Judd began spending hours on his computer. At first Lacey feared the worst—porn or an online affair of some sort. But when she confronted him, he showed her the chat boards on 4chan and Reddit where he was discussing manipulated voting machines and the possibility that COVID was a Chinese-engineered bioweapon. Weird, to be sure, but Lacey had been relieved that was all it was. God, how stupid she'd been.

Lacey pressed her hand into the soft plush of the bathroom rug.

"Judd," she began, her voice faltering. "I'm not coming home. Not until you're..."

She trailed off, searching for the right words. Until you're what? Different? Better? Back to being the man who rubbed her shoulders and asked about her day instead of treating her with cold disdain when she brought up Elliott's troubles at school, like all his issues were her problem to solve alone?

That man felt like a stranger now. Maybe he didn't exist anymore.

"We're not coming home right now," she said instead.

She braced herself.

There was a long pause. Then, "Don't say things you'll regret, Lacey," Judd warned, his voice biting. "He's my son, too."

But he's scared of you, she wanted to say. *And I spend all my energy protecting him from your anger, so there's nothing left for me.*

She exhaled shakily as Judd hung up and let her body sink onto the rug, exhaustion flooding through her limbs. Maybe she could nap here, just for a little while, while Elliott was still glued to his movie. Then she'd figure out what else to try, where else they could stay.

Her stomach growled loudly in protest. She frowned, trying to remember the last time she'd eaten. Dinner? Lunch? Yesterday? With a sigh, she forced herself upright. First, food. Then sleep.

Back in the bedroom, Elliott hadn't moved, eyes locked on his screen. Lacey unzipped the side pocket of her duffel bag and rifled through it for a granola bar. Empty.

She hesitated, listening for movement upstairs. Nothing.

Slipping into the kitchen, she moved as quietly as possible, slathering peanut butter onto slices of bread, stacking up four sand-wiches—it was always good to have reserves. She rinsed and dried the knife, erasing any trace she'd been there.

It had been so long since she existed in a world where she didn't feel like she was treading on eggshells: here at Sarah's, before that with Judd, at her job as an office manager—a glorified receptionist, really—at a carpet installation company, where she'd already pissed off her boss by taking more time off than she could afford, scrambling for childcare now that Elliott's summer camp had ended.

Her original plan had been to leave him with Judd, who worked from home. But that plan, like so many others, was no longer an option.

"Hey," Sarah's voice came from behind her.

Lacey jumped, the knife slipping from her fingers and clattering into the sink. "Jesus, Sar," she said, spinning around. "You scared me."

Sarah stood there, arms crossed, face unreadable. "It *is* my house," she pointed out. She brushed her honey-blonde bob away from her face, her brown eyes, so much like Lacey's, framed by thick lashes that Lacey knew were fake but still envied.

Growing up, Lacey had always been the pretty sister—some had even called her beautiful. She'd had flawless skin, long, wavy hair, and naturally straight teeth that never needed braces. But now, despite being only eighteen months older than Sarah, she knew she could pass for Sarah's *much* older sister.

Sarah's face was smooth, plumped, and rested, while the fine lines around Lacey's mouth and eyes deepened by the day. Sarah's highlights were fresh, her hair perfectly styled, while Lacey's had grown wild and was overdue for a cut. Sarah's toned, sculpted body filled out her expensive workout clothes, while Lacey's wrinkled shorts and two-day-old T-shirt hung loose on her increasingly thin frame. It turned out that watching your life fall apart really killed your appetite.

"Sorry," Lacey said, shaking her head. "I was just trying to stay out of the way."

Sarah's eyes flicked to the pile of sandwiches on the counter. "Going somewhere?"

Lacey forced a smile. "Just... hungry."

Despite being near in age, she and Sarah had never been close

—they were too different. Lacey had been the outgoing, popular one, always surrounded by people, while Sarah hid away in the school's art studio. Still, for a brief time, after they'd both had kids a year apart, it had seemed like that might change.

They'd ended up living in the same New Jersey commuter town, and often met up to take the boys to the park or story hour at the library, and commiserated via text about teething and how annoying "Baby Shark" was.

Then the pandemic hit. The get-togethers and texts slowed. Then, as Elliott's emotional struggles began to appear, and things with Judd started to unravel, they stopped altogether.

Sarah pressed her lips together, then nodded toward the pantry. "There are peanut butter pretzels in there. I know Elliott likes them. Just take the bag—I'll get a new one."

The small, unexpected kindness made Lacey's throat tighten. She blinked rapidly. "Thanks."

"It's no problem." Sarah hesitated, biting her lip before finally meeting Lacey's eyes. "Brett says you guys need to be out by next weekend."

For an instant, Lacey saw something in her sister's expression—regret, maybe, or sadness—but it vanished just as quickly.

Lacey sucked in a breath. "The weekend?" she echoed. "But, Sarah, I—" She cut herself off, pressing her lips together. She wouldn't beg. They'd already been here nearly three weeks. Sarah had done her part.

She gave a curt nod. "Understood." Gathering the sandwiches from the counter, she added, "We'll try to stay out of your way until then."

She was nearly at the basement door when Sarah called her name.

Lacey turned.

Sarah held up the bag of pretzels. "For Elliott," she said, her voice softer now.

As she set them on the counter and walked away, Lacey blinked back hot tears. When they'd lost their mother and father only a year apart, she and Sarah had been united in their grief. Lacey had consoled herself that, despite their ups and downs, at least she would always have her sister. Now, as Sarah disappeared back upstairs, it felt as though she had severed that bond in one swift motion—a cut so deep it took a moment for the blood to rise. But when the pain came, it was breathtaking.

FOUR

Lacey glanced around the parking lot of the squat office building that housed Carpet World, the local carpet installation company where she worked. Then she turned to the backseat.

"Remember, you can watch movies all day, but you have to be quiet," she reminded Elliott, pushing away the guilt that came with the thought of parking him in front of an iPad for the next eight hours. She had no other choice.

"OK, Mommy," he said obediently. She'd forced him into the bathtub the night before and even stayed up late doing laundry, waiting until she was sure everyone at Sarah's was asleep, just to make sure he had a clean shirt to wear.

Steeling herself, Lacey led Elliott into the office. They were the first ones there, intentionally so. She wanted him settled before anyone else arrived, wanted to be seen already hard at work by the time her boss walked in.

The office doubled as a showroom, a cavernous space with high ceilings and rows of carpet and rug samples for customers to page through.

"Wow," Elliott said, eyes wide. "This place would be *great* for hide and seek."

"No hide and seek," Lacey said with a quick shake of her head. "You stay put, OK?"

She flicked on the fluorescent lights in the small, windowless break room, revealing a battered cafeteria-style table, a few plastic chairs, an old fridge, and a microwave. The air smelled like stale coffee and buttered popcorn.

"Welcome to your office for the day," she said, gesturing around.

Elliott sniffed. "Is that popcorn? Can I have some?"

"If you can be on your best behavior, I'll make you some later," Lacey promised. She pulled out a chair for him and unzipped the faded dark green backpack with Yoda printed on the front. "More *Star Wars?*"

He nodded eagerly and slid into the chair as she handed over his iPad and headphones.

"There are snacks in your bag, and the bathroom is right through there," she said, pointing. "I'll check on you in a little while, but try not to come out unless it's an emergency, OK?"

He nodded, already slipping on his headphones and navigating to his movie.

Lacey bent to kiss the top of his head, ruffling his hair. "Love you, buddy."

"Love you," he mumbled back, eyes locked on the screen.

With a silent prayer that they could just get through the day, she stepped back out to the reception desk and got to work.

"Morning, Lacey," her boss, Chip, said as he strode in twenty minutes later, surprise flickering across his face. "You don't usually beat me in."

He was a tall, rangy man with a long, sharp nose that always reminded Lacey of a rat, and pale skin that turned an alarming shade of violet whenever he got upset—which was often.

"Good morning, Chip," she said brightly. "Just catching up so I can make great happen today."

In the few months she'd worked at Carpet World, she'd learned that the best way to stay on Chip's good side was to sprinkle her conversations with the corporate jargon he loved, phrases that sounded like they'd been lifted straight from a self-help podcast, like "Winners find solutions."

Chip nodded approvingly. "That's what I like to see. Good things come to those who hustle." He let his eyes linger on her lips, then slide down to the V-neck of the light-pink T-shirt she wore under a wrinkled linen blazer, before slapping a hand on the reception counter and heading for his office.

Lacey suppressed a shudder and turned back to the inventory report she was reconciling. Mind-numbing work, like pretty much everything at her job, but she wasn't in a position to complain. She'd been lucky to land it at all.

Technically, the position required a college degree—why, she had no idea, since she was fairly certain a well-trained chimp could handle her duties without much trouble—a degree Lacey didn't have, thanks to getting pregnant junior year.

At the time, she had planned to go back and finish her biochemistry degree once Elliott was past the exhausting baby phase. But then came the exhausting toddler phase, and by the time that ended, Judd had gotten promoted to lead a team of designers. His new salary was enough for them to put a down payment on the house in Maplehurst, and moving there to raise a family had seemed like the logical next step. Better than staying in their cramped one-bedroom in the city.

Other employees filtered in, offering greetings as they passed Lacey's desk. She responded with quick hellos, barely looking up from her report, which she was flying through. A glance at her watch told her she'd been in the office for nearly an hour without a peep from Elliott, and relief began to settle in her chest. Maybe this would work after all.

Then, out of the corner of her eye, she saw Marcia sidling up to the front desk. Lacey swallowed a groan.

Most of her coworkers were bland but harmless, but Marcia, who had been promoted out of Lacey's role into a sales coordinator position, seemed to believe that entitled her to a running commentary on how Lacey should be doing her job.

"Good morning, Marcia," Lacey said, pasting on a smile she hoped would preempt whatever complaint Marcia had come to deliver.

"There's a *child* in the break room," Marcia said, pursing her lips as she raised one overplucked eyebrow—the same shade of purple-red as her rigid helmet of hair.

"Yes, my son, Elliott," Lacey replied smoothly. "You met him at the company picnic."

Marcia folded her arms. "This is a workplace, not a daycare."

"It's just for today," Lacey said, her eyes watering from the thick cloud of Marcia's aggressively sweet perfume.

Marcia's lips tightened. "Well, I'm *sure* you cleared it with Chip," she said, voice dripping with faux innocence. "So we'll just have to hope for the best that he doesn't become a distraction."

Lacey's smile faltered, and satisfaction flickered in Marcia's eyes.

"No distraction, I promise," Lacey said, forcing her voice to stay even. Marcia held her gaze for an instant, her chin lifted slightly as if in challenge. Then she turned and stalked back toward her desk, her wide hips swaying.

Steadying herself, Lacey pushed to her feet and made a beeline for the break room.

Elliott was exactly where she'd left him, hunched over his iPad, eyes glued to the screen. She placed a hand on his shoulder.

"Doing OK, buddy?"

No response. She kneaded her fingers gently against his shoulder, then leaned closer to his ear. She knew he probably couldn't hear her through his headphones. Then again, sometimes even without them, he didn't hear her when he was lost in a comic book or deep in a LEGO build. *Hyperfocus*, their pediatrician had called it. A side effect of ADHD.

"I know it seems counterintuitive," the doctor had explained, "that a disorder with 'attention deficit' in the name would cause intense focus, but it's actually very common, especially for kids, that ADHD presents with hyperactivity rather than inattention."

When Elliott was diagnosed at the start of second grade, it felt like a relief. Finally, an explanation for the intense emotional swings, the outbursts, the impulsive behavior that kept getting him into trouble, like the time he couldn't resist cutting off Hadley McAllister's braid during art class.

By then, Lacey had stopped taking him to playdates and birthday parties for fear of a meltdown or that he might accidentally hurt someone. She had assumed she was just a bad mother. That she hadn't read enough parenting books, hadn't fed him enough vegetables, had been too rigid with his sleep schedule, or maybe too lax.

But the diagnosis proved it wasn't *her*. It was something external. Something she could learn how to manage.

"Elliott," she said again, giving him a gentle shake. Touch was the best way to pull him back to the present.

"Huh?" He paused the movie and looked up.

"You good, sweetheart? Need a snack or anything?"

"Can I have popcorn yet?" he asked.

Lacey ruffled his hair. "In a little while, OK?"

He nodded, then turned back to the screen.

Lacey bent to kiss his cheek and inhale his little boy smell of shampoo and the peanut butter crackers he'd had for breakfast, then hurried back to the reception desk.

Fifteen minutes later, Chip appeared in front of her, his eyes narrowed.

"Is that your kid in the break room?" He jerked his head toward the door.

"Elliott, yes." Lacey forced another bright smile. "My childcare for today fell through, and I didn't want to let you down by calling out again. He'll be fine in there, I promise."

She fluttered her eyelashes slightly, tucking a strand of hair behind her ear, then let her hand trail down her neck as she held Chip's gaze, all the while hating herself for it.

Chip grunted. "It's against policy."

Lacey toyed with the button on her blazer just below her breasts. "It's just for today, I swear."

His mouth twisted in indecision. Then another grunt.

"Just for today," he said, giving her a stern look before walking off.

An hour later they were crammed into the conference room for their Monday morning staff meeting, which Chip had dubbed the Hustle Huddle.

"All right, team," Chip had said. "Let's lock in and level up! We'll start with status updates. Marcia, can you kick us off?"

Marcia smiled as though he'd just handed her a medal. "Happy to start," she said, then paused and sniffed the air. "Does anyone else smell that?"

Lacey inhaled. A faint burnt scent lingered in the air, like a crumb stuck in a toaster. She sniffed again and the smell had grown stronger.

BEEP. BEEP. BEEP.

The blaring wail of the fire alarm filled the office.

"Something's definitely burning," Marcia said, frowning.

Lacey's stomach plummeted.

She shot out of her chair, shoved open the conference room door, and sprinted toward the break room. The acrid scent thickened as she got closer. When she stepped inside, she found Elliott standing frozen in front of the microwave, wide-eyed, his face twisted in panic. Smoke leaked from the microwave, which was still running.

"What do I do?" he asked frantically.

"Get back!" Lacey ordered.

Grabbing a towel, she waved at the smoke, then used it to yank open the microwave door. A thick cloud poured out, and she coughed, her eyes burning.

"Shit," she gasped. "Elliott, what did you do?"

Tears welled in his eyes. "I was making popcorn," he whimpered. "I found a bag in the cabinet—I just... I forgot it was in there!"

Lacey dropped to her knees, yanking open the cabinet beneath the sink, desperately searching for the fire extinguisher she knew had to be there. Her fingers closed around it, and she fumbled to scan the instructions, heart pounding.

No visible flames, but she couldn't risk it.

She wrenched out the pin, aimed at the microwave, and squeezed the trigger. A blast of white foam shot out, smothering the smoke. The acrid burn of charred popcorn was quickly replaced by the harsh, chemical scent of extinguisher residue.

A beat of silence.

Then—

"What the hell?"

Lacey spun around to find Chip standing in the doorway, flanked by Marcia and the rest of the team, all staring in horrified fascination.

Tears burned behind her eyes.

"I'm so sorry," she said, her voice barely above a whisper.

An hour later, Lacey sat in the car, her head resting against the steering wheel. Elliott sat silently in the backseat, his backpack beside him.

"Mommy," he whispered, his voice small. "I'm really sorry."

"I know," she murmured. Just forming the words took all her energy.

She wanted to be angry, but she knew she had only herself to blame. Eight was too young to sit unsupervised all morning. But in all the scenarios she'd mentally prepared for, Elliott nearly burning down the office hadn't been one of them. Neither had getting fired as a result.

"It's just not working out," Chip had said flatly as she gathered her things. "I'll have HR reach out later this week."

Lacey hadn't even had the strength to argue. She didn't want the job, anyway, no matter that she needed it. She'd opted to study biochemistry in college, and had wanted to work in public health, helping to create new, life-saving vaccinations or water purification agents for use in developing countries. She'd imagined herself moving to Africa with the Peace Corps for a year, and doing a PhD eventually. Tracking inventory at a budget carpet store had not been on her proverbial vision board.

Her phone rang deep in her purse. She ignored it. It was probably just more bad news.

"Mommy, your phone," Elliott said, reaching into the front seat.

"Just leave it," she said, waving him off.

But he fished it out of her bag and handed it to her. "It might be important."

She sighed, lifting her head just enough to take it from him, intending to silence it. "Sweetheart, I promise it's not—"

Her breath caught as she registered the number. Heart hammering, she scrambled to answer.

"Hello?"

"Lacey, hi," came the voice, breezy and smooth. "It's Regina Cho. How are you?"

"Um, fine," Lacey managed, her throat suddenly tight.

"Good, good. Hey, I was calling to let you know that Tavia, Nanette, and I talked it over, and if you're still interested, we'd love to have you and Elliott join the house."

Lacey's relief was so acute it felt like a lightning bolt through her chest. "Yes," she croaked, gripping the phone like someone might try to take it from her. "Yes, I'm still interested."

Regina let out a warm, throaty laugh. "Wonderful. Welcome to the mommune."

FIVE

On Thursday, Lacey loaded the last of her and Elliott's bags into the car in the driveway of Sarah's house. As she slammed the trunk shut, a pang settled in her chest to see that all their belongings fit into a single car.

Well, all they had now. Her winter clothes, her books, and her beloved baking pans were still at the house she used to call home, along with most of Elliott's toys. At least he got to see his things regularly when she dropped him off with Judd, like she was about to.

But she missed her mixing bowls, the ones she used to whip up cakes, cookies, even the occasional loaf of bread when she was feeling ambitious. She missed the ritual of it, the comfort in knowing exactly the result you'd get if you added the right ingredients in the right order.

If only life worked the same way.

"All packed up?"

Lacey flinched at the sound of Sarah's voice behind her. She turned to see her sister standing on the front steps, shifting on her feet. Dressed in a cream-colored linen jumpsuit, her honey-blonde hair perfectly waved, Sarah looked as composed as Lacey felt scattered.

"Yeah." Lacey nodded, smoothing the frizzy flyaway strands that had escaped her ponytail in the thick August humidity. "I think we have everything." She forced a small, tired smile.

Sarah bit her lip. "OK. Well, if you need anything…" She trailed off, eyes darting away. A guilty expression flickered across her face.

They both knew the truth: Lacey's needs were too much for Sarah.

"I'm sorry," Sarah said suddenly, looking back at her, face tight, eyes watery. "It's just… Elliott, and everything. I wish…"

"I know," Lacey said, shoving her hands into the pockets of her worn denim cutoffs. "It's fine."

But it wasn't fine, and they both knew that.

Sarah stepped forward and wrapped Lacey in an awkward hug —limp arms, bodies held apart. Then she turned and walked back inside, closing the door behind her.

As she drove, Lacey flicked through radio stations, dodging commercials, her fingers moving restlessly across the dial. In the rearview mirror, she caught glimpses of Elliott, his small face turned to the window, his mouth drawn in a tight line.

"Will Daddy be in a good mood?" Elliott asked.

The question hit Lacey like a gut punch and for a moment she couldn't answer. The last thing she wanted was to leave him alone with Judd. While she didn't believe Judd would hurt Elliott—not physically—in the three weeks since they'd moved out, she'd watched her son slowly unfurl. The tense lines had eased from his face, his shoulders no longer hunched up to his ears. He didn't flinch anymore when she raised her voice in frustration, like he was bracing for an explosion, the kind that was common with Judd. It made her ache with guilt, realizing now how far into himself Elliott had retreated.

He'd still seen Judd occasionally, an hour here or there for baseball or a swim at the neighborhood pool, but Judd hadn't pressed for more. Until now. This time, he'd insisted on an overnight.

"Of course Daddy's in a good mood; he's excited to see you," she said, forcing a brightness into her voice that she didn't feel. She adjusted the rearview mirror so she could meet Elliott's eyes in the backseat. "Maybe you can work on planning your next camping trip," she said, and Elliott smiled.

Starting the summer he turned five, Judd had taken Elliott on a father-son camping trip every year. They would pitch a tent at a nearby state park, and, judging by the photos Judd took, spend twenty-four hours swimming, tooling around in a rented pontoon, and eating as many hot dogs and s'mores as their stomachs could handle. Elliott inevitably arrived home sticky and smiling, giggling as he recounted to Lacey how the bear he thought he'd heard in the middle of the night had just been Judd snoring.

Yet now, as they entered their old neighborhood, she couldn't shake her worry. Elliott thrived on routine. Their mornings together always started the same—snuggles first, then breakfast (peanut butter crackers with exactly two raisins per cracker, no more, no less), then movement of some kind to burn off his restless energy. And, of course, his medicine, which Judd definitely wouldn't give him. But Lacey had zipped a pill into the inside pocket of Elliott's backpack.

She shook her head to scatter her concerns. It would be fine. She needed this time to get them settled at the mommune. By the time she picked Elliott up tomorrow, his things would be unpacked, his favorite foods stocked, his new home waiting for him —neat, stable, safe.

But as she turned onto their old street, then into the driveway of their house, a wave of loss crashed over her.

Loss for the life she'd once imagined, for the home she and Judd were supposed to build together, for the stable, happy childhood Elliott deserved.

She took a slow breath, pushing the ache down, and turned to face her son.

"OK, remember, your pill for tomorrow morning is in the inside pocket of your backpack. Promise me you'll take it first thing? Before you go down for breakfast with Daddy?"

Elliott nodded, barely listening, his hand already on the door handle.

The front door swung open, and Judd stepped onto the porch.

"Hi, Daddy!" he said, climbing out of the car.

"Hey, buddy," Judd said, bounding down the walk and wrapping his arms around Elliott.

He kissed the top of Elliott's head, then looked up as Lacey got out of the car, raising her hand in a limp wave.

"Hey," he said. His dark hair had grown shaggy, curling over his ears, and the pale blue of his eyes, so much like Elliott's, stood out against the hollowness of his face. A beard was growing in patches on his chin and cheeks.

"Hey," she echoed, awkwardly holding out Elliott's backpack. "Everything he needs should be in here."

Judd's jaw tensed. "He has plenty of stuff here."

"Just in case." Lacey tried to smile, but her mouth only stretched into a tight, unconvincing line.

She searched his face for some trace of the man she had once loved—the one who had shown up outside her dorm with a bouquet of roses on their first date, who had rubbed her swollen feet every night during her pregnancy, who had kissed her under an arbor of wisteria in her parents' back yard on their wedding day. But all she saw now was the hardness in his eyes, the deepening creases between his brows as he frowned at her.

Her chest ached, wondering how someone went from being your person to feeling like a stranger.

"How are you?" she asked, scanning his face for something—anything—familiar.

"I'd be better if you'd just come home," he said, his chin jutting out. For a brief second the thought flitted through Lacey's mind as an actual possibility. It was replaced almost immediately by a sharp memory of how alone she'd felt living with Judd, and how tense she'd become trying to anticipate his moods and protect Elliott from them.

She exhaled sharply, crouching down to hand Elliott his backpack. "Hey, why don't you run inside and see your toys while I talk to Daddy?" She lowered her voice, pressing her lips to his ear. "And don't forget your pill tomorrow morning, OK?"

Elliott nodded and ran up to the house.

She straightened, locking eyes with Judd. "Don't do that in front of him," she said, crossing her arms.

"Do what?" His gaze flickered over her, and suddenly she felt self-conscious about her wrinkled T-shirt, the bleach-stained cutoff shorts she'd been wearing since being fired, too exhausted to care about fishing something cleaner out of her suitcase.

"Talk about us moving back in," she said. "It gives him false hope."

"This is his home," Judd said, voice tight. "And *yours*, too."

Lacey's throat burned. "Not anymore."

Judd took half a step back. "So it's really over? Just like that?"

Just like that. As if they hadn't been unraveling for years. As if they hadn't spent countless nights in hushed, hostile fights after Elliott was asleep. Judd volleying caustic barbs at her, criticizing her reliance on therapists and medication to solve Elliott's problems when really what he needed was good old-fashioned discipline, Lacey begging Judd to see the faulty logic behind his theories about Big Pharma suppressing the cure for cancer to keep people hooked on expensive treatments. She had asked him to go to marriage therapy, had asked his parents and his friends to intervene. He had only dug in deeper.

For Lacey, having to medicate Elliott in secret had been the final breaking point. She knew she couldn't survive in a marriage where she had to hide her views on what was best for her child.

Lacey swallowed hard. "It's really over."

Her voice cracked, and she blinked back the tears welling in her eyes. She cleared her throat and swiped at them quickly. "I'll pick him up tomorrow morning. Around nine."

Elliott had a therapy appointment, but she wasn't about to tell Judd that.

Judd gave a short nod. "Fine."

For a moment, he held her gaze. Then he turned, stepping inside, and shut the door.

Lacey stood there for a long second, alone on the stoop, saying a silent prayer that all would be well and Elliott would have a good time. Then she turned back to her car.

Pulling up to the house on Wildwood Lane, Lacey took a moment to collect herself. The front yard looked just as she remembered—the bike with training wheels still parked haphazardly on the walkway, the grass in need of cutting but not quite overgrown. She pictured the kids from last time, running through their names in her head to make sure she had them right: Linden, the headstrong five-year-old; Grace, Tavia's two-year-old; and Max and Maddie, Regina's twins, eight years old like Elliott.

Elliott had fallen in with them so seamlessly when they were here last week—had it really only been a week? Time blurred lately, slipping through her fingers as she focused on little more than getting through each day.

Regina answered the door within seconds of Lacey ringing the bell. She wore a rust-colored sleeveless dress, simple but elegant as it hung on her lean frame.

"Come in!" she said, her voice low and warm, reaching to take one of Lacey's bags.

"Oh, I've got it," Lacey said, glancing around for somewhere to set them down.

"Don't be silly." Regina hoisted a bag off Lacey's shoulder with ease, then peered behind her. "Where's Elliott?"

Lacey shifted on her feet. "At his dad's for the night. I figured I'd get us settled first."

"Ah." Regina nodded knowingly. "Well, good. I'm glad you

have a night to yourself." She turned toward the stairs. "Max, Maddie!" she called. "Come help Lacey unload the car."

"Oh, they don't have to—" Lacey started.

Regina raised a decisive hand, cutting her off. "Everyone helps out around here, even the kids."

A thundering noise echoed from upstairs, and then two kids barreled down the staircase, shoving each other out of the way.

"I won!" Max declared triumphantly, still clad in a pair of slightly-too-short *Black Panther* pajamas that barely grazed his ankles.

"Did not," Maddie huffed, rolling her eyes. Her shoulder-length dark hair was unruly, much like her mother's, and she wore baggy surfer-style shorts with an oversized T-shirt.

"Did too—"

"Guys, enough," Regina said, raising an eyebrow. She handed off the bag she was holding. "One of you take this to the yellow room, then help Lacey get the rest of her things from the car."

She turned to Lacey with a nod. "Follow me."

Lacey trailed behind, inhaling the warm, inviting scent of coffee and something freshly baked. Did it always smell this good here?

Upstairs, the house looked exactly as it had in the pictures Regina had shared with her over email. The stairs opened into a small, sunlit alcove, furnished with a loveseat and a mound of over-sized pillows strewn across a soft, dark green rug. A large bookshelf stood against the wall, crammed with children's books.

Regina continued down the hallway, the wood floors worn but freshly polished. She pointed as they passed each doorway. "That's Max and Maddie's room, mine is downstairs—the only bedroom on the main floor. Nanette and Linden are here, Tavia and Grace are across from them, and you and Elliott are here." She paused in front of a door at the end of the hall. "Like I mentioned, there's a Japanese screen you can set up for privacy next to Elliott's bed, and you have your own en suite bathroom. Tavia and Nanette share the other one on this floor, and Max and Maddie use mine downstairs."

Lacey stepped inside. The walls were painted a pale yellow, sunlight streaming through the windows, making them almost glow. Against one wall sat a queen-sized bed with a patinaed metal headboard, a small nightstand beside it. Above the bed hung three framed prints of sunflowers. In the far corner, partially obscured by a freestanding off-white wooden screen, was a twin bed, and in the other corner stood an overstuffed armchair with a weathered blue and white cotton slipcover. A plush cream-colored rug stretched across the floor, and a long bay window lined with plants overlooked the yard. Some leaves drooped, tinged with yellow.

"Sorry about the plants," Regina sighed, following her gaze. "I've been trying to keep up with them, but..." She shrugged. "Feel free to ditch them if you want." She swept a hand around the room, the other still gripping her coffee mug. "And also to replace the pictures, the bedding—whatever you want. It's your room."

Lacey's breath caught. *Your room.* Tears pricked at her eyes.

"Thank you," she whispered, swallowing the lump in her throat.

Regina smiled. "I'll let you get settled. I work from home, but Tavia and Nanette will be back this afternoon. Once you're unpacked, we can stick the kids in front of a movie and have some wine and adult time." She winked and turned to go.

Lacey stood in the center of the sun-drenched room, turning in a slow circle. A wave of relief washed over her, cool and steady, unlike the tight, panicked survival mode she'd been living in for weeks. She could feel the tightness easing in her chest. She and Elliott would be safe here, she was sure of it.

SIX

Lacey awoke to the sound of children's voices. Blinking, it took her a few seconds to remember where she was. The bright afternoon sunlight that had bathed her room while she unpacked—hanging her clothes in the closet, arranging Elliott's beloved *Star Wars* LEGO figurines on the little shelf next to his bed—had softened into the golden haze of early evening.

She wiped a small trail of drool from her cheek, realizing she'd fallen asleep without even crawling under the covers, her feet still hanging off the end of the bed. She had only meant to lie down for a minute, but the second she was horizontal, her body had felt like cement, too heavy to sit back up, her eyes welded shut with exhaustion. Checking her watch, she saw she'd been out for nearly two hours. And yet, she still felt like she could roll over and sleep for several more.

Blinking the grogginess away, she forced herself to sit up. The unpacking was nearly done, but she needed to run to the store, pick up a few essentials, make sure there were snacks for Elliott when she collected him in the morning.

Downstairs, the high-pitched chatter of children's voices mixed with the lower murmur of adult conversation. Lacey padded to the bathroom, splashed cool water on her face, and pulled her wavy hair into a ponytail. Her large brown eyes looked less tired than usual under her thick brows, and there was a pretty flush on her cheekbones from the lingering warmth of the sun-filled room.

"Here I've been thinking I needed Botox, when all I really needed was a nap," she muttered to herself.

Swapping her cutoffs and two-day-old T-shirt for a black tank top and a pair of oat-colored linen pants—wrinkled, but in a way that she hoped looked intentional—she stepped into the hall.

Following the voices, she headed downstairs toward the kitchen. The four kids sat at the table, their chatter punctuated by the clink of silverware as Tavia, clad in a clingy black T-shirt dress, loaded their plates with homemade mac and cheese, the golden-brown breadcrumb topping crisp and glistening.

She stood taking in the kitchen's riot of color—deep green cabinets, coral pink pantry doors, and a bright yellow tile backsplash that somehow all worked together. The stone countertop was flecked with gray and blue, scattered with crumbs, and a sweating container of milk. It radiated warmth and welcome.

The worn floorboards creaked under Lacey's feet and she raised a hand in a shy greeting as heads turned toward her. "Hey."

Tavia grinned. "You're just in time for happy hour," she said in her drawl, nodding toward Nanette, who was standing by the fridge, a bottle of wine in hand. She wore a muted orange tank top tucked into linen shorts printed with a bold, Aztec-inspired pattern and the same stack of jade bracelets she'd had on last time Lacey had seen her.

"Two-for-one glasses, every day from five to seven," Nanette quipped, a smile sliding over her full lips. She held up the bottle. "White or red?"

"Um, white, if it's open," Lacey said. "But just a small glass. I still need to run to the store tonight."

Tavia waved a hand as she set the kids' plates in front of them. The chatter around the table immediately ceased as they dug in.

"Don't go anywhere," she said. "I'm about to throw some

burgers on the grill in honor of your first night. And Nanette's going to whip up a cheese plate, aren't you, honey child?"

Nanette rolled her eyes good-naturedly as she poured Lacey's wine. "Why does the one with the dairy allergy always end up making the cheese plate?" she lamented.

"Because you do those cute little garnishes," Regina said, smiling as she entered the kitchen. To Lacey she added, "Nanette's the artistic one. She makes the most amazing jewelry. And Tavia's our resident Southern belle."

Tavia batted her eyelashes and raised her wine glass in salute. "And Regina's the captain of this crazy ship," she added, nodding toward Regina. "Cool as cucumber, that one. If she'd been in charge of the *Titanic*, it never would have made headlines."

Regina laughed and waved off the compliment. "Did everyone say thank you to Tavia for dinner?" she asked, turning to the kids.

"Thank you for dinner!" came the chorus of small voices.

Lacey marveled at how well-behaved all the kids were, even toddler Grace, strapped into her booster seat, happily munching away.

Tavia caught her eye. "It's not always this peaceful, believe me," she said wryly. "But mac and cheese is a crowd-pleaser."

"Tavia's an *amazing* cook," Regina added. "Everyone's excited when it's her night. Less so when I cook." She gave an apologetic shrug as she took the glass of wine Nanette offered.

"You have other skills," Nanette said diplomatically. Then, to Lacey, "She retiled the whole downstairs bathroom single-handedly last summer."

Lacey took a sip of the crisp, cold wine. "You take turns cooking?" she asked, her mind stuck on Regina's comment.

Regina nodded. "We put up a sign-up sheet on Sundays, and everyone grabs a night or two that works for them. It's easier when you don't have to think about it every day, you know?"

Lacey did know. If there was one thing about motherhood that felt the most unfair, it was that dinner happened every single night. She had lost count of how many times she'd resorted to peanut butter sandwiches for Elliott and a bowl of cereal for herself. The idea of not scrambling to figure it out every night sent a spark of excitement through her.

"But what about groceries?" she asked.

"I use part of the rent money to keep us stocked with the basics," Regina explained. "Milk, eggs, bread, fruits, veggies—the essentials. There's also a second freezer in the garage where we keep meat and bulk items. And if there's anything special you need for something you're cooking for the house just let me know and I'll pick it up when I do the grocery run."

"We each have a pantry shelf for personal stuff," Nanette added, "but everything else is communal."

"Oh, and we take shifts for kitchen and common area cleanup," Tavia said, pouring herself a glass of wine. "And for watching the kids in the evenings or on weekends, depending on everyone's schedules. Like, I have a salsa class on Tuesday nights, so someone else gets Gracie to bed."

Lacey's head buzzed, whether from the wine on an empty stomach or the rush of information, she wasn't sure. Shared meals, communal groceries, built-in childcare—it was a lot to take in. And yet, every part of it sounded wonderful.

"Wow," she managed, taking another gulp of wine.

Regina laughed. "It's a lot, I know. But you'll get the rhythm of the house in no time." She lifted her glass. "Cheers! And welcome."

"Cheers!" echoed Tavia and Nanette, and the four women clinked glasses.

After the kids finished their dinner, Nanette whisked Grace off to bed while Tavia put burgers and fresh sweetcorn on the grill for the adults. Regina cued up a movie for Max, Maddie, and Linden, then set to work on a salad.

Lacey, nibbling a slice of cheese, watched as Regina tossed crisp lettuce with cherry tomatoes and cucumbers. True to Regina's word, Nanette's cheeseboard had been exquisite, the slices arranged just so with delicately fanned-out sliced strawberries adding the perfect touch.

"Can I do anything to help?" Lacey asked.

Regina smiled as she reached for the salad tongs. "Just relax tonight. We'll put you to work soon enough."

Lacey hesitated, taking in the easy rhythm of the house, the seamless way everyone moved together. "So having everyone pitch in like this... it really works?" She tried to keep the note of skepticism out of her voice.

Regina tilted her head, considering. "It's not perfect," she admitted. "But yeah, mostly it works. The chemistry has to be right, though. Not everyone is suited for communal living, and trust is a big part of it—we're essentially helping to raise each other's kids."

She tossed the salad again, then leaned against the counter. "There's a certain amount of letting go that has to happen. At first, it can be hard to give up that control, to stop being the only decision-maker. We try to respect each other's boundaries, but there has to be some give and take." She lifted her chin. "Not everyone's going to fit in here, you know?"

"And you think I will?" Lacey asked softly. Suddenly she desperately wanted to be part of this. Not simply to have a place to live but to have the effortless camaraderie, the way these women moved around each other with ease, caring for each other's kids, cooking dinner without resentment. She wanted to be part of this house with its sun-drenched rooms and good smells, the whole place exuding a certain lived-in comfort. It was so different from Sarah's pristine, gleaming house, where she'd been afraid to move anything out of its place.

Regina met her gaze, something knowing in her expression. "I think," she said, smiling, "we're about to find out."

Tavia bustled back into the kitchen, juggling one plate of browned, juicy hamburgers and another of perfectly charred corn. "Lord, it's hotter than Hades out there," she said, fanning her glistening face. "I can't wait for it to be September next week, maybe get some fall weather for a change."

Nanette breezed back in and began to refill everyone's wine glasses.

"Goodness," Tavia said. "Is my little hellion already asleep?"

Nanette rubbed a hand over her closely shorn hair. "She was out before I even finished the first story."

"Thank God," Tavia said, setting the plates down with a flourish. "Because all I want right now is to sit my butt down with a burger and an inappropriately large glass of wine." She nodded toward the bottle in Nanette's hand. "Don't be stingy now."

Nanette laughed, tipping the last of the bottle into Tavia's glass. "I'll grab another one."

Regina swirled the wine in her own glass. "Lacey and I were just talking about what makes someone a good fit here," she said as the four of them settled at the kitchen table. Its light wood surface was worn with nicks and grooves and the occasional scribble of marker. She glanced at Tavia and Nanette. "You two have been here a while; what do you think?"

"Being able to thrive in chaos is a good start," Nanette observed, raising her glass. "Also, don't walk around barefoot because you'll impale your foot on a LEGO."

Lacey laughed as she accepted a burger from the plate being passed around, her stomach growling. "How long have you all lived here?" she asked.

"I came right before Grace was born," Tavia said, spearing a thick slice of tomato with her fork and sliding it onto her burger. "Right after my husband gave me two black eyes, because one apparently wasn't enough to ensure I'd learned my lesson." Her tone was light but the smile she gave Lacey was strained.

Lacey's jaw dropped in horror. "That's awful," she said.

Tavia shrugged. "Thanks, honey. But it's all trauma under the bridge now. Most days I hardly think about him. Last I heard he was remarried to a woman he met at the gym, poor thing." She clucked her tongue in pity, then added, "Her, obviously, not him."

Unsure how to respond, Lacey swallowed a bite of burger and nodded.

"And I moved in a few months after Tavia, when my husband kicked me out after he caught me on a lesbian porn website," Nanette said.

Lacey choked as she swallowed, and reached for her water glass. She hadn't expected such unvarnished honesty from the women, at least not on day one. "He kicked you out for watching porn?" she asked, eyes wide, when she'd recovered.

Nanette raised a well-sculpted eyebrow. "No—he kicked me out because it turns out I *am* a lesbian." She took a sip of wine, her face darkening slightly. "I hadn't known till then, either. He's very involved in our church, which isn't known for its warm embrace of homosexuality." Her long fingernails, which were painted neon orange, tapped against her glass. "I would have been open to trying to co-parent amicably, but he didn't want to hear it. He tried to get custody of Linden."

Lacey's stomach clenched. Custody. She and Judd hadn't gotten that far yet. She hadn't dared think about it, but had been hoping Elliott would stay with her, the parent most equipped to support his needs. Her thoughts flew to Elliott, wondering what he was doing at that moment. She prayed the night was going smoothly, that Elliott hadn't had one of his meltdowns, which often sent Judd into a tailspin of his own, ratcheting up the tension instead of diffusing it.

"I'm so sorry," Lacey said, swallowing the last bite of her burger. She felt a twinge of guilt for having devoured dinner like a cavewoman in the midst of Nanette and Tavia's stories of heartbreak and domestic upheaval.

Tavia squared her shoulders. "I'm not," she said simply. "And I'd wager Nanette isn't either. But thank God for Regina." She smiled at Regina, who looked modestly down at her lap. "Without her," Tavia continued, "I'd probably be back at my parents' in Tennessee, tail between my legs, watching my mama cook and clean while my daddy knocked us both around."

"Same," said Nanette. "I didn't have any friends outside our church. Who, it turned out, weren't really friends at all." Her mouth pressed briefly into a grim line, then softened as she turned to Lacey. "This house is a soft landing," she said. "A place to regroup."

Lacey let the words wash over her. It sounded as though it was exactly what she needed.

That night after dinner, as the rest of the women wrangled kids into pajamas and brushed little teeth, Lacey drifted upstairs to her room. She felt loose and warm from the wine, full and satisfied from the long dinner, and so much more connected to the other women as they'd shared their painful pasts with her—all except for Regina, Lacey realized as she washed her face and pulled on an old T-shirt to sleep in. While the others had shared, Regina had sat quietly, wearing that same unreadable Mona Lisa smile.

It wasn't even ten, but Lacey was more than happy to crawl beneath the soft sheets. The white curtains rippled lazily under the whir of the ceiling fan, lulling her toward sleep—until her phone rang, yanking her back.

Reaching for it on her nightstand, she saw Judd's number on the screen and scrambled to a seated position.

"Is everything OK?" she asked, skipping a greeting entirely.

"Mommy?" Elliott's voice was small and wobbly.

Fear shot through Lacey. "Sweetheart? What's wrong? Where's Daddy?"

"I'm OK," Elliott said, but his voice quivered. "Daddy's downstairs. He's mad at me."

Lacey was already reaching for the pair of shorts she'd left draped over a chair, her free hand digging through the clutter on her nightstand for her car keys. "I'm coming to get you."

"No." The shakiness in Elliott's voice disappeared, replaced by quiet determination. "I don't wanna leave. I just—I just wanted to talk to you."

Lacey hesitated, her pulse still racing. Slowly, she sank back onto the bed, forcing herself to take a deep breath. "OK, buddy. Talk to me. What happened?"

There was a pause, then Elliott's voice came back, quieter.

"I made him mad," he said. "He was asking me about school starting next week, and I said I wasn't excited because it's hard for me... you know, because of my different brain. And then his face got all red, and he started yelling that there's *nothing* different about my brain, that it's just like everyone else's and that I only think it's hard because I don't like working. And that you let me be lazy."

His voice cracked on the last word.

Lacey's grip tightened around her phone, her throat burning with a mix of anger and heartbreak. Judd could be infuriating—dismissive, stubborn, unwilling to accept anything that didn't fit into his rigid worldview—but this? Making Elliott question himself? It was cruel.

"Oh, sweetheart," she murmured.

Elliott sniffled. "Mommy... am I, like... not smart? Because if Daddy's right, and my brain's not different, but school is still hard for me, then... what if I'm just dumb?"

Lacey's spine stiffened. "Elliott," she said fiercely. "Listen to me. You are *so* smart. Remember last year, when we read that book about the solar system? You still remember every single thing from it. And you can do math in your head that I need a calculator for. School was hard before because we didn't know you had ADHD. You weren't on your medicine yet. But this year, buddy? It's going to be so much better. I promise."

"Yeah?" His voice wavered, but the doubt in it had softened some.

"Yeah," she said firmly.

She could picture him nodding, clutching Judd's phone.

Lacey inhaled deeply. "Does Daddy know you're talking to me?"

A pause.

"No," Elliott admitted. "I took his phone when he went in the kitchen. I'm in the bathroom."

Lacey's heart clenched at the thought of Elliott hiding in the bathroom to call her.

"Sweetheart, let me come get you," she pleaded, even as her stomach twisted at the thought of showing up and facing Judd.

"I'm OK, Mommy," Elliott said, steadier now. "I don't wanna leave Daddy alone. He never gets to see me, and I think he's lonely. He'll calm down, I know he will. We were having fun before."

Lacey wanted to scream at the unfairness of it all—that Elliott, at eight years old, already felt responsible for managing his father's emotions. "OK," she relented, though it physically hurt to say it. "But you call me anytime, OK? No matter what time it is, I'll come get you."

"OK," Elliott said.

"I love you so much, buddy."

"Love you, too. Bye, Mommy."

Lacey exhaled shakily as she hung up then rolled over and buried her face in the pillow, letting out a long, muffled scream.

SEVEN

Lacey did her best to swallow her rage the next morning as she pulled up to Judd's house, forcing her jaw to unclench, pasting on her sunniest smile when Elliott flung open the door and launched himself into her arms.

"Hey, buddy," she said, pressing a kiss into his bedhead hair as she hugged him tight. "Why don't you hop in the car? I'll be right there."

"Hop, hop," he said, frog-jumping down the front steps before turning back as Judd appeared in the doorway.

"Bye, Daddy!" Elliott called, hopping back to wrap his arms around him.

Judd ruffled his hair. "Bye, kiddo. Love you. See you soon, OK?"

"Love you, too!"

Elliott turned back toward the car, hopping the rest of the way, his backpack bouncing against his back.

The second his car door clicked shut, Lacey folded her arms tightly across her chest. "Elliott called me last night," she said, forcing her voice to stay level. "He was upset. You yelled at him, and he was scared."

A shadow of guilt crossed Judd's face, quickly replaced by suspicion. "How did he even call you? Did you buy him a phone without telling me?" He took a step toward her.

"Of course not," Lacey said, refusing to shrink away from him. "He used your phone." She took a breath, trying again. "Look, please can you just be more careful when you talk to him about his ADHD?"

Judd's jaw clenched. "I don't talk to him about it because he doesn't have it. It's a made-up condition—"

"By the drug companies, I know," Lacey cut in, rolling her eyes. "But when you refuse to acknowledge it, what you're really telling him is that he's lazy. Or worse, stupid."

"I never said that," Judd growled, his voice rising.

Lacey's own voice dropped, tight and trembling with restrained fury. "He told me *exactly* what you said."

Judd's forehead creased with regret, but he quickly masked it with a smirk. "So what? He ran to you to tattle? You love that, don't you? The big hero, swooping in to coddle him."

Lacey's nails dug into her palms as she glanced at Elliott in the car, making sure he wasn't listening. Her voice dropped to a fierce whisper. "How dare you make him doubt himself even for a minute? Do you have any idea how far he's come?"

She thought of the countless hours she'd spent shuttling Elliott to his twice-weekly occupational therapy sessions, the weekend mornings dedicated to his therapeutic playgroup to help him navigate social situations. The months of painstaking trial and error in bi-weekly consultations with his pediatrician, adjusting his medication little by little, searching for the right balance that would help him regulate his emotions without dulling the bright, curious boy she loved so much. And now here was Judd, undoing all her hard work with one overnight visit.

Judd's smirk vanished, his stance stiffening. "Oh, give me a break," he snapped. "Elliott's just like every other kid—he needs discipline. Structure. Not some made-up disorder."

Lacey felt a sharp sting behind her eyes, the familiar helpless fury she always felt when arguing with him. "It's not a made-up disorder, Judd. It's a neurological condition. His brain works differently. You think I just wanted to put him on medication? That I didn't agonize over it? That I didn't read every study, talk extensively to every doctor? You have no idea what it took to get him to where he is now. You saw how hard school was for him last year, academically and socially."

Judd let out a short, bitter laugh. "Listen to yourself. You're so brainwashed you actually believe this is helping him."

Lacey's breath hitched. "Are you even listening to yourself?" she hissed. "You think he's better off struggling every day? Feeling like a failure? Do you even know what it does to him when you say things like that?"

Judd took a step forward, lowering his voice, his eyes glinting with something that sent a chill through her. "I'm saying," he said slowly, deliberately, "that if you keep trying to give him those damn pills, I will take legal action."

Lacey's stomach dropped. "What?"

"You heard me," he said, his voice eerily calm. "According to you, we're over. But you need my consent to drug our son, and I won't give it. I'll go to court if that's what it takes to keep you from poisoning him."

Lacey's heart pounded in her ears. "You really think a judge is going to side with you?" she shot back. "You, who doesn't even believe ADHD is real? Who thinks vaccines are a government mind-control experiment? Who believes everything he reads on Reddit is a medical fact?"

Judd's face went red, his hands balling into fists at his sides. "Watch yourself," he said with a dark glance toward the car where Elliott was waiting.

Lacey inhaled sharply, forcing herself to step back.

"You do whatever you think you need to," she said, voice icy. "But I'll do whatever it takes to make sure Elliott gets the support he actually needs."

She turned on her heel, stalking toward the car before she said something she'd regret. As she pulled away from the curb, her hands trembled against the steering wheel. She glanced at Elliott in the rearview mirror. He was humming to himself, looking out the window, blissfully unaware of the battle looming over his head.

EIGHT

When Lacey and Elliott returned to the mommune after his therapy appointment and a grocery run, she had only just begun to settle after her confrontation with Judd. Fortunately, Max and Maddie were home, and Elliott immediately fell into a game of tag with them in the backyard, their laughter filtering in through the open window in the kitchen.

As she unpacked groceries into the pantry, she spotted a neatly printed label on an empty shelf—*Lacey & Elliott*—written in a child's careful handwriting. Something about the small, thoughtful gesture made her chest tighten. But her thoughts refused to slow down.

Would Judd really take legal action to stop Elliott from getting the care he needed? What would that even look like? Could she somehow teach herself enough legalese to represent herself in court? The thought of hiring a lawyer made her queasy—there was no way she could afford one, not until she found another job or reached some kind of financial settlement with Judd, which wasn't likely to happen anytime soon.

Lost in anxious thought, she turned too quickly, her elbow knocking into a bag of flour perched on the shelf. It tumbled to the ground with a heavy *thud*, the paper splitting open on impact, sending a cloud of fine white dust billowing into the air and coating the floor.

Lacey yelped, jumping back.

"Everything all right?"

She spun around to find Regina standing in the doorway. She was dressed more casually today, in olive green linen shorts and a crisp white T-shirt, but somehow next to her Lacey still felt frumpy in her cutoffs and faded Mumford & Sons T-shirt with a hole in the armpit.

"Just making a mess of your pantry," Lacey said, gesturing at the flour-covered floor. "I'm so sorry, I'll clean it up."

Regina smiled. "It's your pantry, too," she said easily. "Broom's in the corner." She ran a hand through her unruly waves. "Coffee? I was just about to make some."

"Yeah, sure," Lacey said, grabbing the broom.

As she swept up the mess, Regina measured out coffee while glancing out the window at the kids chasing each other in the backyard. "I'll be so happy when school starts on Tuesday," she said. "Figuring out childcare during summer break is like an unsolvable Rubik's Cube invented specifically for moms."

"Tell me about it," Lacey muttered, dumping the ruined flour into the trash. She braced her hands on the counter and exhaled heavily, the weight of the morning pressing down on her.

Behind her, Regina moved quietly, the comforting sounds of coffee brewing filling the space. After a moment, she spoke. "Want to talk about it?"

Lacey turned and looked up to find Regina watching her, head tilted slightly in quiet assessment, her eyes kind. She held out a steaming mug.

Lacey reached for the mug, hesitating for only a second before everything came pouring out: Elliott's frightened phone call the night before, the confrontation with Judd, the way his threat still rattled in her chest. Her increasing desperation over her finances, the sinking realization that if Judd followed through, she had no idea how she'd afford to fight him.

By the time she finished, she braced herself, expecting some flicker of judgment on Regina's face. Or maybe regret that she'd invited Lacey, clearly a walking disaster, into her house. But Regina's expression remained the same mild, knowing look she always wore.

"It sounds like you could really use a break," she said simply.

Lacey let out a slow breath, gripping the mug in both hands. "Yeah," she admitted. "I really could." She forced a small, self-conscious smile. "Sorry. I didn't mean to dump all that on you." A hollow laugh escaped her. "You're probably already regretting choosing me as a roommate."

Regina set her mug down on the counter, her eyes steady. "There's no shame in needing help, Lacey," she said. "That's why we all ended up here." She paused. "Also, I think you'll find that we're much more than roommates."

For a brief moment, something shifted in Regina's expression—her gaze sharpening, appraising. Unease prickled down Lacey's spine, but she shook it off. The whole situation with Judd was clearly making her paranoid. Regina looked away, tucking a loose strand of hair behind her ear. Then, she studied Lacey again, lips pressing into a thoughtful line. "I think I can help with a job," she said.

Hope flared in Lacey's chest. "Really? What kind of job?" Then her stomach clenched slightly as she added, "I mean, I'm not exactly qualified for much. College dropout, remember?"

Regina's gaze flickered with something unreadable before she grinned. "Oh, you're qualified for this," she said. "In fact, I'd say you're perfect. It's more about whether you're open to doing something a little... unconventional. Taking a risk or two."

Lacey frowned, a low-level sense of apprehension battling with her curiosity. "What kind of risk?" she asked.

Regina waved a hand dismissively. "Nothing dangerous or anything. And it pays well. Really well." She tilted her head expectantly.

Lacey hesitated, but her curiosity won out. "Tell me more," she said.

"It's an executive assistant job for a startup," Regina said, leaning against the kitchen counter and swirling the coffee in her mug. "But not your typical shoestring-budget kind of place. The owner's already a multi-millionaire and has plenty of his own money to invest."

Lacey frowned. "I really don't think I'm qualified for—"

"They do wearable biosensors," Regina interrupted. "Very popular with the biohacking crowd." She gave a small eyeroll, like she wasn't entirely sold on the trend. "But you studied biomedical stuff in college, right?"

Lacey blinked. She didn't remember mentioning that to Regina, but she must have, at some point.

"Yes," she said slowly. "But I didn't finish my degree."

Late in her junior year—before she had dropped out—she had already been deep in planning her senior thesis. She'd spent months poring over research on biometrics, self-experimentation, and the ethics of human enhancement. She had even picked her thesis title: *DIY Biology: The Scientific Validity and Ethical Concerns of Biohacking*. It felt like a hundred years ago now.

Regina waved a dismissive hand. "No one cares about the degree," she said. "They just care if you can do the job." She lifted her mug to her lips. "I'll send you the job description. Think about it." She paused and offered a small smile. "Things are going to turn around for you, you'll see."

That night, Lacey read Elliott a chapter of *Harry Potter and the Chamber of Secrets* as he curled into her side. After, she stroked his back in slow circles, something she'd done nearly every night since he was a baby. Now that he was eight, she often wondered how much longer he'd want her close like this. But so far, he was as cuddly as ever, and she wasn't about to rush him into growing up.

Once his breathing deepened and his limbs went still, she eased off the bed and padded downstairs for a glass of water. In the kitchen she found the other women gathered at the table, a bottle of white wine sweating between them.

"Welcome to the magnetic pull of the kitchen table," Nanette said, her bangles clinking like distant wind chimes as she gestured to the empty chair. "We seem to always end up here—not that I'm mad about it."

Lacey opened a cabinet in search of a glass.

"The one to the right of the stove," Regina instructed her. Her hair was up in a loose bun, a few strands curling around her temples, softening the sharp angles of her face.

Lacey found a glass and slid into the seat beside Nanette.

"How's Elliott settling in?" Regina asked.

"OK, I think." Lacey gave a half-shrug. "It's just been a lot of change lately." The guilt prickled under her skin as she thought of the upheaval she'd dragged Elliott through in the last month.

"Well, from the sound of things, y'all getting away from that husband of yours might be the kind of change you both needed," Tavia said. The corners of her eyes crinkled in a sympathetic smile. Though Lacey guessed Tavia was younger than her, her face had a worn quality to it, like she'd lived multiple lives already.

Her throat tightened as she thought of Judd, the memory of his angry threats still fresh. She wrapped her fingers around the wine glass Regina had just filled. "He's already talking about getting a lawyer," she said.

Tavia snorted. "My ex didn't even pretend to care. I packed up and left while I was still pregnant. He's never even met Grace— never wanted to."

Lacey looked toward Regina, who pressed her lips together. "It's always just been me and the kids," she said. "Keeps things simple."

"Like anything with kids is ever simple," Nanette said, fingering the leather fringe of her long earring.

"That's for sure," Lacey agreed. "When I had Elliott, I thought, how hard can this be? I'll just take him to class with me. But then he had his first diaper blowout..." She shook her head.

"And you decided you didn't want to be the girl with shit leaking all over her in the middle of class?" Tavia asked sweetly.

Laughter echoed around the table and Lacey laughed too, surprised by how easily it came.

"Linden had colic," Nanette said with a shudder. "I didn't sleep for six months straight."

"There's always something," Tavia said. "Grace didn't walk till she was almost two. I dragged her to every specialist in the county." She tipped her head toward Regina and Nanette. "These two watched me spiral."

"She didn't walk because you just carried her everywhere," Nanette pointed out.

Tavia rolled her eyes.

"Now imagine all that anxiety—times two," Regina said dryly.

"Oof, twins," Tavia said. "You win."

Regina smiled. "I always do."

Lacey sat back and let the conversation wash over her. She felt the coil of anxiety in her chest begin to loosen and her shoulders fall away from her ears. At least moving here, she'd finally gotten something right.

NINE

Labor Day weekend passed in a blur of grilled hot dogs and burgers, the scent of charcoal hanging in the thick summer air as the kids shrieked and darted through the backyard sprinkler. Lacey and the other women lounged on the shaded back deck, sipping seltzers and then switching to wine once the afternoon light softened into dusk.

There was an ease to it all that Lacey hadn't felt in years. The weekend carried the same relaxed, unhurried rhythm as the neighborhood barbecues she used to love, back before Judd changed. Before she started policing herself, trying to control for any little thing that might set him off. She remembered those summer weekends, sitting in folding chairs with the other parents, laughing over drinks while the kids ran wild, everyone easing into the shared responsibility of keeping an eye on them. It had felt safe. Simple.

Now, watching Elliott tear across the grass, his sticky, popsicle-stained grin stretching ear to ear, she realized how much she had missed this, how isolated they had become once Judd's dark moods took over and kept people away. But at last, here was a place where Elliott could just be, where there were always playmates ready to race and build and wrestle until they collapsed in an exhausted heap.

He and Max and Maddie spent the weekend constructing obstacle courses out of sticks, rocks, and lawn furniture, their games evolving in a language all their own. They made mud pies and watched *Minions* movies on an endless loop, while Linden trailed after them, determined to keep up, until she inevitably ran out of steam and crashed in Nanette's lap, her curls damp with sweat. Grace toddled around the chaos, all sunshine and wobbling enthusiasm, while the four women took turns leaping up to keep her from tumbling off the deck or shoving a handful of mud pie into her mouth.

For the first time in a long time, Lacey felt something like peace. Even her worry about the truck she'd hit and driven away from, which she still needed to do something about, began to fade from her mind. The only thread of disappointment she felt curling at the edges of her mind was to do with the job Regina had sent her.

The company, Vetra Vitals, sounded fascinating. The listing described it as a "cutting-edge leader in the biomedical industry, specializing in wearable biosensors that provide real-time health monitoring and promote longevity."

But as she scanned the requirements, her hope faded. The requirements included a college degree, plus three to five years of experience as an executive assistant to a senior leader. She wasn't even remotely qualified.

As she stood at the bus stop with Elliott on his first day of school, a low-grade sense of despair set in. She'd be lucky to land another dead-end office manager job—and she likely couldn't even count on a reference from Carpet World after the popcorn debacle.

"I see the bus!" Elliott's excited cry yanked her back to the moment.

He, Max, Maddie, and Linden stood in a tight cluster, craning their necks to spot the big yellow bus as it lumbered up the street.

"Everyone look at me and smile!" Nanette called, whipping out her phone.

The kids leaned into each other, a tangle of sun-kissed faces and brand-new backpacks. Elliott flashed a thumbs-up just as the shutter clicked and Lacey's heart clenched.

She crouched down and pulled him into a fierce hug. "Have a great first day, buddy," she murmured, pressing a kiss to his cheek. "I love you so much. And remember, I'm proud of you no matter what."

"Bye, Mommy!" Elliott grinned, already wriggling free as the bus rolled to a stop.

Regina caught Lacey's eye as the kids filed up the steps, clocking the tears she was trying to blink away. She reached over and squeezed Lacey's hand.

"He's going to do great," she said. "Max will look out for him."

Elliott and Max had landed in the same class, which had thrilled them both.

"Recess is right after lunch," Max had explained the night before. "So if we eat super fast, we can be the first ones out to the basketball court!"

Now, watching them slide into a seat together through the bus window, Lacey felt like she might collapse under the weight of her gratitude. *There he is*, she thought, her throat tightening. *Happy. Excited. Already with a friend.*

"Happy tears," she managed to say to Regina, her voice thick.

"Not mine," came Nanette's wobbly voice.

Lacey turned to see her standing frozen on the sidewalk, her face streaked with tears as she frantically waved at the departing bus.

"It's just all going so *fast*," Nanette said, swiping at her damp cheeks.

Lacey smiled. "Except when it isn't," she said.

Regina let out a snort. "For real," she agreed. "I mean, I love my kids, but let's be honest, I've spent the last month counting down to this exact moment." She gestured toward the bus disappearing down the street.

Nanette let out a watery laugh. "Yeah, OK... same." She exhaled, shaking her head as she wiped her eyes.

Regina looped an arm around her shoulders and threw Lacey a conspiratorial wink as they started back toward the house.

Back inside, Nanette headed upstairs to get ready for work, leaving Regina and Lacey alone in the kitchen.

Lacey refilled her coffee mug as Regina began to fiddle with the faucet, dropping down to examine it at eye level.

"It's got a slow leak that's driving me crazy," she said. "I'm guessing it needs a new O-ring." She straightened up. "I just need a wrench and a free fifteen minutes."

"Wow," Lacey said, impressed. "I don't even know what an O-ring is."

"Being a single mom will force you to become very handy," Regina said with a wry smile. She crossed her arms and leaned against the counter. "So, what did you think of the job?"

Lacey swallowed a lump of shame in her throat. "I'm not exactly qualified," she murmured.

Regina's gaze was frank and unwavering. "Don't take this the wrong way," she said. "But you're never going to get anywhere in life playing by the rules."

Lacey's cheeks flushed. It was like Regina could see into her soul. Lacey had always been a rules follower, studying for every test, making her five-year plan, checking every box. Even getting pregnant hadn't been her fault—she and Judd had been scrupulous about using condoms, unaware that they weren't failsafe. And where had that gotten her? A life where she was barely scraping by. One misstep away from losing everything.

Regina pursed her lips. "If I can get you the job," she said, "do you want it?"

Lacey let out a small, nervous laugh. "How would that even work?"

"I'll help you massage your résumé," Regina said, her tone as matter of fact as if they were discussing the grocery list. "Make sure it reflects the right experience and qualifications."

Lacey's eyebrows shot up. "Like... make stuff up?"

Regina gave a nonchalant shrug. "If we need to, sure."

"I could never—" Lacey started, shaking her head, but Regina cut her off.

"Look, could you do the job?"

Lacey hesitated, mentally running through the job description. Managing complex schedules, juggling priorities, anticipating conflicts, screening communications, handling logistics... It basically read like a description of being a mom.

"Well, yeah," she admitted. "I could do it, but—"

"Then why shouldn't you get the job?" Regina asked, tossing her hair behind her shoulders. "Why should the fact that you don't have one stupid little credential hold you back?"

Lacey bit her lip. She admired Regina's bravery, but that just wasn't her.

"Did you know that men apply for jobs when they meet sixty percent of the qualifications?" Regina said. "Guess when women apply?" She let the question hang for a beat before tilting her head. "When they meet *one hundred percent*." She leveled Lacey with a pointed look. "So, do you want to keep putting yourself at a disadvantage? Or do you want to actually start making some real progress in your life?"

A series of memories flickered through Lacey's mind in rapid succession, like a slide show on fast-forward. A late night in the college library during finals week, her roommate begging her to come out for drinks, leaving a dog-eared copy of the CliffsNotes version of the novel Lacey was writing a paper on propped on her pillow. She hadn't even considered it.

The early days of motherhood, Elliott howling through his nap window, and Lacey refusing to let him watch a single minute of TV before the recommended age, even when her own nerves were fraying.

And in the past few months, job listings she'd scrolled past without applying. Roles she knew she could handle but hadn't even considered because they required a degree she didn't have.

Her chest tightened, a sharp, hot squeeze of frustration. She couldn't tell if it was aimed at Regina for her suggestion that Lacey was a fool for always playing by the rules, or at herself for not coming to this realization on her own.

She looked down to find her hands clenched into fists. "I'm sorry," she said. "I just wouldn't feel right about it."

There was a pause. "Why don't you at least send me your résumé?" Regina said. "I'm good with that stuff. Maybe I can recommend some changes to tighten it up, or some other jobs."

Lacey felt a surge of gratitude. "That would be amazing, thank you."

The doorbell rang.

Regina glanced toward the sound, then back at the offending sink.

"I've got it," Lacey offered. "I'm headed upstairs anyway."

"Thanks," Regina said, turning back to the faucet.

At the front door, Lacey found a slight man in jeans and a black T-shirt standing stiffly on the porch. A beak-like nose jutted from his thin face and his hands were tucked behind his back.

"I'm looking for Lacey Kessler," he said.

A flicker of unease moved down her spine. "That's me," she replied cautiously.

The man pulled a manila envelope from behind his back and handed it to her. "You've been served," he said, offering a tight, almost apologetic smile.

Before she could speak, he turned and strode briskly down the walkway to his car.

Lacey stared after him, the envelope oddly heavy in her hand. Slowly, she peeled it open.

At the top, in bold capital letters, were the words: COMPLAINT FOR DIVORCE.

Her eyes dropped to the petitioner's name: Judd Kessler.

Under Judd's name, in clean, clinical type, was a sentence that stole her breath.

Seeking sole legal and physical custody of Elliott Kessler.

<h1 style="text-align:center">TEN</h1>

Elliott barreled off the school bus that afternoon after his first day, a grin stretched across his face. Max, Maddie, and Linden trailed close behind.

"Mommy!" he cried, launching himself into Lacey's arms. "Guess what? I won a prize today for being the first person to answer when Mr. Barry asked what 'respect' means!"

Lacey crouched to hug him, her heart squeezing tight. The tears she'd been holding back all day pricked the corners of her eyes.

"That's amazing, buddy," she said, hugging him tighter. "I'm so proud of you for knowing what it means."

Elliott looked up at her. "Well, I didn't actually know. But Mr. Barry said the main thing is I wasn't afraid to share my idea."

Lacey smiled, standing as they began to walk hand in hand toward the house. "Then I definitely agree with Mr. Barry." She squeezed his hand. "Let's go have a snack. I baked cookies." The truth was that baking had been the only way she could force her swirling thoughts about being served divorce papers to focus on something else for a while.

Over the fresh snickerdoodles, the kids rehashed their day. Maddie declared that her new teacher was "way better than last year's." Max and Elliott agreed that Mr. Barry seemed "cool," and Linden proclaimed that kindergarten was "the best," then promptly burst into tears when she learned it wasn't over and that she'd have to go back again the next day.

Lacey couldn't remember the last time she'd seen Elliott so animated. He barely answered any of her questions, but he and Max talked nonstop—about their classmates, the class pet (a turtle named Captain Shell), and the soccer game they'd played at recess.

"Sounds like it was a good first day," Regina murmured, sidling up next to Lacey as they watched the kids demolish graham crackers slathered with peanut butter.

Lacey's voice caught. "Yeah."

Regina gave her a side glance. "You OK?"

Lacey hesitated, then swallowed hard. "I got served this morning," she said quietly. "Divorce papers. From Judd."

Regina raised her eyebrows. "Congratulations," she said. "I mean... you want a divorce, right?"

Lacey pressed her fingers to her lips, trying to keep the rising despair at bay. "He's seeking full custody," she whispered.

Regina's eyes widened. "Oh, damn. Lacey. I'm so sorry." She reached out and gave Lacey's arm a squeeze. Her gaze flicked toward the kids, who were now pushing each other out the back door, already racing for the swing set. "What are you going to do?" she asked.

Lacey tried to laugh, but it caught in her throat, coming out as a strangled gasp. "He can't get custody," she said, her voice raw. "It would be a disaster. He'd take Elliott off his medication, and without it..." She trailed off, swallowing hard as if forcing down memories. "He was almost kicked out of school last year before we figured out what was going on with him. Before I..." Her eyes dropped to the floor. "...before I filled the prescription without telling Judd." She rubbed her forehead, her shoulders sagging against the counter. "And honestly? I don't even think he really wants custody. He's never been able to handle Elliott's ups and downs."

Regina's mouth flattened into a thin, hard line. "It's not about Elliott," she said. "He wants custody because he wants to punish *you*."

Tears welled in Lacey's eyes, and she brushed them away with the heel of her hand, frustrated. She was so tired of feeling raw, constantly teetering on the edge of a breakdown.

"Hey," Regina said gently, catching the anguish in Lacey's expression. "It's going to be OK. We'll figure it out."

"Figure what out?" Nanette asked, stepping into the kitchen, holding Linden's lunchbox. She popped it open and began unpacking its contents—sandwich crusts and untouched carrot sticks. She'd come home early from her IT job in the city to meet Linden after school on her first day.

Regina glanced at Lacey, and Lacey gave a small nod.

"Lacey's ex is suing for custody of Elliott," Regina said.

Nanette let out a low whistle and clucked her tongue. "Oh, honey, I'm so sorry."

Lacey lifted her head. "How did you handle it—when your ex... with Linden...?"

A look of scorn came over Nanette's face. "I got myself a very expensive lawyer and took that son-of-a-bitch to court. He didn't even *want* custody—he just didn't want me to have it. We settled on every other weekend, which he still cancels half the time." She blew out an exasperated breath.

The pit of despair in Lacey's stomach hardened. "I can't afford an expensive lawyer," she said. "I don't even have a job."

Her thoughts spiraled back to the frantic hours she'd spent that afternoon, down online rabbit holes about New Jersey custody law, family court precedents, and attorney fees. She'd come up for air with only two conclusions: There was no way she could represent herself, and no way she could afford someone who could—not on the kind of fifteen-dollar-an-hour jobs she was actually qualified for if she didn't want to lie on her résumé.

"You don't have a job *yet*," Regina said, her tone firm. She squeezed Lacey's arm again. "We'll figure it out," she repeated. "We've got your back."

Lacey tried to smile, but her face crumpled despite her best efforts.

Nanette stepped closer, her voice softening. "It sucks, I know. I'm so sorry. Go take a long shower, have a good cry if you need to. I'll keep an eye on the kids. Then once Tavia gets home, maybe the three of us," she added, gesturing toward Regina, "can go grab a glass of wine before Back to School Night."

Lacey groaned. She'd forgotten all about Back to School Night, where parents sat in tiny chairs while cheerful, smiling teachers stood in front of the classroom explaining how magical the school year would be. The last thing Lacey felt capable of doing was making small talk and pretending everything was fine.

"Sounds good," she said anyway, forcing a smile.

By the time they arrived at school, the emotional whiplash of Lacey's day had been dulled by two quickly consumed glasses of wine. She, Regina, and Nanette had stopped off at a nearby bar, a detour that gave the evening a slightly surreal, floaty quality. At first, Lacey had been anxious about leaving Elliott behind with Tavia—the only one of the four moms not attending the school function, since Grace was still in daycare. It had been ages since anyone but she or Judd had watched him. But when Tavia came bustling in from the train station—like Nanette, she commuted daily to the city—Grace on her hip and calm authority radiating off her as she steered the older kids toward the dinner table, Lacey exhaled.

"I won't be out late," she'd told Elliott, brushing a smear of ketchup from the corner of his mouth as he happily munched on a chicken nugget. "You can read in bed until I get back, OK?"

Still, even with the wine warming her stomach, Back to School Night was the last place Lacey wanted to be. The third-grade classroom was a riot of color and optimism. Clusters of chairs surrounded kid-height tables, a hand-lettered banner read *Welcome to Third Grade!* and laminated posters on the walls proclaimed things like *Don't Be Afraid to Fail, Be Afraid Not to Try!* and *Kindness is Like Sunshine. It Warms Everyone!*

Elliott's teacher, Mr. Barry, stood at the front of the room in khakis and a patterned button-down as brightly colored as his classroom décor, flushed with enthusiasm as he greeted parents and chatted with small groups of them.

With Regina tied up across the hall in Maddie's classroom, Lacey was left to fend for herself among a sea of parents who all seemed to already know one another. Though she was grateful for Elliott's chance at a fresh start in a new school, as she scanned the room she felt like the awkward new girl. She gave up and wandered to the classroom library, thumbing through a dog-eared copy of a graphic novel.

"Big *Captain Underpants* fan?" came a voice from next to her.

She looked up and into a pair of brown eyes that crinkled at the corners with amusement. The man they belonged to was broad-shouldered, with sandy brown hair, a square jaw softened by a few days of scruff, and a slightly crooked smile that caused an unfamiliar—but not unwelcome—flutter in her stomach.

"What?" Lacey asked, caught off guard.

He nodded toward the book in her hands. "You looked like you were deep in the world of Professor Poopypants."

She glanced down at the cover and laughed. "Oh. Right. Yeah, I've read them all," she deadpanned.

He grinned. "And here I thought you looked like someone with refined taste. Glad I was wrong. I don't trust anyone who's too good for a fart joke."

Lacey let out a real laugh, her tension loosening.

He extended his hand. "Simon," he said. "Otherwise known as Ella's dad."

She took his hand, grateful for the human connection. "Lacey," she said. "Elliott's mom. Nice to meet a fellow connoisseur of toilet humor."

He tilted his head. "I don't remember you from last year."

Lacey ran a hand through her hair, suddenly self-conscious about her frizzy ponytail. Why hadn't she taken ten extra minutes to blow-dry it into something resembling a style? "No, um, we're new to the school," she said.

Simon's eyes flicked over her in a way that registered but didn't feel disrespectful. It wasn't like when Chip, her old boss, used to leer. This time she felt a small tingle go through her.

"Well," he said, smiling again, "welcome. We both lucked out; Mr. Barry's one of the good ones." He gestured toward the front of the room. "My older daughter had him last year. He's a total gem."

"Oh?" Lacey said, relieved. "That's good to hear. We just moved last week—I didn't really have time to do the school research thing."

"Then welcome to the neighborhood," Simon said, his voice warm. He looked around the room. "I'll have to introduce myself to your husband. We've got a pretty solid dad crew here."

"Actually, I—" Lacey started, hesitated, then squared her shoulders. "Actually, it's just me and Elliott." It was the first time she'd said it like that out loud, and the words caught in her throat for a moment before settling into place.

"Ah," Simon said, and maybe it was just her imagination, but she could have sworn there was a flicker of interest in his expression. "Same here. Just me and my girls."

"Oh," Lacey said. She suddenly felt overheated in the overly air-conditioned classroom.

"All right, boys and girls," came Mr. Barry's voice, his theatrical tone drawing a laugh from the room. "Let's grab a seat and get started."

"I guess we should—" Lacey said at the same time Simon started, "Looks like we better—"

They both stepped forward at once and bumped into each other.

"Sorry," Lacey said quickly, as Simon gave a low, pleasant laugh.

"My fault. Nice to meet you, Lacey," he said. "Hope I see you around."

"You too," she managed, watching as he walked to a seat near the front, his gray cotton T-shirt stretching across his shoulders.

She barely noticed Regina slide into the chair beside her until she whispered, "Um... who was *that*?"

Heat bloomed in Lacey's cheeks as she stared straight ahead at Mr. Barry, pretending not to hear while Regina watched her with a wide smile on her face.

ELEVEN

Once Elliott was off to school the next morning, Lacey headed up to her room with a fresh cup of coffee and stretched out on the bed with her laptop. Instead of powering it on, though, she reached for her phone.

The link to the job listing Regina had texted was still near the top of her messages. She tapped it open for what felt like the hundredth time, eyes scanning the now-familiar words. She nearly had the description memorized, but something about rereading it made her heart thrum with possibility. What would it be like to work somewhere that genuinely interested her? To have a job that felt like more than just survival? To be able to check her bank balance without a feeling of dread?

Reflexively she flipped over to her banking app as she sipped her coffee. As if maybe, this time, the number might magically be higher. It wasn't. It had dipped into the low triple digits. Not enough for next month's rent. Not enough for groceries, gas, and certainly not enough for a lawyer to help her fight Judd for custody.

The coffee turned sour in her stomach. She set the mug down on the nightstand and pushed her phone away. Opening her laptop again, she logged into the job search site she'd been haunting daily, only to see the same listings from yesterday and the day before—underpaid jobs she was qualified for, and higher-paying jobs she wasn't.

She shut the laptop with a little more force than necessary, shame crashing over her. How had this become her life? Once, she'd had a plan, had hopes for the future. She was going to be someone who did important things and helped other people. Now she felt helpless, batted around by life's circumstances like a plastic bag caught in a windstorm. She'd been fortunate to find Regina and the mommune, she knew, but now it appeared even that stroke of luck couldn't save her.

Tipping her head back against the pillow, she wiped her clammy hands on the bedspread and focused on taking deep, slow breaths to calm her racing heart.

No one is coming to save me, she thought. *It's all up to me.*

By late morning, Lacey's empty stomach was growling, and her nerves were frayed from too much coffee and too many hours reading dense legal websites about New Jersey custody law. She headed downstairs to the kitchen, craving something to eat and, hopefully, a break from her swirling thoughts.

In the kitchen she found Regina crouched in front of the cabinet under the sink, her head and shoulders fully inside it. She reversed out, holding a large wrench. "That ought to do it," she muttered, then smiled as she noticed Lacey. "Oh, hey."

"Hi," Lacey said. It was a relief to see another adult face after a solitary morning of doomscrolling legal forums and job boards. Plus, there was something calming about Regina's presence. No matter what kind of chaos was happening around her—the kids running in circles on a popsicle sugar high or the morning circus of getting everyone to the bus stop on time—she seemed to float along unfazed.

Regina stood up and wiped her hands on the navy linen pants she wore with a matching top. Lacey looked down self-consciously at the wrinkled T-shirt and shorts she'd swapped her pajamas for—not a huge improvement.

"How's your morning?" Regina asked as Lacey opened the fridge.

Looking inside it, she felt a surprising rush of gratitude. Thanks to the communal groceries, she and Elliott were no longer subsisting on peanut butter sandwiches.

She pulled out a container of yogurt and a carton of fresh strawberries, luxuries she didn't take for granted. "Just looking for jobs," she said with a heavy sigh. "What about you?"

"Busy with work," Regina said, setting the wrench on the counter. "My current client's in Europe, so I've been up since five."

"What do you do again?" Lacey asked, spooning yogurt into a bowl.

"I'm a software engineer. Freelance, mostly."

"Oh wow," Lacey said. She felt a stab of jealousy. Regina had an actual career, something Lacey could only dream of. "Did you go to school for that?"

"Yeah, out in California. I worked for a few startups before I realized I'm better off on my own. I tend to get too wrapped up in work, so I've learned to keep a little distance by being a consultant instead of building something myself." She gave a small smile, like she'd just admitted a secret.

Lacey smiled, grateful for the flash of connection. Maybe she and Regina could be friends. It had been so long since she'd had one. "When did you move to New Jersey?" she asked, realizing she knew far less about Regina than she did about Nanette or Tavia. Whereas the two of them seemed like open books, the subject always seemed to shift before Regina got around to sharing much.

Regina's expression changed slightly, like a curtain falling back into place after having been pushed open by the breeze. "About three years ago," she said. "I needed a change."

"Is that when you started the mommune?"

"Mmhmm," Regina acknowledged. "I bought this house for a song. It needed a lot of work, most of which I did myself." A fond smile spread across her face. "Max and Maddie can sleep through anything now because they used to nap to the sound of the drum sander when they were babies."

Lacey shook her head. "I have no idea what a drum sander even is."

Regina laughed. "It's for refinishing hardwood floors," she said. "I like that kind of stuff. It's like therapy. Anyway, I figured it would be an investment property, but then I met Tavia, and she needed a place to stay with Grace, and well." She waved a hand as if to say, *You know how the rest of it goes.*

But Lacey didn't, and she realized she had so many more questions for Regina. Before she could ask them, though, Regina turned away and headed for the door.

"Hang on a sec," she said. "I'll be right back."

Lacey sat down at the table, mixing the fruit into her yogurt. When Regina returned, she slid a crisp sheet of paper across the table.

Lacey looked up, her face a question mark.

Regina smiled. "Your new résumé. I got some of the stuff on it from your LinkedIn and just... added the rest."

Lacey scanned the document, her eyes widening as they landed on the education section, which stated that she'd earned a degree in biomedical engineering—graduated, not dropped out. Her part-time college lab job had been stretched into a full-time two-year position after graduation, and in the time since, she'd supposedly worked as an executive assistant at a medical device company.

"What's NovoMed Technologies?" she asked, pointing, as her stomach began to tie itself in a knot.

"They manufacture white-label glucose monitors," Regina said, tucking a wavy lock of hair behind her ear. "You loved it there, learned a ton, but when the opportunity at Vetra came up, you knew it aligned more with your passion for cutting-edge biomedical tech." She smiled conspiratorially as she fed Lacey the script.

As she continued to scan the document, Lacey had the queer

sensation that she had stepped through a sliding door and was viewing a life that, if things had gone differently, could have been hers. A tingle of excitement came over her, followed immediately by a surge of guilt.

She slid the paper across the table, then wiped her hands on her shorts like they might be contaminated. "This is just... made up," she said, her voice laced with shock. "I could never use this."

Regina smoothed her hair and studied Lacey for a long moment. "Of course. I get it," she said. "I was just trying to help. I'm sure you'll come up with another solution to afford a good custody lawyer." She gave a faint smile and turned to go, pausing in the doorway. "But if you change your mind, I already sent it to the CEO of Vetra. Your interview's Friday."

Lacey's jaw dropped. Words of protest surged in her throat, but before she could utter any of them, Regina had disappeared back into the hall, the door to her bedroom clicking as she closed it behind her.

TWELVE

That afternoon, Lacey volunteered to take the four school-age kids to the park. Nanette had been debating whether to enroll Linden in aftercare—Elliott, Max, and Maddie were old enough to manage on their own until dinner—but Lacey had offered to look after the feisty five-year-old until she found a job. The look of relief that washed over Nanette's face when she'd said it made Lacey stand a little taller. It felt good to help someone else out.

They dropped the kids' backpacks at home, grabbed snacks, and made the short three-block walk to the park. The heat of summer had finally begun to wane, replaced by a breeze that hinted at early fall. Lacey claimed a shady bench with a clear view of the playground.

"Be sure to include Linden in your games," she murmured to Elliott, giving his shoulder a gentle squeeze.

He nodded and made a beeline for the swings. "Hey, Linden, want me to push you?" he called.

Lacey smiled, then pulled out her phone and opened the Vetra Vitals website. Her stomach still bubbled with shock and indignation at what Regina had done, submitting her fabricated résumé. It was so bold—and so unethical.

What's more, Lacey couldn't believe the fake résumé had actually landed her an interview. Which she obviously wasn't going to. Still, for a brief instant it had been nice to enjoy the flicker of hope she felt at the thought of it, bright and sharp, cutting through the dark fog that had surrounded her since being served with divorce papers.

She scanned Vetra's website. What grabbed her attention was a section on their work with emerging technologies—administering medication through wearable devices triggered by real-time hormonal and biometric feedback. She clicked on an embedded video and leaned forward.

The CEO appeared seated outdoors, backlit by a lush wall of trees and greenery. He had a long face, with strong cheekbones and a pronounced jawline under a neatly trimmed red beard. His copper-colored hair was swept back from his forehead in a wave. His light eyes caught the sun, lending a glint of intensity as he spoke directly into the camera.

"Imagine a future where we prevent heart attacks before they happen, or treat panic attacks before they're triggered," he said, his voice animated and confident. "This is the future of biomedicine. This is Vetra Vitals."

"Hey, I know you," came a deep voice.

Lacey looked up, startled, and saw the dad from Back to School Night approaching. She instinctively dropped her phone onto her lap and reached to smooth her hair, which was twisted into a rushed ponytail.

He paused in front of her, brows knitting in mock concentration. "Lacey, right?" he said after a beat. He wore cargo shorts and a navy T-shirt that clung just enough at the sleeves to highlight the quiet strength of his arms—fit, but not trying too hard.

"Uh, yes," she said, laughing nervously. "Good memory." Her brain scrambled for his name. Sam? Stewart?

"Simon," he said, tapping his chest, a smile tugging at one corner of his mouth.

"Right," she said quickly, trying to sound like she'd remembered all along.

He gestured toward the bench beside her. "Mind if I join you?"

"Of course not," she said, shifting her tote bag full of snacks and water bottles onto her lap to make room.

"Watch me on the monkey bars, Daddy!"

Lacey looked over to see a girl in pink leggings and a rainbow T-shirt already sprinting toward the play structure.

"That's Ella; she's in Mr. Barry's class," Simon said, waving at his daughter.

Before Lacey could reply, a whirlwind of children descended. Elliott, Max, Maddie, and Linden barreled toward the bench in a clamor of voices.

"Can we have snacks?" Elliott asked breathlessly.

"I'm literally starving to death," Maddie declared, clutching her stomach.

"Did you bring chips?" Max demanded.

"Me too! Me too!" Linden chirped, bouncing on her toes.

Simon blinked at the sudden swarm. "Wow," he said.

"No chips," Lacey said, laughing as she dug into the tote. "But I've got granola bars."

There was a round of appreciative murmurs as she doled out the bars, which were promptly devoured, the wrappers shoved back into her hands as the four of them stormed back toward the playground.

"Are they all yours?" Simon asked, eyes wide.

Lacey laughed. "God, no. Just Elliott." She pointed toward her son, who was now hanging upside down on the monkey bars, blocking Ella's path. "They're the other kids we..." She paused, unsure of how to explain her living situation. "I live with three other moms," she said. "Over on Wildwood, the house with the wraparound front porch. We kind of all take turns watching all the kids, helping with chores, that kind of thing. Kind of like a sorority, I guess—I mean, I wouldn't totally know since I was never in one, and of course, people don't have kids in college—well, most people don't." She flushed and clamped her mouth shut, willing herself to stop babbling.

Simon coughed. "Interesting," he said when he recovered. "How... progressive."

Lacey instantly regretted sharing so much.

"But also, how handy," he added hastily, noting her reaction. He grinned. "I mean, there are moments when I'd give anything for some backup from another grown-up—usually around bedtime." He gave a dry laugh and took off his baseball cap, running a hand through his tousled hair. "I mean, doing this alone was definitely not my plan. But all things considered, I'm lucky. I work from home, so I can be there for the after-school stuff, homework, you know."

"That is lucky," Lacey said. Her mind flickered back to the résumé Regina had created for her. "I'm job hunting right now," she added with a sigh.

"That's a lot all at once—new house, new school, job search," Simon said. The compassion in his voice caught her off guard.

"Yup," she admitted. "I'm basically completely exhausted." She gave a short laugh.

Simon's kind brown eyes locked on hers. "Well, if I can ever help, just let me know," he said.

The way he held her gaze sent a warm current through her. He shifted beside her, looking toward the playground, where Ella and Elliott were trying to scramble up the slide, laughing wildly every time they slipped back down.

"Looks like they've hit it off," he said.

Lacey smiled, her heart softening at the sight. "That's nice to see. Elliott can be... high-strung sometimes." She hesitated at the word, then realized it hadn't really applied these past few days. Despite the upheaval—new house, new school—he hadn't had a single meltdown. The rhythm of the mommune, the constant low buzz of companionship and structure, seemed to be working for him.

Simon laughed. "Ella's not exactly zen either," he said with a grin. Then, shifting his gaze back to Lacey, he added, "Do you, um, want to exchange numbers? You know—for more park hangs?"

Lacey felt her cheeks flush. "Sure," she said, aiming for casual but knowing she was smiling too much. "That sounds nice."

She had just finished typing his number into her phone when it rang. Judd's name flashed across the screen like a warning flare. Her stomach dropped.

"I'm so sorry," she said, standing. "I need to take this."

Simon gave an easy smile, his attention returning to his daughter, now spinning in lazy circles next to Elliott.

Lacey stepped a few feet away and answered in a low, sharp voice. "What the hell, Judd?" she said, skipping a greeting. "Sole custody?"

"I'm not calling to argue," he said, his voice maddeningly calm. "Let's leave that to the lawyers—once you hire one. I'm calling to confirm you'll be dropping Elliott off Friday, as planned."

"Absolutely not—" she began, but he cut her off.

"According to my lawyer, withholding our child from me won't look good for you," he said. "But if you want to get off on the wrong foot with the proceedings, by all means, go for it."

Her hand clenched into a fist, knuckles white. "Fine," she bit out. "But if he wants to come home—"

"Five o'clock on Friday," Judd said, and hung up.

Lacey stood there, her whole body buzzing with cold, helpless fury at the impossible situation she faced. How could she possibly fight Judd for custody with an empty bank account and a house full of roommates? And, more importantly, how could she be sure Elliott would be safe when she dropped him off with Judd on Friday? The thought turned her stomach. She tried to steady herself with the reminder that, for all his unpredictable moods and volatile temper, Judd had never laid a hand on Elliott. Still, doubt gnawed at her. She ransacked her brain for an answer, for some way—any way—to keep her son safe.

From the corner of her eye, she caught Simon watching her and realized she'd been pacing along the edge of the playground like a caged animal for several minutes. She took a deep breath, painted on a smile, and made her way back to the bench.

Simon was on his feet, calling to Ella. "Time to go, sweetie!" He turned back to Lacey. "Everything OK?"

She forced a smile. "All good," she said. "You're heading out?"

He gave a disappointed nod, checking his watch. "Gotta grab my oldest from practice. But this was nice." He smiled at her. "Let's do it again soon."

"I'd love to," she said, the warmth returning to her body.

After Simon left, Lacey gave the kids another hour at the park, her mind relentlessly replaying the call with Judd and trying to come up with her next move—but every scenario ended up with her backed into a corner. According to the internet, she had thirty-five days to respond to Judd's divorce complaint. Thirty-five days to come up with the money to hire a lawyer to help her keep her son.

Back at the house, the kids collapsed in the living room in front of the TV as fragrant smells of cooking drifted from the kitchen. Lacey found Regina browning ground beef at the stove, humming along to Liz Phair's voice playing through her phone on the counter.

"Hey," Lacey said, her voice tight as she chewed on her lip.

"Hey," Regina replied easily. "So, I forwarded you the interview information for Friday."

Lacey inhaled, her stomach twisting sharply. "I can't do it," she said. "It's not right." Her heartrate accelerated as she pictured the opportunity vanishing like invisible ink.

One corner of Regina's mouth tugged up. "Then I'm sure you'll cancel it," she said.

Lacey swallowed. "Right," she said. "I will."

THIRTEEN

Lacey awoke to her alarm on Friday to find Elliott's leg draped over hers, his face tucked into the crook of her neck. Though he liked having his "cozy corner"—the twin bed tucked behind the folding screen across the room—most nights he still found his way into her bed.

She kissed the top of his head as she reached to silence her alarm, then let herself sink into the warmth of him for a few more precious minutes. But as she wrapped her arms tighter around him, reality crept back in. Friday. Tonight she had to drop him off at Judd's for the entire weekend. And she needed to contact Vetra Vitals to tell them she wouldn't be coming in for the interview.

Her stomach twisted.

"Ow," Elliott mumbled, squirming as he pushed her arm away. "Too tight, Mommy."

She eased her hold and pressed another kiss to his hair. "Sorry, sweetheart. Time to get up for breakfast."

Elliott's eyes popped open, his face lighting up. "It's Friday! Mr. Barry said we get extra flex time. I can play Minecraft!"

"And," she added gently, "you're going to Daddy's tonight for the weekend."

She felt his body tighten next to hers, but then an eager smile spread across his face. "Daddy said we could go buy a PlayStation this weekend," he said. Then his face fell. "But I can only use it if I'm good at church."

Lacey tried to smooth the frown off her face. After the initial pandemic lockdown lifted, Judd had gravitated toward Mount Zion Covenant Church, a squat, brown-brick building on the outskirts of Maplehurst that Lacey only noticed because of its welcoming message on the marquee out front, which never seemed to change: *Sinners repent.* Still, when Judd started attending regularly, she'd tried to keep an open mind. Toward the end, she even went with him once or twice, hoping to reconnect, to find some shared ground that might help pull them back together. But all she found were stiff wooden pews that seemed engineered for penance and sermons thick with dogma and judgment.

She smoothed Elliott's hair. "PlayStation sounds fun," she said. "And you have your phone now, so you can call me whenever you want, OK?" The day before, the anxiety about whether he'd be all right had overwhelmed her and she'd gone out and bought him the cheapest flip phone she could find and programmed her number into it. They'd spent fifteen minutes practicing how to use it.

"OK," Elliott said, yawning.

"Just keep the phone in your backpack unless you need to use it," she reminded him. "And only call me when you're alone."

Guilt tugged at her chest at the idea of going behind Judd's back—again. But getting Elliott a secret phone seemed like a small sacrifice to make to know he had a lifeline if he needed it.

"All right," Lacey said, pushing herself up to a seated position. "Breakfast time."

They were the first ones downstairs, so she started coffee for the adults and toast for the kids. By the time Tavia entered, clad in black leggings and a faded, oversized University of Tennessee T-shirt, a scowling Grace on her hip, Lacey already had a plate waiting: peanut butter toast and banana slices arranged in a little smiley face.

"Oh my God, you're an angel," Tavia groaned as she slid Grace into her booster seat. "When she's hungry she's meaner than a hornet in a hatbox." She paused to adjust her hair, which was falling out of its lopsided bun.

"No problem," Lacey said, feeling a flicker of pride. It felt good to be getting the hang of the house's rhythm.

"What's a hatbox?" Elliott asked, mid-chew.

Tavia laughed. "Just something my mama used to say. Along with 'Bless your heart' and 'Well, butter my butt and call me a biscuit.'"

"Butter my butt," Elliott repeated, snorting a laugh.

Tavia poured herself coffee. "TGIF," she said, raising her mug toward Lacey in a toast. "So, big job interview today?"

Lacey froze, then blinked. "You know about that?"

Tavia winked. "Of course. No secrets in this house. You'll be great, honey."

Lacey gripped her mug so hard she worried it might crack and shook her head. "I'm not doing the interview," she said. "I can't— I'm not... qualified."

Tavia frowned. "Well, that's a shame, now, isn't it?"

Maddie, Max, and Linden clattered into the room, followed by Regina and Nanette, the house coming alive with the chaotic ballet of getting five kids fed, dressed, and out the door. When the older kids finally boarded the bus, Regina fell into step beside Lacey on the walk back to the house.

"So, you'll be meeting with Reid Mercer, Vetra's CEO," she said. "So be ready."

Lacey looked over at her, incredulous. "I told you, I'm not doing the interview." She paused. "And anyway, the email said it was with Marina Silva, the head of human resources, not the CEO."

Regina shook her head. "It doesn't matter. Reid interviews everyone himself. Always."

Lacey's brow furrowed. "How do you know?"

Regina waved a hand. "I worked with Reid, once upon a time.

He's a smart guy but don't flatter him; he'll see right through it. Be direct. Be real. He'll respect that."

Lacey shook her head. "I told you, I'm not—"

Regina's phone buzzed.

"Client," she said, glancing at the screen. She smiled and squeezed Lacey's shoulder. "You'll be great. We'll talk after." Then she hurried ahead and disappeared into the house.

Back inside, Lacey stepped into the shower, lathering her hair in frustration as her unanswered questions piled up. Where had Regina and Reid worked together? How exactly had she gotten Lacey this interview? And, a small voice in the back of her head piped up, why hadn't Lacey canceled it yet?

As she toweled off, she opened her phone and typed *Regina Cho* into the search bar. There were no social media links save for a sparse LinkedIn profile, featuring an old photo where Regina's hair was cut in a sleek bob. The job title listed beneath her name read simply: *Technology Consultant*. No companies. No dates. No details.

By the time Lacey boarded the train into the city, her stomach was a knot of nerves. What was she doing? She felt like she'd stepped outside herself, watching from a distance as she went through the motions—pulling on her least-wrinkled gray work pants, buttoning a plain white blouse, shrugging into a blazer. Still, she clearly couldn't go through with this interview—it was madness to even think about it. But then came the other voice in her head, quieter but sharper: Wasn't it also madness to think she could keep supporting herself and Elliott—and afford a custody lawyer—on a minimum-wage job?

Vetra's headquarters was in Manhattan, just over half an hour by train, but it had been ages since Lacey had come into the city. She stared out the window, her thoughts drifting to the last time she and Judd had made the trip together, a month before COVID shut everything down. They'd found a sitter for Elliott and taken the train into the city for dinner at their favorite little cash-only trattoria on the Upper West Side owned by an Italian expat Lacey was pretty sure kept two sets of books, but whose arrabbiata was worth the moral compromise.

After dinner they'd walked along the Hudson River, its inky surface reflecting the city lights. They meandered all the way to SoHo and, improbably declaring themselves still hungry, stopped for ice cream. She remembered sitting together on a bench, knees touching, talking about the future.

"I'm going to look for a research position once I finish school," Lacey said. "I'll work for a couple of years, until you've made director, and then go for my master's degree, maybe even my PhD, so I can run my own lab one day."

Judd squeezed her thigh. "I won't even need to make director, because you're going to have some kind of scientific breakthrough and earn a Nobel Prize."

Lacey had laughed and leaned forward to kiss him, his lips sweet and sticky with ice cream. In that moment everything had felt so bright and possible.

The ache of that memory pressed at her chest and she shook it off. She dug the printed copy of her résumé from her tote, reviewing the bullet points of her fictional past, even as her stomach roiled. It was just an interview, she reasoned. Maybe nothing would even come of it.

When she found herself rereading the same résumé bullet over and over, she stopped and looked up Reid Mercer on her phone. A Stanford PhD dropout who'd made millions with his first startup, Chomer Labs, Reid was now the brainchild behind the Vetra-Patch. It was an exciting product—revolutionary even, if they could successfully get it through FDA trials.

Lacey watched videos of Reid, who came across as intense and focused. She hoped he wasn't a tech bro type who fasted for twenty-two hours a day and slept in a cryochamber. She tucked the résumé back into her bag, took a deep breath to try and soothe her nerves, and gazed out the window watching as the city skyline came into view.

The Vetra Vitals Midtown office was sleek and minimalist, all white surfaces and quiet angles. Lacey sat on the edge of a curved leather bench, her guilt battling with the small thrill of excitement pulsing in her chest. Twice she stood to leave, to abandon the whole ridiculous endeavor, but each time she found herself sitting back down.

"Lacey Kessler?" a woman called, stepping into the reception area. She wore a sharp, tailored suit and heels high enough to be weaponized. Her dark hair was pulled into a bun so tight it looked like it might be holding her entire face in place. A bold slash of red lipstick offered the only color on her person.

Lacey stood quickly. "Yes, that's me."

"I'm Marina Silva, head of HR." The woman pushed her over-sized, black-framed glasses up her nose and extended her hand. "Thanks for coming in."

She led Lacey down a bright corridor to a glass-walled confer-ence room. They had barely settled—Lacey politely declining coffee and clasping her hands in her lap—when the door swung open again.

The man who entered was casually dressed in dark jeans and an untucked slate-gray button-up shirt, the sleeves pushed to his elbows. The shirt hugged broad shoulders and a lean torso. His eyes—pale and intense—landed on Lacey and seemed to take a slow inventory.

"Reid Mercer," he said, offering his hand.

Lacey rose to shake it, catching a whiff of his clean, woodsy scent. A tingle went through her. "Lacey Kessler."

"Oh, I know all about you," he said, stepping back, hands slip-ping into his pockets.

Panic flared in Lacey's chest. He already knew. Of course he did—it wouldn't be that hard to figure out she was a fraud if anyone scratched the surface of her past.

But Reid just smiled, scanning the sterile room. "Let's get out of here."

Marina groaned. "Reid, I told you, these are first-round inter-views. Let me—"

"I know, I know," he said, his grin like that of a boy who'd been caught sneaking cookies but knew he could talk his way out of it. "Next time, I swear."

Lacey looked at Marina, who pursed her red, shiny lips and gave a tight nod.

Grabbing her bag, Lacey hurried to keep up with Reid as he led her down the hall and through a door into a dim, echoing stairwell, whistling brightly as he went. Her heels clacked against concrete as he took the stairs two at a time. Four flights down, he pushed through a door labeled EMERGENCY EXIT, and they emerged into the pulsing noise of Midtown.

"Ah," Reid said, stretching slightly and squinting into the sunlight. "Fresh air. Or whatever passes for it in Manhattan."

"Not a fan of the city?" she asked as they fell into step.

He held up his palms. "It's where the investors are. But I'm a California guy. I miss the ocean. Actual space to think."

"Mm." She looked around at the crowded Midtown sidewalk. "Are we headed anywhere in particular?"

Reid smirked. "Now *there's* a deep question." He glanced both ways, then took her elbow and guided her across through a break in the traffic, ignoring a cab that blared its horn as they passed.

"Here," he said, pointing ahead at the shaded green of Bryant Park.

They wove through metal tables and seated themselves across from each other at one that had seen better days. Nearby, two elderly men played chess while a pair of athleisure-clad moms pushed double strollers and clutched Starbucks cups.

Reid adjusted his chair to squarely face hers. "Do you know what we're trying to do at Vetra?" he asked.

Here we go, thought Lacey, her heart accelerating. She drew in a deep breath and met his gaze. "You're developing wearable biosensors capable of predictive, real-time therapeutic delivery. The Vetra-Patch. Most intervention tech today is reactive. Yours aims to be preemptive, to outsmart chronic conditions."

Reid's pale blue eyes lit up. "Exactly. Do you think it will work?"

Lacey bit her lip, recalling Regina's advice.

"It's... ambitious," she said cautiously. "And you still need FDA approval. If you pull it off, it'll change the entire landscape of chronic and acute care. The challenges are huge, though. You're building the future, but there are a thousand ways it could go sideways."

She trailed off, worried she'd overstepped, but Reid looked pleased.

"You know your stuff," he said, then frowned. "I just don't understand why you want to be an executive assistant," he said. "I mean, with your degree and lab experience, didn't you think about doing R&D somewhere if you're really into this stuff?"

Lacey's stomach dropped. That was exactly what she'd wanted to do. She swallowed, fumbling for an answer.

"I've done the lab coat thing, but now I'm more interested in the business side of things. How ideas get executed."

Reid leaned forward, elbows on the table. His gaze was penetrating. "I'm not an easy boss," he said. "I research obsessively, then move fast. I expect the people around me to keep up." His eyes dropped briefly to her lips, then flicked back up. "Is that going to be a problem?"

Her mouth had gone dry, and she had to force herself to speak. "No," she said in a low voice. "Not at all."

FOURTEEN

By the time Lacey made it home from the city, it was mid-afternoon. She barely had time to swap her interview outfit for jeans and a T-shirt before heading out to the bus stop. The kids were already tumbling off the bus when she arrived. Elliott darted ahead with Max and Maddie, and Regina fell into step beside her.

"So?" Regina prompted, a smile tugging at the corners of her mouth. "Something tells me you didn't cancel the interview."

Guilt gnawed at Lacey's stomach. "I didn't," she admitted. "And you were right, I ended up meeting with Reid—for, like, almost an hour."

Sitting in Bryant Park, they'd discussed Vetra's product roadmap, the broader landscape of biomedical innovation, and Reid's vision for the company. The reading she'd done online to prepare had been enough to get her up to speed, asking the right questions. Talking science again—real science—had felt like unlocking a room in her mind she hadn't stepped into in years. It was natural, easy, and energizing.

As they finally walked back to Vetra's headquarters, Reid had turned to look at her. "You're clearly smart enough for the job," he said. "But really, it's about chemistry. I need someone I can work with."

Chemistry. The word had landed with more weight than he probably intended. It lingered in her mind, especially when her eyes strayed to his muscular forearms where his sleeves were pushed up, the sunlight glinting on the blond hairs.

"Then he liked you," Regina said now with certainty as they climbed the porch steps behind the kids. "He wouldn't have spent that much time with you if he didn't."

"When did you work with him?" Lacey asked.

Regina shook her head. "Eons ago. We were kids, practically." A shadow crossed her face. "But maybe don't mention me. It didn't end... great. It's all in the past now, but we went our separate ways."

Lacey wanted to press for more, but something in Regina's tone told her not to.

"Mommy, can we go to the park?" Elliott appeared beside her, tugging her arm.

She smiled, though a stone settled in her gut. "We have to leave for Daddy's soon, remember?"

Elliott brightened. "Ooh! I'll get to play video games!"

Lacey's smile faltered. Screen time was always a gamble. Too much and Elliott unraveled—overstimulated, irritable, unable to regulate his emotions. She could only hope Judd was prepared for the crash after hours of Minecraft.

"Try not to play too long," she said gently. "Ask Daddy to kick the soccer ball around or go outside for a while too, OK?"

She wrapped him in a hug, already feeling the hollow ache of the weekend ahead. The thought of being without him until Sunday, worrying if Judd was being kind to him, caused a sharp pressure in her chest.

"Why don't I make you a snack?" she said, guiding him toward the kitchen. "Then you can play in the backyard before we leave."

One side effect of Elliott's ADHD meds was a midday appetite dip. Lacey tried to load him up on calories at breakfast before the pill kicked in, and again in the late afternoon, when the meds wore off and his hunger returned.

Her shoulders tensed as she thought of the pills she would zip into the inside pocket of Elliott's backpack, with instructions that he try to remember to take them when he wasn't around Judd. If he forgot, his emotions would be a roller coaster. And with Judd's short fuse, that was a volatile combination.

After feeding Elliott and sending him out to play with Max and Maddie, Lacey headed upstairs to pack his clothes for the weekend. In their room, she paused as she folded his things, burying her face in his favorite *Star Wars* T-shirt, trying not to cry. Joint custody was already brutal. The thought of losing even that, of Judd getting full custody, was unthinkable. A chill passed through her, the what-ifs pressing heavy against her ribs. The clock was ticking for her to respond to the divorce complaint, but she felt paralyzed knowing she couldn't afford a good lawyer—something Judd probably knew, too.

Her phone rang, the name *Simon* flashing on the screen. A surprising warmth moved through her as she picked it up and swiped to answer.

"Hey," she said, trying to steady her voice.

"Hi," Simon replied. "How are you?"

"I'm... good," she said, hesitating only slightly. She doubted he wanted the real answer: on the verge of tears as she packed her child up for a weekend with the man trying to take him away from her. "How about you?"

"Good," he said, then added sheepishly, "other than the fact that I've spent the last five minutes staring at my phone trying to draft the perfect text to you."

Lacey laughed, surprised. "Oh?"

"Yeah. I wanted it to sound casual and cool—but also confident and maybe a little funny, you know, to show I have a sense of humor. But not *too* funny so it feels forced..."

"That's a lot of pressure for a single text," she said, folding one of Elliott's shirts, the phone tucked between her ear and shoulder.

"Exactly. So I gave up and just called. Which I'm now realizing probably makes me sound neither casual nor cool."

Lacey laughed.

"Anyway," he said, "the reason I'm calling is to see if you might want to grab dinner sometime."

Lacey's stomach gave a small flip. She looked at Elliott's half-packed backpack and answered automatically, "We'd love to, but Elliott's going to his dad's for the weekend—"

"No, I meant..." Simon cut in, then hesitated. "Without the kids."

"Oh." She dropped Elliott's shirt, her heart skipping. "You mean like a..."

"Yeah," he said. "Like a date. Is that weird?"

She sat down on the edge of the bed, her face suddenly flushed. "No," she said quickly, her pulse thudding in her ears. "Not weird at all." Except it *was* weird. She hadn't been on a date with anyone but Judd in years. She hadn't even imagined Simon was looking at her that way. Cute, funny Simon. Wait, did he think *she* was cute?

"Oh, good," he said, and she could hear the relief in his voice. "I wasn't sure if—I mean, I hoped... Anyway, I'm glad. And I know tomorrow is short notice and it's Saturday night, so you probably already have plans..."

Lacey gave a short laugh. "Simon, I'm a single mom to an eight-year-old boy. My Saturday night plans usually involve sweatpants and reality TV."

He laughed. "Yeah, mine too. Well, not the reality TV, I'm more of a History Channel guy. Except my sister has this idea that I should be out there enjoying life, so she comes over every Saturday evening to watch the girls. Normally I just go to the gym, which is epically disappointing to her. But this would be a nice change of pace."

There was a vulnerability to his words that melted something inside Lacey. "I agree," she said softly.

"Great," he said, the smile in his voice unmistakable. "So, um... I hadn't planned this far ahead in my mental run-through of our conversation. How about I text you a couple dinner spots after we hang up? Once I can form coherent thoughts again."

"Sounds good," Lacey said. "See you tomorrow."

"See you then."

She set the phone down next to her on the bed and stared at it for a moment, the corners of her mouth still turned up. Her life might be a mess in a dozen ways, but somehow—impossibly—she had a date tomorrow night.

Lacey's mild high from her conversation with Simon faded with every mile closer to their old house—*Judd's* house, she corrected herself, though it still felt wrong to think of it that way. When they arrived, Elliott launched himself out of the car, brimming with excitement. Lacey lingered for a moment, hands clenched on the steering wheel, forcing herself to take a few steadying breaths before grabbing his backpack and following him up the walkway.

The flower bed she'd once lovingly tended was now overrun with weeds, and the lawn hadn't been mowed in weeks. The place looked unloved. It broke her heart a little.

Inside, she found Elliott and Judd tangled in a hug on the living room floor, Elliott laughing breathlessly.

"That was some tackle," Judd said, grinning up at their son. "We've got to get you on the football team."

"No football," Lacey said automatically. "Too many head injuries."

Judd's smile dropped as he shot her a glare. "Can you not?" he said, voice sharp. "You literally just walked in the door."

Lacey flushed. He wasn't wrong—she did sound like a killjoy. But she had so many fears about the kind of choices Judd would make if left unchecked, the ways he might fail to protect their son.

"Say goodbye to Mommy," Judd said as he stood and swung Elliott up onto his feet.

A lump rose in Lacey's throat. "Bye, sweetheart." She knelt, arms open.

"Bye, Mommy," Elliott said cheerfully, already turning toward his dad.

"Can I have a hug?" she asked quickly, feeling the ache bloom in her chest.

Judd rolled his eyes, but Elliott ran to her and threw his arms around her waist.

"I love you," she whispered, pressing her lips to his hair. "And remember, you can call me anytime, OK?"

He nodded solemnly, then scampered back toward Judd. "Can I play Minecraft?"

"Sure," Judd said.

"Yay!" Elliott cried, racing off.

Lacey tried to hide her annoyance. "Just don't let him play for too long, OK? It makes him—"

"I've got this," Judd cut in, his tone clipped. "You can go."

She held her ground. "Should we talk? About this full custody thing? Judd—why? It doesn't have to be this way."

His expression hardened. "As long as you insist on pumping him full of those poisonous drugs, then yeah, it does."

Lacey flinched, tears stinging behind her eyes.

"Now if you don't mind," Judd said, already turning away, "I'd like to spend my weekend with my son."

Lacey managed to get herself back out the door, jaw clenched and chest tight. She got in the car and pulled away from the curb, resisting the urge to look back. Once she was down the block, far enough that Judd wouldn't see her if he looked out the window, she pulled over and let the tears come.

Arriving back at the mommune—a word Lacey was now using in her head, ridiculous as it was—she let herself in quietly, intending to head straight upstairs and continue her pity party.

Instead, she ran smack into Tavia in the hallway.

Tavia took one look at Lacey's blotchy face and red eyes and shook her head. "I take it drop-off didn't go well?"

Lacey just shook her head as fresh tears welled.

"Oh, honey." Tavia stepped forward and pulled her into a hug. She smelled like Grace's lavender baby soap, and Lacey pressed her face into her soft shoulder, letting herself be held.

"Everything OK out here?"

Lacey lifted her tear-stained face to see Nanette at the end of the hallway, her brow creased with concern.

"No," Tavia answered for her, rubbing gentle circles on Lacey's back. "Lacey needs an IV of chardonnay, stat."

Lacey let out a watery laugh. "I'm fine, really. I was just going to head upstairs and turn in. It's been a long week."

"No, you are not," Nanette said firmly, looping her arm through Lacey's and tugging her toward the kitchen. "You're going to sit at the table while I make dinner, drink something strong, and we're going to brainstorm ways to torture your ex."

She gave Lacey's hand a gentle squeeze. "Shared custody sucks in the beginning," she said, her voice wistful. "I used to cry every time Linden's dad came to pick her up. Still do, sometimes."

Lacey let herself be steered into the warm glow of the kitchen. "But now?" she asked.

Nanette gave a dry smile. "Now I still cry, but I've also learned to enjoy the quiet. No one asking me to play Barbies or wiping peanut butter on my pants for forty-eight hours? That's not nothing."

"Here, hon," Tavia said, pressing a large glass of wine into Lacey's hand. "It won't fix your broken heart, but it'll dull the pain."

Lacey wiped the last of her tears away and moved toward the kitchen table, which was covered by the debris of dinner, half-eaten carrot sticks, crusts from grilled cheese sandwiches, and a pink plastic cup of milk sweating onto the wood. From the basement, she could hear the kids' voices rising in a chorus of giggles and shouts.

She set the wine down and started gathering the plates.

"Sit," Nanette said firmly, swooping in to take them from her. "You're off duty."

Lacey sank into a chair. "Why are you all being so nice to me?" she asked, her voice cracking. "You barely know me. And I'm obviously a complete mess. I'm getting everything all wrong."

Nanette and Tavia exchanged a look. Nanette slid into the seat across from her. Today her earrings were long curtains of brightly colored beads that swayed as she moved.

"We're nice to you because we've been you," she said simply. "And because someone—specifically Regina—was nice to us when we needed it. The universe comes full circle. Karma."

"If you believe in that stuff," Tavia, said, tossing a playful eyeroll in Nanette's direction. "Nanette's got a healthy dose of the woo-woo in her."

Nanette waved her arms near Tavia, her bracelets clinking. "I really wish you'd let me help you unblock your chakras," she said wistfully.

"My chakras will be fine if I just lay off the cheese," Tavia said with a sigh. "That's the only thing blocking me up."

Nanette scrunched her nose and gave a disappointed shake of her head as Lacey suppressed a giggle.

Tavia twisted her long dark hair into a knot and tied it on top of her head. "Lacey, honey," she said, "you just need time to get your feet under you again, and we're here to help." Her eyes shifted, seeming to focus on something in the distance. "Honestly, it feels good to be the one helping for a change. Makes me realize how far I've come."

Lacey felt something inside of her settle. Maybe, for once, leaning on someone else was exactly what she needed to stand up to Judd—and everything else waiting for her.

Her phone rang, slicing through the quiet of the kitchen. She glanced at the screen and saw a New York City area code. Her pulse quickened.

"Hello?" Lacey said.

"Lacey, it's Marina Silva from Vetra Vitals. Is now a good time?"

Her heart slammed into her throat. "Yes," she said, trying to sound composed. "Now is perfect."

"Reid really enjoyed speaking with you today, and we'd like to offer you the role of executive assistant to the CEO," Marina said briskly. "If you're still interested, I'll email you the offer letter with salary and benefits info. I think you'll find them very competitive."

Lacey's eyes widened. "Oh," she said. "OK."

Across the table, Nanette leaned forward in curiosity.

"Fantastic," Marina said. "Once you've had a chance to review the offer, please send over your references and we'll move from there. This is my cell; reach out anytime if you have questions. Even over the weekend. Reid's eager to move quickly."

Cold dread pooled in Lacey's stomach. "Right," she managed. "References."

"Talk soon," Marina said, then hung up.

Lacey slowly lowered the phone and looked up at Tavia and Nanette's expectant faces.

"I... got the job," she said, still half in disbelief.

Tavia squealed. "Honey, that's amazing!"

"What's amazing?" Regina appeared in the doorway, tucking her hair behind her ear.

"Lacey got the job," Nanette said with a grin.

A slow, knowing smile spread across Regina's face. "Congratulations."

Lacey shook her head, the momentary calm she'd felt evaporating. "I can't take it," she said, slumping forward on the table. "They want to check my references—and I don't have any, remember? My résumé is fake." She gave a low groan. "Oh my God, I shouldn't even have gone for the interview. What was I thinking? I have to call Marina back and explain."

Regina stepped forward, her expression steady. "Your expertise is real, Lacey. That's what matters."

Lacey looked at her, stricken. "But—"

"You have references," Regina said calmly. "And a backstory that checks out, if anyone decides to dig."

She glanced at Nanette, who gave a subtle nod, and at Tavia, who offered a quiet, reassuring smile. Then Regina turned her gaze back to Lacey.

"We've taken care of everything."

FIFTEEN

Lacey's brow furrowed. "What do you mean, you've taken care of everything?"

Regina reached into the cupboard and pulled down a fourth wine glass. "Why don't you look yourself up online?" she said lightly.

Lacey's pulse began to thrum in her ears. She picked up her phone and typed her name into the search bar. The first link that popped up was her LinkedIn profile, only now, it featured a crisp, professional headshot she had no memory of ever taking.

Her eyes darted up to Regina, who watched her with a faint, satisfied smile.

Lacey scrolled down. The profile now matched her fabricated résumé exactly. There it was: her degree, her "experience" at NovoMed. She clicked the company link, expecting it to lead nowhere. Instead, a clean, convincing website opened in a new tab.

"But... the photo—this whole thing—" she faltered, unsure what question to even start with.

"I used AI for the headshot," Nanette piped up, taking a sip of wine. "Just pulled a few photos from your socials and used a service to blend them. Not bad, right? I also whipped up the NovoMed site. I'm pretty handy with HTML."

Lacey stared at her phone like it might explode. What the hell was happening?

"But how did you even update my profile?" she asked, her voice faint.

Regina lifted her glass. "You should really use stronger passwords."

"And I'm your reference," Tavia said brightly, twirling her wine glass by the stem. "I'm thinking your boss at NovoMed is British, very posh." She cleared her throat and switched into a clipped accent that contrasted sharply with her normal drawl. "Righteo, Lacey was a brilliant asset to our team—precise, composed, and an absolute pleasure to work with."

Lacey dropped her phone onto the table, her head beginning to spin. "Will someone please tell me what is going on?" she whispered, a dull pressure building behind her eyes.

Her phone buzzed with a new email notification from Marina Silva. *Subject: Vetra Vitals Offer.*

Lacey hesitated, then tapped to open it. She tried to read it, but the words swam in front of her eyes—until one number snapped sharply into focus.

She gasped. The salary was more than she'd hoped for. Way more. Her brain shifted into high gear as she began the math, adding up the cost of rent, food, legal fees for a good lawyer.

A *very* good lawyer.

She looked up at the three women staring back. Nanette's expression was cautious and watchful. Tavia's eyes held a mischievous twinkle. And Regina wore her usual distant smile.

Somehow, impossibly, they had conjured Lacey a second chance. All she had to do now was decide if she wanted it.

Her phone rang again in her hand, startling her so badly she dropped it onto the table with a loud clatter. A California area code flashed across the screen.

"You should answer that," Regina said, her voice soft but firm.

Lacey's heart pounded as she snatched up the phone.

"Hello?"

"Lacey, it's Reid Mercer."

A jolt shot through her, and she tightened her grip on the phone.

"Marina told me she just sent you the offer," he said. "I wanted to call personally and say I think you're a great fit and we'd love to have you on board. I know it's an executive assistant role, but with your background, I see potential for this to grow into something more—something with a research and strategic edge. Chief of staff level. I'm really looking forward to working with you."

The lights of the kitchen seemed to sharpen, and Lacey scrambled for a response, to explain that she couldn't take the job, that it was all a mistake, that he wouldn't even want her if he knew the truth. But the words jammed in her throat.

"Excellent," Reid said, without waiting for her to speak. "Let Marina know if you have any questions, otherwise we'll see you Monday."

As Lacey lowered the phone, the familiar feeling of guilt rose in her. But this time it was dampened by something else: a deep, aching desire to step forward into the persona Regina, Nanette, and Tavia had created for her. To be the mother Elliott needed, to be able to fight for him. To take her second chance.

Tavia clapped her hands as Lacey hung up and set the phone back on the table. "You're gonna knock their socks clean off," she declared.

Nanette leaned in, her sandalwood scent wrapping around Lacey, and placed a warm hand on her forearm. "I'm really happy for you," she said, her voice steady with sincerity.

Regina's eyes gleamed. "This calls for a celebration," she said, reaching up into the cabinet above the sink and pulling down a bottle.

Nanette groaned. "No tequila, please," she said.

"Just one shot," Regina insisted. "It's tradition."

She tipped a generous pour of the clear liquid into four of the kids' tiny juice glasses, and Tavia sliced a lime.

Regina passed out the juice glasses and held hers in the air, her eyes locked on Lacey's. "To new beginnings," she said.

"To new beginnings," Lacey and the others echoed.

The kitchen filled with laughter and conversation as the women drifted out to get kids to bed, then back in to refill their glasses. Lacey sat a little taller in her chair, ignoring the slight queasiness of guilt in her stomach, instead letting herself savor a stronger sensation: the heady sense of possibility.

"I'm not even a tequila person," she said, downing another shot —her third, maybe fourth?—the burn tracing a fiery path down her throat before settling in her belly like a small sun. The house outside the kitchen had gone quiet, the kids long asleep.

Tavia giggled. "You'll learn to like it. It's tradition."

"'Like' might be generous," Nanette muttered, grimacing as she knocked back what remained in her juice glass.

Lacey blinked, the word snagging in her mind: tradition. Regina had said the same thing.

"What do you mean?" she asked, wiping her mouth with the back of her hand. She looked around the kitchen table.

"We drink tequila every time someone officially becomes part of the house," Tavia said, swirling the last of hers.

"Or when we get closer to the goal," Nanette added, her voice looser than usual, head tipped back, limbs slack.

Lacey frowned. "What goal?"

Tavia's eyes flicked toward Regina as she reached for the bottle. "Liberation."

"OK, I think we've hit the philosophical portion of the evening," Regina interjected, waving an arm. "Let's change the subject."

Lacey tried to respond, but hiccupped instead. "I'm lost," she admitted.

Nanette sat up and smiled gently. "It'll all make sense soon. Just trust us."

"Regina got us jobs, too, you know," Tavia said, tugging her hair out of its knot. "Praise be. I had no plan—just me, a baby, and a GED. I'd've been slinging fries for minimum wage."

"Tavia," Regina warned, her tone clipped.

Lacey, suddenly sobered, sipped water and turned to Tavia. "Wait—what do you do, exactly?"

"I'm in HR," Tavia said brightly.

"Where?"

Tavia flashed a grin. "Vetra Vitals."

Lacey choked. "Seriously?"

Nanette glanced down at her lap. Tavia's grin faded a little.

"What about you?" Lacey asked, eyes narrowing.

Nanette gave a small, sheepish smile. "IT department. Also Vetra."

Lacey stared at both of them. "So this whole time...?"

"We didn't want to sway you," Tavia said quickly, casting a guilty glance at Regina. "She thought you should make the decision on your own."

Tavia reached out to pat Regina's arm. "She doesn't like us to talk about her generosity," she stage-whispered to Lacey.

Lacey's head spun—not just from the tequila. She turned to Regina, who for once looked uncomfortable.

"I had connections at Vetra," she said, quietly. "And the company's growing fast."

Lacey felt faint. She pushed back her chair, unsteady on her feet. "I... I should get to bed," she murmured, the room tilting ever so slightly. Her thoughts were spinning. She needed to lie down, clear her head, and start making sense of everything she'd just learned, of what she'd just agreed to.

Regina gave her a gentle smile. "Get some sleep," she said. "We'll talk more in the morning."

SIXTEEN

Lacey awoke early the next morning. The first thing she noticed was that Elliott wasn't snuggled beside her, hogging the covers. The second was the dull ache behind her eyes and the dry, sawdusty feeling on her tongue. The night before came rushing back in flashes, like snapshots: the tequila shots, the fake LinkedIn profile, the job offer with its jaw-dropping salary, Reid's phone call, and finally—Tavia and Nanette's revelation.

She let out a groan and pulled the pillow over her face to block the faint light filtering through the gauzy curtains. If she could just go back to sleep, maybe she'd wake up to find it had all been a dream. Except... she didn't want all of it to vanish. Even though the thought of her doctored résumé made her stomach twist into knots, the fact was that she needed this job. And, if she was being honest with herself, she *wanted* it.

After five more minutes of lying in bed while her brain went into overdrive trying to come up with a way to rationalize moving forward with the job, she gave up. Coffee. Coffee would help.

But the kitchen wasn't empty.

Regina stood at the sink, rinsing the juice glasses from the night before and tossing lime slices into the compost bin. She looked up as Lacey entered, and goosebumps prickled along Lacey's arms. She rubbed at them, wishing she'd grabbed her bathrobe.

"Good morning," Regina said.

Whereas Lacey was still in the T-shirt she'd slept in and her faded flannel pajama pants, and she didn't even want to imagine the bags under her eyes, Regina looked fresh and rested in form-fitting jeans and a loose white button-up shirt.

Lacey rubbed sleep from her eyes. "Morning."

The coffee beckoned, but Lacey leaned against the counter. Her headache pulsed faintly behind her eyes, but she ignored it. She needed answers.

She hesitated, then crossed her arms. "What's going on?" she asked.

Regina turned off the tap and dried her hands slowly on a towel. "You mean, everyone working at Vetra?" she said.

Lacey blinked, caught off guard by Regina's directness. "Well, yeah," she said.

Regina picked up her mug and fiddled with one of her small pearl earrings. She walked over to the table and pulled out a chair, glancing over her shoulder. "Let's sit."

Lacey followed, hesitantly perching on the edge of the chair while Regina settled across from her, perfectly upright, cradling her mug.

"I told you I used to work with Reid," she said. "In California."

"Did you meet at Stanford?" Lacey asked, recalling what she'd read about Reid dropping out of the PhD program there.

Regina gave a dry laugh. "No. I went to a state school, and my parents barely agreed to pay for that."

For the first time, Lacey noticed a few silver strands threaded through Regina's dark hair. Maddie had inherited those same wild, ebony waves, while Max's hair was several shades lighter. Lacey found herself wondering who their father was. Regina had made it sound like he'd never been in the picture. And suddenly, Lacey felt the weight of how little she truly knew about the woman whose house she was living in—the woman who'd handed her a lifeline, and to whom Lacey now owed more than she could name.

"Reid and I met at a biotech summit when I was twenty-four," Regina continued. "One of those hyper-networked, over-caffeinated industry expos where everyone's pitching and posturing. I hated those things, but I liked Reid. He was smart, hardworking, and he wasn't interested in sleeping with me, which is more than I can say for most of the men there." Her mouth turned down in distaste. "He had this idea," she continued. "An early version of a wearable sensor system, and he was getting attention. I could tell he had something, and I felt stalled out at the start-up I'd been working at since college, so we agreed to be partners. I knew how to build, and he knew how to sell. We started Chomer Labs." She blinked. "God, it's hard to believe that was ten years ago already."

Lacey took a sip of her coffee. "So, what happened?"

Regina's face hardened. "After about a year, our idea got some attention. Then a little more." She glanced at Lacey. "Then came the money. Investors. Valuations. Pressure." Her jaw tightened slightly. "Somewhere along the way, things changed. Reid became the face of what we were building, and I was just... the background."

Regina's eyes dropped to her mug, swirling the last bit of coffee at the bottom. She let out a quiet breath. "Two years after starting the company together, he left my name off the patent application for our flagship product. It was right after the twins were born— two months early. They spent a month in the NICU." She inhaled sharply as though trying to push away a memory. After a beat, she lifted her head. "I was on my own, so sleep-deprived, and by the time I caught the omission it was too late. Or at least it felt like it was. I was too tired and overwhelmed with my preemies to put up much of a fight. Then I missed a board meeting, and before I knew it, I was out."

Lacey's stomach twisted. "And Reid... let it happen?"

Regina looked up at her, a hint of coldness in her eyes. "Reid *made* it happen. And in that world, if you don't fight for your credit, people assume you didn't earn it."

She stood and carried her mug back to the sink, rinsing it out. "I sold my shares for pennies before the company really took off. Thought I was being smart. Practical. I was twenty-seven with two kids and no support. I just wanted out." Turning back to face Lacey, her face was stony. "He took our technology and over the next five years he built Chomer Labs into something Vetra wanted to acquire. Now Reid is worth tens of millions—especially because they made him CEO after the acquisition. And he'll be worth even more once Vetra goes public, which I guarantee you is his plan. And all the while I'm..." Her eyes swept the room. "Well, I've got a house full of roommates in a commuter town in New Jersey."

Lacey felt quiet anger on Regina's behalf stir in her chest. "That's..." she started, then trailed off, unsure what word even fit. Unfair? Unethical? The words seemed pale and weak in the face of what Regina had just described. Lacey's thoughts swirled. "But wait, the jobs, why...?"

"Why did I help the three of you get jobs at Vetra after being royally fucked over by Reid?" Regina finished for her.

Lacey nodded.

Regina gave a bitter laugh. "Because as much as I despise Reid Mercer, I know him. I know how he thinks, how he builds, and I know Vetra's going to be a success." She ran a hand through her hair. "And while Reid would never hire *me* again, the three of you are getting in early enough that you'll have equity. And when Vetra goes public, you'll all stand to make real money."

Lacey's eyes widened. "I'm sorry—what?"

"If you take the job at Vetra," Regina said with a tired smile, "eventually you'll likely make a lot of money."

Lacey's breath caught. "But why...?" The question tangled with a dozen others, none of them finding shape.

"Why would I be so generous?" Regina finished for her, her tone wry.

"Um... yes?" Lacey managed.

Regina's jaw tightened. "Because if I can't benefit from all the work I did for Reid, then someone should. Someone who needs it."

Lacey bit her lip, still struggling to process, and Regina's expression softened. "I know how it sounds," she admitted, gripping her mug and looking away. "I should've told you everything upfront. But I wasn't sure you'd say yes if I had. You were already on the fence about taking the job, and if I'd told you it might make you a fortune..." She shook her head, then looked back at Lacey. "You'd have thought it was too good to be true—and you definitely would've said no." She paused, studying Lacey. "I'm telling you now because I want you to trust me. Because I know you, Lacey. I've *been* you—anxious, exhausted, lying awake at night trying to figure out how to make it all work." Her voice was pitched low and urgent. "Do you know how many women are stuck in that same loop?" She straightened her shoulders, her eyes sharp. "Men have systems. They pass each other jobs, money, influence. Especially in tech. It's all backroom deals and old boys' clubs. They help each other without even thinking." She leaned toward Lacey slightly. "Now imagine if we did the same. If women backed each other that way. Imagine what we could build."

A flicker of something wistful passed over her face. "With the mommune, I'm trying to do that—to create a real support network. Not just roommates, but family. And family means helping each other in every way." She cracked a smile. "Picture us a year from now. Vetra goes public, and we're in a bigger house, maybe with a pool. Definitely a housekeeper."

Lacey's thoughts buzzed as she tried to keep up with everything Regina had just shared. She'd been thrilled about the salary alone from the Vetra job, and now Regina was hinting at a payoff that could change everything. Still, knowing the bigger picture did nothing to quell the unease she felt at having accepted the job in the first place. Plus, any payoff would be way down the line, and she didn't want to be financially beholden to Regina; she barely knew her.

"I can't do it," she said with a shake of her head. "It's bad enough that I lied to get the job, but now knowing what Reid is really like—I can't work for someone like that."

Regina's face twisted in exasperation. "Don't be naïve, Lacey. Every time we try and take the moral high ground, we lose and they win."

Lacey bit her lip, her thoughts churning. "What about the mommune?" she asked, turning to the next subject about which she had many unanswered questions. "How did this happen—how do you even start something like this?"

Regina shrugged. "I met Tavia at a story hour at the library. The twins were five, and oh my God, were they a handful. She was so pregnant she could hardly move, but she tried to help me with them. Then I found out she needed a place to stay, and I had this big house..." She paused, her eyes going distant. "Then we met Nanette a few months later, and the rest is history." She shook her head, as though snapping out of the memory. "We built the family we all needed at the time. That we still need."

A sudden lump rose in Lacey's throat. Because, she realized, she needed it, too.

Regina turned to meet Lacey's eyes. "You should take the job," she said, her voice soft and urgent. "Never mind me. It's what's best for you and Elliott. I mean, what else are you going to do?"

Lacey swallowed hard, reality washing over her: In terms of other options, there weren't any.

SEVENTEEN

By early evening, Lacey's hangover had finally faded. Most of the day had passed in a fog of reflection, her thoughts looping back to her conversation with Regina. The more she turned it over in her mind, the less far-fetched Regina's logic seemed. Why shouldn't they all support each other? Regina was right, men did it all the time, without a second thought. And Regina—despite the fact that she hadn't been upfront with Lacey about Vetra—had already done more for her than anyone else in years. First a place to live. Then the job. And now she was offering something even more valuable: a future.

She thought about the last few nights, spent in the kitchen with Regina, Nanette, and Tavia after the kids were in bed, sipping wine, laughing until her sides hurt. It had only been a week, but already this place felt more like home than anywhere she'd lived since those early days with Judd. What would be so crazy about making this her family? Her parents were gone, and it wasn't like Sarah had been there when Lacey needed her, not for the long haul, anyway. Whereas Regina had a plan—something Lacey desperately needed.

By the time Lacey had showered and styled her hair into soft waves, her anxieties about Vetra had quieted, replaced by a new set of nerves.

She had a *date*.

In front of the mirror, she took a final look at herself. She'd opted for jeans, a black V-neck T-shirt, and a simple pendant necklace. Comfortable, low-key. Not trying too hard.

She checked her phone—again. Still no word from Elliott. Earlier she'd texted Judd:

Everything going all right?

His reply had come back quick and clipped:

Yes.

She'd forced herself to let it go. She'd see Elliott tomorrow. Surely he and Judd would be fine together for a mere forty-eight hours.

Downstairs, Nanette was crouched in the living room, dismantling the kids' blanket fort and collecting scattered UNO cards.

"I thought you had a date tonight," she said when she looked up.

"I do."

Her critical gaze swept over Lacey. "Then why are you dressed like you're running to Trader Joe's?"

Lacey blinked. "What? It's a casual dinner." She looked over Nanette, who wore a soft, burnt-orange sweater dress with a colorful, tissue-like turquoise scarf wrapped around her neck.

"Tavia!" Nanette called. Tavia appeared in the hallway, drying her hands on a dish towel.

"I may not be the best judge," Nanette continued, "since I'm not a basic white lady, but does Lacey look dressed for a date?"

Lacey let out a groan and half-laugh, while Tavia gave her a once-over.

"You look lovely, obviously, honey," she said. "But..."

"But?" Lacey prompted.

Tavia wrinkled her nose. "It's giving more PTA meeting than romantic night out."

"It's only a first date," Lacey defended herself.

Nanette grinned. "Exactly. We're dialing this up a notch. Upstairs. Now."

Lacey raised her hands in surrender. "OK," she said, glancing at her watch. "You have ten minutes to make me irresistible."

Tavia tossed her dish towel aside. "Let's go, Cinderella."

Lacey stepped through the glass doors of the Italian restaurant Simon had chosen, taking in the exposed brick and dark wood. The low hum of conversation and clink of silverware rose to meet her. She paused just inside the entrance, smoothing a hand down the side of the dark green wrap dress with the deep V neckline Tavia had pulled from her own closet, claiming it would "show off the good stuff." Her lips were painted a dark berry color that Nanette called "grown-ass woman sexy" and she'd swapped her sneakers for low-heeled boots.

She spotted Simon at a two-top near the window, already half-standing, his hand raised in a wave. He wore a navy button-down with the sleeves rolled up, and when he smiled, it was that same slightly bashful grin that flooded her chest with warmth. As she walked toward him, she caught the way his eyes moved over her—quick, then slower, like he was seeing her for the first time.

"Wow," he said as she approached, rising fully to greet her. "You look great."

A warm flush spread across her cheeks. "Thanks," she said, settling into her chair as the server handed them menus.

"How's your weekend going?" Simon asked.

Lacey bit her lip, hesitating. "Good," she said. "Actually—I got a new job."

His face lit up. "Seriously? Congratulations!"

As she told him about the role at Vetra, the words started to come more confidently. The more she spoke, the more real it all felt —and the more she was able to ignore the pang of guilt that appeared when she thought about how she'd gotten the job. Her nerves eased as excitement crept in.

"It sounds incredible," Simon said, lifting the glass of wine the server had just set down. "Cheers to you."

"Thanks," Lacey said, clinking her glass with his. She took a sip and exhaled, fingers twitching at the corner of her napkin. "I'm also kind of terrified," she admitted.

"Oh?" Simon leaned in, giving her his full attention.

"It's just... I don't know if I'm really qualified," Lacey said, her voice tightening at the edges. She knew she should stop, but the words kept spilling out. "I mean, I didn't finish college. I got pregnant with Elliott, dropped out, and always told myself I'd go back, but I never did." Her cheeks heated. Why was she saying all this? This wasn't first date material; it was way too much, too soon.

Simon frowned, but it was gentle, thoughtful. "Well, they hired you, didn't they? So they must think you can do it."

Lacey swallowed. "Yes," she said, her voice faltering only slightly. "True." She toyed with the stem of her wine glass and forced a bright smile. "Anyway, sorry. Let's talk about something more interesting."

Simon held her gaze. "I'm interested. Tell me more about the job."

Lacey waved a hand. Talking about Vetra suddenly felt like dangerous territory, as though the job was something she should keep separate from "real" life. "Tell me about you," she said. "Tell me about your girls."

Simon's eyes brightened. "I'll start with the girls, since they're much more interesting than me. Ella's super smart, and she loves to sing and dance. She's convinced she's going to be the next Taylor Swift."

Lacey laughed. "Maybe she will."

He tilted his head. "Well, between you and me, she'd have to learn to carry a tune first. Then there's Amelia, in fourth grade. She had Mr. Barry last year, thank God. He was the one who realized she might have ADHD. Before that, everyone, including me, just thought she was difficult." He shook his head, a shadow of shame flickering across his face. "I hate how long it took me to get it. I was just so burned out from trying to manage the roller coaster of her moods all the time, you know?" Pain seared across his face. "Their mom was so much better at all the... feelings stuff. But it's been almost four years since she died. Ella doesn't even have that many memories of her." He shifted in his seat and gave her an apologetic smile. "Wow, I'm really nailing this first-date thing, huh? Light, breezy, super fun..."

Lacey smiled and reached across the table before she could second-guess herself, her fingers closing around his. "I'm sorry about your wife," she said softly. "And Elliott has ADHD, too. I feel like a terrible mom at least once a day. You're not alone. I get it. Really."

Simon looked down at her hand, then back up at her. "Thanks," he said. "That means a lot." The smile he gave her set a fresh wave of butterflies loose in her stomach.

The rest of the evening flowed effortlessly, talking about kids, the school, TV shows. By the time they stood to leave, Lacey felt nearly as relaxed as she did sitting in the kitchen with Regina, Nanette, and Tavia. Being with Simon felt easy.

Outside, the air had turned crisp, the kind of early fall evening that hinted at the colder days ahead. Lacey shivered.

"Cold?" he asked, slipping his arm around her shoulders. "Where'd you park?"

She laughed, pointing just a few feet away. "Right there. Front row."

His face dropped theatrically. "Damn. There goes my chance to walk you to your car and work up the nerve to kiss you."

A spark danced in her chest.

"I had a really nice time," he said, more earnestly now.

"Me too," she said softly.

He hesitated—just a breath—then leaned forward.

For a moment, Lacey let herself lean into the warmth of Simon's kiss, waiting for that familiar rush, the dizzy spark of something new and electric. But as his arms tightened around her, her mind began to drift. She wondered if Elliott had remembered to brush his teeth before bed. She thought about the custody lawyer Regina had recommended, the call she needed to make Monday morning. With a silent sigh, she pulled herself back into the moment with Simon.

He pulled back, his face flushed and grinning. "That was nice," he murmured.

"It was," she agreed, feeling a prickle of guilt about her wandering thoughts. But for now, maybe nice was good enough.

Back at home, the kitchen light spilled a warm glow down the hallway as Lacey stepped through the front door. She heard the low murmur of voices, punctuated by soft laughter, and moved toward the sound.

"Waiting up for me?" she teased as she entered.

Three nearly empty wine glasses sat on the table. Tavia's feet were pulled up under her on the chair, while Nanette leaned in, her elbows on the table, and Regina sat languidly with her arm stretched over the back of an empty chair.

"Of course not," Tavia said, sitting back and flicking her hair over her shoulder.

"Obviously," Regina added with a smirk.

Nanette giggled and gestured to the empty chair beside her.

"So? How was it?" Tavia asked, using the same tone Lacey employed to coax information out of Elliott after school.

Lacey felt her cheeks flush as she took the seat next to Regina. "It was nice," she admitted, trying to sound casual. "He's funny. And easy to talk to."

"Did he kiss you?" Tavia demanded.

"Tavia!" Nanette scolded, half-laughing.

"What?" Tavia said, unbothered. "I haven't so much as even talked to a man other than my car mechanic since Grace was born. Let me live vicariously."

Lacey's blush deepened.

"Oh my God, he *did* kiss you!" Tavia shrieked, clutching her chest.

"Shh!" Regina hissed with mock anger, glancing down the hallway toward Max and Maddie's room.

Lacey ducked her head, smiling. "He did."

Tavia mimed a swoon while Nanette rolled her eyes and swatted at her with a napkin. "I guess our little makeover did the trick," she said, arching a brow at Lacey.

She stood and grabbed a fourth wine glass from the cabinet, setting it in front of Lacey with a flourish. Tavia filled it generously.

Lacey raised the glass to her lips, her smile wide. The date with Simon had been sweet. But coming home to this moment around the table—this felt even better.

EIGHTEEN

Lacey tried to ignore the pit in her stomach as she entered the soaring glass atrium in the Vetra offices. *You can do this*, she told herself. *You* need *to do this, for Elliott.*

Marina greeted her, dressed once again in head-to-toe black. Her hair was twisted into the same severe bun, her lips painted a deep, commanding crimson. She was so sleek and self-contained that for an instant Lacey pictured the seals she and Elliott had watched at the Essex County Zoo over the summer—gliding through the chilly water, popping up now and then to catch a fish mid-air.

Next to Marina, Lacey felt lumpy and unmistakably suburban. She'd ironed her white button-down the night before, but the train ride had rumpled it again, and her only decent pair of work pants sagged slightly from the weight she'd lost that summer under the strain of everything.

"Your access mirrors Reid's for the most part," Marina said briskly as they rode the elevator up to the executive floor. "Inbox, calendar, shared servers, research drive, et cetera." She gave Lacey a sidelong glance, and a flicker of doubt passed over her expression. "I don't have time to walk you through it all, so I hope you're a fast learner."

"No problem," Lacey said, trying to sound confident as Marina led her to her desk, which sat like a sentry in front of Reid's corner office on the far side of the floor from the elevator.

"He's usually in by eight," Marina said, then hesitated, her mouth tightening. "It would be smart to have a matcha latte waiting for him. Large. Oat milk." Her lips curved into the vaguest hint of a smile that, for a moment, reminded Lacey of Regina. "You'll find he's a creature of habit."

Once Marina had left, Lacey settled at her desk, slipping her purse into a drawer and nudging the mouse to wake the oversized monitor. She typed in the password from the Post-it on her desk and as the screen blinked to life, her thoughts drifted to Elliott. He had a vocabulary quiz that morning. They'd spent the evening cramming after she picked him up from Judd's, even though she'd sent the review sheet with him for the weekend. Predictably, Judd hadn't so much as unfolded it.

Judd had offered to bring Elliott home Sunday afternoon, but Lacey had insisted on picking him up. She wasn't ready for Judd to see the mommune. She hadn't told him about the three other women and their kids, or the way this patchwork household had started to feel like home. When he'd asked, she'd simply said she'd found a short-term rental. It wasn't that she was ashamed, but after Simon's confused reaction to her living situation, she realized maybe some things didn't need to be explained. It worked for her. That was enough.

She clicked the email icon on her screen, and Reid's inbox appeared on the screen, an avalanche of unread messages. She opened one at random, from Sunil Bhatt, Vetra's head of research.

Subject: Re: FDA PMA Application

Per our meeting last week, FDA submission by end of Q1 is too aggressive. We're still addressing the algorithm issues I flagged. I need more time to get this right. We get one shot with the FDA and we can't blow it.

Lacey scrolled up to see the thread, noting the clipped back-

and-forth between Sunil and Reid, the tension ratcheting with each reply.

Across the floor, the elevator pinged open. Lacey closed Sunil's email as she heard a jaunty whistle. A second later, Reid appeared, his shoulders back, striding toward her. He raised a hand in greeting, his grin easy, the corners of his pale blue eyes crinkling.

"My savior has arrived," he said.

His light gray shirt looked custom-fitted, the fabric molding to his frame, the top button undone just enough to telegraph casual power. He smelled faintly of warm pine needles and worn leather, and Lacey felt a quick, disorienting quiver run through her.

She flushed. "Good morning."

He nodded toward her screen. "Here's hoping you can save me from myself—and from my seven hundred unread emails."

Lacey straightened, pushing her nerves down. "That's the plan," she said. "How about starting with a matcha latte?"

Lacey's first day flew by in a blur, and by the time she left the office, a dull ache had settled behind her eyes from the sheer volume of information she'd crammed into her brain—everything from which of Reid's standing meetings were absolutely sacred, to deciphering the endless alphabet soup of Vetra acronyms. Still, it had felt good to be challenged, to use her brain in a way she certainly hadn't needed to at Carpet World with Chip. She repressed a shudder thinking of his ruddy, leering face.

It wasn't until her train ride home that Lacey finally found a moment to return a call to Elizabeth Weisberg, the family law attorney Regina had recommended. And while the last thing her exhausted brain wanted was a legal conversation, she was painfully aware that the clock was ticking to respond to Judd's divorce complaint.

"Lacey, hi," came a crisp, no-nonsense voice after a brief hold. "Elizabeth Weisberg here. So, your husband's filed for divorce."

"That's right," Lacey replied, caught off guard and then relieved that Elizabeth skipped the small talk and dove straight in.

"Seeking sole legal and physical custody. Wow." Elizabeth clucked her tongue. "Not something I see often from fathers."

"I don't think it's really about wanting Elliott," Lacey said. "It's more about controlling his medical decisions." Keeping her voice low as she glanced around the packed train car, Lacey quickly filled Elizabeth in on Judd's dramatic personality change and his stance on Elliott's ADHD.

"Mm," Elizabeth said. "Well, here's how this would work, broadly speaking: We'd respond to his complaint with a consent order for interim custody. That gives us a temporary framework while both parties begin discovery and we prepare for the case management conference. That's where the judge hears the facts and issues a formal custody order."

"And if Judd refuses the temporary agreement?"

"Then his only move is to file an emergent motion claiming you're unfit. But based on what you sent me—stable housing, steady job, no mental health or substance issues—he'd have a hard time convincing a judge of that."

A small ripple of relief went through Lacey. "How long would the temporary agreement last?"

"Usually four to six months, depending on how quickly we get on the docket."

Lacey's relief gave way to a heavy sense of dread. Four to six months of sharing Elliott with Judd felt like a lifetime. But then came the guilt. He was still Elliott's father, and to her surprise, Elliott had returned from the weekend smiling, even saying he'd had fun. Maybe there was room for some kind of peaceful co-parenting, if—and she knew it was a big if—she could get Judd to behave reasonably.

"I'll follow up with everything we've discussed," Elizabeth said, her tone softening. "And include information on my fees. Reach out when you're ready to move forward."

"I will," Lacey said quietly. "Thank you."

She ended the call and let her head rest against the seat. Outside, the scenery blurred past—houses growing larger, yards wider, the city slowly giving way to space and stillness. She thought of the paycheck from Vetra that would hit her account in two weeks, her cozy yellow bedroom at the mommune, and Simon's kind eyes across the dinner table. For the first time in what seemed like forever, she felt herself stepping out of the corner she'd been backed into. The weight of feeling trapped had lifted, replaced by something quieter but more powerful: a sense of possibility.

As she walked up the front walk back at the mommune, her phone chimed.

> Are you home? I'm about to drop something off for you. I can leave it by the door, I don't want to interrupt your evening.

Lacey smiled as she typed her reply. She and Simon had been texting steadily in the last forty-eight hours, and the thought of seeing him again so soon sent a small thrill through her.

> Just getting home. You're not interrupting anything.

Seconds later, Simon's Explorer pulled up at the curb. He stepped out with a small brown paper gift bag in hand, wearing jeans and a red quilted flannel over his T-shirt, making him look like an L.L.Bean ad come to life.

"I swear I'm not stalking you," he said, grinning sheepishly as he approached. "But at the park you mentioned you lived on Wildwood, in the house with the huge front porch, so I figured it was this one."

Lacey laughed. "It's fine," she said.

He stopped just shy of the front step, glancing toward the house. "Is, um, Elliott around?"

She looked at him quizzically.

He shook his head. "I just meant, I was maybe going to try to kiss you again, but I didn't want to—I just wasn't sure if he knew..."

He stopped and ran a hand through his hair. "Wow, I'm so smooth, right?"

Lacey stepped closer, slipping her hand into his. "I appreciate your lack of smoothness," she murmured. "And yes, you can kiss me again."

Their lips met for a long minute, and when they finally broke apart, Lacey searched herself for a spark, a jolt, even a flutter. But all she felt was the chill of the crisp fall air against her cheeks. Still, she wrapped her arms around Simon, basking in his comforting warmth and musky scent.

"Elliott's not around, for the record," Lacey clarified.

Simon nodded. "Of course, I get it." He gestured between them. "This is very... new." He stepped back and took a long look at her. "And this is going to sound like a total line when I say it, but I really do feel like I've known you longer than one measly date."

Lacey smiled. "It doesn't feel like a line coming from you," she said. "And besides, I feel the same way." She linked her arm through his. "Maybe we knew each other in a past life."

"Maybe," he said, grinning.

She gestured to the front steps. "Can you sit for a minute?"

They sank down together, shoulder to shoulder. He handed her the bag.

"Oh—this is for you," he said, suddenly shy. "What I was dropping off."

Lacey peeked inside, then gasped as she pulled out a buttery soft pale yellow cashmere scarf. The color was soft and sunny, like early morning light. She pressed it to her cheek.

"It's beautiful," she said. "Thank you."

"I saw it and thought of you," Simon said. "It seemed so full of sunshine. Anyway, happy first day of work."

Lacey turned and kissed him on the cheek. "I love it," she said. She was genuinely touched, not only by the gesture, but also by the fact that someone could see her as full of sunshine when she'd felt so dark for so long.

Simon's phone buzzed. He glanced at the screen. "I should go. The girls are at my sister's and I'm late for dinner."

They rose together. Lacey looped the scarf around her neck, the fabric deliciously soft against her skin.

"Thank you again," she said. "You're incredibly thoughtful."

He placed a kiss on top of her head. "I hope it's not too forward of me to say I hope I get to see you in it a lot," he said.

Lacey's cheeks flushed. She watched him walk to his car and roll down the window to wave as he pulled away. She was still smiling when she walked through the front door, just in time to see Tavia dart out of the living room.

"Was that Simon?" she squealed.

Nanette appeared behind her, an amused look on her face. "Tavia was spying," she said.

"Was not!" Tavia shot back. "OK, maybe a little. But you *were* totally making out right on the porch."

"I was *not*," Lacey hissed, horrified, as her face went hot.

"Whatever you say," Nanette said, waving her toward the kitchen. "Come on, dinner's ready." Then she sang softly, "Lacey's got a boyfriend..."

Tavia giggled.

"You guys!" Lacey said, trying to sound scandalized, but the laughter in her voice gave her away. She unwrapped the scarf as she walked toward the kitchen, still smiling.

NINETEEN

The phone on Lacey's desk rang, and she answered on the second ring.

"CEO's office," she said, her tone bright and polished. Two months into her job at Vetra, the words still gave her a small thrill. She glanced around the sleek, white-on-white reception area outside Reid's office where she sat. It was a nice break from the cozy chaos of the mommune, a place where she felt like a real adult, the kind of person who had her life together.

And slowly, over the weeks, the knot in her stomach, the one tied to all the lies she'd told to get here, had begun to loosen. Each day, she felt a little more confident that taking the job had been the right thing—especially when she checked her bank account to make sure she had enough to pay her lawyer's bills.

"Let me see what Reid has open Wednesday," she said into the phone.

Reid hadn't been lying when he'd said he was a demanding boss. Half the time, Lacey felt like Anne Hathaway in *The Devil Wears Prada*, scrambling to deliver Reid's matcha latte while it was still hot. The other half she felt like she was becoming an integral part of the team. Reid regularly asked her opinion on research proposals and debriefed with her after funder meetings.

"OK, I've got you on the calendar," she told the caller. "And please send any meeting materials twenty-four hours in advance. He'll cancel the meeting if you don't."

"You make me sound so high maintenance," came Reid's voice.

Lacey turned in her chair and raised her eyebrow. "This coming from the man who made me send his açaí bowl back yesterday for not having enough blueberries."

Reid lifted his hands in mock innocence. "You can't call it a superfood bowl without the superfoods."

Lacey gave him a half-amused, half-exasperated smile. "By the way, Marina's looking for you," she said. Marina spent a *lot* of time looking for Reid. She also spent a lot of time talking to Lacey *about* Reid—that he was allergic to cilantro, that he hated fluorescent lighting, that he was always in a foul mood after meeting with Sunil, who rarely had good news about the clinical trials. It was as if she needed Lacey to know that she was the expert when it came to the CEO.

"Were you ever his assistant?" Lacey had asked one day with faux innocence. "You seem to know him really well."

"What?" Marina looked horrified. "God, no. I have a law degree from Stanford." She pursed her lips. "We've just worked together a long time."

Now, standing in front of Lacey's desk, Reid waved a hand. "Marina can wait," he said. "I need some fresh air." He flashed a look in her direction—the kind that usually meant *You're coming, too*.

Lacey suppressed her sigh as she glanced at the growing list of emails in her inbox. "Fine," she said. "Let's go."

It was a bright mid-November afternoon, the sun catching in the steel and glass towers as Lacey and Reid moved along the sidewalk at a brisk pace, talking about a trial of a competitor's product that had been shut down.

"The board got spooked over what looked like a spike in participants' blood pressure," Reid said. "So they pulled the plug. Six weeks later? Turns out it was a data logging error."

Lacey gave a small shrug. "They had to consider the optics. And the liability."

He shot her a look. "You can't innovate if you're afraid of a headline. They should have investigated quietly, in the background. Not blown it up like they did. Now the study's dead, the funding's dried up, and the patients have nothing."

They passed a street vendor hawking pretzels and bottled water.

"OK," Lacey said, "so what, we just ignore red flags now?" She liked that she could be blunt with Reid, no sugarcoating necessary.

"No," he said, reaching out and guiding her by the elbow out of the path of an oncoming cyclist. "We stop pretending every bump in the road is a disaster. Like Sunil—he's so goddamn black and white with these clinical trials." Though the danger had passed, he left his hand on her arm, his eyes locked on hers.

She looked down at where he was touching her, heat shooting through her body. "We should head back," she said, stepping away just out of reach. "Speaking of Sunil, you've got a meeting with him in ten minutes."

"Let's hope he's finally made some fucking progress on the algorithm," muttered Reid.

The rest of the day flew by, and by the time Lacey stepped off the train back in Maplehurst, the sun had long since vanished, leaving the sky a deep navy. She shivered, pulling her coat tighter around her shoulders as she crossed the commuter lot and slid into her car for the short drive home. As she drove, she made one extra turn to avoid going down the street where she'd hit the red pickup truck months earlier. She still felt a pit of guilt in her stomach when she thought about how she'd left the scene, but she'd told herself it didn't make sense to dredge it back up after so much time had passed, not when things were finally going well for her.

Lacey made a point of getting home in time for dinner most nights, then catching up on emails and prep work for Reid after Elliott was in bed. There were nights she worked until long after midnight, trying to keep up with Reid's requests, which rolled in at all hours. The man seemed never to sleep, and Lacey constantly felt a half-step behind and undercaffeinated. Still, she couldn't deny she loved the job.

Given her hours, she'd considered enrolling Elliott in aftercare at the elementary school, but Regina had waved off the suggestion.

"I work from home," she'd said. "He can just come back with Max and Maddie. I leave snacks out and they pretty much handle the rest."

Regina to the rescue—again. Lacey was deeply grateful; aftercare wasn't cheap, and every extra penny was already taken up by Elizabeth Weisberg's retainer, though so far she was proving to be worth every cent of her fees. Miraculously, she and Judd's lawyer had negotiated an interim agreement: temporary shared custody while they prepared for a court appearance where Judd was still lobbying for full custody. And while nausea twisted in Lacey's stomach every time she dropped Elliott off, Judd had, so far, been on his best behavior. Lacey suspected this was likely because lawyers were now watching, and he knew just how much he stood to lose.

Lacey turned onto her street just as the heat in her old car finally kicked on. Her phone lit up with Simon's name.

"Hey there," she answered, tapping speakerphone.

"Hey," he said, the sound of his voice making her smile. She liked how he checked in, the way he'd call just to say he was thinking about her, or to share a funny story he knew she'd appreciate. "How was your day?" he asked.

"It was good," Lacey replied, trying to recall anything specific from the blur of the day. The only memory that jumped to mind in sharp focus was Reid's hand on her elbow, lingering just a second too long. "How about you?" she asked, pushing away the thought of Reid's eyes locked on hers.

"Busy," Simon said. "I'm picking up the girls from Girl Scouts and just realized it's the first time I've left the house since this morning. I changed shirts for my Zoom calls, but I'm still in pajama pants."

"Sexy," Lacey teased.

He laughed. "Business on top, bedtime on the bottom." He paused, his voice dropping into a lower register. "Hey, so, I was wondering, what if we tried to go away together sometime soon? I know this great bed and breakfast in the Poconos."

Lacey's stomach dropped the same way it used to when she and Judd would go ride the roller coasters at Six Flags—equal parts thrill and trepidation. So far, she and Simon had been limited to spending a couple of hours together at a time, over dinner or sometimes a weekend hike if Elliott was at Judd's. It was enjoyable. Conversation flowed easily, and Simon was the only person in Lacey's life who truly understood what it was like to have a child like Elliott. But was she ready to take an entire weekend trip with him?

"It could just be for a night," he said quickly, taking her silence as hesitation. "I know it's hard with the kids. And I know it might feel a little soon, but think about it—we keep grabbing a few hours here and there, barely scratching the surface, or we can spend real time together and find out if we still like each other after it." She could hear his smile through the phone. "Specifically, whether you still like me. I'm pretty sure of where I stand. And we can get two rooms, if you want. No expectations."

Lacey swallowed with nervous anticipation. "One room is fine," she said. An unfamiliar feeling stirred in her: yearning. Simon was right, she reasoned. They were grown-ups. She liked spending time with him. He made her laugh, was a good listener, and never tired of playing catch with Elliott when they all went to the park together. She liked the feeling of his arms around her and his lips on hers, even if she didn't feel any fireworks. It was time to see if this was going to work.

She and Simon chatted until she reached home, and as she hung up, the warm lights through the windows of the mommune glowed, a cozy beacon in the chilly evening. She stepped out, breath fogging, and gathered a small stack of mail from the mailbox before heading up the walk, a feeling of gratitude coming over her.

How lucky she was to come home to this house where Elliott was happy and safe under the watchful eye of three extra mothers, and where dinner would be waiting for her. Lacey's stomach growled, remembering Tavia was making her famous gravy-smothered pork chops.

She thumbed through the mail as she opened the front door, pausing at one addressed to her. Inside was a bill from the ADHD specialist—the one who oversaw Elliott's meds and occupational therapy. The amount made her breath catch. Stamped in red at the bottom: *PAST DUE—FINAL NOTICE.*

Her stomach clenched. According to the interim custody agreement, Judd was supposed to cover Elliott's medical expenses. Occupational therapy wasn't cheap, but it was crucial. She stared at the numbers on the bill, her pulse rising.

Without thinking, she pulled out her phone and dialed.

"Hello?" Judd's voice was wary.

"Why am I holding a past due medical bill for Elliott's therapy that you should have paid months ago?" she said, skipping over a greeting.

"Nice to hear from you, too," he said dryly.

"This is your responsibility," Lacey continued. "Now they're suspending our appointments until it's paid. We were supposed to see his doctor on Friday." She thought of the orange pill jar on her and Elliott's shelf in the pantry with only a handful of doses left in it. They couldn't get a refill without seeing the doctor.

"I agreed to pay for necessary medical expenses," Judd replied coolly. "Therapy for a made-up condition doesn't count."

Lacey's grip tightened on the paper, crumpling it in her fist. "Are you kidding me? ADHD isn't made up, Judd. You don't get to opt out of science just because it's inconvenient."

"I've done my research," he said smugly. "I had the bill switched to your name. If it's so important to you, you pay it."

The line went dead.

TWENTY

Lacey stood in the entryway, her body tense with rage. She wanted to scream. Even with her Vetra salary, she couldn't just cover a multi-thousand-dollar bill at the drop of a hat, not with legal fees draining her account and barely two months of pay under her belt. Her credit card was still nearly maxed out. She put both hands over her mouth and let out a muffled, frustrated cry.

"Everything OK?"

She turned to see Regina framed in her bedroom doorway.

Lacey forced a bitter smile. "Not really," she sighed. "Judd's refusing to pay for Elliott's therapy." She waved the bill in the air. "I'm just so tired of fighting. Every time I take a step forward, he finds a way to drag me back under. I hate who I am when I talk to him."

Regina's expression darkened. "Men and their fucking mind games."

For an instant Lacey wondered if Regina was talking about Reid. Since she'd started at Vetra, his name had rarely come up between them. Initially Lacey had found herself watching him closely, searching for a glimpse of the ruthless operator Regina had described, the man who had supposedly cut her out of her own company without a second thought. But all she'd seen so far was someone driven, exacting, and, yes, often sometimes impatient when others couldn't keep up, but not a villain.

Lacey sighed, her anger ceding to the desire to go hug Elliott and sit down to dinner with the rest of her mismatched family. "Yeah," she said.

Regina's expression softened. "I'm so sorry he's being a dick," she said, tucking a loose strand of dark hair behind her ear. "And I know exactly how it feels to get knocked down just when you're getting back on your feet. Let me cover the bill. Consider it a loan."

Lacey felt her eyes go wide. "Oh no, I couldn't let you do that. I'll call Elizabeth; there's got to be some kind of legal recourse—"

Regina held up a hand. "Please don't start with the whole 'I can't accept help' thing. You've got to let go of that pull-yourself-up-by-your-bootstraps mentality. That's a myth built for men. It doesn't work for women, not the way we're expected to do it all. You're one of us now. This is what we do—we look out for each other." Then, as if the matter were already settled, she stepped forward and linked her arm through Lacey's. "Now, come on. Let's eat dinner and plot your revenge."

Her voice was warm, her touch light, her smile gentle, but beneath it, the message was clear: Saying no was not an option.

Lacey had the sudden feeling she'd waded one step too far into a seemingly calm stream, only to find herself caught in a swift current, unsure if she could make it back to shore. She managed a weak smile and let Regina lead her toward the kitchen. Despite the unease prickling at the back of her neck, her stomach, ever opportunistic, rumbled at the warm, savory smells in the air.

"Mommy!" Elliott shot up from the table and barreled into her arms.

She wrapped him tight, pressing kisses across his cheek. "How was your day, sweetheart?"

"Great!" He grinned, already halfway back to his pork chop and mashed potatoes. "I scored two goals at recess! Max and I were on the same team."

Lacey ruffled his hair as Tavia handed her a plate. "That's awesome. You'll have to walk me through every play."

Later, once Elliott had drifted off in her bed after the latest installment of *Harry Potter*, Lacey slipped from the bed with a yawn. Her brain was drained, but her body buzzed as she thought of Simon's invitation. As she headed downstairs, she smoothed her palms over her waist and hips. Judd was the only man she'd ever slept with—a fact she rarely shared, not out of modesty but because, at thirty, it felt vaguely embarrassing to admit she'd only had one partner. She'd never even thought to regret it before things soured with him. But now, imagining a weekend away with Simon, she wished she had more experience to draw from.

She wasn't surprised to find Regina and Tavia already at the kitchen table, wine glasses in hand. Nanette followed just behind her, like they'd all heard an unspoken dinner bell.

"Right on time," Tavia said, raising her glass in greeting.

Lacey pulled down two more wine glasses, handed one to Nanette, and slid into the seat beside Tavia.

Nanette eyed Lacey, her eyes narrowing slightly. "What's going on with you?" she asked.

"Nothing." Lacey flushed, her mind going to Simon. "What do you mean?"

Nanette tilted her head skeptically. "I'm very intuitive," she said. "Something is up with you."

Lacey made a face. "OK, fine, Simon invited me to go to the Poconos with him for a night."

Tavia let out a delighted shriek. "A night away with the Brawny man? Girl..." She made a show of fanning herself.

Lacey blushed.

"The who now?" Nanette said, squinting at Tavia.

"The Brawny guy," Tavia said, eyes twinkling. "You know, the flannel-shirted lumberjack paper towel mascot? That's Simon's vibe. Totally."

Nanette shook her head. "You lost me."

Tavia grabbed her phone, tapped, then held up an image of the square-jawed cartoon man.

Nanette studied it. "Meh, not my type."

Regina snorted into her wine. "Too many Y chromosomes?"

"You know it," Nanette said, laughing.

"So when is this little romantic getaway?" Tavia asked, clapping her hands.

Lacey bit her lip. "I don't know if I should go. I mean, I haven't even told Elliott about him yet. As far as he knows, Simon is just 'Ella's dad we sometimes see at the park.' We've only been dating a couple of months."

"But you have to go!" Tavia cried, looking offended. "No one in this house ever gets laid; you could change our whole trajectory."

"Maybe some of us are just fine with our 'trajectory,' Tavia," Nanette said, making air quotes.

Tavia rolled her eyes. "Speak for yourself. I'd give my left nipple for a handsome lumberjack to whisk me away to a mountain chalet for a night."

Lacey felt a small stab of guilt, thinking about her kiss with Simon on the porch and how during it her mind had wandered to what to pack in Elliott's lunch the next day.

"Do you like him?" Regina asked. "Simon?"

Lacey's cheeks burned. It was like Regina had read her thoughts. She cleared her throat. "He's really sweet," she murmured.

"Mm," Regina said, her eyebrows briefly knitting together with skepticism. Then, mercifully, she changed the subject. "How's work?"

"Um, good, I think," Lacey said.

Regina gave her a probing look. "How's Reid?"

Lacey tightened her grip on her wine glass. "He's... a lot." She met Regina's gaze. "But I guess you already know that."

"Oh, I do," Regina said, a wry smile playing at the corners of her mouth.

Lacey hesitated, then forged ahead. "It's weird. He's

demanding and blunt, but also funny, even charming. And so far, he seems... fair?" She swallowed. "It's hard to picture him doing what you said he did."

Regina's mouth twitched. "Oh, Reid's great. Right up until you become an obstacle to him getting what he wants. Then he'll flatten you without blinking."

"Everyone in HR is terrified of him," Tavia offered. "Except Marina. But her hero-worship thing is a whole separate pathology." She rolled her eyes and took a long sip of wine.

Lacey turned to Regina. "How did you manage after the twins were born? Being on your own with two babies, and the NICU... I mean, one newborn is hard enough."

A flicker of something passed over Regina's face—grief, maybe, or anger—before it quickly smoothed away. "Yeah, I don't have the fondest memories of that time," she said, her voice flat. "But we got through it." Her tone made it clear there would be no follow-up questions.

Nanette gave a theatrical shudder. "Having a newborn is like boot camp—no sleep and someone's always screaming at you."

"Except boot camp ends," Tavia added dryly. "Our sleepless nights last forever. It's a good thing we're the ones doing it, because no man I know would survive."

Nanette raised her glass. "That's for sure."

As Tavia refilled their glasses, the conversation drifted to potty training, skincare, and the latest celebrity breakups. Laughter bubbled up easily around the table, but Lacey's eyes kept straying to Regina. She felt like she was growing close to Tavia and Nanette, but Regina remained a mystery. Her unwavering calm despite everything she'd been through, the unexpected flashes of vulnerability, her generosity that seemed both instinctive and calculated, it all tugged at Lacey's curiosity. Lacey couldn't stop wondering what, exactly, was beneath that carefully composed surface.

TWENTY-ONE

Lacey had expected it would take weeks to find a weekend that worked for her and Simon, but Regina, Tavia, and Nanette had jumped in, telling her she deserved a night away, that they would handle everything with Elliott, and encouraging her to get it on the calendar. So, two weeks later, in early December, Lacey found herself across from Simon at a cozy, impossibly romantic mountain bistro.

The restaurant was softly lit by the tiny white lights strung around the rustic wood beams. Through the frosted windows, Lacey could just make out the snow-dusted paths of the Christmas market she and Simon wandered earlier, past booths selling handmade ornaments and cinnamon-roasted nuts. She still had a paper bag in her purse from one of the stalls, inside of which was a small carved fox Elliott would love.

It was the first night she'd spent so far away from him in six years. The last time had been a brief weekend in Atlantic City with Judd, when Elliott was still in diapers. They'd left him with Judd's parents in Connecticut, who'd looked like they'd barely survived a natural disaster by the time Lacey and Judd returned. They'd never offered to babysit again.

"How's the wine?" Simon asked, gesturing toward her glass.

His cheeks were still pink from the cold, and his sandy hair was rumpled from the knit hat he'd worn all day. In jeans and a button-down, sleeves rolled just enough to show his forearms, he looked comfortable, handsome, and entirely unaware of the way the waitress had definitely checked him out when she took their order.

"It's good," Lacey said, taking another sip and smiling, trying to stay present. At home, she knew, the kids were probably snuggled into the couch, deep into a movie, bowls of popcorn in their laps. She'd teared up when saying goodbye to Elliott, but he'd been thrilled at the idea of a sleepover in Max and Maddie's room.

"Thinking about Elliott?" Simon asked gently.

Lacey smiled, surprised he could read her that easily. "Yes," she admitted. She reached across the table, resting her hand lightly over his. "But I'm stopping. Right now."

Simon laughed softly. "It's OK. It's weird being away from them, right?"

She smiled. "Weird, but also really nice not having to choose a restaurant based on the kids' menu."

"Cheers to that," Simon said, raising his glass.

Dinner arrived, seared trout and roasted vegetables, hearty and elegant, and the conversation flowed as easily as it had all day.

"Was that your first time on snowshoes?" he asked, slicing into his trout.

Lacey laughed. "Was it that obvious?" She'd fallen over more than once, one time grabbing onto him and bringing them both down in a heap of snow and laughter.

"Not at all," Simon said with a mock-serious expression. "Plus you looked very sexy flailing around in the snow."

Her heart skipped at the warmth in his voice and his hand found her knee under the table.

Up until now, their physical relationship had been limited to a few make-out sessions in his car, headlights off in front of the mommune, like teenagers, because with kids at home they had nowhere else to go. Except Lacey had remembered enjoying it more as a teenager. But maybe she was just getting old, her neck complaining about the odd angles she sometimes found herself in, in the car. But tonight, they had a hotel room. A king-sized bed. Privacy.

"I used to be athletic, you know," she said, nudging the conversation to safer ground. "I played varsity tennis in high school. We were two-time state champs."

Simon smiled. "I bet you were also Homecoming Queen and valedictorian. You seem like the kind of person who's always had it all together."

Lacey blinked. Was that how he saw her? Inside she always felt like such a mess—though less so lately, she realized, as some of the pieces of her life seemed to be falling into place.

"I'm... working on it," she said, folding her napkin in her lap. "My marriage ending kind of threw me. I thought I had everything mapped out."

Simon squeezed her leg as Lacey explained in broad strokes about Judd's dark transformation and their resulting separation, and now the custody battle. It felt extremely vulnerable, but it helped that Simon had also opened up about the pain of losing his wife to a swift and surprising battle with ovarian cancer.

"Where are things with the custody case?" Simon asked when she finished speaking, just as the server set down their dessert, warm apple cake with a scoop of vanilla ice cream slowly melting over it.

Lacey's stomach tightened. Before she could stop herself, she was updating him on Judd's latest stunt—refusing to pay for Elliott's therapy and trying to use the bill as leverage.

"Your ex doesn't sound particularly stable," Simon said, frowning. "Surely a judge will see that."

"I don't know," Lacey said. "On paper, he has the better job, the better living situation."

Simon hesitated. "What does your lawyer think they'll say about your living situation? I mean, it's a little... unconventional."

Lacey stiffened. "My unconventional living situation is the

only reason I could be here tonight," she said, sharper than she meant to.

He looked momentarily chastened, and she forced her shoulders to drop, reminding herself that he wasn't Judd. There was no need to be defensive.

"This looks amazing," she said, redirecting with a smile as she picked up her fork.

Simon accepted the pivot with a small, understanding smile and handed her a fork.

They lingered after dessert, sipping the last of their wine. When the check came, Simon waved her off as she reached for her purse.

"My treat," he said. "The whole weekend. Let me do this."

Lacey hesitated, then nodded. It felt strange to be taken care of, but not unwelcome.

Outside, the wind had picked up. Simon took her hand as they walked the short distance back to the hotel, his thumb brushing lightly across her knuckles. She glanced sideways at him, taking in his easy smile, his calm steadiness.

Back in the room, Lacey slipped into the bathroom, brushing her teeth and staring at her reflection. She smoothed her hair and tried to quiet the nerves in her stomach. She was suddenly hyper aware of her body and how long it had been since she'd used it like this. She and Judd had stopped being intimate long before their split.

She took a breath and opened the door.

Simon stood by the bed, a soft smile spreading across his face as she approached him. He reached out and tucked a strand of hair behind her ear.

"You're so beautiful, Lacey," he murmured, then leaned in to kiss her.

They undressed slowly, gently. Lacey waited for the jolt of desire, the breathless rush she remembered from those early days with Judd, but it didn't come. Instead, there was warmth. Kindness. Familiarity, not fire. It was tender. Sweet. Quietly satisfying.

As they lay curled together afterward, Simon's arm draped around her, his hand absently stroking her hair, Lacey chided herself.

You're older now, she thought. *You can't expect to feel like you did back then. And this was nice.*

And nice was more than she'd had in a long time.

In the morning, they spent another soft, unhurried hour in bed before making their way downstairs to the hotel's sprawling breakfast buffet. Lacey loaded her plate with thick-cut bacon and flaky croissants, savoring the rare indulgence of a morning with no responsibilities, no schedules, just easy conversation and coffee that didn't need to be reheated twice in the microwave.

Then it was time to check out and head home.

When Simon pulled up in front of the house, he got out to retrieve her bag from the trunk. He leaned in for a kiss—gentle, lingering, his hand brushing lightly against her jaw.

"I had a really good time this weekend," he said, voice low and a little hoarse.

"Me too," Lacey said. It was true. There was something comforting about Simon. He made her feel safe, steady. And that counted for a lot.

"I'll call you later," he added.

"OK." She smiled, gave his hand a squeeze, and turned toward the house.

Inside it was quiet—too quiet. Her heart seized. "Hello?" she called, dropping her bag. "Elliott?"

Her phone dinged with a message from Nanette.

Took the kids to Pizza Land for lunch.

Lacey exhaled, relief flooding her limbs. She didn't even know what exactly she'd been afraid of, just that she had an urgent need to see her son.

Just got home. I'll meet you there, she texted back.

Her hand was on the doorknob when her phone rang.

"Can you order me the Cobb salad?" she said automatically, answering without checking the screen. "I'll be there in five minutes."

A beat of silence.

"Sure," came a man's smooth, slightly amused voice. "One Cobb salad coming up."

A jolt went through her. "Reid," she said, blinking. "Sorry—I thought you were... never mind. Um, hi. How are you?"

"All good," he said. "Sorry to intrude on your Sunday, but something just came up. I need to be in San Francisco by lunch tomorrow. Can you coordinate everything with the jet?"

"Yes, of course," she said, already running through the mental checklist—contact the airfield, shift his meetings, book his usual suite at the Four Seasons.

"Just one night. We'll be back Tuesday," Reid added.

"We?" she echoed. "Is Sunil going?" As the head of research, Sunil often traveled with Reid.

There was a short pause, then a low laugh from Reid. "No," he said. "You are."

TWENTY-TWO

When Lacey stumbled into the kitchen the next morning just after four-thirty a.m. she was surprised to find Regina already there, the faint gurgle of the coffee maker breaking the silence.

"You're up early," Lacey mumbled, rubbing her eyes. She'd stayed up late the night before, first savoring a few quiet hours with Elliott, then unpacking from her overnight with Simon and repacking for California.

Regina gave a tired shake of her head. "Another European client."

She studied Lacey for a beat. "Big day," she said. "Jetting off with Reid. That's quite a milestone."

A tingle shot through Lacey despite her exhaustion. The night before, she'd apologized profusely to the other women for the short notice, asking them to cover for her with Elliott. They'd readily agreed. Still, the guilt pulsed just under her skin, especially after Elliott had clung to her at bedtime, his little voice trembling as he asked why she had to leave again. In that moment, she wanted nothing more than to promise him she'd never leave again. But instead, she swallowed the lump in her throat, smoothed his hair back, and told him how much fun he'd have with Max and Maddie while she was gone. Then she held him extra tight as he drifted off to sleep, unaware of her tears dampening his pillow.

Regina poured a mug of coffee and handed it over. "It's good Reid asked you to go," she said. "It means he's starting to trust you. That's not nothing."

Lacey frowned, taking a cautious sip. "Why wouldn't he trust me?" she asked. "He hired me. I have access to everything—his calendar, his inbox. I basically run his life."

Regina leaned against the counter, wrapping her hands around her own mug. "Just... be careful," she said.

A chill crept through Lacey's chest. "Careful?" she echoed. "Why?"

"Reid has a way of drawing people in," Regina said slowly. "He likes to see how people operate under pressure. How loyal you are when the lines start to blur." She gave a faint, cryptic smile. "Good luck." Then she brushed past Lacey, leaving her alone in the kitchen.

After a brief hello when he boarded, Reid barely spoke to Lacey on the flight. He spent most of the time tapping away on his iPad, pausing only to sip the green juice the flight attendant handed him, or to get up and stretch. Lacey tried not to watch the way his navy joggers clung to his legs when he bent to touch his toes.

They were the only two on board, and Reid had taken a seat in the back, leaving Lacey alone near the front. She kept her eyes on her laptop screen, trying to focus on rearranging his calendar for the next two days. But Regina's words looped through her head.

Reid has a way of drawing people in.

"Hey," came Reid's voice behind her as he placed a light hand on her shoulder.

Lacey startled and snapped her laptop shut.

She looked up at him, her pulse quickening as she inhaled his familiar scent of pine and leather.

"Can you bump my lunch meeting back by thirty minutes?" he said. "And for tomorrow don't schedule anything before ten."

"Sure," she managed.

"Thanks," he said, giving her shoulder a quick pat before heading back to his seat.

Lacey's shoulder burned where he'd touched her.

After they landed, Reid disappeared into investor meetings while Lacey set up shop in the conference room next door, fielding Reid's mid-meeting text requests for additional documents or another matcha latte.

In the afternoon, around dinnertime back home, she texted Regina to see if she could FaceTime Elliott.

The second his face appeared on-screen, Lacey's heart sank.

"When are you coming home?" he demanded. His frown was deep, his expression stormy.

"Tomorrow, sweetheart," she said gently.

"When tomorrow? Will you be here when I wake up?"

Lacey hesitated. "I'll be back after dinner," she said. "In time to tuck you in."

"I want you to be here in the morning," he said, his fists balled in frustration. Lacey could see his emotions simmering dangerously close to the surface.

"Elliott," came Regina's voice in the background, firm but calm. "Dinner time, then TV."

Without another word, his face vanished and Regina's appeared in his place.

"He's fine," she said, reading Lacey's stricken expression. "He just misses you. He'll settle down."

Guilt pooled in Lacey's chest like lead.

"How's it going with Reid?" Regina asked, her voice dipping just enough to signal the question's weight.

"Fine," Lacey replied, maybe a little too quickly. "We've both been busy. I've barely seen him."

She watched Regina's expression carefully, but it remained neutral.

"Well," she said breezily, "have a good trip and we'll see you soon."

Just as Lacey set her phone down, it buzzed with a stream of texts from Reid. She looked down.

Move mtg w/ J to Thurs @ 10.

Remind K no metrics till v3 rolls.

Push exec 1:1s if M shows Fri. Clear the rest.

Lacey rolled her eyes and set about decoding his riddle-like texts.

Someone cleared their throat and she looked up to find Reid leaning casually against the doorframe, hands in his pockets, an amused smile tugging at his lips.

"Were you seriously just standing there texting me?" she asked.

"Yep," he said, pushing off the frame. "And I definitely caught that eyeroll."

She rolled them again for good measure, and he laughed. Then his expression shifted.

"What are you doing right now?"

Lacey gestured at her phone. "Well, it appears I'm currently deciphering a series of cryptic texts from my very important boss."

Reid raised an eyebrow. "He sounds like a real nightmare."

She tilted her head. "Nothing I can't handle." Their eyes locked, and a flicker of something passed between them.

He stepped farther into the room. "Add canceling my dinner reservation at Atelier Crenn to your list."

"Sure. Should I rebook you somewhere?"

"Nope," he said. "We're getting out of here."

Her stomach gave a small leap. "We?"

He gave her a slow smile. "Yes. Let's go."

"But I didn't order the car—"

He clucked his tongue in mock disapproval. "You underestimate me, Lacey. I *am* capable of calling my own driver."

She felt momentarily caught off balance by the sense that

something had shifted. Then she stuffed her laptop into her bag and followed Reid to the elevator.

TWENTY-THREE

Outside in the late afternoon sunlight, Reid ushered her into the back of a shiny black SUV.

"Where are we going?" she asked as they pulled away from the hotel. "I didn't see anything on your calendar—"

"Forget my calendar," Reid said, bouncing in his seat like an excited child. "I've spent all day talking about clinical trials, margins, and exit strategies. I deserve some fun." His shoulders sagged slightly as he looked over at her. "I hate investor meetings. The schmoozing, the handshakes, the constant performance."

Lacey felt a rush of sympathy for him, then a pang of guilt as she thought of Regina.

Twenty minutes later, the car pulled up in front of a red-brick restaurant tucked nearly beneath the Bay Bridge, its steel bones cutting across the sky above them.

Reid opened her door and offered a hand to help her out.

"It's a little touristy," he admitted as they stepped onto the sidewalk, "but they have a great patio. If we hurry, we'll catch the sunset—with oysters."

Lacey swallowed as they were led to a prime table on the edge of the patio, nestled beside a palm tree just feet from the bay. She took in the linen tablecloth, flickering candle, and chilled bottle of white wine already waiting in an ice bucket.

"Did your date fall through or something?" she asked. "Not that I'm complaining about being Plan B if it involves oysters and wine."

Reid laughed, loosening the cuff of his shirt. "No date. Just you."

Their eyes met for a second too long, and Lacey looked away, focusing on the view. The sky was already blushing into dusk, streaked with soft orange and violet.

A server appeared and Reid rattled off an order that sounded like enough food for an entire family as he poured them both a glass of wine.

The cold alcohol hit Lacey's empty stomach like a shockwave, awakening her to the oddness of the situation. She was drinking wine on a romantic patio—with her *boss*.

"Any updates on the Vetra-Patch trials?" she asked, determined to keep the conversation focused on work.

Reid's face darkened. "We're still not getting the results we need and Sunil's not making any progress on fixing the algorithm." His jaw tightened. "I can't afford that kind of delay. Investors are already impatient and the board's breathing down my neck."

Lacey bit her lip. "I know Sunil updated the algorithm to smooth out the noise, but maybe it's dampening the real spikes, too, blurring the signal instead of clarifying it."

Reid blinked. "Huh, maybe you should be head of research. God knows Sunil's making a fucking mess of it."

Their server reappeared, bearing a tray laden with oysters, lobster rolls, and an enormous basket of French fries.

Lacey's stomach growled and she reached for a French fry, her eyes going wide with delight as she chewed. "Oh my God, that's good."

Reid's eyes strayed to her lips as she licked the salt off them. A smile played on his lips. "I like to see you enjoying yourself," he said.

His voice dipped low, sending a warm tingle through Lacey. She reached for her wine glass, taking a longer than necessary sip of the cold liquid as her cheeks burned.

"What made you join Vetra?" she said quickly, steering them away from whatever had just passed between them.

Reid took a drink and glanced out over the bay. "I made a lot of money from my last company," he said.

The one you cut Regina out of, Lacey reminded herself.

"And I didn't want to just sit on it," he went on. "I wanted to do something that actually mattered. Something that could change lives."

Lacey tried to listen, but she couldn't stop staring at the way his shirt was open at the throat, revealing the smallest glint of blond hair where his chest began. "What about your life?" The question slipped out, half-formed, before she could stop it.

Reid looked back at her, his fingers tracing the stem of his wine glass. "What about it?"

Lacey thought of the brief flash of exhaustion that had crossed his face in the car, the way he'd talked about hating the endless parade of investor meetings.

"Has all this—joining Vetra, building something big—has it actually made your life better?"

He offered a smile that didn't quite reach his eyes. "I don't have a life," he said, topping off both their glasses. "You know that. You've seen my calendar."

Lacey swirled the wine in her glass. "Well," she said, her filter loosened, "maybe you should do something about that." It came out sounding more flirtatious than she'd intended, and her cheeks flushed.

Reid's eyes seemed to search hers. "Maybe I should," he said, his voice suddenly low.

A wave of heat swept through Lacey's chest. Then, from inside Reid's pocket, his phone dinged. Tearing his eyes from hers, he pulled it out, his face tensing as he viewed the screen.

"Kirk wants to run through some numbers for tomorrow's

meeting," he said, referring to the Vetra CFO, a pale man whose short, dark hair was so thick and wiry it reminded Lacey of a helmet.

"I should get back anyway," Lacey said quickly. "I've got a few things to catch up on."

The car ride back to the hotel passed in silence, each of them absorbed in their phones, though once when Lacey glanced up, she found Reid's eyes on her and quickly looked away.

They stood awkwardly in the lobby elevator.

"What floor?" he asked.

"Fourteen."

A smile played on his lips. "Same."

Lacey's pulse thudded as she moved sideways, deliberately widening the space between them. When the doors opened on their floor, they both moved through it at the same time, bumping each other. Reid caught her arm to steady her, his touch firm.

"Sorry," she murmured.

Still holding her arm, he looked down at her. "Lacey," he said, in a low voice. They stood in the quiet hallway, inches from each other. She could smell his cologne and see the scruff that had bloomed across his jaw since morning. Her heart kicked as she imagined dragging her lips across it.

Stop! she commanded herself. What was she doing? She'd been with Simon only the day before—he was definitely her boyfriend now. She should absolutely *not* be having these thoughts about her boss, of all people.

She stepped back, gently pulling her arm free. "Thanks for dinner," she said with a polished, professional smile. "It was a nice break."

His expression shifted and his posture stiffened. "My pleasure," he said, his tone matching hers. "See you bright and early."

Back in her room Lacey closed the door behind her and leaned against it, her heart hammering. Her phone sounded and she looked down to see Simon calling. Sighing, she silenced the phone, then typed out a quick text, guilt coursing through her.

> Just back from dinner and catching up on some work. So tired. Call you tomorrow? xo

Of course, he replied. *Sleep tight.*

The next morning flew by, and Lacey didn't see Reid again until he boarded that afternoon, dressed in a dark gray suit that hugged his frame, his hair tousled in the way it always was after he raked frustrated fingers through it in meetings.

"Hi," she replied, trying to sound crisp and professional—not like someone who'd fallen asleep replaying the moment in the hallway the night before, wondering what might've happened if she'd leaned toward Reid instead of pulling away.

Reid paused beside her seat, close enough for her to catch the familiar edge of his cologne. His eyes looked tired, but his smile was easy. "If we'd had one more day, I would've dragged you down to Malibu," he said. "Got you out on a surfboard."

Lacey laughed, too quickly. "I'm pretty sure that wouldn't end well."

"You'd be fine," he said, eyes lingering on her just a second longer than necessary. "I'm a good teacher."

His eyes flicked to the empty seat beside her, and he seemed to hesitate. Then he gave a small wave and continued toward the rear of the jet.

As the hum of the plane settled into a low lull, Lacey's eyelids grew heavy. She hadn't meant to sleep, but when the wheels hit the tarmac hours later, she jolted awake. Outside in chilly darkness, two black SUVs waited.

"You were a big help on this trip," Reid said, his hand briefly resting on her shoulder before he headed toward his car and driver. "See you tomorrow."

She nodded, still groggy. As she settled into the backseat of her car, still feeling the warmth of his hand on her shoulder, she pulled out her phone. She frowned when she realized it had been on Do

Not Disturb. Toggling it alive, the screen lit up with a deluge of missed calls and texts—from Elliott's school, from Judd, from Nanette.

A cold wave of panic surged through her.

Her hands shook as she tapped Nanette's name. The call connected on the first ring.

"What's going on?" Lacey demanded.

"Elliott didn't get off the bus," Nanette said, her voice high and tight. "Maddie said she saw him at lunch walking out to the parking lot with a man. Tall, dark hair, beard. We called the school, but they wouldn't tell us anything since none of us are listed as emergency contacts."

Lacey's heart pounded in her ears.

Judd.

He had Elliott.

TWENTY-FOUR

From the backseat of the town car, Lacey dialed Judd's number. It rang, then went to voicemail. She called again. And again.

On the fourth try, he finally picked up.

"Hello?"

"Where is he?" Lacey demanded. "What did you do with him?"

"He's with me," Judd said, his voice clipped. "Obviously. Because the school couldn't reach you. And then I find out—from Elliott—that you're in *California?* You just left him with some random friends?"

"They're not random," she snapped. "They're my—" She faltered. What *was* Regina? What were any of them? "—roommates," she finished weakly. "And I was in California for work."

"*Roommates?* You didn't tell me you had *roommates.* What the hell, Lacey? So you went to California and left our son with people you've lived with for, what, a few weeks?"

Lacey dug her fingernails into the leather seat. "That's not exactly—"

"Oh, and apparently you were also away over the weekend with your boyfriend?"

Heat flushed through her body and guilt mixed with defensiveness. "Simon and I spent one night away," she said sharply. "And then I was gone one night for work. That's it."

"And during neither of those nights did it occur to you to ask *me*—his father—to take care of him?"

His voice was cold and precise, and she hated how effective it was. She opened her mouth to protest, to explain that she hadn't trusted Judd to keep Elliott emotionally safe, but she knew it sounded like a poor excuse, especially when she hadn't even given him a heads-up about her trips.

"I did what I thought was best for him," she said finally. "What happened at school? Why did you take him?"

"He was in a fight. That's why the school called me—after they couldn't reach you." His words were pointed.

Lacey went cold. "A fight?" she said, her voice barely above a whisper. The car jolted slightly as they merged onto the interstate, and she grabbed for the armrest. "What happened?"

"He's not saying much," Judd said, voice dropping.

Lacey imagined Elliott in the room with him, probably wondering where she was and why she hadn't come to get him when the school called. Her eyes filled with tears.

"The principal said it happened in the lunchroom," Judd continued in a hushed tone. "He shoved another kid down. Pretty hard, apparently."

She pressed a hand to her mouth. He hadn't done something like that in months. Not since the move. Not since things had started to feel OK.

"I'm coming to get him," she said. "I'll be there in—"

"No, you're not," Judd interrupted. "He's staying here tonight. I'll take him to school tomorrow. I've already called my lawyer and we're filing an emergency motion to have Elliott removed from you for violating the interim custody agreement."

Lacey's stomach lurched and her throat went dry.

"I want to talk to him," she said. "Please."

"He's taking a shower."

She heard the lie in his voice and gripped her phone tighter in desperation. "Judd, please—"

"There will be an emergency hearing tomorrow," Judd said. "See you in court." And the line went dead.

Regina, Nanette, and Tavia were gathered in the kitchen when Lacey stepped through the front door. Nanette was on her feet in an instant, her face lined with worry.

"I'm so sorry," she said, wringing her hands. "I called the school over and over, but they wouldn't talk to me."

"It's not your fault," Lacey said, collapsing into a chair with a sigh so heavy it felt like it came from her bones. She buried her face in her hands for a moment, then recounted the call with Judd, her voice cracking at the edges.

"An emergency hearing?" Tavia repeated, stunned. "I swear, that man's got more nerve than a bad tooth."

"A fight?" murmured Nanette. "That doesn't sound like Elliott at all."

"I shouldn't have left again, not after the weekend," Lacey murmured, dragging her hands down her face. "I thought he was doing OK, but I pushed it too far."

"Reid needed you." Regina's cool, firm voice cut through the room. "You're allowed to take a business trip."

"Elliott needed me more," Lacey shot back, her voice breaking. "And now I've just given Judd ammunition for his case against me. I walked right into it."

"This is such bullshit," Tavia said, arms crossed, her voice brimming with heat. "You're an amazing mom."

"You can't just play defense," Regina said, her voice low, deliberate. "You need to go on the offensive, to make sure the judge can see Elliott belongs with you."

Lacey gave a hollow laugh. "And how exactly do I do that?"

Regina's eyes locked onto hers. "You need to think bigger."

Lacey's phone buzzed and she saw Elizabeth's name flash

across the screen, returning her call. "I need to take this," she said, brushing away the tears as she pushed back from the table.

"This isn't good," Elizabeth said the second Lacey answered. "Tell me exactly what happened."

"I was only gone one night," Lacey said quickly. "Well—two. One with my... boyfriend"—she stumbled over the word—"and one for work. I didn't think—"

"If you can't be present during your designated parenting time," Elizabeth interrupted, sounding exasperated, "your ex has the legal right to be offered that time first. And he needs to give permission for the child to stay with anyone else."

"I didn't know," Lacey said, voice cracking as shame washed over her. "I thought it would be fine—he was with people I trust—"

"Look, it was an honest mistake," Elizabeth said, her tone softening slightly. "But the judge may not see it that way. Judd's attorney has filed an order to show cause. The emergency hearing tomorrow will determine whether your current custody arrangement should be modified."

Lacey's knees nearly gave out. "Wait. I could lose Elliott? Tomorrow?"

"Yes," said Elizabeth. "You could."

TWENTY-FIVE

Lacey met Elizabeth outside the courtroom the next morning after texting Reid to let him know she'd be in late due to a family emergency. They'd never talked about her personal life or family situation, and now didn't feel like the time to start.

Reid's reply had been a single word:

OK.

Elizabeth stood waiting, statuesque in a sharply tailored navy suit, her blonde bob perfectly blunt and her brow drawn in a stern crease. She looked every bit the force Lacey needed at her side.

"I'll do what I can," she said.

The liquid dread that had pooled in Lacey's chest last night had calcified into something solid and heavy, pressing against her lungs. She could barely breathe.

The courtroom was a small, wood-paneled affair in the family court division of Essex County, sterile in a way that reminded Lacey of a hospital waiting room. An armed security guard stood off to the side, a pair of handcuffs clipped to his belt. Lacey flashed back to the red pickup truck she'd hit months earlier, wondering for one delirious moment if somehow they knew and that she was about to be arrested for it.

Get a grip, she told herself as the guilt of that incident rose in her. She wiped away the clammy sweat that had sprung up on her neck. *You need to keep it together—for Elliott.*

Judd was seated at the opposite table, leaning in close to whisper something to his attorney, a man in his fifties with slicked-back gray hair and a pocket square so precisely folded it looked ironed onto his chest.

"All rise," the bailiff called. Everyone stood as the judge entered.

The judge took her seat, her expression unreadable as she shuffled through the stack of paper she held.

"This hearing is based on an emergent motion filed by Mr. Judd Kessler, against Ms. Lacey Kessler. Mr. Kessler alleges a violation of the previously established consent order for interim custody and parenting time."

Lacey clasped her hands tightly in her lap.

The judge looked up. "Counsel for Mr. Kessler, since you filed the motion that brought us here today, you may begin."

Judd's lawyer rose smoothly. "Your Honor, the facts here are troubling. In the last twenty-four hours the child, Elliott Kessler, was sent home early from school after an altercation in the cafeteria. According to witness statements, he was visibly agitated and physically lashed out at another student. The school attempted to contact Ms. Kessler"—he gestured toward Lacey—"who had custody on that date, but she was unreachable. She had traveled out of state, we understand, leaving the child in the care of unrelated roommates."

Lacey felt her face burn. Her stomach churned with shame.

The lawyer went on. "Furthermore, the child's mother has recently traveled for both personal and professional reasons, including a romantic weekend with a new partner, and a business trip. While the court certainly recognizes a parent's right to earn a living, abandoning one's parental responsibilities without appropriate communication or care plans is reckless and—frankly—irresponsible."

"Objection," Elizabeth said sharply. "She didn't abandon her child."

"Sustained," Judge Rowe said. "Watch your language, counselor. But you may proceed."

The lawyer gave a deferential nod. "Of course. I only mean to underscore the pattern of behavior we've seen. Ms. Kessler has consistently failed to prioritize her son's well-being."

Elizabeth rose next, her voice crisp but measured. "Your Honor, what the opposing counsel has conveniently omitted is the fact that Ms. Kessler arranged care for her son with trusted housemates and friends—an error on her part, to be sure, but an honest one, as she wasn't aware that Mr. Kessler should be notified of this change. But Elliott was not left alone. He was *not* at risk."

She turned, her tone firming. "And let's talk about risk. The reason Elliott needs specialized support is due to a documented diagnosis of ADHD. A diagnosis Mr. Kessler continues to deny, and whose associated medical and therapeutic costs he has refused to contribute to—despite the interim custody agreement signed three months ago, which explicitly outlines his financial responsibility." Elizabeth stepped closer to the bench. "We're not just talking about a forgotten co-pay here. Elliott's therapy was nearly halted because of non-payment. His prescription, essential for managing his emotional regulation, would have been disrupted. *That's* what's been putting him at risk."

"Objection!" Judd's lawyer rose, tossing a disapproving look in Elizabeth's direction. "My client's financial responsibilities are not the focus of today's hearing."

The judge cocked her head. "True," she said. "But if Mr. Kessler is not abiding by the financial responsibilities laid out in the original consent order, that should be addressed."

"Your Honor, he is not," stated Elizabeth.

The judge held up a hand. "Enough. I've heard what I need to hear."

Lacey's mouth went dry as the judge scanned her notes, then looked up with a level gaze.

"Both parents have made missteps. One has been absent due to work and personal obligations, and her living situation is… unusual, to say the least." The judge raised her eyebrows. "The other has demonstrated an unwillingness to engage with his child's medical needs." She folded her hands in front of her. "The interim consent order of shared custody stands, assuming Ms. Kessler now understands that she is not to leave Elliott in anyone else's care without explicit permission from Mr. Kessler." She looked over the top of her glasses at Lacey, who felt her cheeks go hot. "Ms. Kessler, you are also to provide documentation to Mr. Kessler on all parties who live with you and your son. He has a right to know who is in the household—especially since it seems to be"—she cleared her throat—"quite a few people." Then she turned to Judd. "And Mr. Kessler is ordered to attend to his financial responsibilities. Any previously agreed upon therapy, medical appointments, or prescribed medication must stand and be fully funded while discovery continues."

Lacey's brain struggled to process the judge's words, scrambling to her feet as the judge pounded the gavel once to adjourn the hearing. Elizabeth turned to her with a smile.

"That went better than I expected," she murmured.

Over Elizabeth's shoulder, Lacey caught Judd's glare, hot and poisonous.

She had escaped his wrath—for now.

Elizabeth leaned in to whisper something about next steps, but Lacey's mind was already drifting.

You need to go on the offensive, Regina had said.

Suddenly, Lacey wondered what that might look like.

TWENTY-SIX

On her desk, Lacey's phone buzzed, jolting her out of the zone she'd been in as she raced to update the PowerPoint deck Reid needed for his four p.m. meeting with Olivier Marchand, the chair of Vetra's board.

She grabbed the phone: a message from Nanette, sent to her and Tavia.

Lunch?

Once a week or so, the three of them snuck off to a café just far enough from the office—and just dingy enough—to ensure they wouldn't run into anyone from work. It seemed better to keep their relationship outside of work quiet, so people wouldn't ask questions.

Sorry, I'm slammed

Lacey typed back with a wistful glance at her calendar, then set her phone down and cocked her head as the voices in Reid's office grew louder.

"What the fuck, Sunil?" Reid snapped, his voice carrying

clearly through the barely closed sliding door of his office. "Why isn't it working?"

"There's still too much noise in the data," Sunil replied, tight and defensive.

"Then fix it, God dammit! I told Olivier we'd be ready to submit for FDA approval by quarter end."

There was a pause, then came Sunil's voice, sharper, defensive. "It's *your* fucking algorithm, Reid, remember? From Chomer Labs? I didn't build it—you did. I've been trying to reverse-engineer it for weeks, but it's a black box. I can't fix what I don't fully understand."

"I swear to God, Sunil, if you can't fix this, I will find someone who can," Reid growled.

A beat later, the door opened, and Sunil stormed past Lacey's desk, eyes locked on the floor, jaw tight.

Reid appeared in the doorway just long enough to glower at Sunil's retreating back before slamming his office door so hard Lacey jumped.

She blinked and tried to refocus on her screen.

"Sounds like trouble in paradise."

Lacey startled again as Marina materialized beside her desk. Dressed in a sleek black sweater dress under a loose blazer, her trademark red lipstick and tight bun in place, she looked as polished as ever. Lacey, who had started wearing makeup most days and, thanks to Regina's urging, had upgraded her wardrobe with a handful of washable silk blouses and fitted blazers, still felt vaguely frumpy and out of place in comparison.

"Hi, Marina," she said. "How can I help you?"

Marina lifted her chin in the direction of Reid's closed door. "I was going to see if he was free for five minutes."

Lacey rubbed her temples. "I'm going to go with... not a good time," she said.

"Sunil needs to get his shit together or we're all screwed," Marina muttered.

"What do you mean?" Lacey asked.

Marina frowned "Have you not figured out yet that the Vetra-Patch is the golden goose? It's why investors are still throwing money at us. But if it tanks in trials..." She trailed off, studying her crimson nails before meeting Lacey's gaze again with a knowing smile. "Lucky for us, Reid always gets what he wants."

"I'll let him know you stopped by," Lacey said, barely veiling her annoyance. Marina always managed to put her on edge.

Lacey turned back to her computer. If she skipped lunch and powered through with the granola bar she'd found in the depths of her purse, she might just get out on time.

They were nearly two months into the temporary custody arrangement: two days on, two days off, alternating weekends. Simon had done his best to fill the quiet on the nights Elliott was at Judd's, making plans and trying to keep her spirits up. But lately, Lacey found her mind drifting even when she was with him—back to Elliott, sometimes even to work. But today Elliott was hers, so every extra minute at the office felt like it cost more than she was willing to pay.

At three forty-five Lacey realized she hadn't moved from her desk in hours. She arched her back to stretch as she finished the email she was writing, a reply to a journalist from *Esquire* seeking a comment from Reid for an article on biohacking.

Unfortunately, due to his demanding schedule, Mr. Mercer is unable to participate.

When she'd started at Vetra in September, Reid had welcomed nearly every media opportunity, eager to champion the company's ambitious product pipeline. But as Sunil had continued to struggle with the Vetra-Patch trials, Reid had turned down several press inquiries before finally telling Lacey to reject all of them outright.

The door to Reid's office slid open, and he stepped out, pushing up the sleeves of his white button-down. His jaw was tight.

"Everything OK?" Lacey asked.

"I need you to order flowers for delivery tomorrow," he said. "Something big. Roses and peonies. For Julia Smith."

Lacey blinked, caught off guard. "Peonies aren't in season," she said, irrational jealousy curling low in her stomach. Who the hell was Julia Smith? Did Reid have a new girlfriend? And why did she even care?

"All the more reason to send them," he said.

"Fine," Lacey said, trying to keep her voice light. "I just need the message for the card."

Reid waved a hand. "Just write, *Happy birthday, Mom. Love, Reid.*"

Relief swelled in Lacey. "Sure," she said with a laugh. His *mom*.

Reid eyed her. "What's funny?"

"Nothing," she said quickly. "Just, roses and peonies seem like a very romantic arrangement for... your mom."

He rolled his eyes. "You clearly haven't met mine. Once I got my first payout, her tastes leveled up—dramatically." Then he tilted his head, studying Lacey. "But good to know you consider that particular combination to be romantic."

Lacey's cheeks flamed as she turned back to her computer, her eyes snagging on the clock. If she left now she might have time to play a game of chess with Elliott before dinner—he was teaching her—or curl up together on her bed and watch an episode of *Is It Cake?*

"If you don't need anything else," she said, forcing composure into her voice as she glanced back at him, "I was hoping to sneak out a little early tonight."

Reid's eyes lingered on her for a second too long. Then he nodded. "Sure. Go. I know how to find you if I need you."

She gave him a small smile, the heat still burning in her cheeks as he disappeared into his office.

TWENTY-SEVEN

When Lacey stepped out of her car in front of the mommune an hour later, she was greeted by an enormous inflatable abominable snowman looming over the front yard. Max and Elliott were on the porch, wrapping multicolored Christmas lights around the railings, their breath visible in the crisp mid-December air. Regina sat nearby in one of the wicker chairs, bundled in a heavy coat, her mittened hands wrapped around a steaming mug.

"Nice decorations," Lacey said as she approached, eyeing the towering snowman with amusement.

Regina gave a dry smile. "I took these two to Home Depot after school for a few strings of lights, and somehow that monstrosity ended up in the cart." She sighed. "It's hideous. I can't believe I gave in."

"Mommy!" Elliott's face lit up brighter than the lights in his hands. "Did you see what we got?" He pointed proudly at the snowman as he ran over and threw his arms around her.

"It's kind of hard to miss," Lacey said, laughing as she hugged him back.

"Max likes white lights, but I like colored ones, so we got both for the porch," Elliott said matter-of-factly, already bouncing back to his project.

"It looks great, sweetheart," Lacey called after him.

Regina lifted her mug. "Tavia made mulled wine, but fair warning—it's potent." Her lips gave a small twitch. "You're home early. Everything OK at work?"

Lacey zipped her coat up and dropped into the chair beside Regina. "I wrapped up early," she said. "I just... missed him." She gave a subtle nod in Elliott's direction. "It's been a long week. I feel like I haven't really been here."

Max and Elliott stepped back to admire their handiwork, then exchanged a triumphant high-five.

"Want to go do remote control cars?" Max asked.

"Yes!" Elliott cheered, and the boys took off inside.

Regina's expression shifted, and when she spoke, her voice was cool. "You want to stay on Reid's good side," she said. "Elliott's fine when you're not here. We're all looking out for him."

"I know he is," Lacey replied, an edge to her voice. Of all people, Regina should understand how much it mattered for Lacey to be present in Elliott's life, especially in the midst of all the upheaval he'd experienced lately. Regina's face tightened and Lacey quickly smoothed her tone. "It's just... with the custody hearing down the line, I don't want it to look like I'm always working. Like I'm not present. And... he's my son, and I just miss him. I miss hanging out with him." She hesitated, chewing her lip as she glanced at Regina. "Please don't think I'm ungrateful when I say this next part. I mean, you helped me land the job at Vetra—God, I'm so thankful—but lately I've been wondering if it's just... too much. Maybe I should look for something closer to home, something with more regular hours."

Her heart pounded as she gave voice to what had been gnawing at her all week. She *loved* her work at Vetra—the opportunity to use everything she'd once studied, the way Reid increasingly sought her input and brought her into higher-level meetings. For the first time in years, she could see a future taking shape: a career she cared about, a chance to become the version of herself she'd once imagined. But none of it mattered if it came at the cost of time with Elliott.

Regina's eyes sharpened. "That's not possible," she said flatly. "You need to stay at Vetra. If you leave, none of this works."

Lacey blinked. "What do you mean? Tavia and Nanette are still there. They'll make money when the company goes public—"

"It has to be *you*," Regina cut in. There was an edge of desperation to her voice that Lacey had never heard before. She set her mug down harder than necessary. The mulled wine sloshed over the rim, dark red pooling across the whitewashed table.

Lacey leaned back in her chair, caught off guard by this unexpected crack in Regina's normally unflappable composure. "I don't understand."

Regina's eyes pinned her in place. "Vetra's not going public."

Lacey stared. "But you said—"

Regina raised one corner of her mouth. "How are the Vetra-Patch trials going?" She paused. "Let me guess... not as hoped."

Lacey's mind flashed back to Reid's voice behind the office door, angry with an edge of panic. Sunil's evasive emails. The delays. "How do you know that?"

Regina laughed—not her usual soft, easy chuckle, but a sharper, harder sound. "Because he can't do it without me."

Lacey's brow knit together in confusion.

"I wrote the prototype algorithm the Vetra-Patch is built on— the flagship product I told you about," Regina continued, her voice softer now. "Back when Reid and I started Chomer Labs."

The words Sunil had spat toward Reid echoed in Lacey's head.

It's your algorithm, remember? From Chomer Labs? I didn't build it.

Lacey stared at her. "But... Chomer Labs was acquired by Vetra four years ago. They made Reid CEO. The patch—"

"Was built on my work," Regina said. "The IP that got them the funding, the acquisition, the momentum? It was mine. And I got nothing." Her eyes flashed with something fierce.

Lacey's head buzzed. "But if it was your algorithm, why won't the patch work?"

Regina leaned back in her chair as though the whole conversation was exhausting her. "Because what Reid has is incomplete. He took what he thought was finished, but I never finalized it. Right now, he's only just realizing the holes." She reached for her mug. "And I'm the only one who can fill them."

Lacey sat very still as the implications sank in. "But Vetra's future hinges on those clinical trials," she said slowly. "If they fail…"

"Reid goes down," Regina finished, taking a slow sip. Then she suddenly leaned forward again, as though an electric current had shot through her. "That's why I needed you. I need proof—emails, documentation—that shows I was the original creator. That he stole it. Then I sue him for everything he's worth."

Lacey's breath caught.

"You're the only one close enough to get it. You can't back out now." There was an unfamiliar, pleading quality to Regina's voice.

A knot of dread formed in Lacey's stomach. "So that's what this was? You got me the job so I could spy on him for you?" She felt as though the floor had dropped out from beneath her. All of Regina's kindness—was this what had been behind it the whole time? Anger exploded in her chest. "So it was never actually about helping *me*—about the money you said I might make," Lacey snapped, her voice rising. "It was about you getting what *you* wanted."

A flash of anguish rolled over Regina's face. "He already stole a lot more from me than I'm asking you to take from him."

The quaver in Regina's voice cooled Lacey's anger. Her thoughts tangled as a rush of questions filled her head. She felt unbalanced by Regina's sudden emotional vulnerability, and she was certainly in her debt after all that Regina had done for her. Still, Lacey thought of the moment that had passed between her and Reid only hours earlier, the way he'd looked at her and the warmth that had swept over her. She swallowed. "What if I don't want to do this?" she asked. "I mean, Reid trusts me—"

Under the glow of the Christmas lights hurt registered in Regina's eyes. Then she narrowed them in exasperation. "You're nothing to him, I promise. Don't make the mistake of thinking you are. That's not how Reid operates." She pressed her lips together in a disappointed line, then stood and picked up her mug. "I've tried to help you, Lacey. And now I'm asking you to help me. If you do this, if you get me what I need, then part of that money is yours. We both walk away with a lot more than a paycheck." She tilted her head. "Think about it."

Without waiting for a reply, she turned and walked back inside, leaving Lacey alone in the cold, staring up at the towering inflatable snowman as it swayed slightly in the wind.

TWENTY-EIGHT

Lacey awoke to Elliott gently shaking her shoulder.

"Mommy, your alarm's going off," he said.

She blinked groggily, rubbing the sleep from her eyes. It felt like she'd only just drifted off after a night spent tossing and turning, Regina's voice echoing in her head: *You're nothing to him. Don't make the mistake of thinking you are. That's not how Reid operates.*

She shut her eyes again, trying to push away the complicated swirl of emotions in her chest. She felt betrayed by Regina's lies, but now, knowing the full extent of Reid's treachery, she also couldn't help but feel indignant on Regina's behalf. Still, the thought of being wedged between them, caught in the middle of Regina's scheme, turned Lacey's stomach. She hadn't signed up for this, yet she wasn't entirely sure how to extricate herself.

"Mommy," Elliott said, more insistent now. "It's time for breakfast."

"OK," she mumbled, forcing a smile as she ruffled his hair. "Let's go."

Down in the kitchen, Lacey was relieved to find the other kids had already eaten and that Regina was nowhere in sight. She poured a bowl of cereal for Elliott and coffee for herself. Her stomach was too knotted to consider eating breakfast.

After, she gave Elliott his medication, then moved around on autopilot, making sure he brushed his teeth and zipping him into his puffy winter coat and boots. Then she pulled on her own jacket and rushed out to the bus stop with him, where Regina and Nanette stood with Max, Maddie and Linden. Lacey stiffened upon seeing Regina and averted her eyes, not ready to talk yet.

The temperature had dropped overnight, and the morning air was sharp and biting.

"They're saying it might snow today," Maddie was saying as they reached the group of kids waiting on the corner. She bounced excitedly on her toes.

"Snow day!" Max shouted, throwing his arms up.

Elliott whooped. "Maybe school will let out early and we can have a snowball fight," he said, beaming.

Lacey's shoulders tensed. An early dismissal would throw her whole day off. Even though the train ride into the city was only forty minutes, Vetra was starting to feel worlds away. She silently willed the weather to hold off.

The bus rumbled up to the curb. The kids clambered on, waving through the windows as it pulled away in a cloud of exhaust.

Heading back to the house, Lacey turned to see Regina fall into step beside her, her pale cheeks pink from the cold, her dark hair tumbling out from beneath a knit maroon hat.

"How'd you sleep?" Regina asked.

"Not well," Lacey replied tersely.

Regina inhaled deeply. "Understandable. It's a lot to process."

"That's putting it mildly," Lacey muttered, nudging a rock with her sneaker. Then she stopped walking and turned to face Regina. "Why did you lie to me?" she asked. "Why not just tell me the truth from the beginning?"

Up ahead, Nanette glanced over her shoulder, her gaze landing on both of them before Regina gave a slight nod. Nanette turned and kept walking.

Regina rubbed her temples. "Right. So I was supposed to say, 'Hey, I've got a great job for you—just one catch. You'll need to break into the CEO's files and personal documents for me.'" She gave Lacey a pleading look and Lacey noticed the purple shadows under her eyes.

Lacey crossed her arms and sighed. "OK. Fair. But now I feel... trapped." Her voice caught. "What you're asking me to do is *illegal*, Regina. And you know what's at stake for me—I could lose my job, or worse, lose Elliott."

Unexpectedly, her eyes filled with hot tears of frustration and anger. She was so tired of feeling like a passenger in her own life. Just when she'd finally started to find her footing again, when things had begun to feel stable, like she had power and agency over her choices, it was as if the rug had been yanked out from under her—again.

Regina tugged her hat down lower on her forehead, her face softening. "I'm sorry, Lacey, I really am. But I have a plan, and I need to see it through."

They were silent for a moment as they continued toward the house.

"Why me?" Lacey asked. Resentment flared in her chest—at Regina, at herself for her own naivety. "Why not Nanette or Tavia?" Her thoughts turned to the other two women, wondering how much they knew.

Regina's mouth curved into a small, sad smile. "Because I know Reid and I knew he would like you. That he would trust you—as much as he ever trusts anyone." She gave a soft, bitter snort. "And with your background, what you studied in college... well, it was too perfect. When you showed up at my door, it felt like the universe was handing me a second chance."

Lacey's eyes narrowed. "But you didn't know what I studied when we met."

Regina glanced over at her. "Lacey, of course I did. I knew

everything about you before we even met. You think I was going to invite someone to live in my house if I didn't?"

Lacey's cheeks flushed with anger and embarrassment. It had been a setup from the beginning; how had she not seen that? She'd been so trusting, so desperate, all she'd seen was Regina's kindness.

As they stepped through the front door, Regina shrugged off her coat and glanced at her watch. "I'm late for a call," she said, and disappeared down the hall.

Lacey stood clenching her fists. She wrenched off her coat and flung it on a hook, then headed for the kitchen. At the table, Tavia sat beside Grace, who was happily spooning strawberry yogurt into her mouth, most of it ending up on the tray of her booster seat in pale pink glops. Nanette leaned against the counter, sipping coffee from her favorite yellow mug.

Lacey crossed her arms, her jaw tight with anger. "Did you know?" she asked.

Tavia's head snapped up from wiping yogurt off Grace's chin.

Nanette coughed, then set down her mug. "Yeah," she said after a beat. "We knew."

A hot flash of betrayal rose in Lacey's chest. "Since when?"

The small muscles around Nanette's mouth tightened. "Since Regina found you."

Lacey stared at her. "I thought we were friends," she said, wincing at how small and plaintive her voice sounded.

"Oh, honey." Tavia stood quickly and crossed the kitchen. "We *are* friends," she said, pulling Lacey into a hug. Lacey stiffened, but couldn't stop herself from leaning into Tavia's familiar scent of baby powder and lavender.

Finally, Lacey pulled away. "How could you not tell me?"

Nanette and Tavia exchanged a look.

"It wasn't our thing to tell," Nanette said, her arms hugging her sides.

"But you work at Vetra, too," Lacey said, her voice trembling. "You're part of this."

She picked up the mug she'd abandoned earlier when she'd

taken Elliott to the bus stop, the coffee long gone cold. Wordlessly, Nanette reached out. After a pause, Lacey handed it over. Nanette dumped the contents, refilled it with steaming liquid from the pot, and passed it back.

Lacey took a long sip. A thick silence settled between the women, broken only by Grace's off-key rendition of "Baa Baa Black Sheep"—sung as "blah blah black sheep"—as she stacked her banana slices into a tiny tower.

"We do work at Vetra," Tavia said slowly. "For the same reason you do. Regina wanted people close to Reid."

"But it turns out we couldn't get close enough," Nanette added. "Even with my IT access and Tavia's HR credentials. It wasn't enough."

Lacey's eyes widened. "So she tricked you both into doing her dirty work, too?"

Tavia stood and gently unbuckled Grace from her booster seat, wiping her sticky hands with a napkin. "Can you go find your baby doll, Gracie?" she asked softly. Grace clapped her hands and toddled off toward the living room, humming to herself.

"Not tricked," Tavia said once Grace was gone. "We knew what we were doing."

"We knew what Reid did to her," Nanette added. "It was the least we could do. I mean, Regina saved my life."

Lacey frowned. "Let's not be dramatic."

Nanette set her mug down with a quiet clink. "It's not dramatic," she said in a clipped voice. "I had no job, no money, and nowhere to go. I spent two weeks in a shelter with my two-year-old daughter." Her voice trembled slightly, then she squared her shoulders and her eyes locked on Lacey, as though daring her to speak. "I thank God every day Linden wasn't old enough to remember it."

Tavia reached out, squeezed Nanette's hand, then turned back to Lacey.

"I was eight months pregnant with a broken rib when I moved in," she said, her voice quiet and matter of fact. "I went to my mama's for help and she just stood there while my husband dragged me back out." She balled her hands into fists at her sides. "I had Grace two weeks after I got here. Regina was the one who helped me through labor, not him, not my mama. Grace has never met her father, and God willing, she never will."

Lacey bit her lip, any anger she'd felt dissolving into shame.

Nanette spoke bluntly. "Regina just wants what Reid stole from her. And after everything she's done for us, I don't blame her. I'll help her however I can."

"Amen," Tavia said. "And whatever she gets from him she shares. That's what she's promised."

"But it's still not right," Lacey said. "I don't want a cut of blackmail money."

Nanette's eyes narrowed. "That's easy for you to say. You're a pretty white woman. The world will give you a thousand second chances. Me? I only get one. And I'm not wasting it."

She picked up her mug and walked out.

Lacey stared down into her coffee, heat crawling up her neck, the sharp moral lines she'd drawn last night on the porch with Regina suddenly blurring.

"Mama?" came Grace's voice from the living room.

"Coming, baby," Tavia called over her shoulder, then she turned back to Lacey. "Look, I know this is a lot to take in. I remember being in your shoes. But it's not as black and white as it seems. It's not just about the money, or even about helping the woman who save my life. It's about freedom, Lacey. The freedom to live our lives without having to answer to anyone else. That's what Regina's offering. And if you don't want in, that's your choice. But don't ruin this chance for the rest of us."

Then she turned and walked out, leaving Lacey standing in the kitchen. In a house full of people, she'd never felt more alone.

TWENTY-NINE

On Monday when Lacey got to work Reid's office was dark. His calendar showed a breakfast meeting, but she placed his usual matcha order just in case, along with a breakfast sandwich for herself. Her stomach was still queasy from the emotional whiplash of the past few days, but it felt like the kind of nausea perhaps bacon could fix.

That weekend, Lacey had kept her distance from the mommune, still reeling from everything Regina, Nanette, and Tavia had told her. She needed space to think, so she took Elliott into the city to see the Christmas tree and ice skate at Rockefeller Center, returning late Saturday night after the other kids were already in bed. Then Sunday they'd gone to a movie, and later, when Elliott complained he wanted to play with Max and Maddie, Lacey had retreated to her room with a book, trying to ignore Tavia's words looping in her head: *If you don't want in, that's your choice. But don't ruin this chance for the rest of us.*

Now, at the office, she'd just settled at her desk and taken a satisfying bite of her breakfast sandwich when the elevator doors opened and Reid's whistling echoed across the floor.

"Oh, hey," she said as he approached, scrambling for a napkin to wipe her fingers. "I wasn't expecting you yet."

Reid looked down at the drink on her desk. "Looks like you were," he said.

She smiled. "I figured better safe than sorry," she said. As she handed him the cup, their fingers brushed. Electricity passed through her hand, and she pulled it back too fast, bumping her arm on the desk.

"Thanks," he murmured, taking a sip and rubbing his jaw, the scrape of stubble catching the light. His eyes lingered on her a moment longer than usual, sweeping over her with a flicker of curiosity, like it was the first time that day he was really seeing her. "You look... different."

Lacey's hand instinctively went to her hair, which she'd taken the time to blow out that morning until it fell sleek and glossy around her shoulders. She'd recently had a proper haircut for the first time in over a year, and the stylist had talked her into adding some subtle caramel-colored lowlights. Lacey had initially balked at the cost, then remembered Regina's words.

"You have to look the part," she'd said. "Otherwise, you'll never become it."

Lacey had caught a glimpse of herself in the mirror on her way out that morning and, for the first time in longer than she could remember, liked what she saw: someone polished and put together. Someone who looked like she belonged.

"New haircut," she said to Reid now, feeling suddenly self-conscious under his gaze as a warm flush rose on her neck.

She shook her head sharply. What was *wrong* with her? How could she still be googly eyed over a man who had passed someone else's work off as his own and cut them out of millions of dollars?

Reid looked at her strangely. "You OK?"

"Fine," she said, forcing herself to look anywhere but at him.

"Good. Because today's going to be a shitstorm. We're delaying the FDA filing."

Lacey sucked in a breath. "Oh, wow. So Sunil couldn't—"

"Sunil is out as of later today," Reid said, lowering his voice, his eyes glancing over Lacey's shoulder.

Lacey worked to keep her voice neutral. "He can't fix the algorithm? I thought he wrote it." She gave an innocent smile.

Reid snorted. "No," he said. "I did. Well—with some help from someone else." He clenched his fists at his sides. "It should've been airtight. But clearly something's missing." His face tightened. "I'm notifying the board today. I need to be in California on Thursday to meet with investors and try to avoid a complete implosion—you'll come along to handle logistics."

Lacey's mind raced. Wednesday Elliott went back to Judd's.

"How many days?" she said.

"As many as it takes," Reid replied grimly. He tapped his knuckles against her desk. "Have Marina pull together our exit NDA and termination paperwork for Sunil ASAP. Oh, and a slate of candidates for head of research. I want a shortlist on my desk by end of day."

Without waiting for a response, he turned and disappeared into his office.

Lacey sat frozen, her mind spinning. Sunil was being fired for failing to fix an algorithm that, by Reid's own admission, Reid had built with help from someone else.

Regina had been telling the truth all along.

Lacey grasped for an alternate explanation—some kind of misunderstanding, a reason Reid might not have credited Regina. But the puzzle pieces rolling through her mind wouldn't rearrange themselves into a version that absolved him. Her stomach turned, the breakfast sandwich she'd barely touched now a regret.

She put her head in her hands. What had she gotten herself into with this job? And how could she get out of it?

She sent Reid's request to Marina, then glanced toward his office, and picked up her phone.

"Weisberg Law," chirped the receptionist on the other end of the call.

"This is Lacey Kessler. Is Elizabeth in?"

"I'm afraid Ms. Weisberg is in a meeting," the woman replied. "Wait, actually—can you hold a moment?"

A minute later Elizabeth's voice crackled through the phone.

"I don't have any updates, unfortunately," she said without preamble. She'd been trying to get the custody hearing, which was scheduled for late February, moved up, but had cautioned that the courts were always backed up before and after the holidays.

"Oh, no, that's not why I called," Lacey said quickly. "I just... I was thinking about quitting my job and I wanted to know what impact that would have on the, um, case." She had no idea what she'd do if she left Vetra, or how she'd pay her bills, but she had the increasing sense that she couldn't stay.

"Why would you do that?" Elizabeth asked. "Do you have a better one lined up?"

"Uh, no," Lacey admitted.

"Then that's a no," Elizabeth said flatly. "I don't recommend any major changes to your employment or living situation between now and the hearing."

"But what if there's a really good reason to quit?" Lacey closed her eyes, a pit of dread in her stomach.

"Short of bodily harm? Stick it out," Elizabeth advised. "Your current job looks great on paper, but it's still new. You don't want to look unstable."

Something inside Lacey deflated. Short of lying on her résumé again, she wasn't going to find a better job where she could still afford Elizabeth. And no matter how messy things got at Vetra, Lacey could not jeopardize her chances in the upcoming custody hearing.

"Got it," she said faintly, pinching the bridge of her nose. "It was just a thought."

She finished the call and sank back in her chair, her head as muddied as ever. Her eyes went to Reid's closed door and a bitter taste arose in her mouth. As much as Lacey hated it, she could suddenly imagine Reid doing exactly what Regina said he had done. Sure, he'd always treated her well, but maybe that was only because she hadn't exhausted her usefulness to him yet—like Sunil. And Regina.

Lacey's phone buzzed in her hand, and she looked down to see the number for Elliott's school on the screen. Her stomach flipped as she scrambled to answer.

"Mrs. Kessler? This is Mr. Barry."

Lacey's mind raced through a mental slideshow of possible emergencies.

"Elliott's fine," Mr. Barry said, his tone calm and practiced, as though he knew exactly where her thoughts had gone. "I was just hoping to talk for a minute, if now's a good time?"

"Yes, of course," Lacey said, pressing a hand to her chest and trying to steady her breathing.

"First, I want to say I've really enjoyed having Elliott in class. He's a bright, inquisitive kid with a huge imagination. But..." He paused, choosing his words. "We've started noticing some inconsistencies. There are days when he's focused and collaborative, and then others where he's impulsive, emotional—disruptive, even."

"What do you mean by disruptive?" she asked, already dreading the answer.

"He'll interrupt repeatedly, talk over me, or get disproportionately upset if things don't go his way, like if I ask him to wait his turn or choose another group for an activity. It can be upsetting for the other kids."

Lacey closed her eyes, her stomach sinking. She knew this version of Elliott. She'd lived with it before his diagnosis.

"We've had some great days," Mr. Barry added quickly. "But the contrast is... sharp. It's almost like there are two different Elliotts. I just wanted to ask if there have been any recent changes to his medication or treatment plan?"

"No," Lacey said, frowning. "But I'll talk to Elliott," she said carefully. "And to his father. Things are... complicated right now between us."

"I understand," Mr. Barry said gently. "Elliott mentioned he spends time with each of you separately. Just keep me in the loop if anything comes up. I want to support him as best I can."

"Thank you," Lacey said, her voice tight. "I really appreciate the call."

As she ended the call, her hands clenched around her phone and she fired off a text to Judd.

> We need to talk.

Reid's office door slid open and she jumped.

"Anything from Marina?" he asked.

Lacey turned to her computer and quickly scanned her inbox. "She just forwarded the NDA and termination paperwork to you for approval," she said.

"Great," Reid said. "I'm meeting with Sunil in thirty minutes. Before then, I need you to call IT and have them revoke his access—research files, security badge, everything. And have security ready to walk him out."

He said it in the same brisk, casual tone he used when dictating a meeting agenda. Lacey stared at him, struggling to keep the shock off her face.

Reid caught her look and gave a small, cold smile.

"It's just business, Lacey," he said, and disappeared back into his office. Thirty minutes later Lacey watched Sunil emerge from his office and cross the floor, calm, unhurried, and completely unaware he was walking straight into his own execution. Moments after he entered Reid's office, Marina appeared, flanked by two security guards. They swept silently into Sunil's office like a military tactical team.

A beat later, shouting erupted.

"What the hell? You can't do this!"

Reid's voice answered, low and controlled. Lacey couldn't make out the words, but the chill in them was unmistakable.

The door burst open and Sunil stormed out, red-faced. He reached his office just as Marina and the guards emerged with multiple computer towers in tow.

"What are you doing?" he yelped. "I have personal stuff on there!"

"Not anymore, you don't," Marina said coolly. "It's company property." She gestured to his office. "Take five minutes to collect your personal items. Then these gentlemen will escort you out."

"Marina, please," Sunil pleaded. "You know I didn't do anything wrong. Talk to Reid—this is crazy."

Lacey's heart seized hearing the desperation in his voice.

"The decision has been made, Sunil," Marina said evenly. "We wish you all the best in your next endeavor."

"What endeavor?" he snapped. "You think anyone's going to hire me after this?" His eyes darted to Reid's closed door. "How could you let him do this?"

Marina's face remained cool and impassive, and Sunil's eyes narrowed.

"Or was it your idea?" Sunil's voice twisted into a snarl. "Falsifying clinical trial data? As if I'd ever—" He cut himself off, his chest heaving, and shook his head. "I never should've taken this job."

"Get your things and go, Sunil," Marina said, her voice sharpened to a blade.

Sunil stalked into his office, reappearing moments later with his coat and messenger bag.

"You'll be hearing from my lawyer," he hissed.

"I wouldn't advise that," Marina replied smoothly. "Our case is airtight. I made sure of it." A flicker of a smile passed over her lips.

"You bitch!" Sunil exploded.

The guard moved toward him, and Sunil stepped back.

"Fine. I'm going."

As the elevator doors slid shut, Marina turned, headed for Reid's office. Lacey stepped into her path.

"Falsifying clinical trial data?" she asked, her stomach suddenly queasy.

Marina barely paused. "It's sad, isn't it?" she said. "But at least this way, investors see it was Sunil's failure, not the product's." Her mouth twitched, then she turned away and went into Reid's office, closing the door behind her.

A wave of nausea swept through Lacey as the realization hit: This wasn't just business. This was calculated destruction, and Reid was right at the center of it.

THIRTY

Lacey scanned the restaurant as she unwound the yellow scarf Simon had given her from her neck.

She spotted him now at the bar, one hand raised in greeting, the stool beside him empty and waiting. He looked relaxed and handsome in dark jeans, brown leather boots, and a double-breasted gray wool coat.

"Hi," she said, leaning in to kiss his cheek, the familiar scent of his spicy cologne instantly soothing.

"Hi, yourself," he said, smiling. He slid a glass of wine toward her on the bar. "I got you a Pinot." He checked his watch. "I think that's all we'll have time for before the parent-teacher conferences."

"Sorry I'm late," Lacey apologized. "Work emergency."

Sliding onto the stool next to him, she caught the faintly disappointed glance of the woman seated next to Simon—who had probably been hoping the seat would stay empty. Lacey felt another tremor of guilt. Any other woman in her position would be thrilled to call Simon their boyfriend. Lacey wasn't naïve; she knew a good man was hard to find at her stage of life, especially when you had a kid and baggage like she did. She should be grateful they'd found each other, not frustrated when he talked about the latest investing podcast he'd listened to or his Fantasy Football league, despite the fact that he knew it made her eyes glaze over.

Lacey shifted closer so that their legs touched, willing herself to focus on the positive. After all, Simon made her feel cared for. Being with him felt like sinking into a warm blanket while a winter storm howled outside. Safe. Comforting. Easy.

"How was your day?" he asked.

Lacey took a long sip of her wine, the chaos of the afternoon replaying in sharp flashes: Reid's icy calm as he orchestrated Sunil's ouster, Sunil's disbelief and fury, Marina's coy, triumphant smile as the security guards led him out, his career decimated. For an instant, Lacey considered telling Simon everything. But doing so would mean skimming too close to other truths she wasn't ready to share—about Reid, about Regina, about Lacey's own uneasy place in all of it.

"It was fine," she said, forcing a smile, then changed the subject. "I have to go to California on Thursday again," she said.

Simon paused. "You travel a lot for an assistant," he said, a whiff of disapproval in his voice.

"Executive assistant," she corrected. "To the CEO." She sighed. "At least Judd has Elliott those days so I don't have to tell him I'll be out of town again."

Simon's mouth tensed and he placed a protective hand on Lacey's arm. "Will he be there tonight?"

Lacey's stomach tightened. "As far as I know."

Simon squeezed her arm. "I wish you didn't have to deal with all this. You don't deserve it."

"I'm fine," she said quietly. "It's Elliott I worry about. Mr. Barry called and he's struggling again. What he described almost sounded like the Elliott before he started on medication—outbursts, fights, the whole deal." She shook her head. "He said it's like two different Elliotts depending on the day. I think going back and forth between his dad and me is too much."

She lifted her wine glass again, hoping to hide the tears welling in her eyes. Simon slid his arm around her waist, pulling her gently against him.

"Hey," he said softly. "It's all going to be fine. Elliott's a great kid." He gave her a tender smile. "I'm hoping to spend a lot more time with him."

Lacey leaned into him. Simon always knew the right thing to say.

"I just..." She paused, searching for the right words. "I love him so much, but sometimes I wonder what life would be like if he didn't have ADHD. How much easier it would be. For him. For me. And then I feel so guilty for even thinking that. Like I'm wishing away part of him."

Simon pulled back slightly, gripping her hand. "I think it would be weird if we didn't have those thoughts," he said. "What parent doesn't want an easier life for their kid? I mean, I know you probably get all the same Instagram videos I do—the ones with parents crying tears of gratitude about how they'd never change their kid's neurodivergence because it's what makes them amazing. Blah, blah, blah."

He rolled his eyes and Lacey let out a choked laugh.

"But honestly?" he went on. "I'd trade it in a heartbeat. Not because I don't love Amelia exactly how she is. But because I know her life would probably be easier if she wasn't neurodivergent. And, yeah, mine would be, too." His voice softened. "But here we are. All we can do is love them and make the best of it."

Lacey's shoulders sagged and she let out a long exhale. She'd had all these same thoughts, along with the intense guilt that came with them that she must be a terrible mother for wishing Elliott was different. But hearing them come out of Simon's mouth sent a wave of relief through her.

"That's exactly how I feel," she said softly.

He smiled, then tilted his head in thought. "You said Mr. Barry mentioned Elliott seems like two different people... is there any chance—" He hesitated. "Do you think maybe Judd isn't giving him his meds?"

Lacey gave a sharp shake of her head. "The judge said he had to..." She trailed off, a cold dread gripping her. She drew in a long breath, her hands curling into fists. "God dammit," she swore softly as the realization set in.

"I could be wrong," Simon said quickly, seeing the anger come over her face.

Lacey gritted her teeth. "I highly doubt you are," she said, her voice bitter. "Judd refusing to follow the judge's orders and give Elliott his medication would track exactly with the kind of person he's become." Along with her anger, her heart seized at the thought of Elliott suffering unnecessarily because of what Judd had done.

They finished their wine quickly and bundled back up to make the short drive in his car to the school. In the parking lot, he clasped her hand reassuringly.

"I wish I could go with you," he said as they entered the building. He glanced around, worry on his face. "But I've got my meeting with Amelia's teacher."

"I'll be fine," Lacey said. "I'll meet you back here after."

As he leaned in for a quick kiss, Simon said, almost offhandedly, "OK, love you." He froze as soon as the words were out, his cheeks coloring. "I'm sorry, I didn't mean—well, I did—but I mean, what I meant to say was—"

A stunned laugh escaped Lacey. "It's OK," she said, taking in the embarrassed, puppyish yearning on his face. "I, um, love you, too."

Simon's face broke into a broad, boyish grin. He squeezed her hand before turning and disappearing down the hall.

Lacey stood there for a moment, her mind whirling. They'd been dating nearly four months now, spending every spare moment together—which sometimes wasn't a lot, given they were both single parents, but they tried. He knew her coffee order, stocked her favorite ice cream at his house, and had taken her car in for winter tires without her even asking. Of course she loved him.

Didn't she?

Mr. Barry's door was still closed when she walked up, so she paced the hallway, scanning for Judd. Her body felt like a live wire that might spark if anyone touched her. How dare he? The judge had given a direct order to—

Her thoughts snagged as her eyes caught on the "All About Me" portraits taped along the wall and zeroed in on Elliott's. He'd drawn himself with spiky brown hair and a huge, toothy grin. His fill-in-the-blank section read: *I like to play Minecraft. My favorite food is mac and cheese. My favorite thing about third grade is getting to live with my friends Max and Maddie.*

A rush of gratitude swelled in Lacey's chest, battling with her anger. Yes, things might be feeling messy between her and Regina and the others right now, but Elliott was happy at the mommune. That counted for a lot.

She heard a throat clear behind her and turned to find Judd standing a few feet away. Bitter resentment rose in her throat and she took a sharp step toward him.

"What the fuck, Judd?" she demanded.

He blinked, caught off guard by her language—Lacey had never been much for angry curse words; that was his department. "What do you—"

"Elliott's medication." Lacey cut him off, crossing her arms so he couldn't see her hands trembling with anger. "You're not giving it to him."

A small flicker passed over Judd's face as he realized he was busted, then he rearranged it into an imperious sneer. "What I do with Elliott on my time is none of your business," he said.

"It is when you're not doing what the judge ordered you to do," Lacey said, her voice low and loaded. "When it affects Elliott. He's struggling without his medication, so you're actively causing him to suffer."

"If you think I'm going to let some judge—" Judd began.

Just then Mr. Barry's door opened and a couple exited, calling their thanks over their shoulders. Mr. Barry leaned out, sporting jeans and a Hawaiian shirt, and spotted Lacey and Judd.

"I'm ready whenever you are," he said with a warm smile, that faded as he noticed the icy stare Judd and Lacey were exchanging.

"We're not done with this conversation," Lacey said, her tone frigid, then turned and walked into the classroom.

Inside, Mr. Barry gestured for them to sit in the two chairs across from his desk.

"Thank you for coming, Mr. and Ms. Kessler," he said cheerily.

Lacey winced at hearing them lumped together.

"I'm so glad you could both make it," Mr. Barry continued. "Elliott is such a bright kid with so much potential. He asks wonderful questions during discussions and really shines during hands-on projects, especially in science."

"But?" Judd said, his tone sharp, arms folding across his chest.

Mr. Barry's smile hitched and he glanced at Lacey. "Ms. Kessler, we've had a chance to speak about this, but Mr. Kessler"—he turned to Judd—"I wasn't able to reach you today." He cleared his throat as Judd glowered at him. "What I explained to Ms. Kessler is that in the last month I've seen a... change in Elliott. Some days he's focused and social. Other days, it's like he can't settle at all—outbursts, impulsivity, frustration. It's impacting his learning and that of the other students."

"That's because it turns out Elliott isn't on his ADHD medication when he's at his dad's," Lacey cut in, tossing a look of fury at Judd. "Despite very clear orders from the judge to—"

"I'm not letting the court tell me I need to poison my son!" Judd exploded, pushing his chair back from the table.

Mr. Barry physically drew back.

"Are you so blind and stupid that if some judge told you that you were supposed to give Elliott arsenic every morning, you'd just do it?" Judd demanded, pointing at Lacey.

"We're not talking about arsenic, for God's sake," Lacey said, slamming her fist onto her thigh. "We're talking about an FDA approved medication that is *helping* our son. How can you not see that?"

"Because I'm not a brainless sheep letting myself be fed lies by the libs," Judd scoffed. "And I'm not letting my son suffer because of their bullshit."

"Mr. Kessler, please—" Mr. Barry held up a timid hand.

Judd stood, whirling toward him. "You don't know shit about my kid, OK?" he said. Kicking the small chair out of his way, he stormed toward the door.

Lacey's stomach clenched in embarrassment as she watched Mr. Barry recoil from Judd. She realized too late she should have warned him about Judd ahead of time—but she wasn't thinking straight; every day now was a blur of work and preparing for the custody trial.

"I'm sorry," she said, rising to her feet. "This was a bad idea."

Judd was halfway down the hallway, and Lacey called after him. "You don't get to do this, Judd! I'm calling my lawyer!"

All at once she realized her mistake, as Judd froze, then slowly turned and began to walk back toward her.

"No," he hissed as he got close, so close she could see the small drop of spit in the corner of his mouth. "*You* don't get to do this. I'll take him from you, Lacey, you wait. Because while you're off sucking face with your new boyfriend and doing God knows what else in the hippy commune you live in, I am the one who knows what's best for our son."

Lacey leaned forward, her fury rising. "Elliott's grades are tanking. He's getting into fights. He's on an emotional roller coaster that's out of his control. That doesn't happen when he's on his medication! Why can't you see that?"

Lacey's heart hammered in her chest, the heat of Judd's glare burning into her.

"When I get custody, I'm pulling him out of this woke joke of a school and enrolling him at Mount Zion, where he'll get the discipline he needs," Judd said.

A wave of panic rolled through Lacey as she pictured Judd's church. It had its own small, insular school tucked behind it. Lacey had seen a brochure for it on one of the rare occasions she'd attended service with Judd, and remembered it promising a "highly structured environment where discipline and faith are paramount."

"You can't do that," Lacey said, her breathing suddenly shallow.

Judd stepped in closer, his face darkening. "You lost the right to tell me what I can and can't do the day you walked out, thinking you knew better," he said, his voice low and threatening.

Lacey instinctively stepped back, glancing down the deserted hallway. She didn't even recognize the man in front of her, his finger jabbing the air near her chest, his face twisted in fury.

"Lacey?" Simon's voice rang out from the far end of the hallway. She turned to see him jogging toward them, his brow creased with concern. "Hey, man, back off," Simon called, as he approached.

Judd's lips curled into a cruel smile. He stepped back, giving Simon an exaggerated thumbs up. "For sure, man. She's all yours." His voice dripped with mockery.

Then he spun on his heel and stalked away.

"Hey," Simon said, placing a steadying hand on her back. His eyes lingered on Judd as he turned the corner. "What's going on?"

"Can we just get out of here?" Lacey said, her voice unsteady.

"I've got you," Simon said. He wrapped his arm around her shoulders, steering her gently toward the exit.

At first, the weight of his arm felt reassuring, safe. A small part of her wanted to sink into it, let him shoulder the fear and anger still pulsing through her. But another small part pushed back against the comfort. The pressure building in her chest wasn't just fear or gratitude. It was frustration. Sure, it was nice to have someone step in, to protect her. But she didn't want to need rescuing anymore. She wanted to be powerful enough to stand her ground.

THIRTY-ONE

Simon followed her back to the mommune in his car, then got out to walk her to the door, his head swiveling as they walked up the steps as though Judd might be hiding in the bushes.

"Let me stay the night," he said, keeping his hand firmly gripped on her waist. "I'll crash on the couch downstairs. My sister can come stay with the girls—I'll tell her it's an emergency."

"But it's not an emergency," Lacey said, rubbing her palm over her eyes. The adrenaline had drained out of her, leaving only exhaustion. "I'll call my lawyer in the morning," she added, trying to sound more confident than she felt.

Simon shook his head, his features tense. "I don't like it," he said, surveying a passing car down on the street with the intensity of the secret service. "I should stay."

The authoritative note in his voice sent a ripple of annoyance through Lacey.

"I can take care of myself," she said, stepping back from him. The flash of hurt on his face made her instantly regretful. "I'm sorry," she said with a sigh. "I'm just tired."

"I know you can take care of yourself," Simon said, an edge in his voice. "But you don't always have to be so independent. It's OK to accept help."

Lacey wanted to laugh. Or cry. If only he knew how much help she'd already accepted from Regina, how much she owed her. Her job. Her housing. The quiet bailout over Elliott's medical bill before the judge ordered Judd to begin paying. For Lacey, independence was still a dream—one she hoped to reach when the custody trial was behind her, when her legal bills stopped eating her paycheck, when she was free of being tangled between Reid and Regina.

"I'll be fine, I promise," Lacey repeated. "Besides, I don't live alone, remember?"

"Mm," Simon said, and Lacey thought she detected a faint note of judgment in his voice. "Call me before you go to bed?"

She nodded and leaned in to brush her lips against his. "Thank you—for everything."

He hesitated, then gave a small, tense smile and turned to go.

Lacey let herself into the house just as Simon's car pulled away from the curb. She watched his taillights fade down the street, a yawn catching her before she'd even turned from the window. Upstairs, she found Elliott already in his pajamas, lying belly-down on the bed, elbows propped, nose buried in *Dog Man*.

"What's our favorite half-dog, half-man superhero up to tonight?" she asked, climbing onto the bed beside him.

"Hi, Mommy," he murmured without looking up, but scooted closer until the length of him was pressed against her side.

"You brush your teeth already?"

"Mmhmm."

"All of them? Not just the front ones?"

"Mmhmm."

"Then ten more minutes, and then it'll be lights out," she said, kissing the top of his head.

She dozed off next to him a short while later after tucking him in, and awoke with a dry mouth. Sitting up, she crept out of the room to get a glass of water, unsure what time it was and whether she'd been asleep for five minutes or five hours. The whole evening had been so disorienting. Simon's declaration of love. The ugly scene with Judd.

In the kitchen, the light was on and Nanette and Tavia sat at the table. Lacey hesitated before entering, then took a deep breath. She couldn't avoid them forever.

"Hey, stranger," Nanette said, her hands wrapped around a mug. Across from her, Tavia lifted a wine glass in greeting.

"What are you drinking?" Tavia asked. "I've got a nice Cab. Nanette's gone rogue with herbal tea."

"I told you, I'm doing a cleanse," Nanette said.

"Wine is basically fruit," Tavia argued, swirling her glass. "It's rich in antioxidants." She turned to Lacey. "How were conferences?"

Lacey closed her eyes, a flash of Judd's face rising unbidden: the fleck of spittle at the corner of his mouth and the cruel twist of his features as he'd leaned in to threaten her.

Regina emerged from the pantry. Catching the look on Lacey's face, she set down the bag of chips she was holding.

"Lacey," she said, "are you OK?"

Lacey opened her mouth, but no words came. Instead, tears welled and slipped over her lashes.

Tavia patted the seat next to her. "Come sit."

Nanette rose wordlessly and set her mug in the sink, returning with two wine glasses. She poured one for Lacey and one for herself.

"Talk to us," she said gently.

Lacey sat blinking back tears, her fingers tight around her glass as she recounted what had happened with Judd. In that moment, the tension of the past few days loosened, replaced by the startling realization of how quickly she'd grown accustomed to their support and camaraderie. The rest could wait. Right now, she needed them.

"That son of a bitch," Tavia muttered when she finished.

"You're calling Elizabeth first thing tomorrow," Regina said, her voice steely as she joined them at the table.

"It's not even what he said that bothers me so much," Lacey said. "It's realizing that no matter what, I'm stuck with him. Because of Elliott, he'll always be in my life. I'll never be free of him."

Nanette reached across the table and squeezed her hand. "We should burn some sage. Cleanse you of his toxic energy."

Tavia coughed a laugh. "I'm pretty sure the smoke detectors are still recovering from your last sage ritual, Nanette."

Lacey took a long sip of wine. "It's just... how was I supposed to know it would turn out like this?" she asked, anger creeping into her voice. "Things were good with us at first. Before..."

"You couldn't have known," Nanette said.

"Nobody could," Regina added, her voice flat. "That's why you always have to know how to take care of yourself. No matter what."

Tavia raised her glass. "Say it with me: A man is not a plan. I make Grace repeat that in the mirror every day."

Nanette looked aghast. "She's two!"

"I know," Tavia said solemnly. "I should've started with her sooner."

"Should we get a security system?" Nanette asked, glancing toward the front door. "I mean, how unhinged is he, exactly?"

"It's not like that," Lacey said. "At least... I don't think so."

"Ooh, should we all sign up for one of those self-defense courses together?" Tavia suggested, perking up. "I've always wanted to learn the proper way to kick someone in the nuts."

"No, you go for the throat," Nanette corrected, making a precise jabbing motion. "And the eyes."

"Spoken like the pacifist of the group," Regina observed dryly.

Lacey laughed, the tightness in her chest finally beginning to ease. "What would I do without the three of you?" she wondered aloud.

Across the table, Regina caught her eye and smiled.

THIRTY-TWO

The next morning Lacey placed her call to Elizabeth as she speed-walked from Penn Station to the Vetra office, the chilly mid-December air biting at her cheeks.

"Oh no he did *not*," Elizabeth said as Lacey filled her in about both her run-in with Judd and her suspicion that he was no longer giving Elliott his medication. "Sit tight," she said. "I'll have us in court by the end of the day."

"I'm at work all day in the city," Lacey said, her mind immediately trying to work out whether she could somehow clone herself to keep up with her responsibilities for Reid while still appearing in Essex County family court. "I don't know if I can—"

"I'll request a Zoom session; they do those sometimes, depending on the judge," Elizabeth said. "Stay tuned."

Lacey hung up, feeling both a wave of relief that Elizabeth was in her corner, and a stab of anxiety at the extra hours this would add to Elizabeth's already very high bill.

Entering the office, Lacey noticed a charged quiet, like the aftermath of a storm. People watched from the corners of their eyes as she passed, like she might hold the answers to their unasked questions.

Despite the company-wide email Reid had sent about Sunil's departure, full of vague optimism about Vetra's "next chapter," the unease was palpable. Lacey could feel it in the lowered voices, the watchful glances, the way people seemed to instinctively keep their heads down.

The rumors about Sunil falsifying clinical trial data had also spread, and no matter how polished the press releases or confident Reid's reassurances, everyone knew what was at stake: If the Vetra-Patch trials failed, their jobs could go with it.

The elevator in the lobby was about to close when Marina stepped inside, clutching an enormous coffee in one hand and her phone in the other.

"Hi," she said, offering a smile that didn't reach her eyes, under which Lacey noticed faint purple circles.

"Hi," Lacey replied. She waited for the doors to close, offering them some privacy. "How's the, um, mood?"

Marina sipped her coffee. "Well, the board seems mollified by Sunil leaving—for now." She grimaced. "They're like caged dogs sometimes, you know? Like you need to throw them a bone to get them to stop barking at you for five minutes so you can do your job."

Lacey tried not to betray her surprise. Marina had never before spoken to her so candidly.

"This is just such textbook Reid, you know?" Marina continued, rolling her eyes.

"What do you mean?" Lacey asked lightly as the elevator doors opened to the executive floor.

Marina glanced around as they exited. "I mean, he decides he doesn't need someone anymore, and that's it—they're gone. He just throws them overboard with no consideration of the optics. He never learns." She exhaled sharply and caught herself. "Sorry. I shouldn't be venting. I'm tired."

"It's just me," Lacey said with her most trustworthy smile. "And we all need to vent. Especially about Reid."

Marina gave a small laugh and headed for her office. "That's for sure," she called over her shoulder.

Lacey's brain caught on something as she hurried to her desk, a puzzle piece clicking into place. As her screen blinked to life, she opened a browser window and typed: *Marina Silva Vetra Vitals*.

Marina's LinkedIn profile popped up immediately with her current title: *Head of Human Resources & Legal, Vetra Vitals*.

But it was the line below it, her previous job, that made Lacey's breath catch.

General Counsel, Chomer Labs.

"Hey there."

Reid's voice behind her made Lacey jolt, spinning around so fast she knocked her purse off the desk.

"Reading up on Marina?" he asked, his eyes on her computer screen. Though his tailored slacks and button-down were crisp and immaculate, his face told a different story. It was drawn with fatigue, his pale blue eyes dulled, the rims tinged with red.

Lacey let out a shaky breath as she retrieved her purse and straightened up. "Yeah, she's really impressive," she gushed, then paused. "I didn't realize she'd been with you back at Chomer Labs, too."

"We go way back," Reid said. "I convinced her to join the team at Chomer out of law school instead of one of the big IP law firms that was throwing money at people—not that it was much of a team back then." His face softened like he was experiencing a happy memory. "Just me and one other person, really, until Marina came on board. When I started Vetra, she was the first person I brought with me." He paused, his gaze sharpening slightly. "You know how much I value loyalty."

Lacey kept her face smooth, even as her pulse tapped nervously in her neck. She cleared her throat. "Any, um, updates on Sunil's replacement?"

Reid's mouth pulled tight. "Marina suggested some candidates but no standouts yet." He raked a hand through his hair. "I spent the entire weekend staring at the algorithm, trying to see what Sunil missed. But it's like a word stuck on the tip of your tongue—you know it's there, you just can't grab it. That's where I'm at with this hole in the model."

He shook his head and checked his watch. "Anyway, I've got a last-minute meeting with a crisis comms firm—Marina just scheduled it. She thinks they can help us distance ourselves from Sunil." He rapped his knuckles on her desk and then was gone.

The morning passed quickly, and after lunch Lacey was able to slip into a conference room for the emergency hearing the judge had scheduled based on the motion Elizabeth filed that morning.

On her laptop screen a gallery of Zoom squares arranged like a tense game board: Elizabeth, poised and composed from a conference room; the judge, a tall bookshelf of thick tomes behind her; Judd, appearing from his own home setup, and his lawyer from his office.

Lacey felt like anyone who walked by the conference room could hear her heart pounding.

The judge cleared her throat, the sound crackling through the computer's speakers. "All right. I've reviewed the emergency motion submitted by petitioner's counsel. Mr. Kessler, you were ordered to administer your son's prescribed medication during your custodial time. Did you, or did you not, comply?"

Judd leaned toward the camera, his jaw stiff. "I was trying to use my discretion, Your Honor. Elliott seemed fine without it. I don't believe in overmedicating children, and—"

The judge cut him off. "Mr. Kessler, your personal beliefs are not at issue. The court issued a binding directive. This is not a suggestion; it's an order tied to your custody rights."

Lacey exhaled slowly, gripping the edge of the table. Outside the conference room, the faint hum of the office felt like a different universe.

Elizabeth's voice came through next, calm but firm. "Your Honor, in light of Mr. Kessler's noncompliance, we're requesting that the interim custody arrangement be suspended immediately and that my client be awarded temporary full custody. The child's health and stability are at risk."

Judd's lawyer leaned in. "Respectfully, Your Honor, my client misunderstood the boundaries of the order. He's assured me that he will fully comply moving forward."

There was a pause, and Lacey found herself gripping the edge of the conference room table so tightly her fingers ached.

The judge glanced over her notes, then looked up. "I'm not inclined to upend the custody arrangement today. However, Mr. Kessler, this is your formal warning. Any further deviation will be grounds for immediate reconsideration. Is that understood?"

Judd's face remained blank. "Understood."

The judge continued. "In light of this disruption, however, I *am* moving the case management conference up to late January. That gives us four weeks to complete discovery, including home visits for both parents, to take place as soon as possible after the holidays."

Elizabeth made some notes on the pad in front of her in quick, efficient strokes. "We'll coordinate with the custody evaluator's office, Your Honor."

"Good. Then we're adjourned."

With a click, the judge's square vanished, followed by the others. Lacey sat frozen for a moment in the quiet that followed, her hands finally loosening their grip on the table.

Her phone buzzed with a text from Elizabeth.

Not what we hoped for, but good news that the case management conference is moved up. Let's discuss prepping for your home visit. I'll call you after my next meeting.

Dejected, Lacey closed her laptop and pushed her chair back, frustration rising in her chest. Once again, she was at Judd's mercy, forced to trust that he'd follow the judge's orders, despite all evidence to the contrary. She *knew* she was the only one consistently putting Elliott's well-being first, yet she was still expected to share that authority with someone who treated it like a negotiation. The powerlessness of it all was unbearable.

Her phone buzzed again as she walked back toward her desk with a message from Reid.

> Change of plans, heading out for the day. Clear my afternoon.

After she read the message, Lacey's eyes drifted to Reid's office door. With everything that had happened—Sunil's sudden departure, the emergency hearing with Judd—she'd managed to push Regina's request for help from her mind. But now, as it returned, her stomach flipped.

Lacey glanced over her shoulder, then slipped into Reid's office, closing the door behind her. Her pulse quickened as she scanned the room. If Regina was right, the proof of everything— what Reid had done, what he'd taken—was in here somewhere. The desk loomed in front of her, sleek and neat, its surface almost surgically clean. Her hand hovered above the drawer.

He'd taken his laptop with him, but that didn't mean there wasn't something else—files, notes, anything Regina could use to prove her claim.

The office door swung open and Lacey jerked back from the desk as Marina entered.

Marina stopped short, eyes immediately narrowing. "What are you doing?" she asked.

Lacey straightened, her heart hammering. "Looking for Reid's AirPods," she said, voice steady. "He thought he might've left them." She narrowed her eyes, feigning skepticism. "What are *you* doing?"

A flicker of red touched Marina's cheeks. For a brief, electric second, the balance shifted. Lacey had more claim to Reid's office than Marina did, and they both knew it.

"I thought I left a file in here," Marina replied. "You weren't at your desk, so..."

She glanced vaguely around.

Lacey offered a tight smile. "It doesn't look like it's here."

Marina's mouth pinched into a line. "Must be in my office, then."

She turned and left. Lacey stood still, counting her breaths. Then, slowly, she stepped out, easing the door shut behind her, leaving Reid's office untouched—for now.

THIRTY-THREE

Wednesday evening, Lacey pulled up in front of Judd's house with a knot of dread curling tight in her stomach. Pasting on a bright smile, she turned to face Elliott in the backseat.

"OK, buddy," she said gently. "Time to go."

Elliott didn't move. He clutched his seatbelt with both hands, eyes fixed on his lap. "Do I have to?" he asked, his voice barely audible.

Lacey's heart clenched. *No,* she wanted to say. *We'll turn around, go home. Just the two of us, forever.* But breaking the temporary custody agreement would only jeopardize her case—and make things worse in the long run. A spike of helpless rage flared in her chest. How was it possible that after everything that had passed between her and Judd only days earlier—after Judd's *threats*—she was still forced to drop Elliott off with him?

She kept her smile in place with effort. "I know it's hard, going back and forth," she said. "But Daddy's excited to see you." She reached for his hand, giving it a reassuring squeeze.

His gaze flicked up to hers, then dropped again. "Why can't I just stay with you?" he murmured. "I only get to see Max and Maddie at school when I'm with Daddy. And he makes pasta every night and I don't like it. And on Wednesday nights we have to go to church, and after he always yells at me because I get bored." He scowled.

Lacey's throat tightened. She unbuckled her seatbelt and climbed into the back, wrapping her arms around him.

"I'm so sorry, baby," she whispered, pressing her face into his hair, hoping he wouldn't notice her tears. "That's not fair at all."

She pulled back and cupped Elliott's cheek, still smooth and soft with boyhood. "I charged your phone and put it in the inside pocket of your backpack, OK? You can call me anytime."

He nodded, solemnly unbuckling his seatbelt.

When Judd answered the door, Elliott gave him a tentative hug. Lacey tried to peer past him, to get a glimpse inside the house, but Judd stood in the doorway, blocking her view. Then, with a dark look in her direction, he closed the door before she could speak.

Lacey stood there for a moment, staring at the closed door, her breath visible in the cold air. Then she turned, stepping down the porch slowly, silently begging the universe for one simple thing:

Please let him be OK.

Heading home, Lacey stopped at a red light and put on her left turn signal, her mind drifting to Elliott. How was this legal? How could she be forced to hand over her child to a house that felt unsafe—emotionally if not physically? She didn't believe Judd would hurt Elliott, not with his hands. But the damage of being constantly told that your struggles were your own fault, that if you just tried harder, were better, everything would be fine, ran deep. And there was nothing she could do. Not yet.

She needed to convince the judge that *she* was the safe parent, despite her non-traditional living situation. But she couldn't afford to move out of the mommune while she was still paying Elizabeth's legal fees. It was a cruel catch-22, one she couldn't figure out how to solve.

Behind her, a car honked. Lacey looked up to see the light was green. She surged into the intersection to turn left, oblivious to the red pickup coming straight toward her. Its horn blared, long and angry, and her heart shot into her throat as it sped by and she took in the familiar yellow bumper sticker on the back.

It was the same truck. The one she'd hit all those months ago.

Panic flared in her chest. She yanked the wheel hard, veering onto a side street and pulling over. Putting the car into park, she sat there, hands trembling on the steering wheel, heart pounding.

The guilt came crashing back. She'd tried to tell herself it hadn't been a big deal, just a minor scrape, barely visible. And more than once she'd thought about slipping an envelope of cash and an apology note under the windshield in the dead of night. But now it felt impossibly late to make amends.

After a long moment, she forced her breathing to slow. Fingers still clenched around the wheel, she blinked away the sting in her eyes, then eased back onto the road and headed home.

At the house, Regina's car pulled in just as Lacey stepped out of hers. Max and Maddie tumbled out first, Max in basketball shorts and a T-shirt, hugging an orange ball to his chest, jacket slung carelessly over one shoulder despite the cold, Maddie trailing behind, struggling under an armful of library books.

"Hey," Regina called as the twins bounded up the steps and disappeared inside. "Did you just drop Elliott off?"

Lacey nodded glumly.

"I'm sorry," Regina said, her smile sympathetic. "But it's temporary. We're going to make sure you get custody."

"How?" Lacey asked bitterly as they climbed the front steps together. "Elizabeth says even if my home visit is perfect, it could still go either way—unless Judd completely blows his, which isn't likely."

Elizabeth had explained that the next phase of trial prep would involve home visits from the court-appointed custody evaluator for both Judd and Lacey. Lacey had no idea how the evaluator would interpret the sprawling, chaotic home that was the mommune. Would they see what she saw—warmth, safety, community—or just a red flag of unconventionality?

They stepped into the foyer and took off their coats, sidestepping the heap of sneakers Max and Maddie had dumped by the door.

"Then maybe you should make sure he does completely blow his." Regina's voice was casual but matter of fact.

Lacey turned, startled. "What do you mean?"

Regina cocked her head. "I'm just saying... do you really want to leave your and Elliott's future in the hands of the New Jersey court system? Maybe it's time to—"

"Mom! Max hit me!" Maddie came barreling into the foyer, her face flushed with fury, bottom lip trembling.

"Did not!" Max yelled, chasing after her. "I sat on you. That's not the same!"

"Max Wellington Cho, don't sit on your sister," Regina said, pointing at Max. "And Maddie, don't *let* your brother sit on you. You have to stand up for yourself." She gave each of them a gentle push. "Go get a snack and stop terrorizing each other."

When they were gone, Regina turned back to Lacey with a sigh, tucking her hair behind her ear. "So much it's-almost-Christmas energy, ugh. I don't know if I'm going to survive the next ten days."

"You will," Lacey said with a smile. "And then they'll all be home for a week of winter break."

Regina groaned as she headed for the kitchen. "There's not enough coffee in the universe."

Lacey almost followed, wanting to hear what Regina had been going to say about Judd's home visit before she'd been interrupted. But then there was a crash, and Max and Maddie's voices rose over each other again, followed by Regina pleading for them to stop fighting. Instead, Lacey headed upstairs to the calm of her room, leaving it for another day.

THIRTY-FOUR

The house was quiet that night as Lacey smoothed a stack of neatly folded clothes into her small suitcase and zipped it shut. She rolled it over to the bedroom door, her eyes catching on Elliott's empty bed in the corner. She'd texted him earlier to check in, but he hadn't replied. She told herself that was a good thing—that he hadn't needed to sneak his phone out to reach her.

Her phone buzzed in her pocket.

"Hey," came Simon's warm voice as she answered.

"Hey," she said, settling on the edge of her bed.

"Packing?"

"Yeah."

"Take a jacket; it looks like they're having a cold snap."

She laughed. "I will."

"I miss you already," he said.

Lacey smiled. "It's only two days. And it's not like we'd get to see each other anyway."

"I'm trying to be romantic and you're ruining it with your flawless logic," he teased.

"Sorry."

"How was dropping off Elliott?" Simon asked, his voice turning protective. "Did you see Judd?"

"It was fine," Lacey said. "I just..." She rubbed a hand over her tired eyes, unsure whether she wanted to get into it with Simon.

"Tell me," he said.

"I'm worried about the home visit, the custody evaluation." She gave a small, brittle laugh. "I mean, I'm going to have to introduce the evaluator to the three other adults and four children who live with me."

Simon paused and Lacey could almost hear his frown through the phone. "What does your lawyer say about your... living arrangement?" he asked.

That pause, almost imperceptible, was like a pinprick. Lacey felt the familiar jolt of defensiveness rise in her chest. When it came to the mommune, Simon's voice carried that same edge of judgment she'd heard from her sister, from Judd, from strangers.

Elizabeth had been blunt during their last call.

"I know it works for you," she'd said. "But to an evaluator, it might look chaotic. No private room for Elliott, unfamiliar adults, constant activity—it could raise questions."

"But they're not unfamiliar," Lacey had said. "They're... family." The word had caught in her throat. Could she really call Regina that, after everything? Her mind drifted to the night last week when they'd all gathered to decorate the tree: kids laughing, Max and Elliott competing to toss tinsel onto the highest branches, Linden clustering ornaments on one small corner on the bottom of the tree, Tavia belting out "Santa Baby" while twirling Grace on her hip, Nanette laughing at her and rolling her eyes. Even Regina, arms wrapped around Maddie, swaying in time. That night, Lacey had felt a deep feeling of being home.

Now, she pressed the phone between her shoulder and her ear as she opened the dresser drawer to pull out pajamas. "Elizabeth says my living situation is... a concern," she admitted.

Simon paused again. "I've been thinking," he said after a beat, "that we should talk about you and Elliott moving in."

The phone slipped from Lacey's hand and landed with a soft

thud on the rug. She snatched it up, the breath rushing out of her lungs.

"Lacey?"

"Yeah—sorry. I just... wow." She tried to sound steady, even as her thoughts scattered.

"I know it's sudden," Simon rushed to add. "I just—" He sighed. "We love each other. We're adults. It makes sense."

"Makes sense how?" she asked carefully. She had the sudden sense of being high above the ground on a tightwire: One wrong step and everything could tilt in the wrong direction.

"I've been thinking about it for a while now," he said. "And if you're worried about the home visit, about how the evaluator might view your, you know... situation, then maybe it makes sense to do it sooner rather than later. Like if you're here with me, it would show that Elliott has a traditional, stable home."

"I have a stable home," Lacey said, her voice sharpening.

"Of course you do," Simon said quickly. "I just meant it might look better—on paper." A pause stretched between them and Lacey felt herself bracing. "And it's not *just* optics, Lacey. I love you. I want this. I want you here, for us to be together."

She rubbed at the tightness gathering at her temples. "It's a lot to think about," she said softly. "And I truly appreciate the offer. But right now, I should get to bed. I have a car coming at five a.m."

"Of course. Safe travels. Love you."

"Love you, too," she said, the words catching faintly in her throat.

A soft knock came from the doorway. "Knock knock," Regina said.

Lacey looked up, startled. "Oh. Hey."

Regina raised an eyebrow. "Simon?"

Lacey flushed.

"I didn't realize you were dropping the L-word now."

"He's a really good guy," Lacey said quickly, the words coming out more defensive than she meant them to.

"He is," Regina agreed, her mouth twitching.

Lacey narrowed her eyes. "But?"

Regina gave a small sigh. "I mean... he's just kind of, I don't know—he's fine."

Lacey straightened her shoulders. "What's that supposed to mean?"

Regina paused as though choosing her words. "Simon is the kind of guy who mows the lawn every Saturday, subscribes to Consumer Reports, and rents the same beach house the same week every single year. He's... stable. He's never going to let you down."

Lacey pressed her lips together. "You say that like it's a bad thing."

Regina tilted her head. "It depends on what you want."

Lacey opened her mouth to push back, then closed it in frustration. Deep inside her a chord of truth reverberated. "I don't know what I want," she sighed.

Regina watched her for a beat. "I think you do," she said quietly. "And I think it's time you stopped being a bystander in your own life and went after it." She paused in the doorway, her jaw tightening slightly. "And let me know what you decide about Vetra. I can't wait forever."

THIRTY-FIVE

When Reid boarded the jet early the next morning, he whistled cheerfully and gave her shoulder a light squeeze as he passed. It was a gesture that would have sent a charge of electricity down Lacey's spine only a week ago. But this time, all she felt was a faint chill.

From the airstrip, they went straight to the hotel, where Lacey had booked a meeting room for their interview with Eleanor Wang, one of the top candidates to replace Sunil. She was impressive, a PhD in biochemistry from UC Berkeley, followed by several years as deputy director of R&D at a major medical device company.

They'd just arrived at the meeting room when Lacey's phone buzzed. "Eleanor's in the lobby," she said to Reid.

"Bring her up," Reid said without looking up from his laptop. "And I want you to sit in. I'm pulled in too many directions right now; I need another set of eyes."

Lacey greeted Eleanor, who was petite with dark hair pulled back into a neat bun and oversized wire-frame glasses that made her look younger than her résumé suggested. At first glance, she seemed almost fragile. But as she took her seat, Eleanor squared her shoulders and planted both hands on the table in a wide, grounded stance that made her seem more substantial.

Reid leaned back in his chair, arms crossed loosely over his chest, projecting the easy confidence of a man used to commanding the room. "I have to say, Eleanor, your work on the biosensor modulation protocols is genuinely impressive. And your recent paper in *Nature* was intriguing."

Eleanor smiled, modest but unfazed. "Thank you."

Reid gave a broad smile. "If you came to Vetra, we'd love to take a peek at the raw data files you used. Our team could really benefit from seeing how you structured your noise filtering."

Lacey nearly choked on her coffee. That data was obviously proprietary—and Reid should know that.

Eleanor didn't miss a beat. "I'm afraid I can't share any of that. It belongs to my previous employer and is still under licensing restriction."

Reid smiled like he'd been joking all along. "Of course. Worth a shot."

The rest of the interview continued politely, but Reid's demeanor had cooled.

"I thought she was great," Lacey said, once they'd finished and Eleanor had left. "Sharp instincts, asked good questions. I think she'd hit the ground running."

Reid shook his head, eyes on his computer screen. "She's off the list."

"What? Why?"

"She's too black and white," he said. "She's clearly used to working at a big company, with layers and layers of compliance and other bullshit. I need someone who can be more nimble, flexible."

Lacey felt a layer of film lift from her vision, like she'd been peering through fogged-up glasses and had finally wiped them clean.

Reid's phone buzzed. "Shit. It's Olivier." He ran a hand through his hair, already rising.

Lacey pushed back her chair. "I'll let you take that."

He waved her off. "No, I need to stretch my legs anyway. Be back in a few."

The door clicked shut behind him.

Lacey's eyes jumped to his laptop, still open on the table, his inbox glowing on the screen. A jolt passed through her.

Before she could second guess herself, she scooted her chair over.

An email exchange with Marina was open on the screen.

Reid: *Have the research servers been updated?*

Marina: *Yes. Sunil's earlier versions have been wiped.*

Reid: *This is serious. It can't look like he started with the Chomer algorithm. It has to seem like he built it from scratch. If anyone went digging…*

Marina: *It's taken care of.*

Lacey frowned. The exchange had been sent earlier that morning—but she hadn't seen it when she'd checked Reid's email before. She bit down on her lip. He must have used secure messaging, bypassing Lacey's access to his email.

The hair on the back of her neck prickled and she clicked into the file navigator. With no idea what she was looking for, she navigated fast, scanning through folders. There were hundreds, too many to look through in the short time she had.

Then one caught her eye: *CL.* Chomer Labs?

She opened it and a long list of files appeared, their names mostly gibberish: *Software_Patchv8.7*, *Predictive_Model_XSF7.5*. She scanned quickly, her fingers cold on the trackpad.

Haphazardly she clicked on a Word document, yielding a list of dense, technical meeting notes. She was about to close the file when something caught her eye:

Revisions made in transition from RC-era modeling.

Her heart kicked. RC. Regina Cho?

There was no company logo on the page, no context. But the date, April 2017, aligned with when Regina said she'd taken time off after the twins were born.

It wasn't anything that proved wrongdoing, but she snapped a screenshot just in case.

Reid's voice grew closer outside the door.

"Yeah, fine, I'll see you then."

Heart pounding, Lacey closed the document and pushed her chair back to its original position just as Reid stepped inside.

"What's next on the agenda?" he asked, eyes still on his phone, not noticing anything amiss.

Lacey breathed a sigh of relief.

That evening, after a long day of investor meetings where Reid had breezily assured stakeholders that all was well and the FDA filing was imminent, Lacey was more than ready to retreat to her hotel room, order room service, and collapse into bed.

"Grab a drink?" Reid asked, gesturing toward the sleek, low-lit bar tucked into the back of the lobby.

She started to decline, then thought better of it. Whatever was shifting inside her, it was probably better if Reid didn't sense it. Not yet.

"Sounds great," she said, pasting on a smile.

Reid pulled out a stool for her, then signaled to the bartender. "Two glasses of Opus One." They watched the deep red wine arc into their glasses, then Reid lifted his. "To progress."

Lacey took a sip, surprised by the rich, complex flavors that hit her tongue, all in perfect balance. She'd thought she didn't like red wine, but apparently she did—the expensive kind.

She swirled the wine in her glass, words on her tongue. She hesitated, then forged ahead. "The stuff you were saying in the meetings—the timelines, the research results—it sounded a little... rosy."

"It's all a matter of perspective," Reid said with a short laugh. "Investors are like horses. You spook them, they bolt. You keep them calm and they'll follow you right off a cliff."

Lacey bit her lip. "Are we headed off a cliff?"

Reid rolled his eyes. "It's a metaphor, OK?" he said. Then his expression sobered. "Look, I need room to maneuver, not pressure from our investors. I decided we're bringing Ketchum on board in the research role. I'll fix the algorithm, and everything will be fine."

Lacey paused mid-sip. "Ketchum Carter? But you haven't even interviewed him yet." Of the three final candidates, Ketchum was by far the weakest. Barely out of his PhD program, his cover letter read like a fan missive to Reid.

Reid waved a hand. "Formality. The kid's perfect—fresh, eager, and just green enough to follow my lead."

Lacey smiled faintly.

Reid took a long drink, nearly draining his glass, then leaned in, his knee brushing hers. Where once Lacey might have thrilled at the contact, now she had to fight the instinct to pull away.

"Falsifying research—Sunil crossed a red line, you know?" He shook his head.

Lacey felt a tight band between her shoulders tighten. "I was surprised," she said carefully. "Sunil didn't strike me as the type."

"Just proves I need tighter oversight on research," Reid said, his eyes locking on hers. "Ketchum will be easy to guide. Loyal. Like you."

As they boarded the jet the next day, Lacey felt a strange mix of emotions—relief at knowing she'd be home soon and could stop playing the role of Reid's trusted confidant, and dread knowing she'd return to a house without Elliott. But the moment the town car turned onto her street, her stomach knotted.

A police cruiser idled in front of the mommune. As she climbed out of the taxi, suitcase in hand, her eyes darted toward the car, her blood suddenly loud in her ears. *Elliott.*

If something had happened to Elliott, she would never forgive herself for letting him go stay with Judd, custody trial be damned.

She hurried toward the house just as an officer emerged from the car, gun bumping against his hip in its holster.

"Excuse me," he called out. Something in his tone made Lacey want to make a run for it.

"Yes?" she said in a halting voice.

"Are you Lacey Kessler?"

She nodded.

He took a step closer, his face stony.

"We need to ask you a few questions related to a hit and run back in August."

THIRTY-SIX

Lacey felt the ground tilt beneath her, the world narrowing to the pressure of her hand gripping the roller bag handle, white-knuckled. The memory hit her like a flash flood: the rushed drive from her sister's house to the mommune all those months ago. Her adrenaline-fueled desperation to find them a place to live sitting in her chest like a rock, pressing down on her lungs and making it hard to breathe. The shriek of metal on metal as she'd scraped the side of the truck. Elliott's eyes widening in the backseat. Her hurried promise to him that she would come back, make it right.

"Ma'am?" The police officer was saying something, and she forced herself to look up. The second officer had gotten out of the car, shorter and more compact than his partner.

"Is this your car?" asked the taller one. He gestured toward her Ford, parked just down the curb. The scrape along the passenger side, faint beneath the grime and salt of winter streets, was still visible. She'd meant to get it fixed, but repairing a cosmetically damaged car that still ran fine was near the bottom of her list when it came to her financial obligations.

"Yes," she managed.

The tall officer put his hands on his hips, fingers resting a little too close to the butt of his holstered weapon. "We'll need to take you to the station for questioning. You can ride with us or follow in your vehicle."

Lacey inhaled sharply, the cold burning her throat. "Do I... should I call a lawyer?"

They exchanged a glance. "That's your right," said the shorter one. "It might not be a bad idea."

Elizabeth didn't even pretend to hide her irritation when Lacey called from the car.

"I'm not a traffic attorney." She sniffed. Then, after a pause, she gave a long sigh. "But I'll send you someone's name. Call me first thing tomorrow. This is not good, Lacey. We'll need to see what kind of damage control we can do."

Lacey gripped the wheel so tightly her knuckles throbbed as she followed the cruiser downtown. At the station, the officers ushered her into a small, windowless interview room, its cinderblock walls painted a sickly yellow.

"There's footage," the shorter cop said. His round face and soft features gave him an almost boyish look, though Lacey wasn't sure if that made him seem kind, or just disarmingly indifferent. "Neighbor's doorbell camera caught your vehicle driving past the scene."

The taller officer remained stone-faced beside him, arms crossed, eyes unreadable.

"It's rare we ID a hit-and-run suspect months after the fact," the younger one added, almost conversationally. "We never would've made the connection if it weren't for the tip."

Lacey blinked. "What tip?"

A sharp look passed between the officers. The younger one flushed, suddenly flustered. "We, ah, got a call. Someone came forward recently."

The older cop cut in, his voice firm. "That's all we can say for now."

Lacey's pulse pounded in her ears as they left her alone to wait. A tip? After all this time? She closed her eyes and scanned backward through her memory. Who would have known? She'd told no one, except... She froze, remembering that first meeting at the mommune, when, desperate and unraveling, she'd unloaded everything in the kitchen like a dam bursting. Regina. Nanette. Tavia. She'd spilled it all in a torrent—her rock bottom situation, Elliott's ADHD, the "hit and run" as the police were now calling it.

A cold weight settled in her stomach.

Two hours later, the lawyer Elizabeth had recommended finally called her back.

"Someone tipped them off," Lacey said, trying to keep her voice steady.

"Well, what's done is done," the lawyer said in a nasal, dispassionate voice. "I'll file to see if we can get the charges reduced, but no promises. And I hope you have a ride home, because your license will likely be suspended, in addition to a hefty fine and possible jail time."

"Jail time?" Lacey gasped. "But I can't go to jail—I have a son."

"Like I said, I'll see what I can do," the lawyer said. "But don't get your hopes up."

Lacey's hands shook as she ended the call. Her head throbbed and she felt the added pressure of tears gathering behind her eyes. How did this keep happening? Every time she thought she'd dug herself out of the hole, she tumbled right back in. Or, she thought, her mind turning to the anonymous tip the police had received— maybe she was pushed.

Her hands were still shaking fifteen minutes later as she pushed through the station's heavy door. It was nearly ten p.m. and the night had gone cold and brittle. An Uber idled at the curb.

She slid in, silent, and as the car picked up speed, she watched the oncoming headlights streaking past the window like silent accusations. Her breath fogged the glass as she leaned her forehead against it, the word "jail" echoing in her head like a siren. She was such an idiot. Once again, she'd ruined everything. She didn't need Elizabeth to bill her four hundred dollars an hour to confirm the obvious: She'd handed Judd the win. At this rate, she'd be lucky to get visitation.

She managed to hold herself together until she got through the door of the mommune. Then the tears came fast, streaking down her cheeks as she kicked off her shoes and tried to make it up the stairs before anyone could see how completely, utterly screwed she was.

"Hey," came a soft voice from the living room.

Lacey jumped and looked toward the sound, her whole body feeling strung tight, like wire about to snap. Regina sat curled on the couch, her features lit from below by the glow of her phone. When she saw Lacey's tear-stained face, she dropped the phone and crossed the room in three swift strides.

"What's wrong? Is it Elliott?" The genuine concern in her voice made Lacey's heart want to crack in two.

She opened her mouth to reply, and a sob escaped. Trying to close the floodgates, she buried her face in her hands.

"Tell me," Regina murmured, placing a hand on her arm. "Whatever it is, we'll figure it out."

It took a minute for Lacey to steady her breath. By then, Nanette and Tavia had appeared in the hallway, drawn by her muffled sobs, forming a quiet circle around her, like spokes on a wheel.

Lacey wiped her eyes and straightened up, eyeing the concerned faces all turned toward her. Her shoulders tightened as the cold reality swept over her.

"How could you?" she asked Regina in a low, tight voice.

Regina blinked. "What?"

"You know what I mean." Lacey turned to Tavia, then Nanette. "Or maybe it was one of you?"

"Lacey, honey, what are you talking about?" Tavia spoke in a slow, cautious tone, like Lacey was a bomb she needed to defuse.

"You told the police about my car accident."

Lacey's angry tone was met with blank faces, and the three other women exchanged confused, sidelong looks.

"Back in August," Lacey continued. "The truck I hit the day I came to meet you all."

A spark of recognition appeared on Nanette's face. "Right, I remember you mentioning something about that."

Regina shook her head. "But that was months ago. You think we *just* reported it?" Her forehead creased with confusion. "Why would we do that?"

"The police received an anonymous tip," Lacey said, her voice bitter. "And you're the only ones who knew." She searched Regina's face but saw only bewilderment.

"That wasn't us," Regina said, holding up her hands.

"Are you sure no one else knew?" Tavia pressed, her brow furrowed. "Maybe someone saw you?"

Lacey hesitated, her certainty faltering as she took in the genuine looks of concern and puzzlement around her. "Elliott was with me, but who would he tell?" she said.

Even as she said it, the possibility pressed in, sharp and cold. Her stomach dropped. She pulled out her phone.

Judd picked up on the third ring. "It's late," he said flatly. "This better be an emergency."

"Did you report me to the police?"

There was a pause, and then: "That was faster than I expected. Maplehurst PD must be more efficient than I give them credit for. Then again, a hit and run's a serious offense."

A strangled cry escaped Lacey's mouth. "But how..." she began.

"Elliott and I happened to drive down the street where it happened this week," Judd said. "The truck was parked in the same spot, according to him." The note of glee in his voice made her grind her teeth in fury.

Lacey started to speak, then ended the call before she could say something she'd regret.

She turned back to the others.

"Judd," she said simply.

Nanette's expression darkened. "Of course."

Lacey sank onto the stairs, her legs suddenly unsteady. "They took my license. I could go to jail," she whispered. "He'll get custody."

Tavia knelt beside her. "No," she said firmly. "We're not letting that happen."

A deep ache of helplessness started up in Lacey's chest. She shook her head. "There's nothing I can do," she said dully.

Regina crouched in front of her, her voice steady and clear. "Elliott needs you," she said. "You can't give up." She reached out a hand. "Come on."

The women gathered in the kitchen, the tequila bottle on the table. Lacey tossed back the shot without hesitating. It burned down her throat, warm and sharp, before settling in her stomach like a small fire. Across the table, Tavia and Nanette watched her with quiet concern while Regina paced behind them like a storm gathering.

Tavia reached over, squeezing Lacey's arm gently. "It's going to be all right, honey."

Lacey dropped her face into her hands. "No, it's not," she moaned. "I'm going to lose Elliott." Saying it aloud was like ripping open a wound. The pain felt raw, jagged, nearly unbearable.

"You can't just sit there and let this happen." Regina's voice sliced through the room.

Lacey's head snapped up, her eyes blazing. "What am I supposed to do?" she snapped, reaching for the bottle and sloshing more tequila into her glass. How could Regina not understand how helpless Lacey was? That it didn't seem to matter what she did—Judd always had the upper hand.

"If Judd's going to play dirty," Regina said evenly, "then maybe it's time you did, too."

Lacey downed the drink in one gulp, her mouth twisting at the burn. "What, you want me to plant a body in his freezer?" Her voice dripped with sarcasm.

Regina lifted her brows, just barely. "A bit extreme, maybe. But I think you're on the right track."

THIRTY-SEVEN

When Lacey opened her eyes the next morning, sunlight streamed through the curtains. She shot upright. Had she slept through her alarm? Where was Elliott? Her pulse slowed as the fog cleared and she remembered it was Saturday, and Elliott was at Judd's.

Relief gave way to the hollow ache of primal loneliness that always settled in when he wasn't there. At least in California, she'd had work to fill the hours and an unfamiliar hotel room to blunt the sting of missing him instead of being confronted by his socks on the floor or *Harry Potter* open face down on the bed to the chapter they'd last finished.

With the weekend yawning empty before her, she considered staying in bed, sleeping straight through until Monday. She lay back down, surprised to find she didn't have a headache after the night before. Her mouth was dry, but Tavia had made sure she drank water before bed, and Nanette had pressed two ibuprofen into her hand before Lacey headed upstairs. Closing her eyes again, she searched for sleep.

After another half hour of tossing and turning, Lacey gave up and made her way downstairs to the empty kitchen, which still held evidence of the morning rush—toast crusts, jelly smears, a glass of orange juice slowly separating, and cold bits of scrambled egg drying on a plate.

Her heart pinched. She wondered what Elliott had eaten for breakfast. Wondered what he and Judd were doing today—and if Judd had followed the judge's orders and given him his medication.

She closed her eyes, the ache building behind them. Then she poured herself a mug of coffee and pushed the pain away. Just one more day and she could hug her son.

The back door opened, and Regina appeared in the kitchen, wearing a puffy jacket, her cheeks pink from the cold.

"Hey," she said, rubbing her hands together. "I couldn't take another minute out there. I don't know how the cold doesn't bother the kids."

Lacey glanced out the back window to see Maddie and Max working to build a pile of dry, brown leaves for Linden to run through.

"It's supposed to snow later," Lacey observed. "Maybe we'll have a white Christmas next week."

She wrapped her hands around her mug, suddenly feeling like a fraud, like a woman who sipped coffee at the kitchen table and talked of normal things, like the weather. Not a woman who had endured a humiliating Uber ride home from the police station the night before, who had then tossed back tequila shots, enjoying the burn in her throat. And certainly not a woman who'd listened to Regina lay out a plan that, in the moment, had felt not only reasonable but inevitable. The only way, really, if Lacey wanted full custody of Elliott.

Now, though, in the light of day, without the tequila in her system, she felt doubt creep in. A good mother, a mother who deserved custody of her son, would never consider doing what Regina had suggested. Then again, maybe a good mother would never have landed in Lacey's situation to begin with.

Regina moved past her toward the coffee pot.

"The other week I read an article about a mom who pried open a mountain lion's jaw to rescue her toddler," Regina said, looking down at the mug she was refilling. "She lost her own arm in the process. Which of course led me to an article about a mom who lost both her legs after suffering horrific burns running into a burning house to rescue her three kids."

Lacey swallowed. "Jesus," she murmured.

Regina looked up. "What I'm saying is there's nothing unnatural about going to extremes to protect your child. It's instinct. Evolution." She paused. "No one would blame you if you decided to take things into your own hands."

Lacey let out a disbelieving breath, part laugh, part sigh. "Judd would. And I'm not exactly rescuing Elliott from a mountain lion."

Regina took a long sip of coffee. "No," she said. "You'd be rescuing him from something worse: a lifetime with a father who sees him as a problem to fix. Someone who will never love him for who he is."

Lacey closed her eyes, feeling a knot pull tight at the base of her skull, the uneasy sense that Regina was right.

"I have enough problems as it is with the hit and run," she said, opening her eyes. "I can't afford any more trouble."

Regina bit her lip. "If you change your mind, I'll help you with Judd. I just... I need your help, too. With Reid. Please."

There was a raw, pleading note in her voice that melted something inside Lacey. Regina had done so much for her in these past four months. And now all she asked in return was a chance at something she'd already earned years earlier.

"You're asking a lot," Lacey whispered, gripping her mug.

Regina's gaze was frank and unblinking, but not without warmth. "If we don't ask, we'll never receive."

THIRTY-EIGHT

On Monday, Lacey caught an early train to the city. The executive floor was mostly still dark when she arrived, the motion-activated lights flicking on overhead as she stepped from the elevator. The quiet hum of the empty office greeted her like a held breath. She stood there for a moment, staring at the rows of sleek white desks, and thought about turning around. About walking out of Vetra and leaving everything she'd entangled herself in behind. But the image of retracing her steps to the station, boarding a train back to Maplehurst, curdled into fear. She saw her bank account bleeding out with every bill and legal fee, no income to staunch the flow. She imagined the pointed questions at the custody hearing about her lack of employment. A shiver ran through her. No—until she'd secured custody of Elliott, there was no other option but to stay.

At her desk, she hung up her winter coat, then smoothed the front of her pearl-gray blouse. According to Reid's calendar he had a breakfast meeting in SoHo for the next couple of hours. Lacey glanced toward his dark office. She felt the sharp tug of her conscience as she considered her last conversation with Regina, remembering the pleading in Regina's voice. At least, she thought it was her conscience—these days Lacey's grasp on right and wrong felt slippery at best, and moral choices that had previously seemed clearly black and white now faded into a confusing gray. Lacey had always been loyal to a fault, but now her emotions battled within her as she tried to discern loyalty from indebtedness.

She bit her lip, then found herself stepping toward Reid's office as she cast a glance over her shoulder. Her heartbeat accelerated as she eased the door open and slipped inside.

Other than his monitor and keyboard, Reid's desk was bare. His laptop, predictably, was gone—he never let it out of his sight. Behind him, the shelves were just as stark: no framed photos, no knickknacks, no books. No sign that a person spent time here at all. She'd never noticed this before, and now it felt like a reflection of something deeper. Detached. Controlled. The absence of warmth.

She moved behind the desk and opened the top drawer. Empty, aside from a stack of yellow sticky notes, a pen from the St. Regis, and a sample vial of cologne. She uncapped it. The scent, musk and pine with a crisp edge, was unmistakably his. It made her look around as though he was in the room with her. Her stomach turning, she dropped it back into the drawer.

The second drawer held nothing. But pulling open the bottom drawer, she paused.

A laptop.

It wasn't his Vetra-issued silver one. This one was black. She lifted it out slowly, the surface smooth under her fingertips, her heart picking up speed. Could she really do this?

Sucking in her breath, she plugged it in and pressed the power button. Seconds later, the screen flickered on and a login prompt appeared.

The username field was already filled in: *r.mercer@chomerlabs.com.*

Before Lacey could second guess herself, she pulled out her phone and texted Regina.

> I have his laptop from Chomer but I need a password.

Regina replied immediately.

Call Nanette.

"Hello?" Nanette's voice was muffled when she answered, a crackle of voices in the background. "I'm on the train; it's hard to hear you."

"How long until you're at the office?" Lacey asked.

"Fifteen minutes, give or take."

"Come straight up to Reid's office. I found something."

After hanging up, Lacey quickly unplugged the laptop and slipped it back into the drawer. She eased the office door open and returned to her desk, heart still thudding.

She tried to focus on her email, but her attention was on the elevator. Each time it dinged Lacey looked over to see if Nanette would emerge.

Finally, she did, walking briskly across the floor, her eyes scanning. A few other people had arrived and were seated at their desks, but no one looked up.

Lacey stood and opened Reid's door.

Nanette was still in her winter coat, a sheen of sweat glinting on her forehead.

"I ran from the subway," she panted once they'd closed the door. "What's going on?"

Lacey opened the bottom drawer, pulled out the laptop, and set it on the desk. As she plugged it in and the login screen appeared, Nanette's eyes widened.

"It's from Chomer," she said.

"Looks like it," Lacey said. "But I need the password."

Nanette smirked. "No, you don't."

She dropped her bag onto Reid's chair and pulled out her own laptop and connected the two machines with a cable.

Frowning in concentration, her fingers flew across the keyboard. Code scrolled across her screen like something out of a spy movie. It was surreal watching Nanette, who Lacey usually saw bleary-eyed in the kitchen in the morning or wiping ketchup off Linden's face at dinner, drop into this version of herself.

After a few minutes, Nanette leaned back. "OK. I've created a virtual administrator account. That should get us access."

"Seriously? Just like that?"

Nanette clicked her mouse and the screen on Reid's laptop shifted. The desktop appeared. "Just like that, baby," she said, grinning.

Lacey leaned down to look. The desktop was sparse, populated by only one folder, labeled *Archive*.

Nanette stepped aside. "I should go," she said quietly. "In case he gets here."

Lacey nodded, eyes still on the screen. "Thank you," she whispered.

Nanette slipped out, the door clicking softly shut behind her.

Lacey sank into Reid's chair and hovered the cursor over the folder, then double-clicked. A new window opened: dozens of subfolders and files stretching down the screen.

She glanced at the clock in the corner of the screen. Reid's breakfast meeting would be wrapping up. He'd be getting into the town car that would ferry him back uptown. She had time, but not much.

She pulled out her phone and dialed.

"I did it," she said the moment Regina picked up. "Or Nanette did. I'm in. But I don't know what I'm looking for."

There was a sharp inhale on the other end. "OK. Um, I signed an NDA, so let's start there," Regina said. "See if you can find it."

Lacey typed *NDA* into the search bar. Nothing. She tried *non-disclosure agreement*. A few documents appeared. She opened them one by one, scanning for Regina's name. "All I'm seeing are agreements with other people," she said.

"Who?" Regina asked.

"Let's see... John Schmidt, Gustavo Toca, Priya Patel—"

"Priya?" Regina said sharply. "She was just an intern. Why would she have an NDA?"

Lacey opened the document, snapped a photo and texted it to Regina, then went back to reading.

The Recipient acknowledges that they have received a settlement payment from Chomer Labs, LLC (the "Company") in full and final settlement of any and all claims, known or unknown, relating to their prior contributions to the research and development activities conducted by the Company including but not limited to those contributions allegedly related to U.S. Patent No. 923837 (the "Patent"). The Company expressly denies any wrongdoing or liability and this settlement shall not be construed as an admission of liability or acknowledgment of inventorship by the Company.

"I don't know what any of this means," Lacey admitted.

There was long pause on Regina's end. Then she swore softly. "God dammit. It means he stole Priya's work, too. That's the patent for what became the VetraBand."

Lacey's mouth tightened. The VetraBand was currently the company's only product, the one thing keeping them afloat until the Vetra-Patch launched.

"I'll bet you anything Priya built the underlying tech," Regina said, her voice brittle. "And Reid gave her a few thousand dollars to shut up and disappear instead of putting her name on the patent."

Lacey checked the clock. "We're running out of time."

On a whim, she typed Regina's name into the search bar. A handful of results appeared, mostly saved emails. She opened the first one, which appeared to be an email Reid had forwarded to Marina with the note: *Proof I'm not the bad guy here.*

Lacey opened it:

Hey R—

Huge congrats on those beautiful babes! We're all rooting for the three of you. Don't worry about work while they're in the hospital, I've got everything covered. You've written another kickass algo and the patch is going to blow the industry wide open. I can't wait.

xx,

Reid

"This looks promising, right?" Lacey said, snapping a photo of the email and sending it to Regina.

There was a pause on the line as Regina reviewed it. "It's not enough," she said finally. Then, with a bitter edge, "Of course he sent this to Marina. His loyal sidekick. She's the one who drafted my NDA—never hesitated to do his dirty work so he could keep his hands clean." She paused and Lacey heard her give a shaky sigh. When she spoke, her voice was laced with emotion. "But Lacey, thank you for trying. Seriously."

"You're welcome," Lacey said softly. She was about to hang up when something clicked in her mind. Her thoughts cycled back to Reid's insistence that Marina scrub Sunil's research files. Reid was smart—too smart to leave anything incriminating on his own devices.

"Regina, wait," Lacey said, "I think you're looking in the wrong place."

THIRTY-NINE

Lacey shut down the laptop, slipped it and the charger back into the drawer, and nudged the desk chair back into place. She had just closed Reid's office door behind her when a voice cut through the hallway.

"Looking for Reid's AirPods again?"

Lacey turned. Marina was striding toward her, eyes narrowed behind her oversized dark-rimmed glasses.

Lacey straightened her posture and forced her expression into one of mild confusion. "Did you have a meeting with Reid? I didn't see anything on his calendar. He should be back any minute though. Maybe he'll have a minute for you."

Marina's mouth tightened. She tucked a flyaway strand into her bun with sharp precision. "Believe me, I know how to find Reid when I need him. He's on his way up and we're about to call Ketchum to offer him the head of research job."

"Oh, right," Lacey said, feigning knowledge. She lowered her voice and tilted her head just slightly. "I'm glad we're going with Ketchum. It's a critical time, and Reid needs to be the one making the decisions."

Marina blinked, then the suspicion on her face faded. "Exactly," she said firmly. "We just need to get the FDA filing locked down, and everything else will fall into place."

"Agreed," Lacey said. "By the way, did you get everything with Sunil buttoned up? Reid asked me to confirm there's no way to trace the original algorithm back to Chomer." She added a small, knowing smile. "You know how paranoid he can be."

A flicker of surprise crossed Marina's face, so fast it would have been easy to miss if Lacey hadn't been watching for it. Then her expression reset, cool and composed.

"Of course," she said.

Lacey knew it was a risk. Marina could mention her comment to Reid, question why Lacey was suddenly in the loop. It could unravel everything. She'd just have to hope it wouldn't.

Across the floor, the elevator dinged. A familiar whistle echoed, followed by footsteps.

"Is there a meeting I wasn't invited to?" Reid joked as he approached.

"Just waiting on you," Marina said, throwing a glance at Lacey.

"How was your meeting?" Lacey asked with a smile, trying to calm her pounding heart.

He groaned. "Whoever scheduled a business roundtable the week before Christmas should be on the naughty list." He knocked his knuckles lightly on Lacey's desk. "Speaking of, I'm hosting holiday drinks at my place Saturday night. You should both come— I make a mean eggnog."

Marina wrinkled her nose. "I'll skip the eggnog, but sure, I'll stop by."

"I'll check my calendar," Lacey said evasively, knowing full well she had plans with Simon and the kids for a movie night. Her throat tightened as she thought of it. Since he'd brought up moving in together a few days earlier, she'd deliberately avoided talking about it again.

"Great, let me know," Reid said, then turned to Marina. "Shall we?"

She hurried after him into his office, closing the door behind them.

Adrenaline buzzed quietly under Lacey's skin for the rest of the morning. It was dampened only by a call from the attorney handling her hit and run, informing her that their court date was set for January fifteenth—and that her license was suspended until then. Her stomach dropped at the news, but she also felt an unexpected sense of relief. At least there was an end point now. Whatever the fallout, it would soon be over and she could stop waiting for the other shoe to drop.

Her relief was doubled by the fact that she'd done what Regina had asked of her—and gotten away with it. However messy it had been, the slate was now wiped clean and she could move forward. Lacey itched to walk down to Nanette's floor, to fill her in on her revelation, but she kept her distance. Then, at the end of the day, as Lacey boarded the train home to Maplehurst, scanning the car for an open seat, she spotted her.

"Did you find anything?" Nanette asked quietly as Lacey slid into the seat next to her.

Lacey gave a small shake of her head. "Nothing big. But I think I know why." Her voice took on a quiet edge of excitement. "Reid's too careful. There's no paper trail, nothing that ties him directly to what he's done. But Marina..." She turned slightly. "She's been covering for him since Chomer. If the proof Regina needs exists, it's on *her* computer, not his. That's where Regina needs to look."

Back at the house, Regina was setting the table while Tavia pulled a tray of chicken nuggets from the oven.

"Sorry," she said with a tired smile. "I promise I'll cook something that's not dinosaur shaped next time it's my night. Been a hell of a week."

"I think they look delicious," Lacey said, her stomach growling.

Tavia laughed. "Well, help yourself. Just leave the stegosauruses for Linden."

"She's in a vegetarian phase," Nanette explained.

Lacey blinked. "But they're *chicken* nuggets."

"Stegosauruses were plant-eaters," Nanette said with a shrug. "Apparently that's airtight logic when you're five."

Lacey managed to wait until the kids were settled at the dinner table before pulling Regina aside.

"You should be looking at Marina, not Reid," she said, glancing over her shoulder back at the kids. "She's the one who'll have the paper trail, not him."

Regina regarded her, blinking slowly as she processed. "You could be right," she said, and Lacey felt a thrill. "Marina's loyalty to Reid has always been... excessive. She's like a pit bull crossed with a lemming. She was the one who drafted my NDA, and probably dozens of others." She pressed her lips together. "But I'm not sure if Reid trusts her—or anyone—enough to run everything through her."

Nanette sidled up. "How would we even get access to those files if she has them?" she asked.

Lacey's phone buzzed and she glanced down at the screen to see a message from Reid.

> Hey, just confirming whether you're coming tomorrow. Need a final count for catering.

She let out a sigh and set the phone back down. "Reid. He's throwing some kind of holiday party this weekend."

Regina's brows shot up. "Is Marina going?"

"I think so," Lacey said.

"That's perfect." A smile spread across her face, slow and sharp. "That's exactly where we want her if we're going to find out whether you're right about her doing all the dirty work."

Lacey frowned, trying to decipher what was happening in Regina's head. "But I can't go to the party," she clarified. "I realized

I already made plans with Simon and the kids—movie night. We've had it on the calendar for weeks."

Regina grinned. "Oh, you're not going to the party," she said. "But while Marina's at Reid's, we're going to her place."

Lacey stared at her for a moment before what Regina was suggesting sank in. Then panic surged through her.

"Oh, no." She shot both hands up and took a quick step back, bumping against the pantry doorframe. Her heart sank. She'd assumed that after what she'd done that morning, her part was finished. She was off the hook. Her voice rose, then dropped to a whisper as she glanced toward the table where the kids were focused on their nuggets. "I can't believe I even did what I did this morning, so I am definitely not breaking into someone's home. That's about ten steps too far," she hissed. She hugged her arms tight across her chest, her anxiety rising. "And in case you've forgotten, I already have a court date for my accident. I can't afford for anything else to go wrong. I have too much to lose."

Regina's mouth twitched with the hint of a smile. "Come on, you have to admit we make a pretty good Bonnie and Clyde."

Lacey groaned despite herself. "Wait, who's Bonnie and who's Clyde in this situation?"

"You're Bonnie, clearly," Regina said. "All you have to do is look pretty and be the lookout."

Lacey chewed her lip. "That's it?"

"Cross my heart." Regina turned to Tavia. "Can you get Marina Silva's home address?" she asked.

Tavia nodded. "Sure. I've got access to every Vetra employee file."

Regina turned back to Lacey and smiled. "Saturday night," she said. "It's a date."

FORTY

"Tell me again why you have to cancel plans we've had for over a month just to hang out with your boss?" Simon's tone was flat and clipped in a way Lacey had never heard before.

It was Thursday night, and they were still parked outside their favorite pizzeria on Maplehurst's town square. Guilt washed over Lacey. All week she'd told herself she'd never actually go through with helping Regina go to Marina's—it was too reckless, too outlandish. But as she and Simon boxed up their leftovers and stepped into the chill night air, she had finally admitted the truth to herself: She was always going to help Regina.

Now, inside the car, the windows were fogged with warmth from the heater, but between her and Simon the air had turned cold.

"I'm sorry, but it's not optional," Lacey said. She shifted in her seat, worried her face would give away the lie. She'd never had reason to lie to Simon before, and doing it now caused her stomach to churn.

"Parties are, by definition, optional," Simon pointed out.

She reached for his arm, but he shifted away.

"I promise, this one isn't," she said, thinking of Regina's firm gaze in the kitchen.

Simon stayed quiet.

"Are we having our first fight?" she tried, adding a lightness to her voice that didn't quite land.

More silence.

"I'm sorry," she said finally. "I didn't realize movie night meant that much to you." She placed a tentative hand on his thigh.

He scrubbed his hand over his face, then let it drop to rest on hers. "It's not about movie night," he said, his voice strained. "I'm just... I've been excited about us all spending more time together. You, me, the kids. Like a family."

He faltered on the last word, and her heart squeezed at the vulnerability in his voice. He turned toward her, and she saw the sadness in the lines around his eyes. "Ever since I brought up moving in together," he said, "you've felt... distant. Like I spooked you. It's been almost a week, and we haven't even talked about it again."

Lacey felt the familiar push and pull of longing within her. The pull to give herself fully over to the relationship with Simon, to his vision for their life together, to embrace the safety and security that could provide. But she also felt the pressure of that future bearing down on her, of the prospect of slotting into someone else's life, just as she'd done with Judd, sacrificing the chance to be fully in charge of her own life, calling all the shots and answering to no one.

"I'm sorry I've been so busy," she said, curling her fingers around his.

He brought her fingers to his lips. "It's not about you being busy," he said, his voice gruff. "It's about whether we want the same things."

She exhaled. "Elliott's had to live through a lot of change in the past few months," she said gently. "Moving him again right now... it feels like a lot. He's still adjusting to the idea of us being together. You and I only started doing things with all the kids a couple of months ago. I want our next chapter to feel stable, like it's something he can count on."

All of that was true. It was also, Lacey hoped, a way to push off any further conversation about moving in together until she could sort through her tangled feelings about Simon. More than once she'd nearly told Regina and the others that Simon had asked her, but the words always dried up on her tongue. She hadn't brought it up, partly because Regina, Nanette, and Tavia treated Simon with a polite, disinterested caution—like an out-of-town relative they'd been warned to be on their best behavior around—and partly because saying it out loud would force her to confront just how conflicted she felt about him.

In the car now, Simon squeezed her hand. "I get it," he said. "You want permanence. For both of you."

Lacey's shoulders relaxed. "Exactly. I feel like I've been on a roller coaster for the past year. I just want to get off and breathe for a while."

Simon let go of her hand and reached for the steering wheel, his expression softening.

"Sorry I got so bent out of shape over movie night," he said.

"It's OK," she said, smiling. "Believe me, I'd rather be on the couch with you, watching the kids argue over what we're going to watch, than stuck at some work party."

But as he leaned in to kiss her, her stomach did another flip—and not the good kind.

"This is a bad idea," Lacey said, leaning her head back against the passenger seat of Regina's car. A wave of nausea rolled through her. "I shouldn't be here. I shouldn't be involved in this."

"It's a little late for that," Regina observed. "Calm down; I promise it will be fine." She gave the steering wheel a small thump of excitement with one hand. "This is it," she said, her voice hushed with anticipation. "I can feel it. Reid's not going to know what hit him."

Lacey turned to look at her. "How long have you been planning this?" she asked. "I mean, did you move Max and Maddie across the country just because Reid was here?"

Regina's smile faltered and she flicked her gaze toward Lacey. "No," she said. "At least, not totally." She exhaled slowly. "But I've been working out how to do something about this for a while. Long before you showed up."

"Good to know I didn't stumble into some half-baked revenge plot," Lacey muttered, sinking back.

Regina looked over at her sharply, the smile falling from her lips. "This isn't revenge," she said. "It's justice."

Lacey let the word settle over her in silence.

Regina looked away, her eyes back on the road. "You can't imagine how devastating it was," she said after a beat, her voice low and raw. "I put everything into what we were building at Chomer Labs. It was my whole life. And Reid was"—her voice caught—"he was my best friend. We were going to change the world. Together."

Her hands tightened around the steering wheel.

"And then, when I was at my most vulnerable, still bleeding from giving birth, my babies fighting for their lives in the NICU, he cut me out. Just... gone. Out of the company. Out of his life." Her voice took on a hard, jagged quality, like a shard of glass. "He erased me."

It was the most emotion Lacey had ever heard from Regina. Pain radiated off her like heat from a sunburn.

"I'm sorry," Lacey said softly.

They emerged from the Holland Tunnel into Manhattan, headlights sweeping over the wet, gritty pavement as they turned onto Hudson Street, toward Marina's address.

"Don't be sorry," Regina said. "Just help me make sure *he* is."

Lacey's heart thudded and her stomach was in knots. She felt like she was clinging to a rope swing, suspended over a murky, fast-moving river. On one side of the arc lay fear, logic, and the urge to walk away before she did something that couldn't be undone. On the other, loyalty to Regina, and the tantalizing desire for the life-changing freedom this outrageous scheme could provide—if Regina got away with it.

"Ready?" Regina prompted.

Lacey nodded, and before her inner pendulum could swing again, she forced herself out of the car into the chilly night.

She followed Regina across the slick street through a light spatter of sleet, stopping just short of Marina's building.

"So I'll... wait here?" Lacey asked.

"You're the lookout. In case she comes back."

"The lookout," Lacey repeated, but Regina was already striding through the building's wide glass doors.

Lacey tugged her stocking hat low, gripping her phone in one hand. A car rolled past, wipers swiping in time to Lacey's pounding heart as the sleet thickened into snow.

The glass doors swung open, and a uniformed doorman emerged, lugging a bag of rock salt. Spotting her, he tipped his cap.

"Really stawting to come down, huh?" he said, the r in "starting" vanishing into his New York accent.

Lacey shivered. "I'm just waiting for a friend," she blurted, though he hadn't asked.

"Why don't you wait inside? Heat's on full blast," he said, gesturing toward the lobby.

She hesitated, which he mistook for uncertainty, turning on the chivalry full force.

"Come on now," he said, holding the door open. "I can't have you freezing to death on my watch."

Lacey let out a thin, high-pitched laugh as he ushered her inside. The lobby was gleaming black-and-gray marble, a sprawling Chihuly sculpture dripping glass tendrils from the ceiling. It smelled expensive, floral and clean, like the kind of place with a signature scent.

As promised, it was warm—stiflingly so—with two portable heaters blasting to counter the constant gust of cold from the doors. Sweat prickled at the base of Lacey's neck as her eyes swept the space.

She located Regina at the reception desk, where a second doorman stood, stiff and unsmiling behind his navy, gold-buttoned coat and hawkish nose. He looked displeased as he said something, and his hand reached for the phone. Regina raised her arms in protest and Lacey's stomach dropped. Oh God, they were about to be caught.

Lacey's pulse roared in her ears. The heat pressed in, thick and suffocating. Her vision tunneled, the edges going dark, until everything slipped into black.

When she came to, the sharp-nosed doorman was standing

over her, looking stricken. "Ma'am?" he said loudly, staring down at her. "Ma'am?"

Lacey struggled to sit up. "What happened?" she croaked.

"You fainted," he said, alarmed. "I'm going to call 911."

"No!" she said quickly, grabbing his arm. "Please, no. I'm fine, really."

Suddenly Regina was by her side, helping Lacey to a seated position. "Oh my God, are you OK? What happened?"

"I just... overheated," Lacey said, blinking to focus her vision as panic seized her. Now that she'd made a scene, they were definitely going to be caught.

But then Regina was hauling her to her feet.

"Should I call someone?" the doorman asked.

"No, no," Regina said quickly, slipping an arm around Lacey's back. "She's fine. It happens sometimes." She gave Lacey a concerned look. "Let's get you up to Marina's to lie down for a minute." From her pocket she pulled a key and brandished it for the doorman to see. "Found it," she said. "Sorry for the trouble."

The doorman looked between them, still uncertain. "All right," he said. "You take care," he added, glancing at Lacey.

Lacey gave a weak nod, letting Regina steer her toward the elevators.

As the doors slid shut, Regina turned to her, grinning. "Oh my God, that was perfect. Wait, did you actually pass out, or was that you causing a distraction?"

"A distraction?" Lacey rubbed the side of her head, which throbbed. She must have hit it when she went down.

"So I could get behind the desk and grab the key," Regina said, her cheeks flushed with triumph. "That guy definitely wasn't buying my story about being Marina's house guest."

"What? No, that was real," Lacey said, gripping the handrail for balance. She still felt woozy. Watching the numbers tick past above the elevator doors, she frowned. "Wait... where are we going?"

Regina gave her a quick, assessing look. "To Marina's, obviously."

Panic tightened Lacey's chest. "No! I'm supposed to be *waiting* for you. I'm the lookout."

"Not anymore," Regina said breezily. The doors opened with a chime, and she nudged Lacey out into the hallway. "Come on. Let's go."

FORTY-TWO

Lacey's heart hammered as Regina turned the key smoothly in the lock. She glanced behind her, then followed Regina into the spacious, open-concept apartment. Floor-to-ceiling windows framed a view of the inky Hudson River, the lights across the water blurred through the icy rain now falling harder against the glass.

Lacey's eyes scanned the living room: a sleek leather sofa with matching captain's chairs, a formal dining table topped with a sculptural candelabra, and a kitchen that gleamed with white marble countertops and stainless-steel appliances—everything pristine and high-end, like a staged luxury condo ad.

Regina gave a low whistle. "Marina's definitely leveled up since Chomer," she said. "Clearly loyalty pays well."

"I'm not supposed to be here," Lacey said, icy panic gripping her.

"Then help me find her laptop and we'll be able to get you out of here that much faster," Regina said, already heading down the hallway.

Lacey glanced at the door behind her, then gritted her teeth and hurried after Regina, who was poking her head into doors as she went. They needed to get this over with—and fast.

The first room she encountered was a spotless bathroom, and across the hall was a guest bedroom, which was clinically clean with not a single personal item in sight.

The third room—there were so many, Lacey couldn't fathom what one person needed with all this space—was an office. A sleek, dark-wood desk sat beneath a curved brass-and-glass lamp, its warm, moody glow pooling across the surface. She stepped inside, her eyes catching on a neat row of three tiny succulents lined up along the desk's edge. Reaching out, she pinched one of the leaves. Fake.

The rest of the desk was equally curated. A blank notepad, a pen perfectly parallel to it, and an empty docking station where a laptop might usually sit. As Lacey's heart rate began to slow, she yanked open the top drawer: another notepad, a tangle of expensive pens, and a package of gold-foil retinol eye patches. Maybe this was the secret to why Marina always looked so well-rested. Then again, it could also be that she was a single woman who lived alone in a luxury apartment. On impulse—and spite—Lacey slipped a pack of the patches into her pocket.

She turned from the desk, eyeing the rest of the space. A Peloton stood idle in one corner. The opposite wall was lined with bookshelves, most of them stacked with business titles and the occasional Portuguese spine. A side table held a tidy stack of *The Economist*, *Fortune*, and *Inc. Magazine*.

"In here!" Regina called.

Lacey crossed the hall and stepped into what looked to be the master bedroom. Regina was perched on the edge of the bed, Marina's work iPad in hand. She looked up, grinning.

Lacey glanced around the room, which had been done in muted tones of gray and beige, everything symmetrical and perfectly placed. On the nightstand sat a complicated-looking alarm clock and a small jewelry dish holding a single pair of diamond studs, the only accessory Lacey had ever seen Marina wear.

She wondered briefly what Marina was wearing to Reid's party that night. She'd only ever seen her in tailored black dresses or suits.

"I just hope we can get into this thing," Regina said, tapping the screen.

The screen flickered to life, asking for a password.

She flexed her fingers, then began to type.

The screen unlocked.

Lacey blinked. "Are you some kind of hacker? How did you do that?"

Regina's smile was at once modest and smug. "Marina's a creature of habit. Same password she used for everything at Chomer."

Lacey sank onto the bed beside Regina as she clicked through folders, the silence punctuated only by the soft flick of the trackpad and the low hum of the heating system.

"We should get out of here," she said, her dread returning.

"Oh my God," Regina exclaimed, her whole body stiffening.

Lacey leaned over her shoulder. On the screen, Marina's iMessages were open to an exchange with Reid from the night before.

REID, 11:27 PM

You up?

MARINA, 11:27 PM

can't do better than that?

REID, 11:28 PM

It's worked before.

REID, 11:30 PM

Hello? It was just a joke. Come over. You know you're already wet for me.

MARINA, 11:31 PM

Grabbing an Uber.

Regina doubled over slightly, clutching her stomach like she'd been punched. "He's *fucking* her," she said, voice sharp with disgust. "Of course he is."

Lacey stared at the screen, stunned. "Reid and Marina?"

Regina gave a short, bitter laugh. "Marina had a thing for him from day one. Everyone at Chomer knew it. Reid used to make fun of her behind her back—called her desperate and pathetic." Her mouth twisted in scorn. "But I guess he finally decided she wasn't too pathetic for a booty call at eleven-thirty on a weeknight." She reached for her phone and snapped a photo of the exchange.

"What are you doing?" Lacey asked.

Regina didn't look up. "Leverage," she said curtly. "You never know when it'll come in handy."

She clicked out of the message thread and went back to combing through Marina's inbox.

Lacey sat back and ran a hand through her hair. The image of Reid smiling at her from across the table in California the night they'd eaten oysters and shared a bottle of wine bubbled up. She thought of him leaning toward her in the hall of the hotel after, the space between them thick with suggestion, and how she'd stepped away at the last second. Had he been sleeping with Marina then, too?

Next to her, Regina inhaled sharply.

Lacey leaned back in, scanning the email chain Regina was scrolling through.

From: reidwellingtonmercer@gmail.com
To: marinasilva21@gmail.com
Subject: Our discussion
Moving this off the Chomer server to our personal emails, just in case. What are my options in terms of an NDA on what we discussed?

From: marinasilva21@gmail.com
To: reidwellingtonmercer@gmail.com
It's sticky. A request for child support would supersede an NDA in this case. Are you on the birth certificate?

From: reidwellingtonmercer@gmail.com
To: marinasilva21@gmail.com

No.

From: *marinasilva21@gmail.com*
To: *reidwellingtonmercer@gmail.com*
Will she want a paternity test?

From: *reidwellingtonmercer@gmail.com*
To: *marinasilva21@gmail.com*
Not sure. Can a settlement preclude her from requesting a test?

From: *marinasilva21@gmail.com*
To: *reidwellingtonmercer@gmail.com*
The court can still order one if she changes her mind, regardless of what she signs.

From: *reidwellingtonmercer@gmail.com*
To: *marinasilva21@gmail.com*
Fuck.

Lacey's thoughts surged like rapids as she read, words and phrases from the emails flashing to the surface, then disappearing again before she could fully form them into a coherent thought.

NDA. Birth certificate. Reid Wellington Mercer. Wellington— where had she heard that name before?

She shook her head and sat back, her brow creased in concentration as she tried to make sense of what she'd read. Beside her, Regina was already snapping photos of the screen, methodical, efficient.

"What does this mean?" Lacey asked.

But before Regina could respond, they both froze at the soft but unmistakable sound of the front door opening, then closing again.

Lacey's body went cold. Her heartbeat spiked, galloping in her chest.

Regina paled. She dropped the iPad onto the bed with a muted thud. Her eyes scanned the room, frantic, but Marina's minimalist aesthetic left them few options for hiding.

Lacey jerked her head toward a door at the far end of the bedroom. They moved in a quick, silent burst, finding themselves in a bathroom with blindingly white tile, a large, glass-walled shower, and nowhere to hide.

"Shit," Regina breathed in a strangled whisper.

They darted back into the bedroom and flattened themselves against the wall near the hallway. In the kitchen, Lacey could hear the soft hiss of running water, the clink of glass on countertop. She pulled in a breath, then looked to Regina, who had gone pale.

Lacey inched forward, peering into the empty hallway.

Holding her breath, she slipped into the hall, darting to the guest room just down the corridor, pulling Regina with her. Lacey flung open the closet door and they squeezed inside, folding into each other behind an ironing board.

Lacey's breath came in shallow sips and her shoulder pressed into Regina's as they crouched in the dark, barely concealed. If Marina opened the door, she would see them immediately.

From the living room, the TV clicked on. A laugh track blared, too loud at first, then a muted echo as the volume was adjusted.

"Why is she back already?" Lacey whispered. "It's barely nine."

"Maybe because it looked like Reid was going to fuck someone else tonight instead of her," Regina hissed.

The sound of footsteps silenced them. Lacey sucked in her breath as the footfalls passed the guest bedroom and faded.

They huddled in silence for another long minute. "Do you think she's going to bed?" Lacey whispered.

"Not a chance," Regina replied. "Marina's a night owl. She's probably up drafting NDAs, ruining people's lives." The sharp edge of her voice cut through the thick darkness.

Then something clicked deep in Lacey's mind, sudden and absolute.

"Max Wellington Cho," she whispered.

Regina stiffened beside her.

"Wellington," Lacey said slowly, her voice barely audible. "Max has the same middle name as Reid... Marina asked if he was on the birth certificate." Her hand flew to her mouth, stifling her gasp. "Oh my God," she whispered. "Is Reid Max and Maddie's father?"

FORTY-THREE

A thick silence descended over the closet where Regina and Lacey sat crouched in the corner. Then finally, Regina spoke.

"Yes," she said.

In the quiet, the word seemed to swell, ballooning into the space between them, pressing in, absorbing all the oxygen.

Lacey swallowed. "But... why?"

"Why what?" Regina's voice was flat.

"Why didn't you say anything?"

Regina slowly lowered herself from a crouch to the floor. As Lacey's eyes adjusted to the dark, she could just make out the shape of Regina folding in on herself, drawing her knees in and wrapping her arms tight around them.

"No one knew," she said, a slight swell of shame in her voice. "Other than Reid, obviously, who refused to even be on the birth certificate." Regina shifted, settling deeper into the corner.

"It was partly my fault," she admitted, her voice a low whisper. "I didn't tell him until after the twins were born. When they came early..." Her voice caught. "When it looked like they might not make it—I thought he deserved to know. To say goodbye, if he wanted to."

Lacey sank down beside her. "Were you... together?" she asked.

"Not really," Regina said. "Just once. There'd always been something between us—an energy—but we were careful. We knew what we had as partners was too rare to risk. It was like opening a safe deposit box—you need two keys. Alone, we were each capable. But together..." A quiet pride crept into her voice. "Together, we could make things happen." Her voice dipped again. "And then one night, we slipped. It only happened once. We agreed it was best to forget it."

Lacey hesitated. "But did you... love him?"

Regina gave a whisper of a laugh. "Of course. I've always loved Reid. But he's not built for it. And I knew that—or I should have, anyway."

Lacey shook her head, trying to piece it together. "But once you were pregnant, surely he figured it out. I mean, he can do math."

"You know Reid," Regina whispered. "So deep in the work, he barely knew what day it was, let alone counting back nine months."

Lacey could practically hear her eyeroll. "And when you *did* tell him?" she prompted.

"Let's just say he didn't take it well," Regina said. "We were on the brink of something big. Technology nearly finalized, acquisition offers starting to circle. He accused me of trying to blow it all up. Which made no sense, because I stood to gain just as much as he did from an acquisition, or so I thought. I mean, we had one offer for *sixty million* dollars." Her laugh was quiet and harsh. "I didn't know he was already making plans to cut me out. My news just complicated things. Gave him an excuse to speed it up. So, he erased me. From the files. From the patent. From the story."

Lacey frowned. "But if you want money, couldn't you go after him for child support? A DNA test—"

"I don't want his money," Regina snapped in a razor-sharp whisper. "I want *mine*. What I should have made from the

Chomer acquisition. That deal only happened because of my algorithm."

Before Lacey could respond, footsteps sounded in the hall. A moment later, the chime of an incoming text echoed through the apartment. Lacey held her breath, instinctively sucking in her stomach, as if shrinking could somehow make her invisible.

There was a soft *click* as the guest room door opened, then another chime, closer this time. Marina was in the room.

Lacey's heart thundered in her ears and her shirt clung to her, suddenly damp with sweat.

"Where the hell did I leave that..." Marina muttered, just outside the closet. A drawer opened, then closed. Then the footsteps receded down the hall.

Lacey's body sagged with relief, every muscle trembling. A sudden, urgent need to pee pulsed through her. Beside her, Regina stayed utterly still. Lacey focused on counting her breaths, slow and shallow.

They waited. Minutes crawled by, then hours. The glow of Regina's watch eventually read eleven p.m. Only then did they stir.

Noiselessly they crept from the closet and approached the door. Lacey pressed her ear to the wood. Silence. She peeked out. The hallway was dark. The door to Marina's bedroom was closed.

They locked eyes for a brief instant, then together they slipped from the guest room and scurried silently down the hall. The click of the front door unlocking sounded impossibly loud, and Lacey thought she might vomit, but she kept moving until they were through, out, and into the corridor.

Only once the elevator doors shut behind them did Lacey allow herself to breathe.

In the lobby, a different doorman sat behind the desk. They kept their heads down, gliding through the doors into a world transformed. Snow had replaced sleet, dusting the street and sidewalk in a soft white glow. They crossed to the parking garage quickly. Once inside the car, Lacey slammed the door shut and finally spoke.

"Get us the hell out of here."

Without a word, Regina put the car in reverse, the tires complaining against the concrete.

As they reached the street, Lacey stared across toward Marina's building, half-expecting her to burst through the revolving door, chasing after them. But all remained still, the snow drifting gently under the streetlights.

As Regina navigated back toward the Holland Tunnel, the heat in the car blasted to life. But it was several minutes before Lacey stopped shivering.

Only once they'd emerged on the New Jersey side and merged onto the interstate did she finally find her voice.

"Oh my God," she said. "I can't believe we actually did that." She glanced over at Regina, whose knuckles were white as she gripped the steering wheel.

Regina's shoulders relaxed slightly, but her face remained grim. "We sure did," she acknowledged. "And I still don't have what I need." In an uncharacteristic display of emotion, she pounded the steering wheel with one sharp, swift motion.

Lacey flinched.

"Sorry," Regina muttered, swiping at her eyes with the back of her hand.

Lacey stared at her glistening eyes. She'd never seen Regina even close to tears. She bit her lip. "So... what now?"

Regina's voice was calm and steady. "We keep going until I have what I need to get my share of that sixty million."

FORTY-FOUR

Monday morning Lacey awoke filled with gratitude that she didn't have to go into the office for ten whole days. Christmas was on Thursday, and with Elliott out of school, she'd taken the days leading up to it off. After that, the Vetra office would stay closed through the New Year. She didn't even expect to hear much from Reid—he was apparently heading off to ski in Japan before retreating to a luxury resort in Thailand. Lacey wondered if Marina was going with him.

She rolled onto her side and nestled closer to Elliott, who was still snoring softly beside her.

"Good morning," she whispered.

He gave a small grunt, like a little piglet, and rubbed his fist over his eyes, the same gesture he'd made as a baby. Her heart ached with tenderness.

Motherhood was so strange. One moment you were moving through life, thinking you understood love. Then you gave birth, and everything you thought you knew turned out to be a grayscale version of something that was actually bursting with color. What had once passed for love felt, in hindsight, like a black and white photocopy of the real thing. And as beautiful as it was, this kaleido-scopic, visceral love she felt for her son, it also terrified her.

Because now she knew what it meant to see the world in full color. And if anything ever happened to this small, warm being beside her, if the world ever reverted back to black and white now that she'd experienced color, she wasn't sure she'd survive it.

And yet, two nights ago, she'd risked everything—her job, her reputation, even her future with Elliott. She'd committed a crime, for God's sake. Breaking and entering. And for what? To help Regina settle an old score? Yes, the potential payout was huge—if Regina was right that Reid *would* pay—but there were no guarantees.

No guarantees.

The words flashed through Lacey's mind like a faulty neon sign, flickering in and out. Ever since those tense hours huddled in Marina's closet with Regina, the truth had settled in: Doing the right thing didn't guarantee the right outcome. She'd married Judd when she got pregnant, dropped out of college to raise Elliott, and finally left the marriage when it became clear it was no longer safe for her son. And still, despite everything, she stood to lose him. Elizabeth hadn't sugarcoated it—between the hit-and-run charge and her "unconventional" living arrangement, shared custody was now best-case scenario. Lacey was keenly aware that if anything else went wrong, Judd would get primary custody, and she'd be reduced to a weekend mom—if that.

Lacey could not let that happen.

She smoothed Elliott's hair as he slept. As grateful as she was to Regina for all she'd done for her, it was time to step off her merry-go-round and focus on what mattered: protecting her son, keeping him out of Judd's reach, no matter what that took.

She eased herself out of bed and into her robe and slippers. Downstairs, the smell of coffee met her before she reached the kitchen. Regina sat at the table, staring out the window at the snowy yard, her fingers threaded around a mug.

"Morning," Lacey said.

Regina jumped, then turned. "Sorry," she murmured. "Got lost in thought."

"Lots to think about," Lacey said lightly.

Since Saturday night, neither of them had spoken about what they'd done. The weekend had unfolded in a blur of snowball fights, last-minute Christmas shopping, and keeping the front walkway shoveled as flakes continued to fall steadily through Sunday. The storm had passed overnight, but now a light dusting drifted lazily from the sky again.

Regina gave a faint, weary smile, her eyes shifting back to the window.

Lacey poured herself a mug of coffee and slid into the seat kitty-corner from Regina. Outside, the sun hovered low behind a wall of slate-gray clouds. Lacey had the feeling that the whole world had suddenly paused, like a treadmill slowing, allowing her to step off. But where she was headed next, she wasn't sure.

She cleared her throat. "I'm sorry we didn't get what you needed at Marina's," she said.

Regina's hands tightened around her mug. "If I'd just had more time..." Her jaw tensed as she turned toward Lacey. Her eyes were glassy, pleading. "I need you to try again."

Lacey took a sip of coffee, buying herself a moment. She looked away from the desperation in Regina's face, then turned back with a slow shake of her head.

"I'm sorry," she said. "I can't. If Marina had found us..." She shuddered at the memory. "I can't risk it, not with the custody hearing coming up. I could lose everything. I could lose my son."

She expected Regina to protest, to cajole, or even to threaten. But the fight seemed to have drained from her, and her shoulders collapsed inward.

Seeing Regina hunched over like this in despair, her normally bright eyes dull with defeat, caused a pang of guilt in Lacey's chest.

"I'm sorry," she found herself saying. "I wish I could help you. Especially now that I know the truth about..." She paused, thinking of Max and Maddie, how she'd caught herself watching them more closely all weekend, looking for signs of Reid in their eyes or their smiles.

Regina gave a slow, listless nod. "The home visit is soon, right?" she asked, her eyes not meeting Lacey's.

"January second, right after the New Year," Lacey said. "Judd's is the same day."

Regina's eyes remained distant, her fingers loosening around the mug. She gave a weak smile that showed none of her usual spark. "We'll do our best for you," she said.

Lacey spent the day building a snow fort in the backyard with Elliott and the other kids, then baking several batches of her signature candy-cane shortbread cookies—most of which ended up looking like lopsided red-and-white squiggles thanks to Elliott's "help." Still, they were delicious.

After dinner and bedtime, she set a plate of them on the kitchen table and took her seat with the other women.

"No more cookies," Tavia groaned, patting her midsection. "My figure's starting to resemble Santa's."

"Oh, come on," Nanette said, already reaching for one. "'Tis the season."

Tavia sighed and reached for one, too. "So, what's the over-under this year on how early the kids get up Christmas morning? I'm betting they don't even make it to five a.m."

"They'd better," Regina muttered. "I told Max and Maddie Santa wouldn't be finished leaving presents until it was light outside."

Lacey's throat tightened. This year, Elliott would be waking up at Judd's on Christmas morning. The thought nearly flattened the air from her lungs. She planned to pick him up as early as she could, but knowing he wouldn't be here to come tearing into the living room with the other kids left a physical ache in her chest.

"Do Max and Maddie still believe in Santa?" she asked, directing the question at Regina. Ever since Lacey had told Regina she couldn't give her what she wanted at Vetra, there had been a new distance between them that Lacey longed to bridge.

Regina gave a tiny shrug. "I think Max does—he's not as much of a cynic as Maddie. She's been asking a *lot* of questions."

Lacey sighed. "Elliott, too. I'm pretty sure he knows, but he's still playing along for my sake."

"That's so sweet," Tavia said.

"Or it means he's going to need a lot of therapy later on," Nanette said, popping the last bite of her cookie into her mouth.

Lacey snorted. "Well, obviously." Her shoulders sagged. "When he was a toddler, when we were going through all the tantrums and potty training, people used to tell me, 'Oh, it goes so fast.' But I never believed them. Except now I'm starting to see it. Like, how many more years do I have before he just wants to be with his friends and wants nothing to do with me?"

"I know what you mean," Regina said. "Max swears he's never going to move out, that he's always going to live with me." Her eyes went soft. "But one day he'll wake up and won't feel that way, and that kills me."

As much as she didn't want it to, Lacey's mind drifted to Reid. And Tavia's ex, who wasn't in the picture, and Nanette's, who hovered barely on the outskirts of it. How did these men exist knowing their children were out in the world without them—without an ounce of curiosity about their lives, or concern for their health and happiness? There were good men out there, of course, like Simon—Lacey felt a pang of guilt as she thought of him—but by and large around her it was the women who poured themselves into their kids every single day, funneling all their love and energy into making them safe, strong, and whole.

"I can't imagine Linden getting older and not knowing what she's doing every second of the day," Nanette said, looking stricken.

"Same," Tavia agreed. "But it'll happen eventually. And we just have to hope they're ready for the world. That we've done enough."

Lacey looked around the table, her heart swelling with a fierce, protective love she once thought she could only feel for family. "Our kids wake up every day feeling loved," she said. "That's so much more than enough."

FORTY-FIVE

Lacey stood by the front door, zipping up her heavy coat. "Elliott, it's time to go!" she called. "Elliott!"

A door slammed upstairs.

She pinched the bridge of her nose and sighed, then headed up the stairs. "Elliott, Daddy needs you there by five, so we need to leave *now*."

Muffled laughter floated from behind Max and Maddie's door. She walked over and knocked.

"Max?" she called. "Maddie? Is Elliott in there?"

A pause. Some low whispers. Then Max's voice, high and hesitant: "No."

Lacey gritted her teeth. "Max, honey, I'm opening the door."

"No!" shrieked a giggling Maddie, and a burst of footfalls thundered across the room as Lacey pushed the door open just in time to see the red blur of Elliott's shirt disappear beneath the bunk bed.

She crossed the room and crouched. "Elliott, honey, we need to go," she said, trying to keep her voice even. But the idea of dropping him off at Judd's for Christmas Eve, of not having him shake her awake at the crack of dawn Christmas morning and then barrel downstairs to the tree before she even had her eyes open, made her heart feel like someone had put it through a paper shredder.

"I don't want to," came Elliott's voice from under the bed, small and quavering.

Lacey sat back and looked over at Max and Maddie, who were perched in their matching bean bag chairs with exaggerated innocence.

"Guys, can I talk to Elliott alone for a minute?" she asked.

Both twins nodded quickly, looking eager to escape the situation.

Once they were gone, Lacey leaned down. "Would it be OK if you came out, just to talk for a minute?"

Elliott scrunched his face up, but scooted toward her. They sat together on the Pokémon rug. Lacey wrapped her arm around him, and he curled into her, burying his face in her side.

"I know this is hard," she whispered, pressing a kiss to his hair. "Going back and forth. Especially on Christmas."

Elliott looked up at her, tears staining his pale cheeks. "I just want to be with you," he said, his voice cracking. "I don't like Daddy's house." He glanced down at the rug, shame coloring his face. Lacey felt a surge of sympathy for the confusing emotions he must be carrying, and a wave of anger that he had to carry them at all. All because, at least for now, the court still believed that having two parents—even if one treated you like a problem to be fixed— was better than having only one parent who loved you wholly, unconditionally, and would move heaven and earth for you.

"It's OK not to like it," Lacey said. "You can still love Daddy and not always like being with him."

"I'm always in trouble when I'm there," Elliott whispered. "Even when I try really, really, *really* hard not to be." He looked up at her, eyes wide with frustration. "Why can't I just stay here with you and Max and Maddie?"

She pulled him closer, her heart aching. "I'll come get you first thing in the morning, and then we'll have Christmas here," she said. "You'll be with us all day. We'll open presents, have pancakes—"

"And have hot chocolate and watch movies and keep building our snow fort?" Elliott interrupted, his face brightening.

"All of the above," Lacey promised, tracing her thumb over his cheek, brushing away a tear. "And tonight, if you start missing me, just think about how great tomorrow's going to be, and how fast it'll get here. Think you can do that?"

Elliott's smile faltered, but he straightened his narrow shoulders. "OK," he said.

"And I put your phone in your backpack," she reminded him, "if you need to talk."

Lacey's license was still suspended as she awaited her court date in January, so Nanette drove them to Judd's to drop off Elliott. He clung to her hand the entire walk up the front path. The houses on the block sparkled with twinkling lights, yards glowing with inflatable Santas, prancing reindeer, and glowing candy canes. But Judd's house was nearly bare, save for a single, limp strand of multicolored lights tossed haphazardly over the front bush, half the bulbs dead.

She'd always been the one in charge of decorating for the holidays, but still, Judd could have made more of an effort, for Elliott's sake.

She thought of the mommune: how the kids had strung lights around every inch of the porch railing, the Christmas tree so big it had taken all four women plus Max, Elliott, and Maddie to wrestle it up the front steps and into the living room. The warm, cinnamon-sweet air in the kitchen thanks to Lacey's "Twelve Days of Christmas Cookies" baking marathon.

That was the home Elliott deserved. Not this cold, dim shell of a house where his father happened to live.

They reached the door and Lacey pulled Elliott close as she rang the bell. When Judd opened it, Elliott froze, his arms locking around her waist.

"Merry Christmas," Lacey said, forcing a smile onto her face.

Judd craned his neck out to the street, eyeing the car. "You didn't drive here, did you?" he asked. "I thought your license was suspended."

Lacey ignored him, biting back a sharp retort, but only because they were in front of Elliott. She knelt in front of him. "I'll see you tomorrow, buddy. Bright and early," she whispered, hugging him tight. She wiped her cheek against his coat so he wouldn't see her tears.

On the drive home she and Nanette were quiet. Lacey kept her head turned toward the window, watching glowing houses with Christmas trees framed in their windows glide past, streetlamps wrapped in garlands, wreaths on every door. Holiday cheer draped the town like a warm blanket, and Lacey tried to focus on it until she couldn't hold back any longer. She sobbed in big, open, heaving cries, her breath fogging the window. She only paused to wipe her nose with the back of her mittened hand. Nanette laid a comforting hand on her shoulder.

By the time they pulled up in front of the mommune, her tears had run dry, and her gasping cries had faded into ragged, shallow breathing.

Nanette offered her a sad smile. "Tomorrow morning will be here before you know it," she said softly.

Lacey took a moment to scrub the mascara from her cheeks, then they headed toward the house, pausing to straighten the inflatable abominable snowman that was listing sideways in the front yard.

Inside, "Santa Claus Is Coming to Town" blared from the living room. Maddie darted past her, wielding a hot pink bow and arrow, nearly knocking her off her feet.

"I'm coming for you!" she yelled, tearing down the hallway.

Regina appeared a moment later, shaking her head. "I made the mistake of letting them open one gift," she said. "Of course they picked the Nerf bows and arrows."

Lacey tried to smile.

Regina's face creased. She hesitated for a moment, then

reached for Lacey's hand. "I'm sorry," she said softly. "It sucks. Come on. You need a Christmas cocktail and a Jimmy Stewart marathon."

Tavia had outdone herself, roasting both a turkey and a honey-baked ham. Regina contributed garlic-sautéed green beans, and Nanette's sweet potato casserole had a crackly brown sugar topping that shimmered under the lights. Dessert was an avalanche of Christmas cookies, and the key lime pie Lacey had picked up from the local bakery.

That pie was tradition. She and Judd had started it during their first year of marriage, after a trip to Key West had made them fall in love with all things key lime. Elliott loved it now, too, and as Lacey served it, a pang rose in her chest. She wondered if Judd had remembered. If he'd picked up a pie for just the two of them. Just in case, she sliced a piece and set it aside for Elliott for tomorrow.

Later, after the kids were bundled off to bed in a flurry of good-night kisses and firm reminders that Santa wouldn't come unless they went to sleep, Lacey curled into the living room couch, flushed and sleepy from the three glasses of wine she'd sipped through dinner. She felt heavy—in a good way. Full not just from food, but from something deeper. A quiet, anchoring sense of contentment. The ache of Elliott's absence still sat in her chest, sharp and real, but it was dulled now by the warmth around her, by the gratitude she felt for having landed here, in this place, with these people.

She glanced around the room. Regina, Tavia, and Nanette lounged in armchairs and on the floor, legs draped over furniture, blankets pulled across laps. They chatted in low voices, laughing softly, gesturing with half-filled wine glasses. Lacey let herself sink into the warm feeling of belonging. She'd made plenty of mistakes in her life, and would probably make plenty more, but at least she had this.

She had almost dozed off on the couch when her phone sounded. Not its usual ring, but the tone she'd set especially for

Elliott's phone. Setting her wine glass heavily on the end table, she snatched up her phone.

"Sweetheart? Is everything OK?" she said breathlessly.

On the other end of the line there was only the sound of Elliott sobbing.

FORTY-SIX

"Elliott, what's wrong?" Lacey's chest tightened, like someone had cinched a rubber band around her ribs. "Are you hurt?"

"N-no," he managed, gulping for air. "N-not hurt."

"Are you scared?" The words nearly caught in her throat.

Across the living room, Nanette, Tavia, and Regina froze mid-gesture, like the three wise men in a twisted nativity scene, their faces etched with alarm.

"Y-yes," Elliott whispered.

Lacey was already on her feet, the sudden motion making her head spin from the wine. "Where are you?"

"In the upstairs bathroom," came the muffled reply.

"What did Daddy do?" she asked, gripping the back of the couch to steady herself.

"He yelled at me," Elliott said, his voice thick with tears. "I was bad in church. I couldn't pay attention; it was too boring. And Daddy got so mad. As soon as we got home, he started yelling. I tried to go to my room, but he said, 'Don't you walk away from me while I'm talking to you,' and he just kept yelling and—and—he really s-scared me."

The sobs returned in a wave.

"Then it seemed like he got tired of yelling and let me go upstairs."

Lacey flinched at the phrase—*Don't you walk away from me*—one of Judd's go-to commands. She paced in place, still gripping the back of the couch.

"Where is Daddy now?" she asked, her brain racing to assess the situation. Judd had a temper, but would he *hurt* Elliott?

"Downstairs." Elliott sniffled.

"Did he follow you up?"

"No." A pause. "Mommy, can you come get me?"

Lacey's stomach dropped.

"I'll drive you if you need to go," Regina said, reading Lacey's thoughts.

Lacey's heart clenched. Ever since she'd told Regina she couldn't risk her job at Vetra by digging further, there had been a quiet strain between them. But now, when it mattered most, Regina didn't hesitate.

"Yes, sweetheart," she said into the phone, her voice breaking. "I'll be right there."

Minutes later, she and Regina were speeding through the frozen streets as silence pressed heavy between them. Lacey clutched the door handle, her pulse hammering in her ears. By the time they pulled up to Judd's house, she was out of the car before it stopped, sprinting up the front walk and pounding on the door. Judd opened it a minute later, his confusion hardening instantly into a scowl. "What the hell are you doing here?" he demanded.

Behind him, Elliott appeared in the reindeer pajamas she'd packed, his small face pale.

"Elliott!" she cried, reaching for him, but Judd stepped into her path.

"It's *my* night with him," he snarled.

"He called me," she pleaded, trying to push past him. Judd shoved her back and Elliott's eyes went wide, horrified. "He was afraid," Lacey gasped, tears streaming hot down her cheeks.

"Hey!" Regina's voice cracked through the cold night air like a whip as she strode up the walk. "Don't touch her!"

Judd swung toward her. "Who the fuck are you?" He spread his arms wide, barricading the doorway.

"Elliott, are you OK?" Lacey cried, straining on tiptoe to see around Judd.

"Get back!" Judd roared, his eyes wild. Fear sliced through Lacey. He jabbed a finger at Regina. "I don't know who you are. And you"—he stabbed the air toward Lacey—"are not supposed to be here."

"Mommy..." Elliott's voice came small and trembling from behind him.

Lacey stumbled backward down the front steps, panting and swiping at her tears. "He was afraid you were going to hurt him," she said hoarsely. "He called me. He asked me to come."

"This has gone too far. I'm calling the police," Judd snapped, slamming the door.

"Mommy!" Elliott's voice shrieked from inside, high and panicked. "I want Mommy!"

Lacey surged forward and Regina caught her arm and pulled her back, already reaching for her phone.

"Yes," she said as the call connected. "I want to report a possible case of child abuse."

Lacey and Regina stood shivering on the sidewalk for what felt like an eternity before a sheriff's SUV finally rolled up, blue and red lights flashing across the snowbanks.

Two officers climbed out. The taller one, with sparse, prickly eyebrows and razor burn along his jaw, looked unhappy to be leaving the warmth of the car.

"We've had a couple of reports of a domestic disturbance at this address?" he said, as though it was a question.

"Yes," Lacey breathed, relief rushing through her. She pointed toward the house. "My son is inside with my husband—ex-husband. He called me begging me to come get him. I'm afraid his father might hurt him."

"Do you live here, ma'am?" the officer asked.

"No, we're separated."

The second officer stepped forward. He was shorter and stockier, with a shearling-flap hat pulled low over his ears and a nose red from the cold. "Who has custody?" he asked.

"We share it," Lacey said.

"But who has custody *tonight*?" he pressed.

Her throat tightened. "He does," she admitted.

The officers exchanged a glance.

Regina stepped forward. "Officers, with all due respect, there's a very scared little boy in there right now, and—"

"Who are you?" the stocky one cut in.

Regina lifted her chin. "I'm her friend." She gestured toward Lacey.

The taller officer nodded. "Give us a minute."

Lacey and Regina huddled together as the two men strode up the walk, knocked, and disappeared inside.

Lacey and Regina huddled together as they waited. By the time the door opened again, Lacey's fingers had gone numb in her pockets.

"Is my son—Elliott—OK?" she breathed, stepping toward them.

The shorter officer held up his hands as though to ward her off.

"Everything appears fine, ma'am," the taller officer said. "Your husband says there was just some misbehavior, some tears. Normal parenting stuff. Nothing concerning."

"No." Lacey shook her head furiously. "Elliott was terrified when he called. You don't understand." She tried to move forward, but the shorter officer stepped in front of her, hand dropping to hover near his taser.

"Ma'am." His tone was sharp. "Given the custody arrangement your husband relayed to us, I'm going to have to ask you to leave."

Lacey's jaw dropped. "You can't be serious—" She surged forward again, and Regina dragged her back. From the corner of her eye, she caught sight of Judd at the window, arms crossed, watching.

"Elliott!" she yelled, desperation breaking her voice. "Elliott!"

A porch light blinked on next door. Next to Lacey, the officers tensed.

"Not here," Regina hissed in her ear, hauling her toward the car. "Not like this."

Regina shoved Lacey inside the car and slammed it shut, the child locks on the doors preventing her from opening it.

"Elliott!" she sobbed, pounding on the window. "Let me out!" she demanded as Regina climbed into the driver's seat and started the engine.

Regina shook her head. "I'm trying to keep you from being arrested. Let's get out of here and call your lawyer."

As the SUV pulled away, Lacey twisted in her seat, craning her neck for one last look. Judd stood in the window, his dark silhouette framed against the warm light, still watching her.

FORTY-SEVEN

The next morning, Lacey was out the door in an Uber before any of the kids at the mommune had stirred, having hardly slept at all, the image of Elliott's tearful face and reindeer pajamas inked onto her eyelids when she closed them. The sky was still dark as she rode through the frozen streets, still in her pajamas under her long, puffy coat and boots.

Judd's house glowed with light when she pulled up, and she asked the driver to wait. She stepped out and knocked. No answer. She knocked again, louder.

Eventually, the door creaked open. Judd stood there, hair sticking up in all directions, his faded flannel robe cinched loosely at the waist, a hole at one elbow. His eyes narrowed.

"What are you doing here?" he muttered, voice rough with sleep. "It's six a.m."

"Where's Elliott?" Lacey demanded. She leaned slightly to peer around him into the house.

"Mommy!" Elliott barreled into view and ducked past Judd to throw his arms around her.

"You're too early. We just started opening presents," Judd said, crossing his arms.

Elliott tugged at her arm. "Brrr. Come in, Mommy. Let's go do presents!"

Judd nudged Elliott back into the house and stepped out onto the stoop. "I'll be right back, buddy," he called, shutting the door behind him. Then he faced Lacey, his eyes cold. "I'm filing a restraining order," he said.

Cold surged down Lacey's spine. "What?"

"You showed up to harass us last night; you got Elliott a phone without my permission." Judd ticked items off on his fingers as he spoke. He glared. "You're out of line."

The door burst open, and Elliott tumbled out again. "Come on, it's time for presents!" he said, tugging on both of their arms.

Lacey tried to slow her panicky breath, glancing from Judd to Elliott. Last night she'd placed a frantic call to Elizabeth, but she'd yet to hear back from her.

"Why don't I wait in the car while you finish?" she said brightly to Elliott. "Then it will be nice and warm for you when you come out."

Judd's mouth tightened, his gaze drifting toward the waiting Uber. "Go home. I'll text you when we're ready."

"I'll wait," Lacey said, her voice firm. She kissed Elliott on the cheek. "I'll be right out here."

Back in the car, the driver was happy to wait for a hefty extra fee. Since she was paying through the nose, Lacey asked him to crank the heat and turn the radio to a classical station playing Christmas choral music. The warmth and quiet wrapped around her like a blanket and she felt herself beginning to doze.

A sudden rattle at the door handle jolted her awake.

She blinked as Elliott yanked open the back door and climbed in next to her, his jacket slung loosely over one arm. Judd stood behind him in his robe, arms crossed.

"He was apparently ready to go," he said flatly.

Lacey glanced at the dashboard clock. Only twenty minutes had passed.

"Merry Christmas, Daddy!" Elliott chirped, buckling himself in.

As Judd shut the door, Lacey motioned to the driver to pull away, and she didn't look back. In the backseat, she clutched Elliott's hand and tried to choke back her tears as she pulled him close. Looking him over, he appeared unscathed, and she breathed a short-lived sigh of relief.

Back at the mommune, the living room had erupted into full-blown Christmas chaos. Maddie was ripping open a gift while Grace flung crumpled wrapping paper into the air like confetti, with Tavia trying to catch it and stuff it into the recycling bag. Linden had stuck oversized bows to both cheeks, and Maddie spun her in circles until she collapsed in a heap, giggling like a tipsy sorority girl.

"Yay, you're back!" Max cried, looking up from his gifts.

Elliott had kicked off his boots and coat and was already at the gift pile before Lacey had even closed the front door. She drew in a shaky breath and followed him into the living room.

Tavia, Nanette, and Regina closed in on her almost immediately, forming a protective circle. Concern flickered across all three faces.

"Is he OK?" Tavia murmured, looking toward Elliott.

"I think so," Lacey managed. Her voice trembled, but she kept it low as she quickly filled them in, fighting back tears.

"A *restraining* order?" Nanette cried.

"Shh!" Tavia hissed, darting a glance at the kids, who had abandoned their presents and were now shrieking with laughter as they balled up discarded wrapping paper for a "snowball fight."

Regina's eyes burned. "This has gone too far. You can't let him get away with this. You have to fight back."

Lacey shivered as the thought pressed in, hard and undeniable: Maybe Regina was right.

After the morning whirlwind of presents and chocolate chip pancakes, Lacey and Elliott headed to Simon's house for lunch and more gifts. He'd cooked a full spread—bubbly lasagna, garlic bread, and a towering chocolate cake for dessert. It was a welcome distraction from the events of the past twenty-four hours.

"I should've worn stretchier pants," Lacey groaned as they finished eating.

Simon laughed, slipping his arm around her waist. "I'm so glad you're here," he murmured, pressing a kiss just behind her ear.

Lacey glanced at the kids, unsure if they'd noticed. They all knew she and Simon were dating, but they'd kept things low-key in front of them in terms of physical affection. But all eyes were on the cake.

After lunch came more gifts. Simon looked on, visibly excited, as Lacey opened hers: a pair of expensive-looking binoculars in a leather case.

"I got myself a pair, too," he said, bouncing slightly in his seat with excitement. "I thought we could take them over to the nature conservancy in the spring. I read that New Jersey is considered an excellent state for bird watching because of its location on the Atlantic Flyway and its diverse habitats."

Lacey forced a smile. "Fun," she said. She felt a pang of guilt, something that was happening more regularly when she was with Simon. He was clearly planning a future with her, and she couldn't stop thinking that he deserved someone equally excited about doing the same with him—and about bird watching. She worried she might be misleading him. It wasn't that she didn't care about him; she just wasn't sure she cared *enough* to merit his devotion.

Later, with the kids occupied by a movie, they slipped into the kitchen while Simon made coffee.

"I need to tell you something," Lacey said, her voice low.

Simon's face darkened as she recounted Elliott's panicked phone call, the police, and then Judd's threat that morning.

"Oh, Lacey," Simon said, pulling her into his chest. "I'm so sorry."

A chill passed through Lacey despite the warmth of Simon's body against hers. "I can't let Judd get custody," she said, stepping back from the embrace.

"Have you talked to Elizabeth?" Simon asked. He moved to pour her a cup of coffee with the perfect splash of milk, just how she liked it. She felt her shoulder relax. She could always count on Simon to be a good listener.

"I've left a bunch of messages," Lacey said. Her shoulders sagged. "But last time we talked she said the judge would probably stick to the fifty-fifty custody arrangement unless something major happens." Her voice turned grim. "Like me having a restraining order filed against me."

Simon frowned. "There has to be something she can do."

"I hope so," Lacey said, but hope was the last thing she felt.

That night, after they returned home and Elliott was downstairs shooting Nerf arrows with Max, Maddie, and Linden, Lacey texted Elizabeth.

> I really need to talk. It's urgent.

Elizabeth called within seconds. "You're aware it's Christmas?" she said by way of greeting.

"Sorry," Lacey said. "But it's important."

"Talk to me."

Lacey relayed everything. The call. Elliott hiding in the bathroom. The police. When she got to the part about Judd threatening her with a restraining order, Elizabeth sucked in a breath.

"Let me get this straight," she said. "The police had to escort you off the premises?"

"Well, sort of," Lacey admitted. "But I needed to make sure Elliott was all right—"

"Was there any physical harm to him?" Elizabeth interrupted.

"No," Lacey said, "but Judd scared him. And—"

"I understand," Elizabeth said. "But without documentation of harm I don't have much to work with. Especially when you're the one showing up outside of the custody agreement."

"Elliott called me and asked me to come get him!" Lacey said, her voice rising. "And he doesn't *want* to be there. That should count for something."

"It should," Elizabeth agreed. "But at his age, the court isn't going to let him choose. The judge will prioritize which parent can offer a more stable environment. And on paper, Judd's a home-owner with a high income and a long-term job. You live with room-mates. You have a traffic trial pending. Your income's good, but nowhere close to his."

Lacey felt her jaw clench. "So what am I paying you for if this is already decided?"

"To make sure Judd doesn't get *full* custody," Elizabeth said, cool and direct. "Which, frankly, is still a real possibility, especially after what you've told me about last night. I told you that from the start. Realistically, joint custody is the best outcome you can expect. And if Judd does file a restraining order, even that starts to look like a long shot."

"That's not good enough," Lacey said, her desperation rising into her throat.

"I understand," Elizabeth said. "But it's better to go into this with clear expectations than false hope."

Lacey hung up, feeling limp and wrung out. Why was she fighting so hard, spending so much money on legal fees, just to end up in a situation where Judd would still have control over Elliott's life?

She dropped the phone onto the bed and buried her head in her hands as despair rushed over her like a rising tide.

FORTY-EIGHT

Lacey crept downstairs before sunrise. After the call with Elizabeth, she'd barely slept—tossing and turning until she'd finally crawled into Elliott's bed to avoid waking him. All night, she'd imagined escape plans: fake passports, fleeing to some far-off island, learning to bartend in a tourist town while Elliott played barefoot in the sand.

Now, though, with morning seeping in, she could see the absurdity of her idea.

She padded into the hallway, surprised to smell fresh coffee. The kitchen light was already on.

"Hey," she said, stepping in.

Regina sat at the table, wrapped in a white waffle-knit robe, laptop open in front of her.

"You're up early," Lacey added. She shifted on her feet, aware of the faint thread of tension still stretching between them.

Regina rubbed her forehead. "Too much excitement yesterday, I guess," she said with a tired smile.

Lacey nodded toward the laptop as she reached for a mug. "Working?"

"Always," Regina murmured, lifting her own cup. "How's Elliot?" she asked after a beat.

"Better now that he's back here," Lacey said, curling her fingers around the mug's warmth. "But he already said he doesn't want to go back to Judd's." She pressed the heated ceramic to her cheeks, as if bracing herself. "I think I've been too optimistic about the custody case."

Regina looked up. "What do you mean?"

Lacey exhaled, slumping further in her chair. "Elizabeth's told me from day one that I probably wouldn't get full custody, but I kept hoping we'd find a way. But now, if Judd files a restraining order, I'm terrified I won't see him at all." Her voice cracked. "And Judd—"

She broke off, wiping a tear that had slid silently down her cheek.

"No." Regina snapped her laptop shut with a loud thwack. "You can't let that happen."

"But Judd has the house. The job. On paper, he looks—"

"Fuck how he looks."

"But the judge—"

"Stop." Regina's voice was sharp.

Lacey blinked, startled.

Regina's eyes blazed with exasperation. "Seriously, how are you still playing by the rules? Haven't you realized yet? The game is rigged."

The heat rose in Lacey's face. "Oh, so your answer is to sneak around, break into apartments, all to support some half-baked revenge scheme?" Her tone was defensive, and heat built in her chest, seeking release. "Pressuring other people into going along with your schemes because the rules don't apply to you? You used me, Regina. You lied to me. The only reason you wanted me here was so I could get you close to Reid."

Regina didn't flinch. "That's true," she said. "But I also helped you."

"You helped me because it helped *you*," Lacey said.

Regina leaned forward. "If the game is rigged, Lacey, you either keep losing, or you change the rules. I've been trying to show you that, but you've been too busy wallowing in self-pity to notice." She stood, pushing her chair back. "You're not helpless, Lacey. You never were. So stop acting like it."

They stared at each other, the air charged.

And then, as if someone had pulled the plug on her anger, Lacey deflated. The fight drained from her body and tears spilled freely down her cheeks.

"I'm scared," she whispered. "I can't lose him."

Regina's posture softened. "I know." She took a small step back toward the table, her narrowed eyes smoothing into a look of concern.

Lacey wiped at her face, but the tears kept coming. "I'm doing everything right. And it's still not enough."

"Because the system isn't made for people like us to win," Regina said quietly. "No one's going to hand you anything. You have to take it."

This wasn't the first time Regina had said something like this, but this time it landed differently. Lacey shook her head. "But how? I can't run away with him; that's not fair to Elliott. And how would I support us?"

Regina removed her hand and tightened the belt on her robe, as if considering the idea. "I agree. That won't work." She paused. "But what if something happened to Judd?"

Lacey's eyes flew wide.

Regina raised a hand. "Not like *that*. Jesus. I mean... what if something happened that made him look unfit?"

"Well, that would certainly solve a lot of my problems." Lacey tried to make her voice light, to suggest this was all a game to her.

But Regina's gaze was serious and unblinking. "Yes," she said. "It certainly would."

FORTY-NINE

Lacey descended the stairs and paused in the doorway to the living room. Tavia, Regina, and Nanette turned to her, while the kids remained glued to the screen, immersed in a New Year's Eve *Minions* marathon.

"Wow," Tavia said, sitting up straighter. "Honey, you look *stunning*."

Nanette gave a low whistle.

"Is it too much?" Lacey tugged at the neckline of her forest green silk dress. When she'd picked it up earlier that week from a boutique on Maplehurst's main square, telling herself she deserved something beautiful, it had struck her as just the right balance of flirty and elegant. Billowy sleeves, a plunging neckline, and soft ruffles that skimmed down to the floor. She'd styled her hair in loose waves, half pinned up, the rest cascading to her shoulders. Her makeup was simple, save for the berry lipstick Nanette had lent her for her first date with Simon—now her signature shade.

"Definitely not too much," Regina said, smiling. "I mean, he *is* taking you to Le Bernardin."

Lacey smiled at her, grateful that the tension between them seemed to be dissipating. "I don't know why we couldn't just stay in," she groaned. "I hate going out on New Year's Eve. Everything's crowded, traffic into the city will be a nightmare..."

Nanette waved a hand. "Well, feel free to cancel and join us for pizza and the last sad crumbs of the Christmas cookies."

"I'd kill to go to Le Bernardin," Tavia sighed. "Especially on someone else's dime."

A knock sounded at the door. Lacey opened it to find Simon in a long wool coat, cheeks pink from the cold. His breath caught as his eyes traveled over her.

"Wow," he said, with a quiet, stunned laugh. "I'm... speechless."

She flushed. "You didn't have to come to the door."

"And let you walk that icy walkway alone in those heels?" he said, glancing down. "Not a chance."

He helped her into her coat, then turned and waved at the trio of women.

"Happy New Year, ladies."

"Happy New Year," Nanette and Tavia echoed.

Simon offered Lacey his arm. "Our chariot awaits."

Lacey gave a small wave. Regina, still perched on the couch, lifted a hand in farewell.

"Have fun, kids. Be good," she said. Her eyes met Lacey's for a brief moment, and a subtle shiver ran down Lacey's spine—half nerves, half anticipation. She thought back to their early-morning conversation in the kitchen. What had begun as a caffeine-fueled spiral of half-jokes and what-ifs had, over the course of the next few days, started to take the shape of something far more real. A plan. As Lacey replayed it in her mind, her pulse quickened. There were a hundred ways it could go wrong. Still, beneath the anxiety curling through her chest, a colder truth settled in: She was out of options. In the back of the black SUV speeding toward the city, Simon reached across the seat to clasp her hand.

"You didn't have to get us a such a fancy car," she said, eyeing the sleek leather interior. "I would have been fine in a regular taxi."

"I wanted everything to be perfect tonight," he said, squeezing her hand.

Lacey felt a familiar stab of guilt thinking about all the thought he'd clearly put into the evening, and forced a smile.

The dining room at Le Bernardin exuded sleek elegance, all warm wood paneling, soft gray tones, and luminous golden light that glowed from artfully recessed fixtures. The low murmur of conversation and the clink of glassware hummed in the background like white noise, punctuated occasionally with a trill of subdued laughter.

As Lacey and Simon were escorted to their table, she felt Simon's eyes on her and had the sudden feeling of being on a film set, hoping she could remember her lines.

When they sat down, the server handed over thick leather-bound menus. Simon immediately dropped his, knocking over his water glass.

"Sorry," he blurted, scrambling for a napkin and rattling the silverware.

The server stepped in smoothly, mopping up the spill with a practiced ease before resetting the table.

Simon flushed. "Sorry," he repeated once the server walked away. Under the table, his leg jiggled so much the hem of Lacey's dress rippled against her shin.

"You OK?" she asked gently.

"Fine," he said quickly, his voice a little too bright. "Should we start with oysters?"

He was quiet during dinner, and Lacey felt the weight of having to make conversation. Once their plates were cleared, a silence descended between them. Lacey wracked her brain, but she'd exhausted her go-to conversation topics: the kids, the kids' teachers, work, and the complicated plot of the historical fantasy show they were watching.

Then, a server appeared at their table, pushing a cart topped with a silver ice bucket, in which was nestled a bottle of champagne, and two flutes.

Lacey blinked. She waited for Simon to intervene, to correct the mistake, but when he didn't, she began to speak. "I'm sorry, we didn't order—"

But then from the corner of her eye she saw him reach into his coat pocket, withdraw a small black velvet box, and slip from his chair.

She froze, knowing what was about to happen when she turned toward him and unsure how to stop it. Around them, the tables quieted as the other diners took notice.

Simon sank to one knee, looking up at her with a nervous smile.

"Lacey Kessler," he said. "Will you make me the happiest man alive and marry me?"

FIFTY

In the back of the SUV, Lacey stared down at the ring now glinting on her left hand, a tasteful round solitaire on a silver band dotted with tiny diamonds. It wasn't flashy, but the stone was significantly larger than the one from her first engagement ring, the modest gold band with a freckle-sized stone that Judd had bought on an entry-level salary. Under the passing glow of streetlights, the diamond caught the light and scattered it across the dark interior of the car. She stared at it, unblinking, until her eyes blurred.

Beside her, Simon reached over and gently stroked her hand, his thumb brushing across the band.

"It looks good on you," he murmured.

Lacey attempted a smile, her head still buzzing with the champagne and the shock of Simon's proposal. She replayed the moment: the hush that had fallen across the dining room, the server poised with the champagne bottle, Simon down on one knee, looking up at her with hopeful, slightly watery eyes.

She'd sat there, stunned, for a long moment. Long enough for the silence to stretch uncomfortably, for Simon's smile to falter. For people to start glancing around.

"Y-yes," she'd finally wheezed, her cheeks flaming. Because, in that moment, what else could she say? She couldn't bear to humiliate him in front of everyone, to suggest they slow down, talk it over, that there was no rush. To tell him—God, the truth—that he deserved better than someone whose feelings were still tangled, still uncertain.

Back at the table, he'd taken her hand again, his eyes shining as he raised his glass. "I know your divorce isn't final until later this month after the hearing," he'd said, "but I wanted you to know I'm serious. And that I heard you."

"Heard... me?" Lacey said faintly, taking a gulp of the cold champagne.

"About wanting stability for Elliott." He gave her a small, regretful smile. "I'm sorry about asking you to move in the way I did—that was presumptuous. I should have known you'd want something that felt permanent after everything you've been through." He squeezed her fingers again, gaze dropping to the ring. "And now I hope it does."

"It's very, um, sudden," Lacey said, with a high, thin laugh.

"I know, right?" Simon leaned back in his chair, beaming. "But I've known for a while that I wanted to marry you. And with everything going on—the custody hearing, the home visit—I figured, why wait? We can get you and Elliott moved in before the evaluator comes. Or reschedule the visit if you need more time to pack. And I can testify at the trial, if you want, as Elliott's stepdad-to-be. Whatever will help the most." He hesitated, then added with a sheepish smile, "Sorry. I'm talking too much. I'm just... excited."

Lacey drained the rest of her champagne. Magically—thankfully—the server appeared and refilled her glass. She murmured her thanks.

Of course Simon was thinking about the home visit, the custody trial—about how to help. He was so... good. Exactly the kind of man she *should* want. And he was probably right: Living with him, with plans to marry, in a stable home with a Christmas-card-ready family, would almost certainly help her case. It all made sense. On paper, it was exactly what she needed.

• • •

Lacey woke to the weight of Elliott's small body draped over her arm, his breath warm and slow against her shoulder. The ring pressed uncomfortably into her skin beneath him. She'd been so exhausted when Simon dropped her off that she'd stepped out of her dress, leaving it in a puddle on the floor, and climbed into bed without even brushing her teeth.

Carefully, she slipped her arm out and tiptoed to the bathroom. After splashing water on her face and running a toothbrush over her teeth, she caught a glimpse of the ring glittering under the harsh overhead light. In one motion she wrenched it off and placed it inside the medicine cabinet, shutting the door with a click.

Downstairs, Regina was already in the kitchen, the rest of the house still quiet.

"We meet again," she said as Lacey walked in. "How was last night?"

Lacey's shoulders tensed. She moved toward the counter, poured a mug of coffee, and slowly lowered herself into a chair. She took a sip, then cleared her throat.

"Simon... proposed."

Regina's mouth dropped open. "Wait—what?" Her eyes darted to Lacey's bare hand. "What did you say?"

Lacey rubbed her thumb over the empty ring finger. "The ring's upstairs."

Regina stared. "So... you said yes?"

Lacey pulled the mug close, cradling it in both hands. "He's really sweet. And he's doing this for me, to help with the custody case. So Elliott and I can move in and present a stable home life in court."

Regina blinked. "OK... skipping over the part where you imply *this*"—she gestured around the kitchen—"isn't a stable home life..." She sat back, her voice strained as though she was choosing her words. "So, Simon proposed... in order to help you win custody of Elliott?"

"No," Lacey said. "He proposed because he loves me."

"And you said yes because you love him," Regina prompted.

Lacey gave a hesitant nod.

"Not because it will make you look better in court?" Regina's voice was edged with disbelief.

Lacey set her mug down harder than she meant to, coffee sloshing over the rim. "That too, obviously. It just makes sense." She met Regina's gaze, her chin lifted. "You're the one who told me to stop playing by the rules, remember?"

Regina gave a short, incredulous laugh. "Yeah, and I didn't mean marry the next nice guy who offers you a lifeboat. Remember our conversation about taking care of Judd? You still have time. His home evaluation visit isn't until tomorrow."

Lacey swiped at the drops of coffee on the table with her palm. "Well, now I don't need to," she said coolly. She hated that Regina could see right through her—could see how she was wrestling to tamp down the rising panic of having boarded a train already gaining speed toward a destination she hadn't chosen.

"Lacey, come on." Regina's voice was soft, urgent. "You've worked so hard to rebuild your life. Don't throw that away just because someone came along with an offer that feels... good enough."

Lacey's nostrils flared. "Why can't you just be happy for me?" she snapped. "Or is that too much to ask now that I'm not jumping through hoops for you at Vetra anymore?"

Regina flinched. "This isn't about that."

"Oh, please," Lacey said, the words rushing out. "You've been distant ever since I told you I wouldn't help you anymore. Don't act like this isn't about that."

Regina's eyes darkened. "Even if I was, it doesn't make what I said any less true." Her voice sharpened. "You're settling. And deep down, you know it. I thought you wanted more than that—I thought you *were* more."

Lacey opened her mouth to argue, but the words withered before they formed. Her shoulders slumped, and she let her eyes fall shut. "Well," she said flatly, "I guess you were wrong."

"Good morning," Tavia mumbled, shuffling into the kitchen,

hair wild, eyes barely open. "Actually, I wish to amend that statement—there is nothing good about it. Grace either had a bad dream or we're starting another sleep regression." She reached for a mug. "Dear, sweet Lord, please let it be a one-off."

She paused mid-pour, picking up on the tension in the room. "Wait, what's going on?"

Regina jerked her head toward Lacey. "She has news."

Tavia glanced at Lacey, coffee pot in hand.

Lacey forced a smile. "Simon and I got engaged."

Tavia's smile flickered on like a lightbulb that wasn't quite screwed in. "Wow, congratulations," she said. Her eyes dropped to Lacey's hand. "Wait, where's the ring?"

"Upstairs," Lacey said with a vague gesture. She crossed her arms. "OK, go ahead. Say it."

"Say what, honey?" Tavia asked, eyes wide, smile frozen.

"What you're *actually* thinking."

Tavia glanced at Regina. Then she sighed and leaned against the counter. "It's not that I'm not happy for you," she said gently, ripping open a Splenda packet. "It's just..."

"Just what?" Lacey asked flatly.

"Just that Simon seems a little more smitten with you than you are with him," Tavia said, stirring. "Which isn't necessarily a bad thing," she added quickly.

"What's not a bad thing?" Nanette asked as she strolled into the kitchen, reaching for a mug. She glanced around. "Wait, how in the world are all the children still asleep? It's a New Year's miracle."

"They *were* up pretty late last night," Regina pointed out.

"And Grace—well, don't ask," Tavia muttered, bringing the mug to her lips. She jerked her head in Lacey's direction. "Someone has news."

"Oh?" Nanette said, perking up.

Lacey slouched in her chair, gripping her mug. "Simon proposed last night," she mumbled. "And no one's happy for me because you all think he's boring."

Nanette froze like she'd been caught in someone's high beams. Then her eyes darted to Regina and Tavia, who studiously looked away.

"Uh... congratulations?" she said.

Tavia cleared her throat. "Honey, no one said he's boring." She hesitated. "He just talks about the weather an awful lot."

"And his intramural disc golf league," added Nanette.

Tavia snorted a giggle.

Lacey groaned. "You're not helping," she said, but the urge to laugh rose up and a reluctant smile tugged at her lips.

"Ignore us," Tavia said, waving a hand. "All that matters is that *you're* happy, honey."

Regina turned to look at Lacey, the smile vanishing from her face. "Are you?" she asked.

Lacey swallowed hard. "Happy enough," she said. She tried to keep her words light, but in the quiet of the kitchen with the other three women looking on, they dropped like stones into a well.

Later that day, Lacey and Elliott were supposed to go to Simon's for homemade pizza and board games, but she called to cancel, feigning a migraine.

"Oh," Simon said, his disappointment evident. "I was hoping we could tell the kids together. About the engagement."

"I'm so sorry," Lacey murmured, adding what she hoped was a sickly rasp to her voice. "Could we try for the weekend?"

"Of course. Let me know if you need anything. Love you."

"Love you, too," she said, and hung up before the guilt could deepen.

Instead, she and Elliott baked banana bread, laughing and spooning large dollops of dough into their mouths, and then played UNO until their eyes crossed. He beat her nearly every game, her mind drifting too often to follow the cards. When he wandered off to join Max and Maddie for another Nerf war, Lacey stayed behind at the kitchen table, staring out the window as the last of the light faded behind the trees.

The engagement ring was still in the medicine cabinet. She

hadn't wanted Elliott asking questions, and the thought of wearing it made her stomach twist. She imagined sitting in Simon's kitchen instead of this one, imagined falling asleep next to him every night. Elliott would have his own room, putting an end to their sleep-overs. Maybe they'd buy a new house. A fresh start.

She turned to gaze around the cheerful, colorful kitchen and felt a sharp ache in her chest. Yes, the cabinets were worn, and the counters were always sticky no matter how many times a day they wiped them down, but it felt like home. She thought of the hours spent at this table with Regina, Tavia, and Nanette. Of Elliott tearing through the house with the other kids, hooting with laughter, and of how their shoes, backpacks, and toys were constantly underfoot. The chaos had grated on her at first, but now she couldn't imagine life without it. Could she find that same feeling of ease living with Simon? Did she want to?

Later, after dinner and bath time, she read aloud to Elliott until his eyes drifted closed. She stroked his hair until he surrendered to sleep, then padded into the bathroom. Opening the medicine cabinet, she pulled out the ring and slid it onto her finger. It felt cold and loose, like it belonged on someone else's hand. Someone who wanted the life Simon was offering, because they were deeply in love with him, not because it was convenient.

Tucking the ring back into the cabinet, she headed downstairs.

Regina sat on the couch, a book open in her lap, the lamp casting a soft pool of light around her.

Lacey paused in the doorway, her heart pounding with quiet certainty.

"I can't do it," she said. "I can't marry him."

Regina looked up sharply, her hand suspended mid-page turn.

"I know," she said simply. Then she rose, set the book aside, and crossed the room to Lacey. "Tell me what you want to do."

FIFTY-ONE

"You're sure he'll be gone?" Regina asked as Lacey parked in front of Judd's two hours later. Around them houses were still draped in twinkling lights, but the holiday magic had faded, the block lined with several Christmas trees discarded on the curb, their brittle, brown needles littering the snowbanks.

"Yes. That's why I have Elliott until tomorrow," Lacey said. "He's spending the night at his parents' place in Connecticut." She wrinkled her nose. "It used to be torture when the three of us went. His parents are country club people and are very into the right outfit for the right occasion and table manners—things eight-year-old boys aren't exactly known for. They never really clicked with Elliott."

Regina nodded. "My mom was like that. Not pearls-and-linen, but just as judgmental in her own way. Traditional Korean mom. All about obedience and becoming a doctor or lawyer. Me joining the freewheeling world of Bay Area tech start-ups was not on her bingo card."

"Do you ever see your parents?" Lacey asked.

Regina gave a hollow laugh. "Not since bringing shame on them by getting knocked up and refusing to name the father," she said. "My mom hung up on me when I called to say the twins had been born. But my dad came to the hospital the next day. Brought me soup and some cash." Her eyes turned distant. "After that, I'd stop by to visit him with the twins when I knew my mom was out at her mah-jongg game. But I haven't seen him since I left California."

"Family is... complicated," Lacey murmured, thinking of her own mother in those final, frail days, and of Sarah—how her texts always contained vague wishes to see Lacey, but never plans.

Regina gave a small smile. "Family's what you make it. And who."

Warmth bloomed in Lacey's chest. As messy as things had gotten between her and Regina, and despite the roller coaster of the last few months, the women of the mommune had become something like family, the safe harbor she'd been searching for since her parents had died. The one she thought she'd found with Judd.

She felt a pang of guilt, thinking of everything Regina had done for her—and how, in return, Lacey had essentially abandoned her in her quest to seek justice from Reid. And how Regina, despite having the upper hand, had let it go.

"Thank you," Lacey said quietly. "For not pushing when I said I was out."

Regina tilted her head back against the headrest. "I'm not a monster," she said dryly. "I mean, yeah, I wish you'd come to your senses and help me extort your boss and the father of my children for millions of dollars, but hey—your loss. I'll get it done one way or another."

Lacey smiled, shaking her head. "What would you do with it? The money?"

Regina closed her eyes. "Travel. Like, for three months at a time, so the twins could still be in school, but see Asia, Australia, Europe. I've never been anywhere, you know?" She opened her eyes. "What about you? Hypothetically, that is, since you're officially out and have no claim to your share of my sixty million."

Lacey let out a small laugh, settling back into her seat. She knew exactly what she'd do with the money, without having to think about it. "I wouldn't travel, actually. At least, not right away. After nearly ending up homeless earlier this year, I'd just want a house, somewhere I could be long-term. Near the water, maybe. With enough room for people to come stay."

"Like friends?"

"Sure. But also, maybe people who need a... soft landing. Sort of like I did." Lacey glanced at Regina shyly, who returned her smile.

For a moment, they sat in silence, warm in the cocoon of the parked car.

Then Regina straightened up, glancing at the dashboard clock, which had ticked past eleven. "I think we're stalling."

Lacey sighed, her pulse quickening again. "Yeah. Probably." Her fingers gripped the door handle. "All right," she said, the nerves back in her throat. "Let's do this."

They tightened their scarves around their necks and moved quickly along the sidewalk and up Judd's front path.

"Let's hope he hasn't changed the locks," Lacey muttered, brandishing the key she still had.

But the door opened smoothly, and the house was still and dark.

"So... where are we putting this?" Regina asked, pulling a small bag of white powder from her coat with gloved fingers.

"Should I ask where you managed to get cocaine on such short notice?" Lacey said, stepping inside.

"The internet is a wild and wonderful place," Regina replied.

Despite the pounding in her chest, Lacey let out a small, stunned laugh. She couldn't believe she was actually doing this. It was dangerous. Illegal. Probably insane. And maybe exactly what it would take to change the rules of the game.

"Upstairs," she said, gesturing Regina forward. They walked up the staircase, which still creaked in all the places Lacey remembered, and down the hall. Past Elliott's room, past the master bedroom, to the small hall bathroom that Elliott used.

"I was thinking the medicine cabinet. I read that the evaluators typically look around in the bathroom to make sure there's soap and toothpaste and stuff, and to make sure any medications are secured."

Regina extended the baggie to Lacey. "Would you like to do the honors?"

Pushing aside the small whisper of guilt in her chest, Lacey took the bag and quickly placed it in the medicine cabinet, positioning it so that it poked out from behind a box of Band-Aids. Now she just had to hope Judd didn't open the cabinet before the evaluation visit the next day.

They headed back down the hall, Regina slipping ahead toward the stairs.

"Be right there," Lacey called, pausing at Elliott's room, feeling a rush of nostalgia. It felt strange to realize she hadn't been in it since she'd moved out months ago. It looked the same, with Elliott's poster of the quarterback of the New York Giants still taped to the wall and a stack of Judd's old Marvel comic books next to his bed.

She wandered over to the bulletin board above his dresser, to which he'd attached some of the comics he'd drawn, plus a photo of the two of them at a street fair last spring, each holding an ear of sweetcorn, their smiling faces shiny with butter.

"You coming?" Regina's voice called.

But another voice echoed after hers.

"Who's there?" Judd called, his voice gravelly but sharp.

Lacey froze and heard the thud of footsteps in the hall outside, followed by a strangled cry from Regina.

"Don't move!" Judd shouted, the footsteps speeding up. "I have a gun!"

There was a crash. A thud. Then, a scream.

Lacey's blood turned to ice.

"Oh my God—shit!" Regina shrieked from below.

Lacey bolted into the hallway and down the stairs, hurtling so fast she stumbled and narrowly missed colliding with Judd, who lay crumpled at the bottom.

Regina looked up, eyes wide with shock. "He's not moving," she said.

<h1 style="text-align:center">FIFTY-TWO</h1>

Lacey stared down at Judd's body, which lay in a heap at the base of the stairs, his neck twisted at an angle so unnatural it made her stomach lurch. A small black pistol lay beside him on the floor.

"When did he get a gun?" she whispered, unable to tear her eyes away.

"I don't think that's our biggest problem right now," Regina hissed. She crouched beside Judd, hands tangled in her hair. "Shit, shit, shit."

Lacey blinked hard, forcing her gaze back to Judd. Cautiously, she nudged his shoulder with the toe of her boot. His head lolled toward them with a sickening limpness that made both women gasp. His eyes were wide open, staring blankly, pupils wide. Heart hammering, Lacey pressed two gloved fingers to the side of his neck.

Nothing.

"I think he might be..." Her voice faltered.

She stared at Judd—his pale skin, the slackness in his jaw, the stubble along his cheek. And suddenly, a cascade of memories flashed through her mind: Judd's shy smile the day they met in their college lecture hall. His tear-stained cheeks when he held Elliott for the first time. His face twisted in rage when she told him she'd had Elliott evaluated for ADHD. The cold fury in his eyes when she told him she was leaving.

A strange pressure built in her chest, the tsunami of conflicting memories crashing into one another with a loud roar inside her head.

They sat there, frozen next to Judd, for a long minute.

"We should call someone," Lacey murmured eventually, rocking slightly in place.

"No," Regina said with a sharp shake of her head, her eyes coming back into focus. "What we need to do is leave." She extended a hand to Lacey and pulled her to her feet.

"But what if he's not—"

"He is," Regina cut in. "Trust me." She bent down and picked up the gun between two gloved fingers.

"What are you doing?" Lacey's voice was thin with panic.

"If the police find a gun, they'll assume foul play," Regina said, a slight tremble in her voice. "No gun, and he could have just fallen down the dark staircase. Come with me."

Holding the gun carefully, she walked back up the stairs and down the hall to the master bedroom, pulling Lacey behind her.

Inside the room, Lacey's eyes traveled around the room, taking in the bed, with Judd's side rumpled and the other smooth, the empty space on the dresser where their wedding photo had been, and the pile of Judd's dirty clothes on the floor near the closet that always reappeared no matter how much she complained about it.

Regina opened the nightstand drawer and dropped the pistol inside, shutting it with a quiet thud. Then she placed a hand on Lacey's shoulder. "I'm so sorry," she murmured, her face pale. "This wasn't supposed to—oh God, Lacey, I'm so sorry."

Lacey stood with her arms clutching her sides as Regina steered her toward the door.

Downstairs Regina pulled her hat back on and tucked her hair under it. Once they were out the front door, she locked it behind them, her fingers fumbling only slightly with the key.

"Head down," she muttered to Lacey, lowering her gaze.

They hurried down the walkway, breath puffing in front of them in the cold.

As Regina pulled away from the curb, Lacey's mind raced. They didn't have a doorbell camera, not unless Judd had installed one recently, but she'd checked carefully as they'd arrived earlier and hadn't noticed anything different, so that was good. And Mrs. Alderino, next door, was in her nineties and didn't even have Wi-Fi. Lacey wasn't sure about neighbors on the other side, but they'd have to hope for the best.

In the driver's seat, Regina hunched forward, gripping her stomach as she drove.

"Shit, shit, shit," she muttered, like a prayer.

Lacey watched, panic rising in her chest at the sight of Regina —normally so cool and collected—coming undone. "No one saw us," Lacey said after a minute, her voice faltering. "There's no forced entry. No fingerprints. It's going to be fine." She was trying to convince herself, she knew.

Regina swallowed, then went pale and turned the car sharply to pull over to the curb. Putting it in park, she flung the door open and vomited. When she finally sat back up, she wiped her mouth with the back of her glove, face drawn and clammy.

"Here," Lacey said, handing her a tissue from her pocket with a shaking hand.

Back at the mommune, the house was dark except for the warm glow spilling from the kitchen down the hall. Lacey and Regina slipped off their coats and boots and walked in silence toward the faint hum of Tavia and Nanette's laughter.

The moment they stepped into the kitchen, the laughter stopped. Tavia's eyes flicked over Regina's pale, drawn face, then to Lacey's stricken one.

"You both look like death," she said, her smile vanishing. "What in the world happened?"

Death.

The word rolled slowly through Lacey's head as tears blurred her vision.

"What is it?" Nanette asked, leaping to her feet. Regina slumped against the counter, and she steered her toward a chair while Lacey stayed standing, tears running freely down her cheeks.

"He's... dead," Lacey whispered, gulping air. "Judd."

"What?" Tavia gave a high-pitched gasp.

Lacey forced out the story, her gaze locked on Regina, who sat motionless, eyes lowered.

"Oh, God," Nanette breathed, hand clamped over her mouth. "This is bad. Really bad."

"What have I done?" Lacey murmured, clutching her sides as the room tilted.

Tavia rose swiftly, catching her by the arm and easing her into a chair. "Breathe," she urged.

Nanette sat back, her face pale. "This is bad," she repeated.

Tavia's lips twitched with an unreadable expression. "OK, it's bad, yes," she said. "But maybe also... a little bit of a relief?"

"Tavia!" Nanette shot her a look of pure horror as a hot flare of guilt detonated in Lacey's chest.

Tavia looked chagrined.

"No," Lacey said, shaking. "I wanted custody of Elliott, not to erase Judd from his life entirely. Now my son will grow up without a father." Her throat tightened around the words.

Tavia rubbed her back gently. "Growing up without a father isn't always the worst thing," she said softly.

Lacey thought of Grace, of Linden, of Max and Maddie, thriving despite—or maybe because of—their fathers' absences. Still, the guilt clawed at her. Who was she to take matters into her own hands, to believe she could ever be in control of her own life?

"I'm so sorry," Regina said suddenly, her voice splintered. She straightened from her hunched position, eyes glistening. "This is all my fault."

A dull ache pulsed in Lacey's temples. She shivered, suddenly cold, and knew she couldn't sit there another second. She needed to see Elliott, to bury her face in his hair, to reassure herself he, at least, was safe.

"I'm going to bed," she said, rising unsteadily.

Regina gave an anguished nod, then stared back down at the table.

Upstairs, Lacey brushed her teeth and slipped into bed beside Elliott. She lay still, trying to sync her short, shallow breaths to the slow, steady rhythm of his, but panic pressed down on her like a boulder. She pulled Elliott close, holding him so tightly he stirred, murmuring in his sleep. She loosened her grip but stayed wrapped around him, her mind replaying the events of the evening on a cruel, unrelenting loop. She stared at the ceiling as the hours crawled by, and sleep remained stubbornly out of reach.

FIFTY-THREE

The day of Judd's funeral was bright and cold, one of those January days that leaves you momentarily blinded when you step outside, the sun reflecting off the snow, and the frigid air scraping your lungs with every breath.

In the church bathroom's full-length mirror, Lacey smoothed the front of her black wool dress and tucked her hair behind her ears. Her makeup-free face looked as grim as she felt. She was dreading the whole affair: seeing Judd's family—and whatever friends he might still have—enduring the stiff wooden pews of the stuffy church, and, worst of all, standing in the receiving line, fielding condolences while her guilt suffocated her from the inside.

After that first night, she'd found she'd gone strangely numb, which only magnified her guilt. That morning, though, she'd understood. It wasn't that she wasn't grieving the father of her child; it was that she'd already done it, months ago. She'd lost Judd already, a long time ago, to his paranoias and conspiracy theories, to his late-night Reddit threads and vitriol, and she'd been mourning that loss ever since. So, while everyone else was just entering the raw, early stages of grief, Lacey was at the tail end of hers—ready, finally, to move on. To try to find a way to shoulder the burden of what she'd done.

She stepped out of the bathroom into the small waiting room off the sanctuary. Elliott sat on a bench, hunched over a comic book.

"It's time, sweetheart," she said gently. When he didn't look up, she placed a hand on his shoulder and held out the other. "Elliott."

He sighed and surrendered the comic. "How long will this take?"

He had cried the day she told him, which she'd done after the call from the police—a conversation that had left her collapsed on the couch, trembling with relief that it had ended in condolences rather than a knock at the door and a pair of handcuffs.

Since then, Elliott had been mostly quiet, his brow furrowed with worries he couldn't or wouldn't put into words. The only time his emotions cracked through was when Lacey tried to leave the house briefly with Tavia for a quick errand. His meltdown had been so fierce it left them both in tears. Since then, he'd refused to leave her side. He sat on the bathroom floor while she showered and clung to her at bedtime, his limbs wrapped tightly around her like a velcroed octopus.

"It's not unusual," said Dr. Levin, Elliott's old psychologist, whom Lacey had finally felt free to call again, realizing she now had sole discretion over Elliott's medical care. "He's lost one parent. It's normal he'd be scared to lose the other. It's a good time to restart treatment."

Now, in the church anteroom, Elliott tugged on her arm. "Mommy, I said how long until it's over?"

She smoothed his hair. "The funeral? Probably longer than either of us wants." She tried for a reassuring smile.

A soft knock at the door interrupted them. Pastor Dale—as he'd introduced himself—stepped in, his long, narrow face drawn into a solemn expression. His gray hair was slicked meticulously to the side, and he looked like he belonged in a black-and-white photo from a tent revival.

"Brother Judd's parents have finished their final blessings," he said with hushed gravity. "Would you and young Elliott like a moment with him?"

Lacey drew back. "You mean, like, with his casket?"

Pastor Dale pressed a hand to his Bible. "I'd be honored to offer a prayer."

Lacey looked at Elliott, who gave a violent shake of his head.

"I don't want to," he said, clutching her waist.

Lacey folded an arm around him. "We'll pass, thank you," she said.

A flicker of judgment crossed the pastor's face. "As you wish," he said. "Please take your seats, then. We'll begin shortly."

Elliott buried his face in her coat as Pastor Dale left the room.

"I don't want to see a dead body," he whispered. "But will Daddy be mad if I don't?"

Lacey knelt beside him. "No, sweetheart. He won't. That's just his body. He's already gone."

"Gone, like... to heaven?" Elliott sniffed.

"Maybe," she said. "Nobody really knows. But it can help to think of it that way." Her heart twisted with guilt, wishing she had more to offer Elliott in the way of spiritual reassurances. But after everything, Lacey found there wasn't much she believed in anymore.

"Then I'm going to imagine him in heaven," Elliott said. "There's probably always a football game on in heaven. Daddy would like that."

Lacey smiled, her throat tight. "He would," she said softly. "He really would."

After the service, which was long on oration and short on actual remembrances of Judd, Pastor Dale invited everyone downstairs for a "fellowship meal." In the church basement, tables were lined with foil pans of baked ziti and lasagna, stacks of garlic bread, and a limp-looking platter of raw vegetables with a puddle of ranch dressing in the center.

Regina, Nanette, and Tavia made their way through the crowd toward Lacey and Elliott, shepherding the kids among them.

"How are you holding up?" Tavia asked, Grace perched on her hip.

"Fine," Lacey said with a tired smile. "Just... ready for it all to be over."

Nanette, holding Linden's hand, glanced over the buffet. "I've never seen so much melted ricotta in one room in my life."

Lacey smothered a laugh, her emotional exhaustion turning to giddiness.

"Do you need anything?" Regina asked quietly. Max and Maddie had flanked Elliott and were flipping through Pokémon cards.

Her eyes met Lacey's. After the first night, neither had spoken about what happened at Judd's house, as though silence might transform the whole thing into a fever dream that would fade with time. But when Lacey had pulled Regina aside after the police called, she'd watched her friend sag onto the couch, knees buckling, hands pressed to her mouth in palpable relief.

"So they don't suspect anything?" Regina had whispered. "Oh God, thank God." She shook her head. "I know you think I'm some kind of vigilante, but I never meant for this. Not really—"

"I know you didn't," Lacey had said. "I know."

In that moment, Lacey saw Regina not as the fearless, unflinching force she'd always leaned on, the one who had it all figured out, but as someone remarkably like herself. Wounded. Scrappy. Scared.

Now, Lacey gestured toward Elliott, who had moved to sit on the floor with Max and Maddie, their heads bent over their Pokémon cards. "If I can convince him to leave, would you mind taking him home?" she asked Regina. "There's no reason for him to be stuck here with me. Everyone will understand."

"Of course," Regina said. "Whatever you need."

It took some coaxing—and the promise of a movie and ice cream sundaes—but eventually Elliott relented.

"When will you be home?" he asked, his arms wrapped tightly around her waist, his voice tremulous. She could see the effort it took for him to keep his tears in check, and her heart seized with love for him.

"As soon as I can, sweetheart," she said, brushing his hair back gently. "I'll be home before the movie ends, OK?"

He pulled away reluctantly. The kids were herded together, and the women offered quiet waves and murmured goodbyes as they headed out.

Simon, who had been lingering at a polite distance, stepped forward.

"Hi," he said softly, placing a hand on her back.

She leaned into him, letting herself rest there for a moment, taking in the warm, familiar scent of him. "Hi," she murmured. "Thanks for being here."

"Of course." His brow furrowed as he looked down at her. "I'm always here for you."

"I'm sorry I've been AWOL these past few days," she said.

"I get it," he said, brushing it aside with a wave of his hand. "You've been through a lot. I'm just really sorry."

His eyes drifted down to her left hand, which was bare.

"I haven't had a chance to talk to Elliott about it," she said, catching the look and brushing her thumb over her ring finger. "It just felt like... not the time."

Simon frowned. "Of course. I understand."

"Lacey, dear, is that you? I haven't seen you in ages!"

Lacey turned to see her and Judd's elderly neighbor shuffling toward her.

Simon leaned in and whispered, "Do you want me to wait and give you a ride home?"

"That would be great," Lacey said, giving his hand one last squeeze before letting go, her stomach sinking.

Lacey hovered on the edges of the overheated, lasagna-scented fellowship hall for the next hour, accepting hugs and handshakes with a tight smile as exhaustion began to seep in. What she wanted, more than anything, was to go home, curl up on the couch with Elliott, and fall asleep while he watched *The Empire Strikes Back* for the hundredth time.

But there was one last thing she needed to do.

She scanned the room as she pulled out her phone.

Ready to head out if you're still here, she texted.

I'll pull the car around front, Simon replied almost instantly.

Her chest tightened at his thoughtfulness, but she tamped the feeling down. There wasn't room for it right now.

Upstairs, she grabbed her coat from the anteroom and walked back through the empty church sanctuary, where Judd's closed casket still rested at the front, surrounded by floral arrangements, including a large bouquet from Vetra. Lacey wondered who Reid had had send it—normally that would have been her job. He'd been understanding when she'd reached out to tell him about Judd, had told her to take as much time as she needed.

In the stillness, she walked forward. The scent of lilies filled her nose. She placed her hand on the lacquered wood. It was cold beneath her palm.

She stood in silence for a minute, her head bowed. "I'm sorry," she whispered. "For everything. And I think, deep down, you were sorry, too."

Simon's car was already at the curb when she exited the church. Seeing her, he leaped out to take her arm and guide her down the steps, opening the car door for her.

"Thanks for waiting," she said.

He reached over and gave her leg a reassuring pat. "Of course."

She rested her head against the seat, grateful for the gentle quiet between them as he drove.

When they pulled up outside the mommune, Lacey hesitated, her mouth suddenly dry.

"Thank you," she said, turning to him. "For everything these last few months."

Simon smiled. "It's been a really good few months," he said, his eyes crinkling into a warm smile. She thought, for the millionth time, how she didn't deserve him. And then, from somewhere deep inside, another voice chimed in. It wasn't that she didn't *deserve* him, but that she didn't want... this. Not with him. Not in the way he wanted her. And he deserved someone who did.

"Simon," she said, her voice cracking. "You are... wonderful. But I can't marry you."

His smile faltered. "I get it," he said quickly. "With Judd gone, custody isn't hanging over your head anymore. I've thought about that. We don't have to rush anything. We can slow down, take our time."

Guilt seeped through her, soaking every nerve and muscle, but she shook it off. "It's not just that." Her voice was soft, apologetic. "I'm not ready. Not for any of this. Not with you."

He sat back, pain flickering across his face. "So you're breaking up with me?"

Lacey's eyes brimmed with tears. "I'm sorry," she whispered, brushing away a tear.

"Lacey—" he started, but she held up a hand.

"Please," she said. "You're so good, and kind, and logical—God, so logical—that if you start talking, you'll probably talk me out of it. But please don't. I know this is right."

He took a long breath, then nodded slowly. "OK," he said. "OK."

She reached out, squeezed his hand one last time, then opened the car door and stepped out into the cold.

FIFTY-FOUR

Lacey had been prepared to take more time off work, to let Elliott stay home from school as long as he needed to process the loss of his father. But after their initial session, Dr. Levin recommended that the routine of school could be good for him.

"Every child is different," he said carefully, "and I trust you'll keep a close eye on how Elliott's doing. But I think returning to a familiar routine might help, especially if school is a place where he feels safe and supported."

"Then let's give it a try," Lacey said.

"Just keep an eye on how he adjusts," Dr. Levin replied. "And let's check in again next week."

That night, as Lacey and Elliott snuggled in bed, she broached the subject.

"How do you feel about going back to school tomorrow?" she asked softly.

He shrugged. "OK."

"Are you excited to see your friends?"

"Yeah."

"And Mr. Barry?"

"Sure."

Lacey smiled, brushing his hair off his forehead. "You're a creature of few words tonight."

He just gave another shrug and nestled closer.

They sat quietly for a moment, and just as Lacey was about to give up and start reading, Elliott spoke, his voice barely above a whisper.

"Sometimes I'm not sad," he said. "About Daddy. Because... he yelled a lot. And now I get to stay with you all the time."

Lacey didn't move, afraid that even the smallest shift might stop him from continuing.

"But those thoughts make me feel bad," he went on, his voice trembling. "I'm worried I'm bad."

She tightened her arms around him. "You are not bad, Elliott. Not even a little. It's OK to feel that way. I do, too," she confessed.

He lifted his head to look up at her. "You do?"

She kissed the top of his head. "I do. I think Daddy was having a really hard time, especially these last couple years. And sometimes he was... hard to be around. Or even scary. And it's OK to feel relieved that things are calmer now. That doesn't mean you didn't love him. And it definitely doesn't mean he didn't love you."

She paused, a fragment of a memory flitting through her mind: Judd insisting they test the new swing set he'd built for Elliott, the two of them side by side, swinging higher and higher, laughing like kids. "It helps me to try to remember the times when I felt that love," Lacey said. "To have that be how I remember him."

Elliott was quiet. Then a small smile tugged at his mouth. "Like last summer, at my baseball game," he said. "When he put me on his shoulders and ran around the field after we won." He closed his eyes. "I think I'll remember him like that." He opened them again. "Is that good?"

Lacey smiled through the blur of tears in her eyes and kissed the top of his head. "That's perfect."

After they finished reading, she lay beside Elliott, gently stroking his hair as she glanced around the yellow room she'd called home for the past four and a half months. It had been a refuge—

warm, safe, comforting. A real home. But was it where she pictured Elliott growing up?

He was getting older, fast approaching the age when he'd want more space, more privacy. Hell, *she* wouldn't mind more privacy. As much as she loved living under the same roof with the women who'd become her best friends, there would come a point when she would outgrow the mommune. But when she tried to imagine what came next, all she saw was a blurry image that wouldn't come into focus no matter how hard she tried.

She shook off the thoughts and pushed herself up from the bed to wash her face and brush her teeth. It was odd to think of going back to Vetra the next morning after nearly three weeks away. Since Judd's death she'd completely tuned out, not even checking her email. A ripple of anxiety went through her as she thought about stepping back into life there, wondering what would be waiting for her.

The next morning, Max and Maddie were ecstatic to have Elliott joining them at the bus stop. The three kids linked arms and shuffled triumphantly off into the chilly dark morning.

An hour later, Lacey stepped off the elevator at Vetra. When she reached her desk, she found a massive gift basket waiting—gourmet teas, artisanal chocolates, a pastel rainbow of macarons.

It was early, and the floor was mostly quiet. She had just docked her laptop when the elevator dinged again and Reid strode out, phone pressed to his ear.

"You're making a huge fucking mistake," he barked, voice echoing throughout the empty floor. "I'm serious—you'll never work in the industry again." He stopped short, mid-stride, his face reddening. "Goddammit, Ketchum, listen—"

Jerking the phone away from his ear, he stared at the screen.

"Fuck!" he yelled, hurling the phone to the floor. It bounced off the carpet and as he scrambled to retrieve it, he noticed Lacey.

"You're back. Thank God."

Lacey frowned. "What's going on?"

He glanced around the open floor, then jerked his head toward his office. She followed, coat still on.

"Close the door," he snapped. His pacing resumed. His hands were in his hair. "Shit. Fuck. Ketchum quit."

Lacey blinked. "But he just started a week ago."

"Apparently that's enough time to blow everything up," Reid said, collapsing into his chair. His beard stood out starkly against his pale skin.

"Can we go back to another candidate? Eleanor Wang—"

Reid cut her off. "He's going to the press."

Her stomach dropped. "What?"

"I thought he'd go along with it," Reid muttered.

"Go along with what?" Dread coiled in Lacey's stomach.

"The trial data. For the Vetra-Patch." He met her eyes briefly. "I altered the results. Just until we got the algorithm cleaned up."

Cold shock rolled over her. "Wait—what you accused Sunil of doing—falsifying trial data—*you* did that?"

He waved a hand. "Come on, you knew that was bullshit. We just needed Sunil out."

He was right, she had known—and she'd stayed quiet. A sick awareness crept in as she wondered whether being an accessory to corporate fraud was something the police would now add to her rap sheet, after her hit and run and her soon-to-be-ex-husband's accidental murder.

"But Ketchum figured it out," Reid continued. "He quit on the spot. Said he's going to the press." He dropped his head into his hands. "Lacey, this could kill us. If the investors find out—"

Her stomach rose into her throat. If the company imploded, where would that leave her? Out of a job, with a résumé built on a lie. She stared at Reid's sweating, ashen face, fury spiking in her chest. Because here she was again, despite her best attempts: collateral damage to yet another man who thought he could call all the shots, bend reality to his will.

"I'll get Marina," she said, trying to keep her voice from shaking with anger.

Reid's phone buzzed again. He picked it up, read the screen, and his face went gray.

"Too late," he said quietly. "The *Journal*'s already reached out. They want a comment. There's blood in the water. We're fucked." His voice dropped. "The only thing that could save us is if I fixed the goddamn algorithm and filed the FDA paperwork with real data—but it's impossible. I've tried everything."

Deep in the back of Lacey's mind, something clicked. Slowly, she turned and walked out of Reid's office.

"Hey, where are you going?" he called after her. "Lacey, I need you to—"

But she was headed down the hall, ducking into the privacy of a conference room as she pulled out her phone.

"Hey," she said when the call connected. "I have an idea."

Fifteen minutes later, she walked back into Reid's office, where Marina now sat, typing furiously on her laptop.

"Sorry," Lacey said. "I just needed to take care of something."

"This is about framing," Marina said to Reid, ignoring her. "We lead with the patch's potential, not the timeline. Call it realigning goals, not failure."

"We still need a scientific voice," Reid muttered. "Someone credible. Lacey, take notes," he ordered.

Lacey remained quiet as they sketched out Reid's talking points for the board, until, a short while later, her phone rang. She glanced at the caller ID—*Vetra Security Desk*.

"Ms. Kessler?" the guard said. "We have a visitor here to see you. Should I send them up?"

Reid shot her an annoyed glance.

"Yes, please," Lacey murmured into the phone.

Moments later, there was a knock at Reid's office door.

"Get rid of whoever it is," Marina ordered Lacey.

Lacey stood, opened the door wide, and stepped aside as Regina walked in.

FIFTY-FIVE

Regina was wearing her long white wool coat cinched at the waist, her dark hair tumbling in waves over her shoulders. Her cheeks were pink from the cold, but her eyes glittered with a sharp, electric intensity.

Reid paled. "What the fuck are you doing here?"

Marina's eyes narrowed.

Regina's lips curled into a smile. "I heard you were having trouble with your algorithm," she said sweetly, addressing Reid. "Or should I say—*my* algorithm?" She arched an eyebrow.

Reid's eyes darted from Regina to Lacey.

"It's a lot to take in, I know," Regina said coolly. "We could waste time explaining it, or I could get to work." She tilted her head. "From what I understand, your company is hours away from total implosion. And I can save it." She brushed her hair over her shoulder. "But hey, you tell me how much time you have to burn."

"You can't be here," Marina snapped, surging to her feet. "It's in your—" She faltered, her eyes flicking nervously to Lacey.

"My NDA?" Regina finished, her eyes wide with faux innocence. "And you'd remember that, wouldn't you, Marina? Reid's favorite fixer, always cleaning up his messes."

Marina's face flushed a mottled red. "You need to leave—"

"Stop." Reid's voice was low, tight. Slowly, he rose, planting both hands on his desk. "Tell me," he said, his eyes on Regina.

She paused just long enough for the room to thicken with tension. "It wasn't finished when you stole it," she said, a smirk tugging at the corner of her mouth. "But I can see how you made that mistake. My first drafts look like most people's finished products. Then again, you know that."

Reid's jaw tightened. "But you know how to finish it."

Regina raised her chin slightly. "Of course."

Marina's voice shot back in, sharper now, edged with panic. "Reid, you can't seriously—"

"You can go, Marina." He flicked his head toward the door, not even looking at her. Then his glare turned on Lacey. "And you."

Lacey glanced at Regina, who gave the faintest nod.

"Reid, please—" Marina started, her voice cracking.

"*Leave.*" Reid stabbed a finger toward the door.

Marina sucked in a sharp, furious breath. She glared at Lacey as she snatched up her laptop, eyes blazing at the indignity of being thrown out alongside her.

Marina whirled on her as soon as they were outside, stepping in close, her voice a hiss. "What the hell do you think you're doing? How do you know her?"

Lacey swallowed but kept her voice steady. "Reid will do anything to save Vetra," she said. "You know that better than anyone." She stared at Marina, daring her to deny it.

Marina's mouth twisted in fury and her whole body looked coiled to strike. Then with a sharp, angry grunt, she turned and stormed away.

Lacey sat at her desk, straining to catch the muffled rise and fall of voices behind Reid's door. Her inbox pinged with messages from panicked investors and board members, and the voicemail light on her desk phone glowed an ominous red. She tried to focus, but her eyes kept drifting back to Reid's office.

Finally, the door swung open. Reid appeared, his face tight, jaw clenched, giving a sharp jerk of his head to summon Lacey.

The air in the office felt charged and thick, like just before a thunderstorm. Regina sat on the couch, her white coat folded neatly beside her, legs crossed at the knee. She wore a fitted black sweater dress and tall, gleaming black leather boots. To the casual eye, her face seemed calm, expressionless. But Lacey caught it—the flicker of satisfaction in her eyes, the tiniest lift at the corners of her mouth.

"I need you to get Regina set up in Ketchum's old office, on the research floor," Reid said. "She'll need all the access and permissions he had—ASAP. And reschedule the board meeting for tomorrow morning, citing new developments. I'll call Olivier; you handle everyone else. And hold off the press until then."

Regina stood. "I'll need access to the full historical data and even the earliest trials," she said to Reid. "This is not the time to get selective."

"The early trials are garbage," Reid said. "You'll waste time starting there. All you need are—"

"—the dynamic test sets, I know."

"—the predictive loop, that's where the work is," Reid said. "Start with the—"

"I *know*," repeated Regina, more forcefully.

Though his eyes remained stormy, Lacey thought she saw the faintest smile on Reid's face.

"I'll expect hourly updates," he said.

Regina rolled her eyes and scooped up her coat. "I'll update you when I have something," she said.

Lacey waited until they'd crossed the open floor and the elevator doors slid shut behind them.

"It worked," she breathed, clutching her arms around her waist. "I can't believe it. He's actually letting you fix the algorithm."

"Of course it worked," Regina said, smoothing her hair. "Reid's not about to let Vetra implode. His ego's too oversized for that." She glanced over, a smile softening her sharp features. She reached out briefly, touching Lacey's shoulder. "It was a good plan—holding the completed algorithm hostage like this. I wish I'd thought of it months ago."

Lacey felt an unexpected swell of pride. "Thanks," she said.

When they stepped onto the research floor, an IT guy was already waiting outside Ketchum's old office.

"This office is like a revolving door lately," he muttered as they entered, running a hand through his spiky hair and pushing his black-framed glasses up his nose.

He turned on the monitors and typed a few commands, then stood back with a flourish. "You should be good," he said.

"Wait, I need the larger monitor on the left," Regina said, stepping forward. "And move the second one up on a stand. I don't want to crane my neck all day."

The guy blinked at her. "Uh, I just handle system setup, not furniture arrangement."

"I also need the backup drive closer to the right side—not shoved behind the tower," Regina continued, as though he hadn't spoken.

"I just said, I don't—"

"You do today," Regina said, hands on her hips.

Once things were set up to her liking and they were alone, Regina settled in front of the array of glowing screens and flashed Lacey a triumphant smile.

"Now, let's see how badly Reid's screwed things up this time, shall we?"

FIFTY-SIX

Lacey's shoulders tensed as the elevator opened onto the executive floor. She could only imagine what was waiting for her—after all, she'd walked Regina straight into Reid's office, a direct shot at the thing he prized most in his people: loyalty.

Just as she reached her desk, Reid's door swung open.

"We need to talk," he said, his face stony.

Without a word, Lacey followed him inside. The fading winter light slanted across the room, casting long shadows. Reid perched on the low arm of the couch, his whole body taut, his knee jiggling.

Lacey stayed just inside the doorway, her arms folded.

"How long have you known her?" Reid said finally, his voice low.

A dozen explanations flickered through Lacey's mind, but she batted them all aside. For the first time in a long time, she'd stumbled into a mess that wasn't hers to clean up.

"Not as long as you have," she said quietly.

Reid's jaw clenched as understanding settled in. "So, you know," he said.

Lacey paused. "What I know," she said, "is that you needed help. And she can help."

Reid's shoulders sagged for an instant as he swiped a hand

across his face. "Fuck." Then his whole body shifted forward like a snake about to strike.

"You have no idea what you've gotten yourself into with her," he hissed. "You think she's your friend? She's not. She's only out for herself. Always has been. Whatever she's promised you, it's a lie, I guarantee."

He stood, his mouth twisting into a menacing grin. "You bet on the wrong horse with her, Lacey. And now that I see where your loyalty lies, I'll make sure no one will ever hire you again, not anywhere."

She waited for his words to have an impact on her, for the familiar sensation of fear to wash over her. She'd spent so much of her time these last few months being afraid. Instead, as she looked at Reid, she felt almost nothing. Just a cool, quiet disgust.

Without a word, she turned and walked out, crossing to her desk to pick up her purse.

Behind her, Reid's voice rose, sharp with fury. "You're fired!"

She turned back, a small, pitying smile on her face. "No, Reid," she said. "I quit."

On her way out, Lacey stopped by the research floor. She heard the music as soon as the elevator doors opened—the raw, raspy edge of Karen O's voice snarling over the pulsing synth riff of "Heads Will Roll" blasting from behind Regina's closed office door.

Lacey knocked loudly, then let herself in.

Inside, Regina was hunched over the keyboard, her head snapping between three enormous monitors where she scrolled through rows and columns of numbers. Just looking at it made Lacey's head throb.

"Hey," Lacey called over the music.

Regina glanced up, then twisted the volume knob, lowering it just enough to talk over. "Hey. Sorry, this album always helps me think."

Lacey shifted on her feet. "I just wanted to check on you."

Regina rolled her eyes, already turning back to the screens.

"Tell Reid he'll hear from me when I have something worth sharing."

"He didn't send me," Lacey said quickly. "I'm just—I'm heading out for the night." She hesitated, her fingers brushing the strap of her purse. "I, um... I quit." A small, strangled laugh escaped her. "Actually, he tried to fire me."

Regina's eyes flicked across the data. "No surprise," she muttered. "Reid's nothing if not predictable."

"Yeah," Lacey said softly. But Reid's words from earlier echoed in her mind: *Whatever she's promised you—it's a lie, I guarantee.*

She looked at Regina, this woman she'd bet her future on. She thought of the fragments of herself that Regina had shared over the past few weeks—and how much Lacey still didn't know about her.

Sensing her gaze, Regina turned, offering a small, crooked smile. "Hey. It's all good. Go home." She gave a light wave toward the screens. "This is going to be an all-nighter, and Tavia and Nanette can't handle all the kids by themselves. I'll see you tomorrow."

Lacey hesitated one beat longer, then nodded. After everything that had happened, she longed for the warmth of the mommune, for the comfort of wrapping her arms around Elliott.

"Sure," she said softly. "See you tomorrow." As she turned to go, she glanced back at Regina. They'd come this far—what else could Lacey do but trust?

FIFTY-SEVEN

When Lacey arrived home, the sun had set, but the mommune glowed with the Christmas lights still strung across the porch and windows. She paused for a moment on the walkway, smiling softly. Maybe they should leave them up all year, she thought—they were oddly comforting against the dark.

Inside, the savory smell of tomatoes and onions simmering on the stove wrapped around her, and her stomach gave a sharp, demanding growl, reminding her how little she'd eaten all day while riding the roller coaster of Vetra's potential implosion. She felt as though she'd lived an entire week in the space of one day.

"Mommy!" Elliott darted out from the living room, flinging his arms around her waist.

"Hey, sweetheart," Lacey murmured, bending to hug him. "How was school?" She smiled as she wiped away a sticky smear of peanut butter from his cheek, a leftover trace of his after-school snack.

Elliott smiled. "Good!" Then he grimaced. "But we started fractions. And we have homework. It's hard."

"I can help you!" piped up Maddie, appearing right behind him, tugging at his hand. "Come on, let's play school—I'll be the teacher."

Elliott looked over at Maddie, then up at Lacey, his reluctance to leave her written on his face.

"It's fine," Lacey said gently. "Go play. I'll just be in the kitchen."

Elliott bit his lip, but let Maddie lead him back into the living room.

Lacey slipped off her shoes and coat, then paused at the edge of the doorway to the living room, smiling as she watched the little scene unfolding: Max, Elliott, and Linden were arranging themselves crisscross applesauce on the floor while Maddie dragged over the battered old chalkboard they kept in the corner.

"Chalk chalk!" crowed Grace, toddling eagerly toward it, her little arms outstretched in delight.

In the kitchen, Nanette was stirring a bubbling pot of tomato sauce while Tavia stood beside her at the counter, arranging carrot sticks in neat rows on the kids' plates. Seeing Lacey, Nanette immediately set her spoon down, both women turning toward her, their questions written on their faces.

"So?" Nanette asked.

Tavia wiped her hands on her apron and peered over Lacey's shoulder, scanning the doorway. "Where's Regina? She said she was going to meet you."

"Still there," Lacey said, moving closer and leaning against the counter, feeling the weight of the day pressing into her bones.

Nanette's eyes widened. "With Reid?"

"Yes—well, no," Lacey corrected herself. "She's working. Trying to fix the algorithm."

"*Her* algorithm?" Tavia echoed, her voice rising with disbelief. "Why would she help him with that?"

"Because he needs it," Lacey said.

Nanette switched off the burner as Lacey filled them in— Ketchum's sudden exit, the board scrambling to meet, the investors' nonstop calls, the press circling like vultures—and most importantly, the moment she'd handed Reid the one thing he needed most: Regina.

"Oh my God," Nanette breathed, her face lighting up. "What a ballsy move. I can't believe Reid actually went for it."

"I don't think he had much choice," Lacey said, running a hand through her hair. "It was that or let the world find out Vetra's crown jewel is basically worthless."

Tavia sucked in a sharp breath, eyes gleaming. "So... how much did she ask for?"

Lacey hesitated, a small knot tightening in her stomach. "I don't actually know," she admitted.

The two women exchanged a quick glance, but before either could reply, Lacey let out a shaky laugh. "Also... I quit my job." She pressed her lips together, then added, "Well—I was fired. But I quit first, so... maybe it's a draw?"

Nanette's mouth fell open. "Wait, what? Lacey!"

Tavia reached over to touch her arm. "Oh, honey. You've had one hell of a day."

"Don't worry," Nanette said with a grin. "If Regina pulls this off, none of us are going to need day jobs much longer."

Lacey tried to match their smiles, but a whisper of doubt slipped through her chest like a draft. All she could do was hope Nanette was right.

Lacey slept fitfully that night, waking every couple of hours to check her phone for any message from Regina—but the screen stayed tauntingly blank. When her alarm finally buzzed, she pried her eyes open and forced herself up, rushing Elliott through breakfast and into his coat and boots for school.

Coming back inside and rubbing her hands together for warmth, Lacey instinctively started up the stairs to shower and get ready for work—then stopped, remembering she had nowhere to be. She reached for her phone again. Still nothing from Regina. With a frustrated sigh, she flopped back onto the bed, pulling the covers up over her eyes.

When she awoke a short while later, the sun had risen, pale light filtering through the crack in her curtains. She grabbed her phone from beside her. Still nothing.

Padding downstairs, the house was quiet, everyone gone to school or work. As Lacey passed the front window, a flicker of motion caught her eye. Peering out, she watched a shiny black SUV glide to a stop at the curb. The door opened, and Regina stepped out, her long white coat almost glowing against the dark car.

Lacey's heart began to pound as she watched Regina approach, searching her face, her posture, her stride—anything for a clue as to what had unfolded the night before.

She stepped back just as Regina opened the front door.

"You're back," Lacey breathed, a million questions rushing into her throat.

Regina's eyes were bleary and rimmed red, but as soon as she spotted Lacey, a slow, triumphant grin overtook her face.

FIFTY-EIGHT

Lacey watched as Regina unbuttoned her white coat, hung it neatly on a hook, then sat to unzip her tall boots. She ran her hands through her dark, slightly limp waves, fanning them out, her face tired but composed.

"Is there coffee?" Regina asked.

"I was just about to make some," Lacey said, moving automatically to the kitchen.

Regina followed, yawning. Lacey couldn't hold back anymore. "So?" she asked as she scooped grounds into the filter, her voice tight with anticipation.

Regina let out another long yawn, then smiled faintly. "I did it," she said simply.

Lacey's relief nearly knocked her sideways. "Oh my God. And Reid...?"

"Reid got what he needed," Regina said, a brief flicker of something unreadable crossing her face. "And then he asked me to come on board as Vetra's head of research."

The spoon in Lacey's hand slipped and clattered to the floor. "You're working for Reid?" she said, stunned. Her thoughts collided in her head, coming out in fragments. "But I thought... why would you—"

"Lacey." Regina's tone held a note of disappointment as she bent to pick up the spoon and drop it in the sink. "I didn't take the job, obviously." A wistful look came over her face. "But I'll admit, being there with him last night, working together, part of me felt like... why not? We were always better together. I'm sure that sounds crazy, but it's the truth. And working on the algorithm again with him... it was like it reminded me who I am. I felt alive in a way I haven't in years."

"You worked *together* with him all of last night?" Lacey said, confused. "But you hate him."

Regina gave a slow, sad shake of her head. "I could never fully hate him," she said. "He's the father of my children. I know you understand."

A dull ache rippled across Lacey's chest as she thought of Judd. "I do," she said softly.

Regina pulled her phone from her pocket, tapped it a few times, then blew out a breath as she turned the phone toward Lacey.

Lacey leaned in. The banking app on the screen displayed: *Cayman Trust Bank. Account Holder: Regina M. Cho. Balance: $30,000,000.*

Lacey gasped, setting down her mug before it slipped from her hand.

Regina gave a small, shaky smile, wiping under her eyes. "I really did it," she whispered. She pressed a hand to her face, shoulders shaking briefly, then gave a watery laugh. "Max, Maddie—we never have to worry again."

Lacey leaned back, her thoughts racing. She bit her lip. "And Reid... with Max and Maddie?" she asked cautiously.

Regina's breath hitched. "Honestly?" she said after a pause. "I'm grateful he doesn't want to be part of their lives. I don't want to compromise on how I raise them."

Lacey let out a soft exhale. "Yeah," she murmured. "I can relate to that."

Regina straightened up, her eyes sharp. "Now, first things first, you're going to need your own Cayman account. Because part of this is yours."

Relief flooded Lacey. Regina caught the look on her face, a flicker of hurt crossing her features. "You look surprised," she said.

Lacey shifted, swallowing. "Reid said..."

Regina locked eyes with her. "No matter what Reid may have told you," she said, "I keep my promises."

FIFTY-NINE

After Regina finally crashed and retreated to her room to sleep, Lacey wandered upstairs in a daze. She made the bed, smoothing the heavy comforter into place, picking up Elliott's balled-up pajamas from the floor, and dropping them into the hamper. Then she collapsed into the window seat, pulling a blanket over her shoulders to guard against the winter chill creeping through the seams of the old windows.

Outside, the sky was a crisp, brilliant blue, and the snowy backyard sparkled like it had been dusted with diamonds. But inside, Lacey's mind wouldn't settle. Her thoughts ricocheted wildly—about Elliott, the money, the mommune, what came next. She fixed her gaze on a bare tree at the far edge of the yard, its crooked tire swing swaying lightly in the wind, and forced herself to take slow, measured breaths.

Gradually, her racing pulse eased, and a single emotion rose to the surface from the crashing swirl of all the rest: sadness.

She'd made a home here, carved out something safe for herself and Elliott. Now everything was about to change. Yes, she'd long craved the freedom Regina's promised payout would give her, the ability to shape her own life on her own terms. But standing on the edge of that freedom, it suddenly felt overwhelming, even suffocating. Was this just what happened after living too long under other people's constraints?

"It's like I have Stockholm syndrome in my own life," she muttered, shaking her head.

To shake the thoughts loose, she threw herself into doing laundry, scrubbing the bathroom, and wiping down the kitchen. When she finally sat down for lunch, she carried her plate into the living room, feeling decadent as she flicked on the TV at midday. It had been left on a business news channel, where a sharp-looking man with bright white teeth and a crisply knotted red tie was talking earnestly to his co-anchor, a Black woman with sharp cheekbones and perfect red lipstick.

Lacey raised the remote, about to change the channel—then froze.

"After a wild twenty-four hours of speculation and mounting investor concern," the male anchor intoned, "biomedical company Vetra Vitals CEO Reid Mercer released a video statement this morning aimed at calming the markets."

The female anchor nodded. "That's right, Carl. Just yesterday the word on the street was that the Vetra-Patch wouldn't advance to FDA trial—but Mercer's statement seems to have stabilized things, at least for now."

"Let's listen to a clip from that statement," Carl added.

The screen cut to Reid, standing confidently in the airy atrium of the Vetra headquarters, his expression calm but commanding.

"We remain fully committed to delivering the groundbreaking therapeutic technology Vetra is known for, and want to assure investors that the Vetra-Patch is fully on track for FDA trial submission effective immediately," Reid said smoothly.

The screen flashed back to the news anchors, the one named Carl raising his eyebrows slightly. "Will this be the reassurance investors need after a rocky twenty-four hours for Vetra? Only time will tell."

. . .

Rather than wait the extra thirty minutes for Elliott to get home on the bus, Lacey decided to surprise him by taking an Uber to pick him up herself. She stood outside the school bundled in her puffy coat, watching the front doors, her breath making clouds in the cold afternoon air. She pulled her phone from her coat pocket to check the time, and when she looked back up, she saw Simon walking briskly in her direction. His eyes were down, but he was too close for her to slip away unnoticed.

"Oh," he said, stopping short as his gaze finally landed on her. "Hey."

"Hey," Lacey echoed, lifting a small, awkward hand in a wave. "How, um, are you?" She felt a pang, both of guilt, thinking of their final conversation after Judd's funeral, and of loss. Simon had been a good friend to her.

He shifted on his feet, clearing his throat. "I'm fine. How about you?" His face, carefully composed, flickered with a trace of concern. "I saw the news about Vetra—sounds like it's been a rough couple of days. Hopefully it hasn't been too stressful for you."

Lacey tilted her head, puzzled. "Where did you see the news about Vetra?" she asked.

Simon's cheeks colored faintly. "I, uh, I forgot I had a news alert set for them."

Her brows lifted, the confusion still clear on her face.

"I wanted to keep up with them," Simon added quickly. "You know... because I know your job is important to you. I wanted to be able to talk about it with you." His mouth twisted in a self-conscious half-smile. "I guess I can turn those alerts off now."

Lacey reached out and gave his shoulder a quick squeeze. "Simon," she said softly, "you are such a good person."

"I know," he said with a sad smile.

The piercing blare of the school bell cut the moment short as students began pouring out of the building. Simon raised a hand in farewell and shuffled toward the parking lot, leaving Lacey to watch him go.

"Mommy!" Elliott's voice rang out, his face lighting up when he spotted her near the doors. But as he ran over, his smile faltered into a worried frown. "Why are you here? Did something bad happen?"

"What?" Lacey laughed, kneeling to pull him into a hug. "No, sweetheart. Everything's fine. I just thought we'd go do something fun."

"Cool!" Elliott grinned, skipping a little as they headed for the car. "Like the arcade?"

Lacey inwardly winced at the thought of the noisy, blinking arcade—Elliott's favorite place, but a guaranteed headache for her. She smiled anyway, brushing a hand over his hair.

"Sure, sweetheart," she said. "Whatever you want."

When they arrived home hours later, bellies full of pizza and milkshakes, Elliott was proudly clutching a cheap green plastic lightsaber he'd won after nearly an hour of Skee-Ball.

The air inside the mommune felt far from their normal school-night vibe. From the living room came the sound of the kids, sprawled out together, watching a movie—their giggles and shrieks punctuating the background noise. In the kitchen, the warm glow of the overhead light revealed Nanette, Tavia, and Regina gathered around the table, a bottle of champagne open and sweating onto the table, along with the remains of a cheese plate, complete with Nanette's signature artistic fruit garnishes.

"You're back!" Tavia called as Lacey stepped in. "How was the arcade?"

Lacey made a face. "Endless fun if you're eight, endless flashing lights and noise if you're over thirty." Her eyes flicked to the champagne.

"We're celebrating Regina's coup." Nanette grinned, tipping her glass toward Regina.

Regina gave her signature restrained smile, but beneath it Lacey sensed a swell of emotion.

"Well," Regina murmured, "I'd say we all have a lot to celebrate." She cleared her throat, her fingers toying with the stem of her glass. "The wire transfers will take a couple of days to clear, but the money is on its way to all of you." Her eyes, uncharacteristically wet, swept across the table, pausing on each of them in turn. "I couldn't have done this without you." Her voice caught slightly, and she raised her glass. "Thank you."

There was a moment of thick, emotional silence. Then Nanette hoisted her glass high, breaking the stillness.

"To being fucking riiich!" she crowed, and they all burst out laughing.

Lacey thought of her bank account, of the money now heading her way, and felt the faintest bubble of guilt begin to rise to the surface, that creeping, familiar voice whispering she hadn't really earned this. But then, just as quickly, the bubble popped, vanishing. Because she had earned it, she realized—through grit, through pain, through sheer stubborn survival.

She let her eyes linger on the three women at the table, the ones who'd held her up when her world had crumbled, who'd seen her raw, flawed, scared—and still supported her. She flashed back to the first day she'd met them, when she'd shown up trembling and teary-eyed, clutching Elliott by the hand, spilling out the broken, jagged pieces of her life to these strangers at the kitchen table. And instead of turning away, they'd opened their arms. They weren't just friends, not anymore. They were the family she'd chosen. The one she hadn't even known she was allowed to want.

"Get a glass!" Nanette commanded, snapping Lacey out of her thoughts. Smiling, she grabbed one from the cabinet and held it out as Nanette filled it to the brim, the bubbles threatening to spill over.

Tavia raised her glass. "To finally pulling it off."

"To karma," Nanette chimed, her eyes twinkling.

"To finally getting what we deserve," Regina said, wearing a defiant smile.

The three of them turned to Lacey, expectant, waiting.

She lifted her glass, her throat tight, her heart full. "To the mommune."

SIXTY

FIVE MONTHS LATER

The mid-June sun was strong and warm as Lacey and Elliott walked along the path. They passed under a dogwood tree, its pink blossoms bursting forth as if they'd been rehearsing all year for this very moment.

"I found it!" Elliott called, waving her over from a few rows ahead.

Lacey wound her way between the neat rows of headstones, her eyes brushing across the names and dates etched in stone, until she reached him.

Judd's headstone was simple and low, carved from red granite, no flourishes or ornamentation. Just his name in clean, strong letters, the years of his birth and death, and beneath that was carved, *Loving son and father*.

Lacey hadn't chosen the inscription—his parents had handled all of that—but standing here now, she was quietly relieved at how simple it was. Honest. Straightforward. Like the Judd she'd fallen in love with all those years ago.

Elliott shifted his weight, looking unsure. "Um... what do we do now?"

Lacey handed him the bouquet of sunflowers she'd been carrying, Judd's favorite. "You can set these down next to it," she said.

Elliott placed the flowers carefully on the neatly trimmed grass. "Now what?" he whispered.

Lacey laughed. "We don't have to whisper, buddy," she said. "It's not like church."

"Oh, OK."

"But we can just hang out here for a while, if you want, and, um, be with Daddy."

Elliott looked at the headstone as though considering, then plopped down in the grass in front of it. "Did you bring UNO?" he asked.

Lacey smiled. "You bet I did." She withdrew the game from her purse and began to shuffle the cards.

After two games, both of which Elliott won, Lacey placed her hand gently on his arm. "OK, sweetheart," she said. "I'm going to go sit over there and give you some time with Daddy." She pointed to the dogwood tree they had passed.

Elliott looked nervous. "But what do I do?"

"Well, if you feel like it, you can talk to him. You could tell him about the end of the school year, or how you feel about moving to California."

Elliott hesitated. "Can he... hear me?"

Lacey smoothed back his dark hair, which had grown shaggy the last few months. "Anything's possible," she murmured, squeezing his shoulder.

She walked over to the dogwood, plucking one of the delicate pink blossoms and turning it between her fingers. She'd always loved how dogwoods tracked the seasons—first flowers, then berries in the summer, then brilliant, red leaves in the fall. But she and Elliott wouldn't be here to see those colors this year.

She let herself sit on the grass under the tree, tilting her face to the sun. The winter had been long and record-breakingly cold, but they'd survived. Despite Lacey's sudden influx of wealth, very little had changed at first. She'd still had to show up for court to deal with her hit and run, where she'd been beyond relieved to avoid jail time and grateful to have the means to pay the exorbitant fine in exchange for having her license reinstated.

But as the weeks passed, change had slowly seeped in, gentle but unstoppable. Tavia and Grace were the first to go, back to Tennessee. Not to Tavia's hometown, but to a quiet Nashville suburb where she'd bought a house with a pool. "Y'all better visit," she'd said, laughing and tearful, as the last box was hauled into the moving truck.

Nanette and Linden left in March, chasing a dream of opening an art gallery in Santa Fe.

Then finally, Regina, Max, and Maddie had moved into the city in April after Regina had accepted a job as chief operating officer at one of Vetra's competitors.

"I don't get it," Lacey had said when Regina had shared the news. "You don't need the money."

Regina shook her head. "It's not about the money," she said. "It's about the impact I can have."

"I'll never understand you," Lacey said, only half joking, and Regina had replied with her familiar enigmatic smile.

Lacey and Elliott had visited Regina's new apartment on Central Park West several times, Elliott marveling each time at the view of the park from the tenth floor.

"I always saw myself as a downtown person," Regina had mused, during their most recent visit two weeks earlier. She and Lacey sipped coffee in her gleaming marble and steel kitchen while the kids played an increasingly chaotic ping pong match on the far side of the expansive living room. "But the commute's easier from here, and the neighborhood school's good."

"How are Max and Maddie adjusting?" Lacey asked.

"To school? Great. To everything else?" Regina had grimaced. "They hate the nanny. They miss coming home and having Elliott and Linden around. They even miss Grace trying to chew on their Pokémon cards." She'd smiled, but there was a flicker of loneliness underneath. "They'll come around, I know. It's just... quiet here with only the three of us."

"Oh, I know," Lacey said. The weeks she and Elliott had spent alone in the mommune had felt strange and lonely without the constant smears of peanut butter on the counter and LEGO underfoot. Even with so many empty bedrooms, Elliott still chose to sleep with her. Regina technically owned the house, but she'd promised not to sell until Lacey figured out her next steps.

"What about you?" Regina asked. "Have you figured out where you'll go when school ends?"

That was when Lacey had pulled out her phone and shown her the house.

"Wow." Regina had whistled. "It's beautiful, and what a location. A lot of space for just you and Elliott, though."

"It is," Lacey had agreed. "But I have a plan."

Now, sitting under the pink-blossomed tree, Lacey took in one deep breath after another, savoring the warm sun and the scent of fresh-cut grass and flowers in the air. A few yards away, Elliott was sitting cross-legged in the grass, waving his arms and talking animatedly to the man they'd both had to let go.

At home, their suitcases were packed for their flight the next day. They hadn't arrived at the mommune with much, and they weren't leaving with much either, but that was OK. They could get everything they needed where they were going.

SIXTY-ONE

"Just one more minute, please!" begged Elliott, brandishing a yellow plastic shovel. He was wet from the waist down, his legs caked with sand. Nearby stood the elaborate sand creation they'd been working on most of the afternoon, a maze of walls and turrets decorated with shells, sticks, and the odd bottle cap that had washed up on the beach.

Lacey stood and shook out their towel, grains of sand scattering on the warm, salt-tinged breeze. "Very last minute," she relented with a smile. "Then for real, we have to get home and clean up before they arrive."

Elliott cheered, scooping up his plastic bucket and running back to the ocean's edge, filling it with the slosh of waves. Above them, the August sun blazed in a bright blue sky dotted with puffy clouds.

She'd loved every one of the long summer days she and Elliott had spent in their new town, a sleepy beach community outside of Santa Barbara. They'd spent the last months slipping into the slower rhythm of the place, biking together along the bluffs and getting cones from the local ice cream shack. Sometimes in the evenings, if Lacey wasn't too tired from her days of repainting their new house, room by room, they'd walk down to the beach and have a bonfire, roasting marshmallows, and curling up under a blanket on the sand to watch the sun melt into the Pacific, licking the sticky goo off their fingers while they told knock-knock jokes.

Elliott seemed happy, too. He'd spent a couple of weeks at a local day camp, making new friends and hunting starfish in tide pools. He'd even transferred to a new therapist in Santa Barbara, an old med school colleague of Dr. Levin's. And though their lives were quieter now, Lacey, Regina, Nanette, and Tavia stayed tightly connected, trading photos and messages almost daily in their group chat, their friendship stretching easily across the miles.

It had been a beautiful, almost dreamlike summer—just the two of them, cocooned in a simpler life, free from the stress and noise of what they'd left behind. But now, as August drifted toward its close, Lacey knew it was time. Time to open the door to what came next, to fill their home and their days with something more.

In September, she was going back to school. First to finish her undergraduate degree, and then, she'd decided, to law school. She had a vision of opening up a family law practice and offering as much pro bono work as she could manage, ensuring that women who truly needed it had access to help in the way that she hadn't before Regina and the mommune had come along.

"Elliott!" she called now, waving her arms.

He came running back up the beach, where she was packing up the sand toys. They walked the three short blocks back to the charming, slightly weathered six-bedroom coastal Craftsman Lacey had purchased, its white clapboard siding faded by salt air and sun, with a wide wraparound porch home to a set of wicker chairs with faded blue cushions leftover from the previous owner. She gave Elliott an initial rinse with the hose, the water spraying in rainbow droplets past him onto the low, silver-green sagebrush and lavender bushes that bordered the yard. Behind them a twisty old lemon tree shaded the soft, scrubby grass where Elliott liked to hunt for lizards.

Inside, she herded Elliott into the shower then padded toward her own bathroom to wash away the remains of their beach day.

After, she pulled on linen pants and a tank top, and joined Elliott at the kitchen island, where he was elbow-deep in a bag of tortilla chips. Together they mashed fresh avocados from the neighbor's tree and arranged a snack platter of fresh fruit and thick slices of soft, mild cheese. Lacey glanced around the bright, softly furnished living space. Big windows bathed the rooms with natural light, and French doors opened to the sunlit back patio. She loved every inch of it, the wide-plank oak floors, the layered linen slipcovers, the natural textures and muted blues, the big rustic dining table, all of which she'd chosen herself.

She knew she was lucky to have as much as she did, and well aware of the consequences she'd sidestepped along the way. There were still nights when she woke, haunted by dreams of Judd, and days when the sight of a passing police car made her whole body tense. She had sinned and gone unpunished, she knew—yet she'd also been the victim of so many things beyond her control. Maybe, she thought, this was the universe's way of evening the score.

Her gaze caught on a framed photograph among the snapshots of her and Elliott on the bookshelf: Elliott perched on Judd's shoulders, both of them grinning, taken last summer. The sight of Judd's face staring back at her each day pierced her with equal parts guilt and grief, yet she knew the photo belonged there. Elliott deserved to hold on to the good memories of his father.

Stepping closer, she brushed her fingers lightly across the frame. "I promise I'll take care of our boy," she whispered. "And I'll make sure he remembers you as the father you wanted to be." She finished arranging the fruit and cheese platter just as a knock sounded at the door. Elliott raced to open it.

On the doorstep stood a thin, pale woman with curly red hair clutching the hand of a little girl with the same bright hair. The woman's face was tight with exhaustion, her voice apologetic. "I'm sorry we're late," she said. "It took longer to pack up—which is funny, because we really don't have that much stuff." She gave a shaky laugh, gesturing toward a battered sedan on the street.

"I'm hungry," the little girl announced, her bottom lip poking out.

The woman squeezed her hand. "Honey, we'll go to the store as soon as we unload, OK?"

Lacey smiled softly. "The grocery store can wait," she said. "We've got plenty here. Come in, have something to eat first." She bent to the little girl's eye level. "My name's Lacey. Do you like chocolate?"

The girl gave a quick, eager nod.

Straightening, Lacey met the woman's tired eyes with a warm smile. "Come on in," she said, stepping aside. "Welcome to the mommune."

A LETTER FROM THE AUTHOR

I want to say a huge thank you for reading *The Good Mothers*. I hope you enjoyed reading about Lacey as much as I enjoyed writing about her. If you'd like to keep in touch and hear all about my books with Storm, you can sign up here:

www.stormpublishing.co/caitlin-weaver

And if you'd like to join other readers in hearing all about my new releases and getting access to giveaways and bonus content, you can sign up for my newsletter—I promise not to bother you too often.

caitlinweaver.substack.com

If you enjoyed this book and could spare a few moments to leave a review that would be hugely appreciated. Even a short review can make all the difference in encouraging someone else to discover my books for the first time. Thank you so much!

In August 2025, *The New York Times* ran an article titled *11 Women, 9 Dogs, Not Much Drama (and No Guys)*, about a group of women living communally with the explicit goal of keeping one another company into old age and even possibly until death. My phone blew up. Every group chat I was in lit up with the story, my girlfriends sharing it with a kind of giddy recognition. It was clear to me this was more than just a news piece. It was a collective female fantasy made real.

By then, I had already written a draft of *The Good Mothers*.

The idea of living in a tight-knit community of female friends has always spoken to me on such a deep level that I was driven to write a book about what it would be like to live with other women and support each other through the thorny, sleep-deprived early years of motherhood—and beyond.

Lacey, my protagonist, is someone who has always tried to play by the rules. She believes that doing all the "right" things—working hard in school, marrying when she gets pregnant in college, throwing herself into advocating for her son when he's diagnosed with ADHD—will lead to the "right" outcomes. What she doesn't realize is that, for women, the game is often rigged. Instead of a straight line forward, her life takes a downward spiral. It's only when she stumbles into a mommune—a chosen family of women— that she begins to see a new truth: The way to the life she wants won't come from following the rules, but by making her own.

Like Lacey, I've always been a rules follower. It took me years to understand that sometimes survival—and joy—come from bending, breaking, or rewriting the rules entirely. I wrote this book for the other women who know that feeling. At its heart, this is a story about identity, friendship, and the courage it takes to forge your own path—hopefully with the support of an extraordinary circle of women beside you.

I hope it resonates with you as much as it has with me!

Thank you for joining me on this journey and I hope you'll stick around. I have many more stories to entertain you with!

With love and gratitude,

Caitlin Weaver

https://www.caitlinrweaver.com/contact

ACKNOWLEDGMENTS

I must start by thanking the entire Storm Publishing team for their support of this book and my writing career as a whole. I'm especially grateful to my brilliant editor, Vicky Blunden, whose sharp insights and thoughtful guidance continually push me to grow as a writer.

I'm equally indebted to my wonderful writing group—Amanda Vink, Ojus Patel, and Renee Ryan—whose encouragement, wisdom, and honest feedback not only strengthened this book but also sustained me through the writing process. I truly couldn't have done it without you.

Special thanks to Alexis Laufer for generously lending me her family law expertise, which was critical to the plot. Any mistakes are entirely my own.

Thank you to all my incredible mom friends who make up my own version of a "mommune." Even though we don't live under the same roof, you've each been an essential part of my journey through the wild, wonderful, and sometimes terrifying adventure of raising children in today's world.

Thank you to my dad for always asking about my "book news," and to my mom for unfailingly declaring, "This is your best one yet!" Your belief in me means everything.

I'm forever grateful to my husband, Marcus, and our sweet boys, Elijah and Sam. You make everything possible, and I am so lucky to have you by my side.

And finally, thank you to *you*, dear reader. With so many books out there, you chose mine—and for that, I am truly grateful.